NOTES FROM A LADY'S DIARY

I remember well that sultry evening when Col McCallum walked into the loggia and our lives. The moment he entered the room it was charged with the crackle of unseen forces, like the electric tension of a coming storm.

With his bright golden hair and dazzling smile he looked like a young god. A chill wind blew through me. It might have been premonition, or merely the breeze off the blue-green sea foaming against the rocky shore so far below our sheltered terrace.

Everyone seemed greatly intrigued by him. I was the only one who held back. I wanted to dislike him, but found myself drawn against my will.

Perhaps I sensed even then, in some subtle way, that he was the kind of man who made things happen. Once he entered our lives, it was inevitable that they would be—that *we* would be—changed forever.

Also by Marianne Willman

Silver Shadows
Yesterday's Shadows

Available from
HarperPaperbacks

The Court
of Three
Sisters

 MARIANNE WILLMAN

HarperPaperbacks
A Division of HarperCollinsPublishers

This is a work of fiction. The characters, incidents, and
dialogues are products of the author's imagination and are not
to be construed as real. Any resemblance to actual events or
persons, living or dead, is entirely coincidental.

HarperPaperbacks   *A Division of* HarperCollins*Publishers*
10 East 53rd Street, New York, N.Y. 10022

Copyright © 1994 by Marianne Willman
All rights reserved. No part of this book may be used or
reproduced in any manner whatsoever without written
permission of the publisher, except in the case of brief
quotations embodied in critical articles and reviews. For
information address HarperCollins*Publishers*,
10 East 53rd Street, New York, N.Y. 10022.

Front cover art courtesy of Alinari/Art Resource, N.Y.
Spine art courtesy of Scala/Art Resource, N.Y.
Step-back cover illustration by Bob Sabin

First printing: April 1994

Printed in the United States of America

HarperPaperbacks, HarperMonogram, and colophon are
trademarks of HarperCollins*Publishers*

❖ 10 9 8 7 6 5 4 3 2 1

For all the dreamers and all the rememberers
and the weavers of stories and song.

And especially for the two dreamers who complained that I hadn't dedicated a book to them yet: With love to my sons, Jeffery Ky and Daniel Willman, who might someday weave a few stories and songs of their own—and a special welcome to the newest bud on the family tree, Miss Haley Rose Willman.

Whatever may befall you, it was preordained for you from everlasting . . . from eternity spinning the thread of your being.

—Marcus Aurelius, *Meditations, X, 5*

PROLOGUE

In a place somewhere between reality and mythology, where what was and what will be *are*—some call it Heaven—three women were at work. Call them Fates or Norns, or Guardian Angels, if you will.

They stood before one of the tapestries they were weaving. They were not pleased with it. The background was too dark, and the paler threads were lost against its heaviness. "It needs light and contrast and surprise," one said at last.

After consulting together, they began to alter their initial pattern that, like all of their works, directed the destinies of human lives, fixing them in time and place.

One took the bright golden thread that was Summer Fairchild, another the fluffy pink filament that was her younger sister Fanny, and the third, the cool blue silk of Thea, the eldest of the three.

Pretty, but lacking strength. The three filaments were too delicate and the one that was Summer Fairchild's life was already badly frayed. A few more twists and the fragile strand might break off prematurely. It had almost happened once before.

"Here," the chief angel said to her companion Fates, "let us take this bright red and twine it with the gold. We'll put a rich green with the silvery blue for contrast, and perhaps a bit of violet with the pink, for substance and balance."

"Very nice," the most artistic of the angels said when they had gathered the other threads and tied them together, "but we still need something more."

Her hand hovered over another tapestry that had been discarded nearby. She tugged loose a new fiber from it: a complex strand spun of rich indigo twined with garnet and shot with quicksilver that changed from dark to light depending on how one looked at it.

At first glance the strand looked too rough to weave among the delicate colors of the Fairchild sisters. She held them up beside the others.

The chief angel cocked her head. "Yes, I believe that is exactly what is needed."

And so the three Fates spun their threads and wove them into the lives of the Fairchild women, binding them together with the unexpected, dark-bright, masculine one that was Colin McCallum. They stepped back to examine what they'd done.

It was very different. A good mixture of simplicity and intricacy. The three murmured in approval. It worked.

"See how the colors and textures bring one another out? I believe God will be pleased with this new pattern," the youngest angel said excitedly.

"Yes, I think so." The second agreed.

The chief angel smiled and shrugged. She liked the new pattern, but then, God always had the final word. She held up her jeweled shears, opening and closing the sharp blades. Their snip determined the length of the lives the three Fates wove.

"If not," she said, "we can always cut the threads and start over."

1

LETTERS

Notes from a lady's journal

*"The seed is in the deed, and will bear fruit or
flower, according to its sowing . . . and woe,
when the Devil plants it."*

*That is what our Nana always told us, when
she felt we were being naughty or headstrong.*

*It's evident that none of us listened well
enough.*

*The seed that blossomed into poisoned fruit
germinated for me, for my two sisters, when our
mother was suddenly taken from us. No, I suppose that is when we first became aware of it;
but it began even earlier. Burrowing under-
ground, tendrils snaking out beneath the placid
dullness of our lives, tangling and twisting away
from the light.*

*Then the Devil came into our lives in the form
of handsome Col McCallum. Reckless explorer,*

part-time archaeologist, scholar. Full-time charming rogue. Involving himself in our secrets. Digging among the dark roots of our past, finding things best kept hidden in darkness, forever.

But that was in August, on the beautiful island of Ellysia, set like precious jade amid the deep sapphire waters of the Mediterranean Sea. We went there weary of our humdrum days, full of hope and aching for change.

How could we know then that our individual lives would be spun and twisted like Arachne's threads, into webs of strange new patterns? How could we anticipate the events that would occur there? Adventure and discovery. Sorrow and joy. Love. And death.

I should go back to the beginning: The story—or at least our particular part of it—really began, of course, in England on a gray, February day.

England, February 1888

Three sisters, one dark and two fair, were arrayed on rose-colored velvet chairs near the drawing-room fire, as if posed for a Sargent watercolor. The brunette had her sketchbook before her, and the others were supposedly engaged in embroidering a tablecloth, but their threads had gotten as frayed and tangled as their tempers. All three were weary of winter, and of each other's company as well.

Summer, the middle sister by six years in either direction, let her charcoal fall into her lap, where several smudges already streaked her blue skirt, and looked out the window. The view was stark. England was caught in winter's frost-rimed hand, blasted by its bitter breath. For three days snow and sleet had blanketed the island from Hadrian's Wall all the way to the Channel.

She stared beyond the frosted traceries on the window-panes to the blurred shapes of the oak trees that lined the carriage drive on the west side of the house. There was always something eerie and otherworldly about them, even at high summer. To her fanciful imagination they appeared like a procession of ancient, gnarled druids, draped in thick white cloaks.

Years ago, one misty summer dawn, she had thought that there *were* druids moving among the oaks. She'd told Nana and Fanny, but they had scoffed at her. And when she'd persisted, she'd been scolded for making up tales.

Later she'd heard Nana talking to Father about the episode, referring to it as one of "Miss Summer's queer spells." It had been followed up with a trip to a bearded doctor in Harley Street, who had asked her a number of very strange questions and sent her home with bottles of foul-tasting tonic. After that incident she had learned to guard her tongue.

Summer jumped as lightning flashed amid the snow, followed by a deep grumble of thunder. Who had ever heard of such a thing? The weather had gone mad. She couldn't remember such a terrible winter. Not since . . . not since . . . *Before.*

Before was a stout oak door, sheathed and hinged in iron, with only a narrow, barred window through which she could view fleeting glimpses of her past. Sometimes that door swung open in her dreams. Then she would find herself running barefoot along a rocky shore, feeling the squelch of damp sand beneath her feet and the heat of a blazing sun on her face.

Each time, she woke up screaming.

Another flare of bright light dazzled her. Summer couldn't tell if it came from outside or if it was a flash of memory from *Before*. She caught a sudden image of herself in a swing hung from a low limb of a soaring tree. Sensations flooded in. She felt herself pushed high, high into a bright blue summer sky. Felt the surge of exhilaration, of blood rushing to her head as she leaned back. Back and back until her body and legs were horizontal to the grass below and she could see the filigree of branches and sun-dappled leaves high above her.

Then the door swung shut with terrifying finality. She was startled to find herself back in the parlor with her sisters. For a few seconds it had been so real! But there were Fanny and Thea sitting side by side, their blond heads bent over their embroidery frames, just as before. In and out their needles flashed, with only the crackle of the flames to break the silence.

The blaze in the hearth gave little warmth and the cranberry-glass shades of the lamps cast false cheer on walls papered in cream and tan. Although it was only three of the clock, a false twilight had fallen over the countryside, pressing against the lace-curtained windows of the rambling stone house. From time to time one or another glanced at the mantel clock. Their father's return from London was long overdue.

Thea, the eldest, had almost finished the corner she had started after luncheon. Fanny, who had just put her hair up a week earlier, had not been gifted with either patience or skill. Her fair brow was knit with irritation. The only reason she was even attempting to embroider was that she felt it was expected of her, with her new grown-up status.

The wind rattled the panes and Fanny jumped. "You are pulling your threads too tight, Fanny," Thea scolded. "Look how the fabric is puckered."

"I am doing the stitches *exactly* as you showed me," Fanny retorted in an aggrieved tone. She shot a challenging look at her sister.

Earlier Summer had tried her hand at embroidering, more out of boredom than anything. She had made a series of awkward stitches along the edge of a stenciled leaf that would have to be picked out and redone. Thea and Fanny had both noticed but said nothing. Of course, she had known that they wouldn't. Perhaps that was why she'd done it so badly. At times she gave in to an irresistible compulsion to do something, anything, no matter how small, to spark them into treating her—just once—as if she were normal.

As if she were like them.

It never worked. And Summer knew that today or tomorrow, when she was out of the room, Thea would unpick the stitches that she had made and quickly redo the leaf edge. Fanny would not say a word about it. As unlike as they were in temperament and interests, Thea and Fanny were allied by their very wholeness in a way that Summer never could be.

"Would you like me to do another bit of the embroidery?" she asked, anticipating their response.

"Oh, no," Thea said, a little too quickly. "Fanny and I are in a fair way to finishing this section. Keep on with your drawing, dear."

It was no use, Summer reflected. She would get no satisfaction from them. They rarely rose to the bait. They bent their golden heads together in a maddening conspiracy of misguided kindness. How alike they were in appearance, with the Fairchild golden hair and light blue eyes.

The major difference was in their personalities. It even showed in their dress. Thea, in her restrained tea gown of striped tone-on-tone ivory, had a reserved elegance that would do credit to a duchess. It matched her refined manner, her careful speech, the extraordinary ease with which she always managed to say and do the right thing.

Fanny was at the opposite end of the scale: She had an outgoing nature accented by a (usually) charming willfulness, and a candy-box prettiness that drew people to her. Her sapphire day dress was a copy of a new Paris fashion, done up by the local seamstress from a French pattern book, and meant— at least by its wearer—to be the height of afternoon sophistication. Instead, Summer thought, it made her look touchingly young and vulnerable. Poor Fanny, pining for the glittering joys of a London season, and stuck instead at Kingsmeade, with only her sisters for company.

A stranger might be forgiven for thinking they were unrelated to dark-haired Summer with her sharp, gypsy cheekbones and winged brows. Even her eyes were different, a blue as deep as Persian lapis, and flecked with the same bright specks of gold. She felt like a plain black crow, camouflaged by her sisters' showier plumage.

At the moment they were busy once more, ruffling each other's feathers. Summer tore off the top sheet of her sketchbook, a drawing of the oak trees lining the drive beyond the window, and picked up her charcoal again.

With a smooth flick of the wrist she sketched in the line of Thea's regal neck, and the annoyed frown between her delicately arched brows. Another squiggle of charcoal across the white paper became Fanny's dimpled cheek and stubborn chin.

Her sisters' voices rose in mutual irritation. It was essential to work quickly. At any moment, one or the other of them would leave the room. It was as inevitable as sunrise and sunset. If only she could capture the way the light shone in Fanny's eyes just now, and the way she caught her full lower lip with her teeth.

"You are pulling the tablecloth, Francine," Thea said through clenched teeth.

"I did not pull," Fanny retorted. Her face took on a familiar, aggrieved look. Thea *knew* how she loathed her full given name, and it was hateful of her to use it! Positively *hateful*.

She punched her needle into the taut circle of fabric. When Thea had first come to stay, while her husband went abroad on government business, Fanny had been glad of her company. Now she prayed every night that Martin Armstrong would return soon and take his wife away with him. For good.

Thea sent Fanny an icy glare. "You just did it again. See how the threads are pulled awry? You've quite ruined this entire corner!"

Fanny stabbed her needle into the cloth, leaving it fixed in place. "I am weary to death of constantly being told what to do and how to do it and—and being blamed for everything, just because I am the youngest!"

"Your outburst does you no credit, Fanny."

"You are *not* my mother, Thea! And if Mama were still alive I *know* she would not let you treat me so condescendingly."

If she expected her reference to their late mother

to gain her sympathy, she was wrong. Thea drew herself up with dignity. "If our dear mother had lived to see you now, I am certain she would be appalled by your atrocious manners. You are growing into a—a spoiled little prima donna!"

Fanny's face reddened. She threw down her embroidery hoop and started toward the door. "Then I shall leave you to—to wallow in your own perfection!"

Thea, usually so in control of her emotions, was exasperated to the point of wanting to slap her youngest sister's pretty, mulish face. The girl was sadly spoiled. It was too bad that Papa hadn't sent Francine off to boarding school.

She gritted her teeth. It didn't help her to hold back the angry, unthinking words. "Not a half hour since, I chided Summer for smudging charcoal on her collar! She didn't flounce out of the room like an ill-tempered child!"

Summer set her sketchbook aside. "Only because I would look ridiculous even attempting it," she said baldly.

An awkward silence fell, punctuated by the hiss and pop of the fire. Any mention of her deformity, no matter how oblique, froze the others in their tracks. Thea and Fanny were both silenced: the one in agony over her terrible faux pas; the other in shock because oh-so-perfect Thea had been so cruelly indiscreet. Both felt a embarrassed pity for Summer, and a genteel revulsion that she would be so crude as to remind them that she was crippled.

Summer made a point to do so at least once a day.

At times, it angered her to fury when Thea and Fanny pretended to ignore the one thing that she could not. Some days, when they were particularly tiresome, and when her pain was very bad, baiting them became her chief form of entertainment.

She rose from her place on the sofa and made her way slowly toward the window with the aid of her ivory-handled cane. Her sisters followed her progress surreptitiously. Nana was right, Thea thought in dismay, this cold weather was worsening her condition.

Summer put her hand against the pane to melt the thick frost that was forming. She looked through the irregular patch of clear glass that resulted. It was snowing again, fat mothlike flakes thickening the air. She couldn't even see the drive and the elms were ghostly shapes in the gathering gloom.

A rattle of china and silver came from beyond the open double doors. Nana bustled in with the tea tray. She was wearing her best dress of black bombazine with her watch pinned to her ample bosom. She beamed at her former charges through her small, round spectacles. It was lovely having all three of her little chicks under the same roof once more. Miss Summer and Miss Fanny and Miss Thea . . . Mrs. Armstrong, that is.

Nana had been with the family for years, coming to Kingsmeade when Thea was only a month old. Now she earned her wages by looking after Summer and acting as unofficial lady's maid to the daughters of the house. Except for the graying of her hair, pulled back into a prim bun, she had not changed in all the time the three sisters had known her.

Summer made her painful way back to the sofa again. Nana set out porcelain plates filled with tiny sandwiches and jam tarts. Tea was in the funny, pumpkin-shaped pot that had always been used in the nursery. Nana shook her head. Ah, those had been good times.

Of course, if not for that and Miss Summer's accident, she would have gone off to some other upper-class family years ago, to rule their nursery with a firm but gentle hand, and raise another generation of little English ladies and gentlemen.

Summer smiled when she saw the teapot. The bright orange-yellow pot with its curving green vine leaves for handle and spout was cheerful, and it annoyed Thea, whose sense of propriety was offended. That was, of course, one of the reasons that she had asked Nana to use it today: Thea had always been prim and proper, but she had grown much too stiff and formal. If marriage did that to one, Summer was glad that she would never have a husband of her own.

"Such a gloomy afternoon," Nana said as she set the china pot in front of Thea. "I thought you might do with a bit of refreshment and a bit of news to brighten you up."

The sisters looked at her with varying degrees of curiosity. It was plain that Nana had a tidbit of interesting gossip to dispense with the Lapsang Souchong and jam tarts. But where had she unearthed any in such frightful weather?

"Do tell us," Fanny prompted. "You look as if you are fairly bursting with it!" She was always the first to pump the servants for news of the countryside.

Thea gave the old retainer a quelling look. Gossiping with the servants was beneath a lady's dignity—even if that servant had dandled one on her knee years ago.

The older woman's air of mock gravity piqued Summer's curiosity. "It must be something rare. Tell us, has the squire's wife run off with the new young curate?"

"Oh!" Nana was scandalized. "What would your dear father say to hear you, Miss Summer?"

"Most likely that I have been reading too many novels." Summer added more sugar to her tea. Thea never made it sweet enough.

Sure of her audience now, Nana settled in for a good coze. "Mr. Jenkins kindly brought over a letter for the master this afternoon. From abroad."

Thea lowered her eyes. Her complexion had gone from pink to pale. "From Brazil?" Her husband had been in South America for almost six months now, on official government business.

"Lord bless us, no, Mrs. Armstrong. I'm that sorry to have gotten your hopes up, so I am. It was from some other foreign place."

"That's nothing out of the ordinary," Fanny said. "Papa receives letters from foreign lands quite regularly."

Summer was intrigued. Before her accident, their father had traveled far and wide, studying the ruins of ancient Greece and Rome. Except for brief carriage rides in the countryside and one or two disastrous trips to London, to consult with specialists in Harley Street, her world was circumscribed by the walls of the house and the tall hedges surrounding its modest gardens.

Drawing was her chief occupation. Otherwise, she only escaped in the pages of the books she read from her father's extensive library, and in the tomes of history and archaeology she took from his private study to read at night.

And in the strange dreams that haunted her sleep and ended in nightmares and cold, shaking fear.

"Ah," the old nursemaid went on, barely able to contain herself. "But one is a thick packet from Mr.

Briarly. The master must have stopped in to see him on his way to the City."

This time her revelations met with the proper response. Mr. Briarly was the business agent of their father's friend and patron, Sir Horace Chriswell, who had underwritten several of his earlier ventures abroad. Their ennui vanished as they tried to interpret this startling news.

Could her father be planning an expedition? Summer wondered. She couldn't bear to be left in Thea's charge, as if she were an infant, while their father went away. The same idea had occurred to Fanny, and was equally unwelcome.

Thea was no more enamored of being left to look after her sisters than they were. She had been the butt of Summer's needle-sharp wit more than enough times, and as for Fanny, the girl was already a rare handful, with a pert and most unbecoming manner about her that quite set Thea's teeth on edge. She rubbed her temples. A headache was rapidly coming on.

Nana saw the gesture and instantly became all starch and self-importance. "Ah, you've been worrying yourself to flinders, poor pet. I'll bring you a headache powder, Miss Thea. As for you, Miss Summer, it's well past time for your daily nap. It wouldn't do to neglect your fragile health in this nasty, wet weather."

"I am not an invalid, I am a cripple," Summer replied more sharply than she'd intended. "Nor am I tired." She stopped to listen as she saw Mary, the parlormaid, hurry down the corridor to open the front door. A murmur of voices was audible above the sound of the wind and a gust of cold air swirled through the room. "Father is home."

Nana saw that her influence over her little chicks was of no use now, and retreated to her lair in defeat. She climbed the stairs with a briskness that did credit to her years. Oh, for the days when she had ruled the nursery, supreme!

Richard Fairchild entered the room. That in itself was unusual. Summer had always wondered if he avoided this particular parlor because of the portrait of Orelia Fairchild that hung over the mantel. She had noticed that he could never quite bring himself to look at it.

He had to duck under the lintel. The winter parlor was in a very old part of the house, built well before the time of Elizabeth, and people had been considerably shorter then. He was a tall man himself, with grizzled dark hair and a scholar's stoop, caused by long hours spent poring over books and maps and his field notes. He coughed into his handkerchief and made for the warmth of the hearth.

"A touch of bronchial trouble," he said, dismissing their concern before it could be voiced. "Nothing that a little warm weather and sunshine wouldn't cure."

Fanny sighed. "Sunshine! It seems eons since we've seen any. If you hadn't given up excavating, Papa, we could be spending the winter in Egypt at Shepheard's Hotel, like Lydia Peyton and her family."

"I haven't given it up," Richard Fairchild replied, chafing his cold hands before the fire. "It takes many years to correlate one's findings and write them up properly."

That was true. Thea had offered to help him by copying his notes over in her perfect hand but he had refused her, as he had refused Summer before. Yet Summer knew something that neither of her sisters even guessed at: The work was already finished. The main notes were transcribed, the papers ready to present, the manuscript completed but never sent on to his waiting publisher. It lay in the second drawer of his desk, where she had found it by accident over a year ago.

Her father spent a good deal of time closed up in his study, but did nothing at all. Except to sit and think. Of what, she had no idea. Perhaps he dreamed of better days. Surely they had been better days—*Before*.

Summer examined the portrait of the woman in white above the mantel. The painted face was ethereally beautiful, as lovely as the pastel roses that framed it. *Her mother*. The words echoed hollowly. They meant nothing. She had no memory of the woman who'd given her birth. Indeed, Summer had no recollection of her life before the age of twelve, when she had suffered the accident that had left her badly crippled.

Until her twelfth year she had been an energetic, outgoing child. She had been able to walk, to run, to dance. Or so she had been told. Her memories of all that were locked behind that ominous barred door that was the boundary between now and *Before*.

Having no past was difficult for Summer. She had no childhood memories to nourish her. It left her incomplete and unattached to life, like an uprooted tree that survived the trauma, even though it had been torn away from the earth. There was one like that at Kingsmeade, fallen in some long-ago storm, yet clinging by one fragile root to the ground. It still put out leaves in spring, but each year there were fewer. Soon it would be a dead hulk, with only lichen to color its branches.

In just one area the amnesia that plagued Summer

was a blessing. It was easier to pretend that she had been born lame, as she was now. That way she could at least hold some of the bitterness at bay.

Richard Fairchild glanced at the drawing book beside Summer's chair. He took in a deep breath, then straightened up and turned suddenly.

His glance swept over the three women. He didn't know if he was making the right choice or not, but he was sure that it was the only real choice he had. "I have an important announcement to make, one that will affect us all."

Fanny clasped her hands together tightly as her thoughts went to the most important event in her universe: the promised London season. Thea had said that she was too young and that Father would not finance an expensive debut when he considered the whole notion absurd, but Fanny had never given up hope. She was eager to see something more of the world than Kingsmeade village, and equally eager for the experiences that would surely come with it— every one of them romantic in the extreme.

There was the problem of Summer, though. She could not imagine her in London. Once Thea had taken them to the assembly at Nunford, and that handsome lieutenant had made up to Fanny so delightfully, and then they had been forced to leave so suddenly, because Summer had fallen on a loose rug. It wasn't fair! Summer hadn't even wanted to go in the first place.

An idea struck Fanny. How simple. Papa could surely arrange for someone to come in and stay with Summer. Aunt Leonie, perhaps? A calculating look came into her wide blue eyes as she enlarged on her theme. Even better if Aunt Leonie came to London to chaperon her and then *Thea* could stay at home with

Summer. That would kill two birds with one stone. Fanny almost hugged herself with glee. She would be free of them, free of this humdrum life they led, at least for a few wonderful months.

Richard Fairchild's words came as a definite anticlimax. "I've had a letter from my old patron, Sir Horace Chriswell. He believes there are interesting discoveries to be made in the Mediterranean. A small island, named Ellysia." Major discoveries, if John Carruthers was already poking about there. The thought of Carruthers beating him to it made Richard's mouth run dry. Their rivalry went back many years.

Fanny was momentarily distracted from planning her debut. "I can still remember the sunshine in Greece, and how I sobbed and sobbed when we reached England in the rain and fog!"

Richard fell silent at Fanny's words, remembering the thrill of discovery at Ilykion, followed so shortly by disaster. Summer saw the shadows flit across their father's face.

Her hand itched to slap Fanny. How could she be so insensitive? Papa had wept too, when they had reached England ten years ago. She remembered it clearly. How could he not, when he saw his wife's lead-lined coffin brought up from the hold and placed upon the dock?

It had been a terrible time: she, weak and recovering from her accident, had not been able to dredge up the tiniest memory of her mother, yet she'd been weighed down with grief. Her tears on homecoming had been for her father, for Fanny, for herself. Only Thea had been spared that mournful arrival. She had been on her honeymoon with Martin, and still unaware of the tragedy.

The moment was engraved indelibly on Summer's mind. The chill drizzle, the tattered fog, and her father's wrenching agony formed her earliest recollections.

The memory triggered something. Against her will, Summer felt that inner door of *Before* swing slowly open. She was suddenly lost in images of the past. The white houses tumbling down the hillside to the bay, blinding in the noonday brilliance. The emerald and sapphire waters surrounding Ilykion. The ruins of the ancient palace crowning the rise inside the natural harbor . . . the murmur of the waves against the cliffs that guarded it . . . her hat blowing away and the fiery kiss of the hot, hot sun on her unshielded face . . . the sand squelching cold beneath her bare feet . . . ahead, the tide pools shimmering along the rocky shore, glittering like secret jewels . . .

She drew in a ragged breath. The scenes faded and vanished. The mental door slammed shut. The aura of utter horror lingered. Summer's hands trembled with reaction and she hid them in her skirts. She had no conscious memory of that little cove she'd just envisioned, but she knew that it existed, somewhere. Her hands were shaking and she clenched them into tight, hard fists.

Thea handed her father a cup of tea. "The servants—"

"Will be put on half salary. We'll close up the house."

"I can't believe you would seriously consider it!" Thea said in dismay.

Summer blinked. How long had she been lost in reverie? It had seemed like seconds, yet the conversation had apparently gone on for some time without her. She cleared her throat. "Consider what?"

Her father drew a letter from inside his waistcoat and regarded it as if it were something magical.

Richard smiled. In a way it was. With a wave of his pen, Sir Horace had transformed him from a stolid, aging academic into an eager adventurer, willing to give up comfort and convenience for the thrill of discovery.

"The opportunity of a lifetime," Chriswell had called it. Richard had run out of opportunities long ago, and although he was still strong and vigorous, who knew how long a man of his age had left? No, he could not let this pass.

He looked suddenly younger and filled with energy. "I have no wish to be separated from my family. I am going to Ellysia, and I want you to join me there for the season."

The sisters had never heard of it. "Ellysia is a small island in the Tyrrhenian Sea," he explained, "halfway between Naples and Sicily. The climate is warm and invigorating, certainly a beneficial change from this accursed weather!"

Summer was rigid with alarm. Leave Kingsmeade? Leave England? He couldn't mean it. Even going to the village, to be stared at and whispered about, was sheer agony. To read of foreign lands and ruined temples was one thing; actually to journey to them, quite another. No, she couldn't do it! She might chafe at the limits of her narrow world, but she was safe inside them.

Thea, ever the practical one, was overwhelmed by her father's announcement. "But Father, only consider—"

"There is no need to pull such a long face. Martin won't be back for months. You can wait for him as well on Ellysia as you can here. Or, if you choose, I suppose you may remain behind and go to your great-aunt Leonie for the duration. But I admit that you would be a great help to me and to your sisters on the journey. I shall, of course, ask Nana to accompany us."

"But Summer couldn't possibly."

Summer heartily agreed, yet her tongue seemed frozen. Her fingers gripped the arms of her chair, her knuckles as white as her porcelain teacup.

Her father avoided her eyes. He knew how difficult it would be for her and realized there were risks involved. He had consulted Dr. Creighton in London before coming to his decision. Dr. Creighton could give him no firm answer. "While there is no guarantee that your trip would aid in the return of her memory—the mind is a mysterious thing and follows its own rules, Professor Fairchild, as you are well aware—I do feel that remembering is vital to her mental fitness. I see no reason why your daughter should not accompany you. Indeed, it may do her a deal of good."

Richard turned so he could not see his middle child and the fear on her face. For too long that same fear had lived within his own heart. It wasn't as if she would be out of reach of medical care. Sir Horace had mentioned that his old friend, Dr. Paolo Ruggieri, had left Rome and retired to Ellysia. Dr. Creighton had felt that discovering the truth of what had happened to her might be the only means of banishing the demons that tormented Summer. Richard feared that remembering would only create a new set of nightmares to haunt her.

There were times when he himself would have given anything to forget.

His gaze went to her sketchpaper again, where clever strokes of her charcoal had rendered a strange drawing. He recognized the oak-lined drive to

Kingsmeade, clotted with recent snowfall, but the trees rising against the stormy sky had twisted and taken on unfamiliar lines. With the hints of human features she'd added, they looked frightening and weird, like a procession of ghostly druids, draped in heavy ermine cloaks.

Richard felt a terrible ache. Summer probably wasn't even aware of what she'd drawn. More than once, of late, he'd seen her glance at a sketch she'd done in surprise, as if the result had nothing to do with what she'd intended. He must take the risk.

With his decision made, Richard was impatient to start. "The season has already begun in the Mediterranean and there is little time for me to spare in arguing. I've already set things in train to assemble my crew, and I mean to be on Ellysia by month's end. You know I need your assistance. Tell me, Thea, what is your decision?"

His eldest daughter swallowed her frustration. She recognized the tone in Father's voice. He sounded *exactly* like Martin at his most adamant. How alike men were, making plans and leaving the women to make do. Father, expecting her to trot off to the far corners of the earth with her sisters in tow, as if it were the most natural thing in the world; Martin, leaving her to kick her heels for the good part of a year while he went off to Brazil. He hadn't asked her to go with him. In the ten years of their marriage they had spent more time apart than together.

She fingered her wedding ring, symbol of their marriage vows. Not all of their separations had been due to government business. But, Thea thought in shame, that was mostly her doing. It didn't bear thinking of. A change of scene might be a welcome distraction.

"I cannot help but feel that the entire plan is ill-advised. However, Nana is not as young as she once was, and must have someone to help her with Summer. If you are set on it, of course I will come," she said reluctantly.

"Excellent. Make out a list of what you anticipate you will need to purchase here before setting out. Fanny and Nana can help you."

Ordinarily Summer would have been outraged at being left out, as if her brain were crippled as well as her body. Yet her emotions were too roiled. With a few words her entire world had been turned upside down.

Father looked upon this as a wonderful opportunity to add to the world's knowledge and his own fine reputation as a scholar of note. Romantic little Fanny saw it as a grand adventure, and Thea as an unwanted task, which she would bear with noble martyrdom.

To Summer the proposed journey to Ellysia was something else. It was an escape from the tedium of life at Kingsmeade. But, like a bird caged too long, she could not conceive of freedom from the home that had become both refuge and prison.

Her overwhelming emotion was terror.

Havana, February

Early sun warmed the bare wood floor and put rainbows around the beveled edge of the mahogany-framed mirror. Col McCallum stood before the shaving stand, naked from the waist up, stropping his razor until the edge was keen and deadly. The mirror reflected a square, stubborn chin, already lathered,

THE COURT OF THREE SISTERS 25

hawklike nose, and a pair of thick-lashed eyes as green and fathomless as the sea visible beyond his open windows.

At the moment his irises were surrounded by networks of tiny red lines. It had been one hell of a night. Champagne at the embassy reception, followed by cheap gin at a sailor's hangout on the waterfront. Odd how something that was so pleasant by moonlight could turn out to be so painful in the glare of day.

Col laughed shortly, and immediately regretted it. His head felt like the inside of a marching drum. But he'd had a damned good reason for hitting the blue ruin. Yesterday had been Alistair's birthday. He would have been thirty-six years old if he hadn't shot himself in a hired room in Athens fourteen years ago.

It had been neat, as far as such things go. With his usual thoroughness and consideration, Alistair had written his suicide note, left the name and direction of his solicitor on another sheet, and loaded his pistol. Then he had carefully wrapped his head in a pillow slip and put his bundled coat behind him, to spare his landlady a grisly cleaning chore. The words of Alistair's last note were burned into Col's mind.

August 12th, Athens

My dear Colin,

What I am about to do requires every ounce of courage I can muster, yet some will no doubt brand me a coward, as well as a thief. I only pray to God you will know that I am neither.

For the record, I swear by everything I hold most dear, that I am not guilty of stealing the Venus of Ilykion. The two things I value most

*are my good name and your happiness. Through
no fault of my own, I have lost the one. There is
nothing for me to do now but protect the other.*

*By the time you are ready to take your place in
the world this sorry scandal will, I devoutly pray,
be forgotten. Good-bye and God bless you.*

Your loving brother,
Alistair

Col's hand shook suddenly and a stinging line of
crimson beaded along his jawbone. *Christ, Alistair, I
miss you like hell!*

As he daubed at the razor cut with the edge of the
linen towel there was a groan from behind him. He
glanced at the reflection in the mirror. On the other
side of the room, a sinewy sailor with a grizzled beard
was still fast asleep in the big armchair. As bad as his
own head felt, Col was sure that Vincenzo would feel
a damned sight worse when he woke up.

Col dipped the brush in water and whipped it over
the shaving soap to make more lather, and slapped it
on his throat. Vincenzo moaned, opened his eyes and
took in his surroundings, and closed them again, as if
the bright light of morning were too painful to contemplate. "Thank God!" he rasped in Portuguese-accented
English. "I dreamed I was clapped in irons down in the
dank hold of a ship, bound round the Horn!"

"And so you would be, if I hadn't hauled your
mangy carcass here. Those two fellows who were so
free with the whiskey had 'shanghaiers' stamped all
over their greasy faces."

Vincenzo grinned. You could always count on Col
when the tides ran against you. Vincenzo didn't know
much else about him, but then, that was all he needed
to know.

Sometimes, when the mood was on Col, Vincenzo could get him to tell stories. And wonderful stories they were. Of strange places and strange people. Lost cities, buried beneath desert sands or hidden in the jungles of the Yucatan. One-eyed giants and three-headed dogs. Ladies with snakes for hair. You never knew what he was going to come up with, once you got him started.

Col could be the best of companions, but other times he went silent and kept to himself, brooding in that quiet way he had, as if there were some black secret locked in his heart.

Church bells tolled and Vincenzo shot upright. "Santa Maria, is it that late? I was supposed to meet Pietro, to get my winnings from him before he sailed."

He rose and staggered out, slamming the door behind him.

Col winced at the explosion of sound reverberating in his head. There would be no more carousing on his part for a while. It was time to move on. His godfather's most recent letter had seen to that. The damned thing had come halfway around the world before finding its way to him in Cuba.

His eyes darkened. It seemed significant that it had come on the anniversary of Alistair's death, when he was feeling more restless and wild than in the early months after it first happened. A gift from beyond the grave.

Col glanced at the letter lying harmlessly on the night table. A single page covered with fine, spidery script. Such a small thing in itself, yet it had opened up old anguish, piercing through an accumulation of years like a scalpel lancing an infected wound. Odd, he hadn't even known the pain was still there, as raw as ever, as though echoes of old anger had been stirring to life.

The letter, in Carruthers's distinctively eccentric style, began without preamble:

> *Damn your eyes, Col, why in God's name can't you stay in one place for more than a fortnight!*
>
> *If, by some miracle, this reaches you, and God only knows if and when it will, get yourself to the Mediterranean and to the island of Ellysia with all due haste. I've found something here you won't believe. I can hardly believe it myself. We shall rewrite history! And that's all I can damn well say just yet. I can't trust it to a letter. There is just too much at stake.*
>
> *I've only a few men and basic equipment, but I mean to get started before Sir Horace Chriswell even learns I'm here. The dainty little bastard has caught wind of something. I lie awake at night sweating that he will get to Ellysia before I'm ready to begin.*
>
> *Col, this is bigger than anything I've encountered before, and bigger than your damned pride. Swallow it, because I need you here. There's something else going on*
>
> *And if you won't do it for me, you damned, hardheaded young fool, do it for Alistair.*

Yes, definitely a message from the Great Beyond—whatever the hell *It* might be. Col rinsed his razor in the now-soapy water. The long blade clanged against the china bowl like a Siamese temple gong. He winced again and cursed roundly.

The letter's postscript had been filled with tantalizing hints of discovery and danger. Carruthers wasn't an alarmist but Col knew him well enough to read between the lines. Beneath the excitement was an undertone of concern. Sir Horace Chriswell was sniffing around.

That in itself was significant. Chriswell had the money to sponsor any number of archaeological investigations. He did it, not to advance knowledge, but to advance Horace Chriswell. The queen had made him a knight, but rumor was that the merchant king wanted even more.

Col's razor glittered in the light as he carved away a layer of lather and whisker. He was a man who thrived on danger. Carruthers knew that nothing intrigued his godson so well as a mystery. Damn the man for being so vague! Col grinned. And for knowing which strings to pull to make him dance to the tune of his old friend's piping.

Col had been to the Aeolian Islands, scattered off the coast of Sicily, halfway between Italy and the coast of Africa, but he'd never seen Ellysia. It was a small, out-of-the-way island, with another nearby. From what he recollected, it had never been a major center of trade or culture.

"We shall rewrite history," Carruthers had written again near the end of the letter, "but come quickly or . . ." The last part had been scratched out. What was this marvelous discovery that had gotten the old man's blood stirred up? It wasn't like him to be so damnably excited.

Somewhere in the street below a man was singing melodiously as he opened his shop for business. The notes slammed into Col's brain like glass knives. Another man with a hangover might have shouted for quiet. Col endured the pain. He usually enjoyed

Antonio's singing, and far be it from him to make another man suffer for his own mistake.

The melody swelled to a piercing resonance. Col winced in agony. Christ, Antonio could really hit those high notes! He shut the casement with more force than he'd intended and winced again. The song faded as the singer wandered away down the street.

Col rinsed his razor blade again in the china basin of water on the shaving stand. The near silence was sweet. The only sounds loud enough to torture his hangover were the twitter of birds and the hiss of the razor.

Then the door of his room door was thrown open with a terrible bang and a woman burst in, alternately sobbing and shouting. Col cursed as the blade slipped in his soapy hands and cut his chin near the deep cleft in the center.

"Damn it, Lulita, you know better than to burst in like that when a man's shaving. I could have cut my throat."

"I wish you had!" she cried in her native tongue. Her golden eyes flashed like amber as she threw herself down upon the bed. When Col didn't respond she shot him a resentful look from beneath her long lashes. "Bastard! I wish that you were dead at my feet!"

He sighed and set the razor down, pressing the thin towel against his bleeding face. "It's a bit early for grand opera. What is it this time?" His Spanish was faultless.

"This time!" She sat up, eyes blazing. She would have been almost beautiful, had her face not been distorted by the storm of emotions. "You make it sound as if I am always upset."

He hid his grin behind the towel. Nothing riled her more than knowing that her temper amused him.

Living with her these past few weeks had been like camping out on the flanks of an active volcano.

She clenched her hands. "Antonio says that you are leaving."

"You knew that."

"Liar!"

Col threw down the blood-spotted towel in disgust. "Be fair, *carita*. I've never told you anything but the truth. You knew from the first that I'd be leaving Havana tomorrow."

She tossed her heavy hair back and glared at him defiantly. It was true that he had told her he would go. It was just that she hadn't really believed him. "Bah! I hate you, you—you deceitful bastard! "

His brows drew together. "If you're calling names, let me remind you that you neglected to mention one little fact yourself, that you are a married woman."

She pushed her heavy hair back from her face. Her husband had gone to visit his relatives at the other end of the island after Christmas—supposedly for two weeks—and not yet returned. "If Alfonso wanted to be a husband to me, he would not stay away so long. And when he is home, he cares more for his gambling and his drinking than he does for me."

Col laughed. "I doubt that most sincerely, *querida*. Only a dead man could ignore a woman like you."

She pulled a dagger from her skirts. "If you leave me, I will kill myself!"

His laughter died. He moved so quickly he was only a blur. A split second later the dagger was in his hand. "Not very sharp," he said. "Nevertheless, I'll remove the immediate temptation."

Placing the thin knife across his knee, he snapped it in two. Lulita's eyes widened. Her alarm mingled with admiration. What a man he was.

Col leaned down and took her face between his hands and kissed her thoroughly. The anger went out of her and Lulita pulled him down on the bed with her. Her breasts were ripe and full against him and her lips parted invitingly. She knew he could not resist making love to her. She would do everything she could to hold him.

Col's arms wound around her like coils of steel. She sighed against his tanned throat and nipped at his skin with her sharp little teeth.

He buried his hands in her thick, dark hair. "It won't work, Lulita. I can't stay. I've already dawdled here far too long."

Exciting as she was to him, Col McCallum was a man more in love with his work. It was his life, his joy, his ultimate mistress in a way no woman could ever be. He hadn't even set sail yet, but he was eager to reach Ellysia.

Still, Lulita was warm and willing, and life would surely be less interesting without her. The sun was much higher in the morning sky before Col finally finished shaving.

He sailed the next day with the tide. He'd given Lulita a fond kiss, a present of a gold comb set with amber, and the advice to write to her husband and make up their difficulties. Then he boarded the ship and turned his face east, where new adventures beckoned. They were the only thing that mattered to him now.

With the scandal and Alistair's death, something had died in Col. He had no ties except to the past, and wanted none. He would place his trust in no one but himself. A man who didn't trust—who didn't love—could never be hurt again. And that was exactly the way Col wanted it.

Before the ship reached the straits of Florida his thoughts had flown ahead on the wind and sun to Ellysia in the far-off Mediterranean Sea, and Havana was already fading in his mind like a pleasant, half-remembered dream.

Col checked into his favorite inn on the Bay of Naples, where he found a letter waiting for him at the desk. The handwriting was unfamiliar. Who the devil was writing to him in Italy? No one knew his itinerary except Carruthers. He saw the return address and a coldness formed around his heart. It came from Ellysia.

Col took the letter up to his room. There were long windows in this end room, one facing east toward the slopes of Mount Vesuvius, the other overlooking the bay. He sat down on the wide edge of one and slit open the letter. His gaze dropped to the signature. Dr. Paolo Ruggieri. A prickle of apprehension danced up his spine. Whatever it was, it was sure to be bad news.

He started at the beginning and scanned the first paragraph. The language was English, the style foreign, and the words cold and clear. Col felt as if he'd been hit in the stomach. Carruthers was dead.

Col crumpled the letter in his fist. The view of the bay, with its colorful fishing boats, blurred before his eyes. Carruthers had been more than a friend or godfather. He had taken the place of the father that Col had never known. And he had believed in Alistair when everyone else had turned against him.

Goddamn it, he couldn't be dead!

He stood at the window, grieving, as dusk gathered and the stars winked like fireflies above the dark waters of the bay.

Three days later Col came down to settle the bill for his lodgings and went out to the loggia, where a last-minute meal of bread, cheese, and strong hot coffee awaited him. A sleepless night left him feeling vague and lightheaded, and he wanted his wits about him.

Scraping back a wrought-iron chair, he sat and poured himself a cup of coffee from the waiting pot. Although it was early the sun was already warm, promising fine weather. In less than an hour the *Minerva* would sail with the tide for Ellysia. He was impatient to be off. He'd made up his mind that he would follow up with Carruthers's great discovery— whatever the hell it might be. He owed the old lion that.

A soft *ziss-zisst* caught his attention. A wizened woman was nearby, plying a broom across the terra cotta tiles, although there was nothing to sweep up except a few scarlet petals that had fallen from the ornamental vine in the night.

Col had never seen her before. Dressed in the traditional black with a fringed shawl over her plump shoulders, she looked like hundreds of other old women in the city. But with her harsh squint, skin like a dried-out orange peel, and quivering hairy mole, she seemed the typical *strega* of Italian folklore. They certainly would have hung her for a witch in England a hundred years earlier, Col surmised. All she needed was a black cat at her heels. He smiled.

That seemed to be the signal she'd waited for.

Tucking the broom against the trellis, she came up to his table. He set down his cup. *"Buon giorno,* Signora."

She nodded in response to his greeting, not surprised that he spoke her language so flawlessly. Her own Italian had a hint of Calabria in the accent. "I will tell you your future, Signore, for you are a man of destiny. Dame Fortune has placed her golden hand upon your head."

Col leaned back in his chair with a sardonic smile. "A golden hand? I was beginning to think it was her black, cloven hoof!"

"You must not mock." Her eyes closed. "I see a boat."

He shifted impatiently. He knew this game. "Signora, who does not? The bay is filled with them." Withdrawing a handful of coins, he shook them gently in his cupped hand. "Here. Take your payment, but spare me your performance."

She reached out with a swiftness that belied her age, pushing his hand aside. The coins clinked against the saucer and rolled off to the tiled terrace floor. "Fool! I do not want your money. You must hear me out." Her voice took on a queer, droning quality. "I see many women. They will surround you."

His mouth quirked up. He certainly hoped so. "Interesting. Tell me more, Signora!"

"They will change your life. Two, especially. One dark as night, one golden bright. I see death . . . an old man . . . foul murder! The old lion calls out to you for justice in his name."

Col sat up so abruptly he almost overturned his chair. He and Alistair had always called Carruthers "the old lion."

"What else!"

The woman's eyes were rolled up in her head until only a thin line of white showed between her half-closed lids. "A long and troubled road lies ahead . . . and three Fates . . . dancing."

A cat yowled and hissed behind his chair. It startled Col. He uttered an oath and turned to look over his shoulder. There was no cat to be seen.

And when he turned back the other way, there was no broom resting against the trellis and no old woman, only an empty, sunlit terrace and a scattering of scarlet petals that had fallen from the vine during the night.

The last of the stores were loaded on the *Minerva* for its monthly run to Lipari and Stromboli. Col had hired it to take him to Ellysia first. A shadow fell across the scrubbed boards of the deck and he looked up.

A man with unruly dark hair and a rumpled brown suit appeared on the dock, carrying a battered valise. He appeared to be about twenty-five, but that might be due as much to his boyish good looks as to his guileless blue eyes. The tweed of his garments was good quality, but had seen better days. He hailed the captain, who went forward to find out what he wanted.

"The name's Adams," the man said. "Jethroe T. Adams. I'm looking for transportation to Capri, so I can catch the steamer to Stromboli. I understand that you're headed there yourself."

The captain didn't understand the man's poor Italian. Col strolled over and took charge. "Few Americans visit the Aeolians, Mr. Adams. They're rather off the beaten track."

"Yes, sir! And that's why I'm headed there." He

pulled a card out of his wallet and handed it to Col. "I'm a newspaper reporter, doing a series of articles on volcanoes for my paper." He hiked a thumb over his shoulder, where Vesuvius was wreathed in veils of mist. "I hiked up to the caldera Tuesday. Spent most of yesterday in bed with a bottle of medicinal brandy. Whew! Quite a climb."

Col glanced at the card. "The *New York Monitor*, eh? The managing editor is an old acquaintance of mine. How's old Rolly Joe doing these days?"

Jethroe Adams's ingenuous blue eyes lit with laughter. "Roland Joseph is with the *Albany Sentinel*, and he'd have a fit of apoplexy if he heard you call him that. What's more, he wouldn't be caught dead crossing the *Monitor*'s threshold, as I'm sure you know. He calls us 'scurrilous scandalmongers and seething sensationalists.'"

Col grinned. "And so you are. Welcome aboard, Mr. Adams. You can stow your things in the aft cabin."

They cast off almost immediately. Col went forward and scanned the horizon after they were under way. The sea was a deep and tranquil blue and Capri only a dark smudge in the distance. The brilliant sun turned his thick hair to threads of spun gold and the wind whipped his dark coat out behind him like a raven's wings. The good weather would hold awhile. His spirits lifted and he felt a sudden surge of exhilaration.

A shrill cry off the starboard bow made him turn. Three gulls, bright as the *Minerva*'s canvas sails, arced across the blue sky.

Jethroe Adams joined Col. He was a poor sailor, and already looking pale and seedy. Col wondered how long it would take before the reporter was either throwing up over the rail or collapsed, face down, on a bunk. Adams shoved his hands in his pockets and followed the path of the gulls' flight, with a faint attempt at nonchalance, as he fought to fend off seasickness.

"Three birds, three wishes," he said. "That's what my grandfather always told me."

"Is that so?"

Adams didn't answer. The vessel lurched suddenly and he stumbled back, turned, and bolted for the cabin, leaving Col to enjoy the scene alone.

As he watched, the white birds swooped and soared like the notes of a Neapolitan lovesong. Three birds, three wishes, eh? Col scanned the waves. There was something on the wind beside the smell of salt sea—the uplifting tang of adventure and discovery, and perhaps the faintest undernote of danger.

A wry smile creased his face. If he could have three wishes, that was exactly what he would ask for.

The gulls shrieked with laughter, and wheeled up, up, up, like shining harpies, into the fierce blue sky.

2

TRAVELS

Notes from Col McCallum's diary

Except for certain acts of God—typhoons, avalanches, desert dust storms—I have always subscribed to the belief that I, as a rational man, was the complete master of my destiny. Brash fool! From the moment I set foot in the Court of Three Sisters I began to realize my error.

Life's lessons are sometimes enjoyable, other times harsh, but always unexpected. My blind arrogance would prove my downfall: We cannot prevent ourselves from being pawns in a much larger game.

Italy, March

"Is it very bad?"

Fanny and Summer sat stiffly on the horsehair sofa

in the pensione's parlor, while Thea and their land-lady hovered over Nana. She was stretched out on the worn carpet in obvious agony and they were all in a state of shock.

Nana had always seemed to be frozen in time, the ageless, unchanging symbol of authority and comfort for as long as any of them could remember. Now she was suddenly reduced to an old woman, exposed and unfamiliar. How very small and fragile she looked!

Summer had sensed disaster from the moment of their arrival yesterday. There was something heavy and dark in the atmosphere of the pensione, a malign miasma that filled every nook and cranny. And now disaster.

The local doctor had been called from his surgery and knelt beside Nana, making stern tsk-tsking sounds as he examined his patient. Summer was terri-bly frightened. Poor Nana had taken quite a fall down the steep back stairs. All the rosy apple color had faded from her cheeks, leaving her face strangely withered. Her skin had gone quite as gray as her hair.

It was hot in the small parlor with the strong sun coming through the dark velvet curtains at the win-dows. Fanny glanced at the picture of Queen Victoria that the landlady, an English expatriate, had placed prominently on the mantelpiece. The pensione with its antimacassars, heavy furniture, and Sheffield fig-urines had been a grave disappointment. Why, one might imagine oneself still home in England! And in much reduced circumstances.

The doctor finished his examination and rose to address Thea.

"I am most sorry to inform you of it, Signora," he said in heavily accented English, "but this good lady has broken her leg quite badly."

Thea wrung her hands. "Oh, dear. This is terrible news."

The sisters' journey had seemed cursed from the start. Their father had gone on ahead to make preparations, leaving the two younger women in Thea's chaperonage and Nana's capable hands. Although the trip across the Channel had been smooth enough, Fanny had been violently ill the entire overnight voyage. She had never been a good patient, and her bout of mal de mer had been a nightmare for all concerned. That had been enough for Thea to realize that they must change their plans and make the longer journey by land to Naples, instead of sailing for Ellysia directly from Marseilles. From the start nothing had gone as it should—and now this!

"Can you set her leg properly?"

"But of course," the doctor responded, greatly offended. "This is Naples, not the wilds of the jungle! First I shall sedate her." He took a dark blue bottle of fluid from his pocket and held it to Nana's lips.

She drank it down gratefully. "So sorry, M-Miss Thea, that is, Mrs. Armstrong. D-don't know h-how I came to f-fall."

The words had cost the woman a terrible effort. Thea knelt beside her and took Nana's hand in hers. "Don't worry, I shall take care of everything. You shall have the best of care until you are well again."

"But not here!" the landlady, Mrs. Bartlett, exclaimed. "I assure you, Mrs. Armstrong, that I am deeply concerned for your nurse. However I cannot take it upon myself to look after an invalid for so many weeks with just myself, Cook, and one maid-of-all-work. Why, they would give me their notice over all the extra chores. We are not equipped to deal with something of this nature, and I—"

Thea raised her eyebrows in disdain. "There is no need for you to put yourself in a taking. My sister Fanny and I will do all the fetching and carrying." She turned to Summer. "You could keep Nana company, perhaps read to her to while away the hours."

Mrs. Bartlett flushed. "Much as I would like to accommodate you, it is *not* possible. You hired the rooms for two days only. I have other guests arriving tomorrow afternoon. The Stantons come every year and I cannot disappoint them."

The doctor frowned at the landlady with disapproval. "I pity anyone who falls ill beneath this roof, Signora." He turned to Thea. "I understand that you and your sisters are en route?"

"Yes. Our father is Professor Fairchild, and we were to join him on Ellysia for several months. This, of course, changes everything." She wrung her hands.

The physician thought rapidly. "Perhaps not. You see, this poor lady will be laid up for some time. Six, eight weeks, perhaps. Travel, of course, will be out of the question. My suggestion is that you settle your servant with the good sisters at the Convent of St. Francis. They are highly skilled in nursing. Then you may proceed with your journey, safe in the knowledge that she is in the best of hands. Once the leg is healed properly, the lady will be able to continue on to join you, or return to England."

Nana moaned. Bad enough to be in such sorry straits, but it was even worse for a staunch but simple Presbyterian to be placed in the hands of papist nuns, who were foreigners, to boot. Grandfather Semple must be spinning in his grave. But her station in life gave Nana a measure of comfort: Miss Thea and the doctor knew best.

The sedative had begun to take effect, but only a

reduction of the fracture would truly ease her agony. She shifted and gave a hoarse scream. Her lips took on a purplish hue and beads of sweat stood out above them like a glistening mustache.

Summer was greatly distressed. She had no faith in a universe where someone as strong and healthy as Nana could be brought low by tripping over a loose rug string. It was sad and unsettling to see someone so formidable reduced to total helplessness. The doctor was prepared to act, and she sincerely hoped he knew what he was about.

The dapper man removed his well-tailored coat and turned to the landlady, rolling up his sleeves. "I will require assistance with setting the leg."

Mrs. Bartlett may have come down in the world from when she was Miss Hemsley of Bath, but she had no intention of playing the role the doctor assigned to her. "I will send in the maid," she said quickly. She smiled at Thea graciously. "If you would care to accompany me, I will have refreshments brought to you in the garden."

Fanny jumped up eagerly but Summer balked. She wanted very much to escape the stuffy parlor, and the unpleasant drama about to unfold, to the tranquillity of the garden, but couldn't imagine abandoning Nana at such a time. Nana had never abandoned her. "I shall remain here."

"You cannot mean it!" Fanny said, aghast. Anything to do with the sickroom made her squeamish. Why, just looking at Nana's graying face had upset her digestion.

Thea was in no mood to humor Summer. She sent her sister an exasperated look. "You are a single young lady, with no training. It would not be seemly for you to remain. Come into the garden."

Summer would not be dissuaded. "Nana will want a familiar face nearby during her ordeal."

Thea swallowed her irritation. She knew from past experience that there would be no use arguing. Not when Summer spoke in that coolly obstinate tone. In her own way, she could be as willful as Fanny. Her sisters were a handful at times. Indeed, how could they help but be spoiled, having been raised alone by Father and a houseful of doting servants? Well, she would soon change that. Meantime, if Summer refused to heed her advice, let her take the consequences.

She gathered her skirts and followed the landlady toward the hallway. "A glass of lemonade would be quite refreshing. Come, Fanny."

After they left Summer endured a most unpleasant half hour. The maid, a stout girl with a merry disposition, held the patient down while the doctor applied steady traction to her broken leg. It was a difficult task and hard on all concerned. Nana fainted. When Summer heard the grating of the displaced bones she almost did the same. It was horrid.

Afterward Nana came to and was much more comfortable with her leg safely splinted. They put her on the couch with a pillow for her head and a quilt over her legs. She was transferred to the nearby convent later that day, more frightened for her charges than for herself.

"My poor little lambs, what will you do without me?" Nana fretted, her voice slurred with the effects of laudanum and exhaustion. She turned to Thea and her voice lowered to a rough whisper. "Who will see to Miss Summer? What will happen if she takes one of her queer turns?"

Thea caught her lower lip between her teeth. What indeed! She'd had her hands full at Kingsmeade, despite the help of Nana and Cook and a half dozen other servants. The idea of taking it all upon her own shoulders—especially if Summer had . . . *problems*—was daunting. She kept an outward calm.

"You must rest now, Nana. Please don't concern yourself overly. I can manage until we reach Ellysia, where I am sure I can make some other arrangements."

Despite her words, she wasn't very confident. Everything had gone wrong from the moment they set out on their journey. Why, oh why, had they ever left home?

Thea was greatly vexed. Because of many delays they had missed the scheduled monthly sailing of the supply boat.

The thought of waiting three more weeks was intolerable, and they were running low on funds. Inquiries brought the news that they must travel on to Sorrento, where they could make other arrangements.

Fanny examined her feet in their scuffed half-boots morosely. She didn't see why they couldn't stroll along by the bay. Everyone else was. And she didn't see why she couldn't remove her braided jacket.

Summer agreed. Thea was being unusually tiresome. No one else was wearing jackets except the three of them, and she'd noticed the averted smiles and shakes of the head from the Neapolitans amused by their quaint English ways. She removed her pelisse, daring Thea to chide her for it. The long journey had taken a greater toll of her energies, and her temper, than she would admit. Let Thea say one word about it, one single word!

The view from the inn's garden showed the wide-flung arms of the bay enclosing a vast expanse of bright water. It was just possible for Summer to make out the island of Capri, floating like a distant mirage. A line of turbulent clouds rose up like ramparts on the far horizon. They were dark as ash below, yet crowned with boiling white thunderheads. They looked impossibly high above the bulk of Mount Vesuvius, rising behind the city.

A shiver rippled up her spine. It was odd to realize that this was the mountain of smoke and fire that had buried Pompeii in a deadly rain of soot and ash. Harder to believe people still lived and worked in its shadow, either accustomed or resigned to its threat.

A ray of sun lit the steeple of a nearby church. Perhaps, she thought, the Neapolitans expected that God and the saints would protect them from the volcano's wrath, where the Romans' pantheon had failed. She wished she had her sketching materials at hand to capture the intriguing scenes.

With several hours on their hands, the sisters were to dine at a hotel catering to British travelers. Summer would rather have spent the time at one of the local inns with their soft gold walls and blue-shuttered windows, hiding secrets and shadows. The Three Crowns, where Thea had reserved a private parlor ahead of time, was done in false half-timbering outside and dark paneling inside, in imitation of an old English inn.

Summer was dismayed. After the balmy air and sunshine it was like plunging into a mausoleum.

It was worse than Mrs. Bartlett's pensione, she thought. "We might as well be in Kingsmeade, at the Hare and Hounds," she remarked aloud.

Thea was not amused at the comparison. Their village inn catered to the lower elements of Kingsmeade society, while the Three Crowns had housed English nobility. "I think you are both exceedingly ungrateful," she said frostily. "I am doing my best to keep you in surroundings that are safe, familiar, and in keeping with our status in the world."

Fanny was bored and wanted to go out. "I should love to explore those quaint little shops in the streets just behind us."

Summer sent her a cynical look. "You just want to hear the young men call out *'bella, bellissima!'* when you stroll past. One would think you would grow tired of it by now."

"You are hateful," Fanny snapped, embarrassed that Summer had seen through her. "I think you are jealous because . . . because . . ."

"Because no one will ever call me beautiful?" Summer shrugged. "I don't care. They won't call me 'vain little widgeon,' either, and that is exactly what you are."

Fanny's quick pang of remorse turned to an acute sense of injury. "You've been out of sorts all day. Nana was right, this trip is too much for you. I don't know why you even wanted to come along."

Summer turned away. "I didn't."

Thea's temper was stretched dangerously thin. "We have come to expand our horizons and improve our minds, not to snipe at one another, nor to shop and perhaps expose ourselves to unpleasant situations. This is an opportunity for you to see history at

firsthand, and to polish your Italian, which is shame-
fully limited."

"How can I practice it if the only people I see to
speak to are you and Summer?" Fanny replied. "Do
say we can take a stroll along the street, dear, dear
Thea."

"You know that I gave Nana my word that
Summer would continue her afternoon rests. I cannot
go back upon it."

Fanny's lower lip stuck out in a familiar pout. "But
I saw a lovely fan in one of the windows that would
be perfect with my yellow muslin."

"You have enough fans for a young lady scarcely
out of the schoolroom, and we cannot leave Summer
here alone at a public inn," Thea snapped, "and I am
sure she does not wish to be stared at any more
today."

"What does she care if they look at her? They are
total strangers."

But Summer did care, very much, although she
couldn't bring herself to admit it. It was very difficult
to be the focus of curious stares and to pretend not to
notice. It was worse to be the object of pity. She had
never got used to eyes that wouldn't meet hers, but
fixed intently on her chin or a space just above her
brows, as if she were a severed head served up on a
silver platter.

Still, she found what she had seen of Naples to be
unexpected and charming. If she could get about like
Fanny and Thea she would have wanted to explore
the city on foot. Instead she satisfied herself by sitting
at the window of their private parlor to watch the colorful street traffic. The hands of the clock crept
around with exasperating slowness. Her back ached
abominably.

Fanny was still pouting. How would she ever meet any dashing young men if Thea kept her as close to her side as she did in England? Thea wanted to box her sister's pretty ears. She lowered her voice. "And we cannot leave Summer alone in a public place even if we have our own parlor."

Summer filtered their voices out. If they were going to continue brangling she wanted no part of it. Instead she let her mind wander where she could not go, through the narrow streets and up past the terraced fields and vineyards, up and up to the summit of Mount Vesuvius. What would it be like there?

She knew there were fumaroles, vents that poured out sulfurous gases and steam so hot it could boil an egg. She'd read of bubbling mudholes amid a landscape more barren than any desert, in the caldera. In her mind's eye the volcano seethed like buried emotions, ready to explode, to burst open in a fury of heat and sound. She felt a strange kinship with it.

A soft *ziss-zisst* caught her attention. Looking through the open window, she saw an old woman sweeping the spotless steps of the little inn across the way. She was dressed all in black and looked exactly the way Summer had always imagined the witch from *Hansel and Gretel* would. She stared at Summer quite intently, then smiled and gave a little wave in greeting. Surprised, Summer gave a polite nod and smiled back. *Ziss-zisst* went the twig broom again, and the woman went inside.

Later, as they left the inn, they passed two lovers entwined in the shadows of an arch, murmuring endearments in one another's ears.

Thea didn't seem to notice, but Fanny watched them eagerly. Someday she would have young swains courting her. Someday she would have a husband, who would be madly in love with her. A wave of excitement crested inside her as she wondered who he might be. *Who will love me?* she thought, lapsing into rosy daydreams.

Summer saw the lovers, too. Their world was one forever closed to her. She looked down and compared Fanny's dainty half-boots to her own sturdy, more serviceable ones. Quite like the hiking boots that Miss Quindling, the odd old spinster who lived down the lane from their home in Kingsmeade, wore.

How symbolic, Summer told herself. Fanny would marry someday, as Thea had, but such a life was not for the likes of her. The carriage turned a corner and another pair of lovers strolled hand in hand. A sudden pang smote Summer. Who would ever love her? she wondered sadly, and closed her eyes.

Ellysia, March

"Ah, Signore McCallum! Come in, come in!"

Dr. Ruggieri invited Col into his parlor. He was a vital little man, trim and nattily dressed as if he still imagined himself to live in a large city. His soft black eyes and easy, congenial manner conspired to make the doctor look vague, yet Col realized he took in everything. "I hope I am not disturbing you at your work."

"No, no! I am pleased to make your acquaintance, although the circumstances are mournful," Ruggieri said, waving his hand dismissively at a pile of papers by his armchair. "Signore Carruthers spoke most highly of you."

"And of you," Col replied.

The doctor brought out two glasses and a bottle of an exquisite local wine, as pale and clear as distilled sunshine. Col looked around the little parlor. It was a soothing combination of clean lines and village simplicity with the interesting clutter acquired in a lifetime in Rome. It smelled of garlic sausage and lemons with a comforting overlay of leather and old books. The walls were lined with them. He glanced at the volume open on the table beside the comfortably worn leather wing chair.

"The third volume of Lord FitzRoy's adventures," the doctor said with a gentle smile. "I enjoy your countryman's tales very much, although I doubt they are all true."

Col laughed. "I can say on good authority that they are."

Ruggieri's face lit up. "You know this FitzRoy?"

"We've been acquainted many years. He's full of bombast, I suppose, but a fairly honest fellow, as his type goes." Col was amused. So the doctor hankered for vicarious adventure in Africa, did he? The taste seemed at odds with the homely, civilized surroundings.

A bunch of early wildflowers stuck in a blue glass vase had dried to an elegant skeleton, shedding crisply curled petals across a bust of Bacchus. The carved lips still smiled, about to nibble from a bunch of marble grapes, but half the sculptor's work had been sheared off in a past catastrophe, returning it to the raw stone from which the likeness had been wrested.

Ruggieri offered him a glass and they drank to the memory of Col's godfather and toasted one another's health. When the conversation got around to Carruthers's demise, the doctor's easy flow of talk faltered. Now that Signore McCallum was here, he wondered if he should speak up or keep his own counsel. Perhaps better to wait until he received a reply from the letter he'd sent to a friend in Rome. He would know if anything more was required of him once the letter arrived.

Ruggieri was troubled and not even his exquisite manners could hide it. The signs were evident in the set of the older man's shoulders and the small but persistent furrow between his eyebrows.

Col had been hoping the doctor would bring up the subject that hovered between them, unspoken, but he seemed reluctant to do so. There was nothing for Col to do but broach it himself.

"I wish Carruthers were here with us today, sharing a glass of this excellent wine. I still cannot believe he died of something so minor as an infected insect bite."

Ruggieri flashed a glance at Col. "Nor I. Signore Carruthers was a good man. And a stubborn one." He sighed. "At times I wonder, if I had been here during his final illness, perhaps he would still be alive."

Now Col knew that his instincts had been right. A dangerous, golden spark burned in the depths of his green eyes.

"Let us stop this fencing. I've guessed from the moment we met that you are not easy in your mind over the circumstances surrounding his death. I want to know why."

"When I left for Lipari, he seemed well on his way to recovery from a mild case of sepsis. His death was most unexpected."

Col wasn't satisfied. "There's more."

"Yes." The doctor frowned. "I have no ready answer." Ruggieri's dark eyes were shadowed. "I can only tell you this—his symptoms, reported to me afterward, were not what I would have expected."

"It's a great leap from unusual symptoms to suspected murder. And that's what we're talking about, *isn't it?*"

Ruggieri was the kind of man who could be led, but not pushed. "As I said earlier, Signore McCallum, I am a man of science. My leaps of intuition spring from a solid base of fact—what you might call the evidence. At this point I have nothing. Except a feeling that makes the hair stand up."

"And that is truly all?"

There was just the slightest pause. "That is all."

Col knew he'd get no more out of Ruggieri just yet. "In your own way, doctor, you are as obdurate as Carruthers, and such stubbornness, I feel obligated to point out, sometimes proves fatal."

"A warning, Signore McCallum?"

"A word to the wise." Col regarded the little man intently. "Will you give me your word that if you find out anything . . . *anything* that confirms your suspicions, you will discuss it with me before acting?"

Again that telltale pause. The doctor nodded. "If I should come across pertinent information, you may be certain that I will inform you at once."

Col had to be satisfied with that. For now.

Although Ruggieri wouldn't come forward without proof, the doctor did have grave doubts as to whether Carruthers had died of natural causes. Despite his natural discretion and courtly manners, he had a bulldog's tenacity. Once he was sure if and how Carruthers had been poisoned, his next steps would be to discover why—and by whom.

He felt better for making that decision. "The equipment and goods are still up at the cottage along with Signore Carruthers's personal effects, but under the circumstances . . ."

His dark eyes twinkled. "I know all too well how professional jealousies can overcome a seemingly rational person, so I have kept the journals and papers of your learned friend here where I can keep an eye on them. It is your own field, yes?"

A shadow crossed Col's features. "Yes. However I have been engaged in other ways for several years."

Like getting roaring drunk in Athens after settling a slur on Alistair's name, signing on with a merchant sailor on a voyage that lasted six months, and getting roaring drunk again the moment the ship docked.

In his checkered career Col had explored the California high country, which had led to several seasons digging for gold followed by a sobering few months among lepers in the Sandwich Islands, and a stint as a laborer in a diamond mine. The last had been devilishly hard, but it was damned easy compared to those weeks with the leper colony. The images still haunted him.

"Come, I will show you," the doctor said, rising.

"Of course." Col followed him. The house, like most of those on the island, was built like a hollow square. They went through a door from the parlor directly into a small, sunny courtyard and across to another door.

Inside it was cool and dim, but when Ruggieri threw open the shutters Col whistled in amazement. He'd expected a few journals and the maroon leather folders in which Carruthers had always kept his field notes, but the floor was filled with crates and cartons of notebooks and journals, with boxes of books, and even a flat-topped trunk. He opened it. Maps, journals, papers, notes to the brim. He picked up a few at random: all recent, all apparently filled, and in Carruthers's familiar, sprawling hand. Christ, there was six months of work here!

Well, there was nothing he could do for Carruthers, except to see that he got the recognition for whatever it was that he had found. And, by God, Col vowed, he would see that the old lion got the credit due him!

The doctor looked from crate to crate. "Signore Carruthers was a most prolific man."

"Yes. He'd been working on several books, in addition to his fieldwork. Some of this is bound to be parts of his manuscript." He thanked Ruggieri for taking charge of the papers. "I'll have them conveyed to the cottage tomorrow."

The doctor nodded. "Whenever it is convenient for you, Signore."

Ruggieri led Col back across the courtyard and into the parlor.

"You will want to go up to the cottage and get settled in before nightfall, I am sure. Signore Carruthers's original lodgings were much larger, but too far away and too inconvenient."

"Actually, I would like to go up to the temple complex and have a look around."

"Ah, I will take you up and introduce you to Professor Fairchild, if you like. But first there is one other thing I have for you. The cottage belongs to me. I therefore went with my sister to clean up the cottage after Signore Carruthers passed on, as the place was in grave disorder."

Col's eyebrows met in a frown. The old lion must have been very ill. He was ordinarily a man of almost monkish austerity and neatness.

Ruggieri looked slightly embarrassed. "The cottage, like this house, was built by my father on the site of an old *villa rustica*. He was afraid with all the political changes of fortune, that he might lose everything one day. To this end he built a special hiding place near the chimney to keep his gold. I looked inside, thinking perhaps Signore Carruthers had discovered it for his own use. I will show you when we go to the cottage, for that is where I found the curious little black wooden coffer."

Col was suddenly energized. "You found *what?*"

Dr. Ruggieri looked startled. "Perhaps you are right to think that it was not my business to remove it, but you see I knew that you were coming, and there was a paper fixed to the top of the coffer with your name written upon it."

A mixture of feelings poured through Col like the rush of a river in spate. "What was in it?"

"I do not know," the doctor said, offended. "It was not addressed to me."

"Where is it, man?"

If Ruggieri was taken aback by Col's vehemence, he hid it well. He went to the huge cabinet that almost filled one wall. It was a curious affair, with dozens of pigeonholes and narrow drawers, and wide cupboards both above and below.

"An apothecary's cabinet," Ruggieri explained. "Perfect for cataloging my specimens and papers. I am so attached to it that I brought it with me from Rome."

He opened a narrow drawer and looked in, then shut it and opened another. This one was as empty as the first. Ruggieri was puzzled.

He began to search the entire cabinet, drawer by drawer, cupboard by cupboard. His hands were trembling. Suddenly he gave an exclamation of relief. "Here it is!"

But as he removed the small coffer from the drawer he was filled with consternation. The colored twine that had bound it was gone, the wax seals broken. Stricken, he turned to Col, holding the coffer on the flat of his palms. He looked suddenly old.

Col slid back the lid. *Empty!* He felt as if he'd been punched in the stomach. But that was to be expected. If Carruthers had located the missing Venus, he'd surely have trumpeted it to the world.

"The last time I saw this little box it was on my brother's worktable in Ilykion, with a priceless golden statuette inside it," Col said.

Priceless not only because of the precious metal and the artifact's age, but because of its likely provenance. At the time of its discovery, it was thought to have been the only work in existence of the great ancient sculptor, Praxiteles. Its theft and the resultant scandal had been the cause of Alistair's suicide. To come so close to solving the mystery . . .

He examined the box. Alistair had sealed it himself. Col detected a fingerprint in the edge of the wax seal and felt his heart turn over. He placed his own fingertip against it, as if the contact could leap the boundaries of time, of death, and touch his brother's hand again. *Oh, Alistair! Oh, bloody hell!*

Ruggieri watched Col's bleak face in great distress. "I am distraught. From its former weight and the fact that it was hidden away, it is probable the statue was still inside when I brought it here, for safekeeping."

Col looked up, shocked beyond words. How in God's name had Carruthers found it? True, he'd promised to put his considerable resources to work locating it, but fourteen long years had passed.

Perhaps, Col thought, he was jumping to the wrong conclusions. If the box *had* held the statue, then Carruthers might have had a damned good reason for not revealing it just yet; or perhaps the old lion had merely been waiting for his arrival.

He resisted the urge to dash the coffer against the whitewashed wall. "Damn it, man, it couldn't have walked off on its own! When was the last time that you saw the box?"

Ruggieri sighed. "It was the day we had a memorial service for Signore Carruthers. Several of us repaired to my humble house for refreshments. I was looking for my old microscope, which I keep in the drawer next to it. I brought it out to show Professor Fairchild, as he is interested in such things. I opened the wrong drawer by mistake, but I am sure no one saw it."

Col was thinking furiously. If someone had been looking in the mirror on the side wall at that exact moment, it *was* possible. "Who else was here at the time?"

"Signore Pierce and his charming wife—they have returned to England. Signora Morville, a widowed Englishwoman. Young Signori Forsythe and Gordon."

"All from the excavation team?"

"All except Father Nunzio."

"It's vitally important that I have the contents of that box," Col said softly. "It is necessary to right a great wrong."

"Perhaps the paper will help. Because of its width it would not fit in the drawer, so I put it with my own papers."

Col took the envelope and slit it open. There was no letter, only a bill of sale from a shop in Cairo that

Col knew. While outwardly respectable, it was suspected of dealing in illicit antiquities on the side. Across the bottom, in a darker shade of ink, Carruthers had written, "The Venus of Ilykion."

Col looked grim. That explained the state of the cottage. Someone had ransacked the place, looking for the statue. If Carruthers had identified the piece by name, then he was damned sure that it was the same one stolen from the dig at Ilykion, fourteen years earlier. But how on earth had he stumbled upon it? And more importantly—who had sold it?

The shadows stirred in the depths of Col's soul. Once he had the answer to those questions, he might be able to uncover the trail to the real thief, and clear Alistair's name.

Col set the box down. "Don't blame yourself for its loss, doctor. Someone knew that Carruthers had it, and was determined to find it."

He tucked the bill of sale into his inner pocket along with his personal papers. Now he had two mysteries to solve, and he was more sure than ever that Carruthers had not died a natural death.

The wind blew strongly off the sea, stirring the wild grasses along Ellysia's jutting headland. McCallum and Dr. Ruggieri walked beneath the branches of a grove of gnarled trees, once sacred to some forgotten god. The breeze blew through the leaves, like the echo of long-dead voices.

Col looked around keenly. "An atmospheric spot. There is something in the air that makes the hair prickle at the nape of my neck."

The doctor smiled. "Yes. Even I, a man of science, feel it. The villagers do not come here often."

They continued out of the grove, into the rich, warm sunlight. Col liked the retired scientist, but noticed that whenever the talk came back to Carruthers, Ruggieri became just the slightest bit stiff. Perhaps he felt that he had failed his patient in some way. Col didn't think so. The man knew more than he was telling, Col was sure of it.

Ahead were the first signs of the temple complex that Carruthers had been exploring at the time of his death. The light poured over the broken walls and columns and pediments like a honeyed glaze.

"The ancient ways have not died out completely," Col commented. Someone had set a fresh bouquet of yellow wildflowers before the remains of a crude wayside shrine that had already been old when Julius Caesar ruled the Roman Empire. "To placate any shades of the old ones that might linger?"

His companion smiled absently. "Or some local youth or maiden, invoking every possible means to win the heart of his or her true love. The shrine is rumored to have been erected to the goddess of love."

They were almost at the main archaeological site.

They crested the low hill, and paused to view the sprawl of the ruined temple complex in silence.

"There is the professor coming along the path now," Ruggieri said, and hailed him.

Col propped his boot up on a crumbled wall and surveyed the area with puzzlement. The exposed remnants of the temples crowned the heights backing onto the cliffs of the headland. Those still standing were well preserved, but the greater part of the complex was only hinted at beneath the overgrowth.

But nothing he could see fit his godfather's hints of an extraordinary discovery. He frowned against the glare. What was there about these ruins to make Carruthers think he had made "the find of the century"?

Professor Fairchild came up the slope of the meadow and joined them. The doctor introduced the men to one another. "Signore McCallum has come to Ellysia to see to the affairs of Sir John Carruthers." Richard's air of bonhomie changed to sudden wariness.

Col offered his hand. "I understand you've found something rather special here on Ellysia."

"Ah, yes." Richard waved at the work in progress with the barely concealed pride that a proud papa of a newborn might display. "I'll show you over the site if you like."

The doctor, his commission accomplished, said his good-byes and left. Richard led Col up a well-trodden path toward the ruins. "Well, Mr. McCallum, there it is. What do you think of it?"

The site covered several acres with Roman architecture, with a few older remnants of classical Greece. Nothing went back much more than two thousand years.

"Very impressive. Yet I am surprised that Carruthers chose something this recent. After visiting Mycenae, he had planned to make their ancient culture his main subject of study."

Fairchild was very defensive of the site. "But the extent of it, man! And in such a remote place. I think that is what intrigued Carruthers so. The *why* of it, you see, on this small island plunked down in the middle of nowhere."

"Yes. Perhaps it had important sacred associations to the ancients."

The professor looked rather disgruntled, as if Col had appropriated his pet theory. He recovered and pointed to the massive temple in the center of the ruins. Although the roof was gone the structure was largely intact. Twelve massive columns framed the front of the deep porch and twenty-four more columns marched along the sides of the rectangular building.

"Marble," he said, "imported from the mainland, which means that this site was indeed of great importance in the ancient world."

"You seem overly sure of it," Col replied cynically. "It may be that a wealthy senator was celebrating a triumph, or, more likely, trying to appease his gods after a lifetime of corruption."

Richard's jaw squared. "Shall we be frank? I cannot blame you if you are disgruntled that Count DiCaesari gave jurisdiction over the excavation to me, rather than to John Carruthers. That was the doing of my patron, Sir Horace Chriswell. By the time I reached Ellysia it had all been settled amicably."

Col lifted his eyebrows. "Indeed? I find that a great surprise. I've never known one archaeologist to give way to another without threat of lawsuits and great bodily harm."

Richard flushed. "There is a good deal of rivalry in this profession of ours, as you well know. I admit that I would have had difficulty accepting the disappointment, if Count DiCaesari had given the concession to Carruthers instead."

As the professor surveyed their surroundings a fervent light shone in his eyes. His voice took on a deeper timbre. "I have high hopes for this site."

Col recognized that look. Richard Fairchild was a well-respected scholar and archaeologist, but that was rarely enough for men of his ilk. They wanted more—a piece of history, with their names carved prominently on it for all the world to see. But Col knew something else: Whatever it was that Carruthers had found here, he had not seen fit to take Fairchild into his confidence, and Fairchild had not found it. He didn't even know that there was anything else to find.

Col shot the older man an assessing glance. The professor had very much the air of a man in hopes of courting Lady Luck, not that of one who had already won her fickle heart.

Of course, Richard Fairchild might be more than a fine scholar, he might be a damned good actor, as well; but Col knew in his blood that Carruthers's mysterious find wasn't at the temple site. And if he hadn't known, he would still have figured it out readily, because if the find were here, there was no way in hell that the old lion would have given the site up so easily. He would have argued for it, fought for it, moved mountains, called in every favor from every person of influence he knew, until the count was worn down.

Col clambered over a test trench sunk through the site beside the professor. Damn it, what had Carruthers found?

He took another tack. "I appreciate your showing me around. God knows, there is never enough time or enough staff to do everything that needs to be done before the season ends."

"My pleasure." The professor led him at right angles to the main complex and stopped before an area cleared of centuries of soil and debris. He indicated a newly uncovered pavement. "We believe this to be all that remains of another large temple. A quite good mosaic, don't you think?"

"You have a gift for understatement."

Col hunkered down on the stone threshold for a closer look. He'd never seen such exquisite work in all his broad experience. The colored stones were fit together as closely, as expertly as pieces of marquetry. The border was dark blue and white, with rows of leaping dolphins enclosing the main design. The detail was phenomenal.

In the center was a man with a gold crown and trident, riding the foaming waves in a chariot made from a giant seashell and pulled by dolphins and sea horses. The king of the ocean himself, Poseidon Earthshaker.

"It's the best I've ever seen," he said finally. "The artist was a genius, but you don't need me to tell you that."

"Yes, I have to admit we're excited about it. I haven't seen its equal among those uncovered in Pompeii, or even in Rome."

Col agreed. But, wondrous as the workmanship was, he knew without a doubt that it had nothing to do with Carruthers's discovery.

They left the headland together, but their paths split up where the trail forked. Richard brought up the subject most on his mind.

"Carruthers intended to stay on here, working on his manuscripts. I have reason to believe that he also hoped to excavate one of the earlier sites on the island. To be quite frank, I am wondering if you mean to do the same."

Col shrugged. "I'm not sure. From the looks of all the papers, I'll have enough on my hands just sorting them through and getting his manuscripts into shape."

That seemed to satisfy the professor. He said goodbye and went along to the main excavation site.

*   *   *

Col settled into the cottage. The older part had begun life as some noble Roman's country estate and was built in the old courtyard style. The later additions opened to the outside and views of Ellysia's rugged beauty.

The boxes and trunks had been brought up from Dr. Ruggieri's place in the village. Col hoped to put the work in some kind of vague order, but it seemed a near hopeless task. All he could do now was continue with his mentor's work. That was the rub. After several days he still had no idea of what Sir John had found, or where. Or if he would ever locate it, himself.

After a lunch of bread, cheese, and the pale local wine, Col sat at the unvarnished table scrubbed almost white and stared out the open window at the distant hillside. The blue-painted shutters framed the temple site in the distance.

It was still cool inside the thick cottage walls but the sun glinted fiercely from the fluted columns of the ruins, turning them to pillars of gold.

Col turned his attention to the stacks of field notes. There were boxes of them, not to mention the day book and odd scraps of paper where Carruthers had jotted inspirations and ideas as they occurred. He rued the discretion that had confined Carruthers to opaque hints as to the nature of his "astounding discovery."

He set aside the papers finally in frustration. It was like beating his head against a stone wall. A ride across the open fields might clear his thoughts, he decided.

Taking his hat from a wall peg, he went out into

the sunshine again. Church bells rang faintly on the clear air. He'd forgotten. This was one of the many saints' days clogging the local calendar. Col saddled his mare. As he rode down the track toward the village of Appolinaria, he couldn't shake off his growing unease. Years ago he'd been in Greece, when a series of great earthquakes had struck. Just before the first shock he'd felt a strange vibration from the ground beneath his feet, like a low note just below the threshold of hearing. Then all hell had broken loose.

He pushed his hat to the back. Funny, he had almost the same feeling now. And this time it didn't come from the ground, but from some well of primitive instinct, deep inside him.

After several days' travel, Thea's patience and Fanny's cheerfulness were almost exhausted. Summer was exhausted in every sense of the word. They arrived in Sorrento in the late afternoon and prepared to embark on the last leg of their journey.

The sun was warm and Thea and Fanny unfurled their parasols. At dawn and sunset, the groom told them, the bay was ringed with all manner of fishing boats. At this time of day there were only a pair of fishermen mending their nets and a band of urchins playing with a canvas ball. They turned to watch the foreigners dismount from the carriage and gaped at the luggage set down from the roof and from the commodious boot.

Summer's cane-backed invalid chair attracted equal attention. One boy argued that the chair was some sort of throne. Why else was the one lady lifted carefully down by the groom while the others descended on their own power? Surely the dark-haired signorina was a princess from another land. The older boys hooted him down. They recognized the women as English by their clothes and mannerisms. The wheeled chair was merely an eccentric fashion.

Everyone knew that the English were mad.

Thea, whose Italian was quite good, became greatly annoyed. Summer laughed softly and her sisters turned to look at her in surprise. It was not something they heard often. In fact, neither could recall the last occasion, although they were much too well bred to comment on it.

There was only one boat in sight. It was small and seemed to be in need of refurbishing. It looked like a larger version of the fishing boat, but they learned that it was to be their ferry to the island. There was no regular transportation to Ellysia, the groom explained. The people who lived there were self-sufficient, between their crops, livestock, and the bounty of the sea. It was only since the Englishmen had come recently that there was any need for regular traffic to and from the mainland.

The baggage was loaded and the women made as comfortable as possible for the overnight voyage to Ellysia. The other occupants of the vessel—the sailors and two servants going to visit relatives farther on the ship's itinerary—were intrigued and amused by their straightlaced English companions. They grinned at their heavy cloaks and veiled hats embellished with feathers and bows, and shook their heads at the white gloves the sisters wore despite the afternoon warmth.

The tiny passenger cabin, with its narrow bunks, was hot and airless. Thea found them a sheltered bench outside and snapped open her sunshade defiantly. The spotted organza parasol, lined with pink silk, looked utterly frivolous against the blistered blue paint.

Summer's invalid chair had been loaded aboard, but there was no place to store it. The sailors anchored it on deck with ropes. She sat down in it, made herself comfortable as they cast off, and looked out over the shimmering blue waves. Soon Naples and the scattered islands beyond the bay grew smaller with distance. She couldn't quite believe that she was really on her way to Ellysia. It was still unreal. Frightening . . . and marvelous.

Fanny spent the first part of the trip leaning over the side with another terrible case of mal de mer. Then she went inside the tiny cabin and fell into a childlike, exhausted sleep. Summer stayed out until it grew dark and Thea insisted that she retire for the night.

The morning sun lit the sea like a wash of gold on cobalt glass. Summer was up at dawn, keeping a lookout for the first sign of land. Her attention was distracted as Fanny stumbled out of the cabin, pale and green as celery root. "Will we never reach Ellysia?" She gasped, clutching the rail.

Although their reasons for it were quite different, Summer felt the same. She was anxious to see the place that would be her home for the next several months. Seeing the moving waves made Fanny feel even worse, and she retreated hastily to the cabin again. Summer made her slow way forward.

Mario, a walnut-brown man with a thick thatch of white curls, pushed aside a coil of rope he was mending. "A fine day, Signorina. A good omen for your visit to Ellysia."

"I hope you may be right."

She was no longer self-conscious of her awkward gait before the sailors. Her command of Italian had delighted them from the start, and they issued their melodious greetings as she limped to the bow. She was grateful to them for their cheerful good nature, for the way they accepted her as she was. There was curiosity without malice, and never once did their eyes slide away from her, as if she were some monstrous creature, better relegated to the family garret.

Despite her affliction, they saw her as a person. No one told her to come away from the rail before she fell overboard, or hovered over her looking for signs of strain, the way that Nana had, or that Thea did now. Summer smiled at an old sailor.

He pointed with a gnarled, sun-brown finger. "There, Signorina. Your destination."

She spied a tiny black dot that grew over time to a thin smudge on the horizon. There were actually two islands, their father had told them, Ellysia and Hades, the one verdant and inhabited, the other hostile and barren. The Aeolian Islands, home of the god of winds, who had feasted Odysseus and sent him on his way, were another full day's sail south and west.

Summer stood like a living figurehead as they drew closer, grasping the rail tightly. Thea joined her, strangely silent. The steamer swung south to avoid the shallows.

The island's northwest tip was a jutting, prowlike headland. As they approached it the boat was plunged into shadow. Rounding the rocky cliffs they were confronted by a stretch of steely water and the irregular outline of Ellysia's dark twin. The other island was dominated by a range of dull-colored hills, surmounted by a smoldering, ash-covered mountain.

At fairly regular intervals a cloud of thin gray steam issued from its summit.

"Hades," Summer murmured. The mythical underworld of the ancients guarded by Cerberus, the fierce, three-headed dog. Yes, she could imagine the boatman, Charon, ferrying the souls of the dead across the river Styx to the forbidding island.

Thea gave a ladylike shudder. "What a melancholy place! How fortunate that it is not our destination."

As the little steamer passed by Hades's windward side, a rain of fine sooty particles fell upon the open decks. The top of her frilly parasol had changed from white to dirty gray. She made a sharp sound of disgust and darted up a step and through the forward door of the cabin, forgetting for a moment that her sister could not easily follow her. An instant later she popped back out like a jack-in-the-box, flushed with embarrassment, her tongue tripping over itself with apologies.

"Oh! So sorry—I—I didn't think! Here, let me help you inside."

"I don't mind, really. I'd much rather stay outside." Summer peered at the back of her white gloves and her dimity skirt, peppered with myriad black grains. They smelled of sulfur and mystery. She drew off her glove and touched one of the specks. A tiny thrill ran up her spine. They had come from inside the volcano, from deep inside the hidden, fiery heart of the earth.

The contact subtly changed her. At Kingsmeade she was insulated from life, wrapped in a cocoon of protectiveness that, at times, came near to suffocating her; yet she had clung to it as her shield against the world. Despite that, she had often felt like a piece of the furnishings, with no more control of her place within the house than a fat sofa pillow, casually moved at the whim of others. Touching the volcanic granules she felt a little frightened. This was something totally foreign. It made her feel real in a way she had never been.

Except perhaps . . . *Before.*

She had a sudden prickling between her shoulder blades. It was always followed by a glimpse of *Before.* This time there was no opening of the great barred door of lost memory, but she had the uncanny feeling that a tiny lock had come undone, that one of the chains that bound it had fallen away.

By the time Thea finished ministering to Fanny, Ellysia's high green hills and towering cliffs had come into view above rocky shores. The slanting sunlight picked out the ruins crowning the highest hill. Either a temple facade, or part of a loggia, overlooking the jeweled sea. The slim columns, some mere stubs, stood out against a leafy backdrop like polished bones. Summer could not take her eyes from them. Her future was inextricably joined with their past.

The boat swung away to skirt the shore. Shielding her eyes against the sun, she looked over her shoulder. Summer saw a flutter of white, like an angel's wing, between the fallen blocks and truncated columns. An instant later an object hovered at the edge, then dove in a tumble of white and black against the sharp-faced cliffs. A large seabird swooping down for a tasty fish, Summer thought. Its ultimate fate was lost in the bright glare of sunlight on the water.

A cool breeze came off the sea, and she pulled her shawl close about her shoulders.

*   *   *

The sea washed restlessly at the base of Ellysia's headland. Col knelt beside the broken body of the man who'd fallen from the cliffside ruins. "Stone dead. Poor sod."

By a fluke of fortune, he had been less than two hundred yards from the victim when it had happened. If he hadn't turned at just that exact moment he wouldn't have witnessed the tragedy. A flash of white and black against the blue had been the only sign. He hadn't heard the victim's cry. The wind had carried it away.

The dead man was dressed in dark twill trousers with a white shirt. Drying blood streaked one side of his face and his dark brown hair was matted with it.

Col's breath hissed between his teeth as he recognized the man. Jethroe T. Adams, the reporter sent over by the *New York Monitor*. He closed the staring blue eyes and addressed the assistant who had followed him down from the cliff top.

"I didn't know he was on the island. When did Adams arrive?"

"He came over from Stromboli on one of the fishing boats this morning. Hired it specially, just to bring him here. He said he'd heard we'd made some interesting discoveries and thought that his editor might be interested in him doing a series on them."

"Poor bastard." Col sat back on his heels. "You were in a better position than I, Lewis. Did you see how it happened?"

The assistant, a university student on holiday, shook his head. "No, sir. Earlier, I heard Professor Fairchild warn the fellow to stay away from the path along the cliff's edge because the ground was unstable."

"Yes, and treacherous when the wind gusts."

Lewis's hands shook just a little. He had never

seen death at such close hand before. He took a deep breath and went on. "I was looking for Angus when Adams went past me, saying that he was going to examine the dolphin mosaic. That was the last I saw of him. The next thing I knew, Mrs. Morville was shrieking like a bloody banshee."

Yes, Col thought, that was an apt description of the screaming he'd heard. There'd been enough noise to wake the dead, but if terrified screams could really rouse the deceased, the fellow would still be alive. With his stringy, athletic build, Jethroe Adams should have had a long and active life.

Col rose, brushing the sand from his palms. "A damned shame he met his end this way." He glanced upward. "No sense in trying to haul his body back up the cliff. Stay with him. I'll get a boat and we'll bring him around to the village by water."

The senseless death filled him with melancholy. Adams had been so eager and full of life. It was a hell of a note for a man to travel halfway around the world just to die.

Col started off, glancing up to the ruins on the summit. There wouldn't be time to go looking for the elusive solution to the puzzle that Carruthers had left uncompleted at his death. He wished that he could find the map Carruthers had made before he died. One of the notes made reference to a map, yet it was not among the man's papers.

Of course, it was possible that Carruthers had destroyed it while in the grip of delirium, or out of professional caution. Col rejected that theory. He had known Carruthers too well. The man was a consummate scholar: He would never have destroyed knowledge that would benefit the world or add to its store of history.

A cloud passed over the sun and that warning hum inside Col grew stronger, deeper. His eyes gleamed green as a cat's. Something was very wrong on Ellysia.

The boat carrying the three sisters moved in closer to shore and entered a small natural harbor. They had reached their destination. Summer looked about anxiously. Immediately ahead the water turned from brilliant blue to shifting shades of green. A stone jetty jutted out from the shallower water into depths safe enough for the larger supply boat. Two fishing boats were beached for repairs at the far end of the harbor, and a larger one drifted at anchor nearby.

"Appolinaria," one of the seamen told them, pointing to the rows of white houses tumbling down the hillside to the shore.

The smallness of the village surprised Summer. She knew it was only one of two settlements on Ellysia. A scattering of whitewashed buildings rose above the tiny harbor, perhaps three dozen in all, the largest surmounted with a square steeple and cross. The buildings ended abruptly, replaced by neat walled fields and olive groves.

Fanny was enchanted. None of them was larger than the caretaker's house at Kingsmeade. They looked like doll's houses, with tiny blue doors and shutters, and bright flowers climbing their facades. Summer was struck by their air of having sprung organically from the rocky bones of the island.

"This is the larger of the two villages," the sailor added. "Other than Appolinaria and Kyraeus, there is only the villa and the castello on the entire island."

Fanny's emotions plunged from the heights of

delight into the abyss of despair. Where were the shops and inns? The homes of the families with which they were to mingle?

Thea decided that she was rather glad. They would be horridly cramped, but the climate was mild and she enjoyed being out of doors. It seemed there would be a great deal of time upon her hands. She needed time. Alone. Solitary walks along the shore and over the meadows, while she thought through her plans and sorted out her future.

Summer was pleased for almost the same reason. Her greatest fear had been that, in a small community, they would be thrust into the midst of local society. Her mouth curved in a smile. It didn't appear that there was any society for them to be thrust into. The fewer people she had to deal with the better.

A glance at her younger sister showed that Fanny was close to tears. "Little goose! Surely you can't have been expecting grand balls and high tea here, such as those your friend wrote about from Cairo?"

"Of . . . of c-course not. I'm not nearly as ignorant as you and Thea think me! It's just . . . I hadn't expected that the island would be so . . . so primitive."

A soft glow illuminated Summer's features. "Perhaps that is what I like about it."

Fanny sniffled into her handkerchief. Lydia had written that she attended two or three balls or receptions a week, and that she'd received two proposals of marriage since arriving in Cairo. The chances of it happening to Fanny on Ellysia looked bleak.

Thea had skipped ahead to the next problem. Not only did there not appear to be a suitable dwelling to house them all, but there was no sign of their father. He'd written that he would spy their boat approaching and meet them himself. She'd looked forward increasingly to the moment when she could turn over the responsibility for her two sisters to him. Not that she wouldn't still have to look after them, but at least there would be an ultimate authority to whom she could appeal when Fanny or Summer challenged her decisions. Thea sighed. There was no one on the jetty at all.

The boat was tied up and the sailors piled their luggage into a huge heap at the end of the dock. The trunks and bandboxes looked ridiculous against the backdrop of the whitewashed houses and dusty fields. The men helped the ladies disembark.

The captain of the vessel handed Thea a packet. "A letter for Dr. Ruggieri, from Naples."

She stared at him blankly. "I do not know a Dr. Ruggieri, nor do I have any idea of where to find him."

The man shrugged his shoulders. "You will meet him soon enough. Everyone knows Dr. Ruggieri. He is a very famous man." He stepped back toward the boat. "We must sail on to Hades. Someone will come for you soon."

Thea's protests were of no avail. The boat left with a load of goods for the fishing settlement on the dark island. They were alone on the beach. She felt abandoned as the vessel cast off and moved out of the harbor. It was not an auspicious start to their sojourn on Ellysia.

"I shall speak to Father of this," she vowed, with fire in her eye. "It is bad enough that Fanny and I have been abandoned, but poor Summer!"

Thea caught herself at the edge of panic and took a deep breath. She must stay calm and think of what to do next. She was responsible for her sisters' welfare. "Fanny! Don't wander off. Summer, perhaps you had better sit down. Here, I'll remove these bandboxes from this trunk."

Fanny had gone a little distance along the beach, but she turned back at her sister's insistence. "How can anyone live in such a place?" she said with a delicate shudder.

Time passed and even the village, deserted as it seemed, began to look inviting. "Perhaps they take siestas, or whatever they are called," Summer said. It was certainly hot. She wished she'd thought to take her fan in her reticule.

She sat on the flat top of her steamer trunk while Thea and Fanny took a turn along the strand. They had been kicking their heels for half an hour. The village appeared deserted, windows shuttered with weathered boards against the fierce noonday sun.

Summer examined the houses. Now that she was closer she found them intriguing. They were all two storeys high, with the top portions overhanging small, columned porches. Vines spilled over them, some bearing vivid lavender blossoms. The doors and shutters of each were freshly painted the identical shade of blue, as rich and deep as Bristol glass.

Turning to the water, she noticed a long rowboat skirting the shore. The oarsman was well muscled, his skin tanned as dark a gold as his hair. A piece of canvas covered the contents of the boat and the rower cut through the waves with ease. He seemed about to turn the boat toward the beach, but changed his mind when he saw the sisters waiting on the jetty. Instead he pulled away and headed farther down the coast.

Suddenly Fanny gave a cry. "There is Father now." Summer turned back toward the village. A cloud of dust came into view on the road above the buildings, moving quickly along. After a moment they could make out wooden wheels and churning hooves in its midst. It rumbled down through the narrow dirt road toward the cobbled wharf.

The cloud resolved itself into a blue-painted wagon, drawn by two rust-colored oxen with yellow horns. The driver was a complete stranger, a thin young man with sandy hair above a sunburned face.

"Angus Gordon at your disposal, Mrs. Armstrong, ladies." His voice was deep with a jaunty American drawl. "I'm with Professor Fairchild's team. I've been sent to fetch you and your baggage and take you to the villa."

He was pleasantly surprised by the professor's daughters. His admiring gaze acknowledged Thea's cool beauty and Fanny's ripe prettiness. It stopped at Summer, making her awkward way toward him, then went on as if she were invisible. He indicated the sturdy wagon with its team of stalwart red oxen. "Your chariot awaits."

The sisters eyed it in dismay. It was not at all the sort of vehicle they were used to. Summer dreaded the painful jolting almost as much as Thea dreaded the inevitable dirt and loss of dignity. Fanny was rather in awe of their proposed mode of travel. "I never expected to ride in a farm wagon," she confided to Angus.

He sent her a jaundiced look. Hoity-toity English girls weren't his type. "I imagine not," he said curtly. "But if you want to get to the villa this afternoon, you'll go by wagon or walk."

Her mouth dropped open and her face flamed. How dare he speak to her in such a manner! But Angus had already turned away, advising them to get in while he threw their things into the back.

Thea was upset. "Our father was to meet us at the boat."

"The professor was detained. He asked me to fetch you back to the villa in his stead."

Summer knew that she should be used to it by now, but the way Angus ignored her very presence filled her with unreasoning anger. It flashed in the stormy depths of her eyes and was reinforced by the stubborn line of her jaw. She forced him to notice her.

"Is something wrong, Mr. Gordon? I cannot imagine our father sending a total stranger to greet us! It is quite unlike him."

Angus flushed a dull red to the roots of his hair. "Circumstances prevented it."

"And what circumstances might those be?"

His jaw jutted out. What a cursed unpleasant girl. Immediately he was ashamed of himself. Poor crippled creature. It was no wonder she was so sour and full of vinegar. But he was young enough to let his pricked pride win out over his pity.

"You'll find out anyway, I suppose." He pointed to the headland. "There was an accident up at the ruins a short time ago. A man fell from the cliff and was killed."

Summer paled as she remembered the flash of white and black against the soaring gray cliffs. She had witnessed the accident without realizing it. Had seen the victim plunging down, down, down to his death upon the glistening black rocks.

She felt dizzy and disoriented as the door to *Before* swung open, this time violently: She was standing at the edge of a rocky shore while the wind whipped her hair away from her face and snatched away her frenzied screams. She ran down the rugged path, cutting her bare feet and not even realizing it. For a few seconds the view was obscured by a tangle of wild vines growing over a dying tree.

Then she was down on the beach, running along the sand to the tide pool. Crabs scuttled away as she reached it. The waves foamed over the deep tide pool, shattering the sky's reflection into a hundred shining ripples. The sea retreated and the surface smoothed to wavery glass. She held her breath and leaned down.

Something bobbed among a mass of matted weeds. Suddenly her feet slipped on the slimy rocks, and she fell headlong into the pool. She shook the weeds from her face and scrambled up, but not before she saw . . . she saw . . .

The vault slammed shut like a clap of thunder. Summer pitched forward in a dead faint.

3

BEGINNINGS AND ENDINGS

Notes from a lady's diary

The French have a name for it: déjà vu. The sense of experiencing something for the first time and knowing what is going to happen, or of recognizing as familiar a place that one has never visited before.

I do know one thing: On the day I arrived at the Court of Three Sisters I felt, for the first time in my life, that I was truly home.

After spotting the little group waiting on the beach, Col muttered an oath and kept rowing. It wouldn't do to land with a corpse in front of the ladies.

He was fighting against the current, with no shelter from the afternoon sun. Sweat glistened on his chest and arms and trickled down his back. Damn, until he'd seen them sitting with their mountain of luggage, he'd almost forgotten about Richard Fairchild's daughters. From the looks of it, they'd brought enough for a world tour. But then, he'd never known a female who didn't travel with most of her wardrobe and all of her creature comforts.

He changed course to avoid the offshore rocks, black and serrated as shark's teeth. The sea foamed around them until it seemed they were gnashing in primitive hunger. It was a struggle, with the waves trying to push the dinghy onto them with every surge. Six months pulling lines and hawsers aboard the *Mary Eddington* stood him in good stead. Col put his back into it, and escaped.

It took a quarter hour and more to round the tongue of land. That made the rowing much easier, and he had time to speculate on the newcomers. Why the hell couldn't they have stayed in England? They were sure to interfere with the work at hand. Women always did.

Except, of course, those like Cynthia Morville, who was one of the experts on the professor's team. She had her hands full trying to preserve and restore the mosaics that were her specialty. Col was surprised that her excellent reputation hadn't circulated to his ears in the past.

There were several women who worked alongside their husbands, unpaid and unrecognized, except by their peers. Mrs. Morville was a rare exception, by virtue of being a widow, yet hired on because of her expertise, despite the risk of scandal. But the fair Cynthia seemed above reproach. Col grinned. The few lures he'd thrown out to her had been appreciated but ignored, except for a faint, amused smile.

But these three new arrivals had no tasks to keep them occupied, and they would expect to be entertained in the same manner in which they were at home. It would be worse for Fairchild and the members of his team—which might be to his own advantage, Col thought. The professor would be too busy to look into his whereabouts. All the same there would be dinners and picnics and, God forbid, musical evenings. Col grimaced. He devoutly hoped that Fairchild's daughters were tone deaf. Every last one of them.

Then he looked at the motionless heap beneath the canvas. Hell, here he was complaining about a few good meals in the company of three pretty Englishwomen, while this poor bastard was cold clay. It always shocked him to realize that life could be snuffed out so quickly. All a person's hopes and dreams and memories gone in an instant.

Even with the dead man's face covered, Col could still visualize his startled features. Had he seen death coming? Or had he, even to the end, hoped for a miracle. Col had learned early in life that miracles were as rare as living saints. He'd never seen either one in his many travels.

He took the rowboat down the coast to a cove on the far side of the village. The unexpected detour doubled the time it would take to get back. Lewis had been watching for him and brought the donkey cart down to the strand as they'd arranged.

Lewis helped Col lift the stiffening body into the back. "Dr. Ruggieri was in his garden, trying one of his vegetable experiments. He said to take the body to the village midwife's house. She'll bathe him and lay him out. Ruggieri will be by later, to fill out the papers and death certificate."

"That's good." The death of a foreigner and shipment of a body were sometimes complicated. Ruggieri, with his contacts in high places, could smooth the process considerably.

Col opened the man's buttoned pocket and removed a thin leather packet. Inside was an assortment of paper money and coins, a notebook, and a calling card case. There was no address on the card other than that of the newspaper he'd worked for.

"Professor Fairchild might have information on whom to contact in case of illness," Lewis said doubtfully.

Col wondered who would mourn the dead man back in the States. Fond parents? Colleagues? Loving wife and children? It was a sad thing for a man to die among strangers.

He turned the card over and the motion was suddenly arrested. A name had been scrawled across the back, in a spidery hand that would have looked familiar even if Col hadn't been reading through pages and pages covered with the same script since his arrival on Ellysia. So was the name Carruthers had written on it: "Colin McCallum."

As he took the card, Col wondered what in hell the connection could be between Carruthers and Jethroe Adams, except for the ominous fact that they were both quite dead.

Summer's brief faint had upset everyone. "I've quite recovered," she said, pushing Angus away.

He bent over her in concern. She had only been in the swoon for half a minute and was embarrassed by all the fuss. Her attempts to struggle upright were futile until he lifted her up in his wiry arms.

"What happened?" Thea and Fanny were frightened. Summer shook her head. She had no idea of what had caused the faint. The memories were locked up safely again.

"Well, you've had a long and tiring journey," Angus said as he deposited Summer on a blanket he'd arranged in the back of the wagon. He was ashamed of his earlier behavior and determined to make up for it. "You can rest when you get to the villa. It's not far."

Once everyone was secure he started the team. They skirted the village and wound their way up toward the hills dominating the southern section of the island. The road was not a real road at all, but more of a worn cart track. The same wildflowers— yellow, white, mauve, and blue—that thronged the wayside and untilled fields, poked their bright heads up between the bare soil of the wheel grooves. Summer had never seen so many. They were everywhere, forming intricate, swirling patterns, like gay daubs of paint on an artist's palette.

Delicate white almond blossoms showered petals on a stone fence where two startled goats peered out. In the pasture beyond, a spotted cow turned to watch them with benign curiosity.

"Far," it appeared, was a relative term. Thea punctuated the minutes by asking Summer at frequent intervals if she felt well. After ten minutes of it Summer felt a headache coming on.

Angus directed the team off the cart track and over a tangle of low, purple-spiked plants. As they reached higher ground the fertile earth gave way to sandy ocher soil studded with agave and fat little pads of the prickly pear cactus. Most of the other plants were strange to her as well.

Fanny lacked her sister's interest in the island's flora. There was not a house or farm as far as the eye could see, nor a single soul in sight. What would she do with herself here for six months or more? At least the sun was warm and bright, and she comforted herself with that. A kid bleated off to the left. Perhaps Papa would let her have a goat to keep as a pet. It was a small comfort.

Past a clump of olive trees was another house, this one bigger than anything in the village itself. Large terra-cotta pots stood at intervals along the colon-naded porch and a low wall enclosed the side garden. A portly man, with thick white hair and a mustache to match, was picking vegetables in his garden as they drove by. Angus reined in.

"'Morning, Dr. Ruggieri. These are the professor's daughters. I'm taking them up to the villa."

The older man set down his basket, removed his straw hat to reveal a shiny, sunburned pate, and pre-sented the ladies with a courtly bow. "Welcome to Ellysia. If there is anything in my power that can make your stay more comfortable, you have only to ask."

Thea thanked him on their behalf and gave him the packet of letters. She noticed that one bore an ornate crest embossed on thick linen paper. "The captain who brought us to the island asked me to deliver these to you. I didn't expect my task to be quite so easy."

Dr. Ruggieri smiled. "Ah, news from my old friend, Count DiCaesari," he said with genuine delight. He glanced at the other letter for the split second that politeness allowed. When he saw the return address a thoughtful expression crossed his features.

"Thank you, Signora. I have been expecting this." And hoping not to get it. It was from the friend to whom he'd confided his doubts about the nature of Signore John Carruthers's sudden demise. By its very thickness he could guess at the news it contained.

Thea completed the introductions. The doctor's quick glance was arrested when he heard Summer's name. Summer had the discomfiting intuition that he knew all about her. It was confirmed by the quick, keen look he gave her before smiling and turning to Fanny.

They spoke the usual pleasantries for a few minutes. The sun was hot and Fanny was very thirsty. She was anxious to get on to the villa, too, and hoped that her sister didn't mean to spend the entire afternoon conversing in the middle of the road. She wriggled impatiently.

The doctor seemed to read her mind. He bowed to her, a twinkle in his dark eyes. "Ah, I am keeping you from finishing your journey. You wish to see your new home, no doubt. Have no fear, Signorina. The Court of Three Sisters has stood for hundreds of years—it will wait a few more minutes for you."

Fanny flushed and made a polite demur. Dr. Ruggieri's smile widened. The young were so hasty always, rushing here and rushing there. They didn't know that all roads in life, like those on Ellysia, led to the same destination. He presented them with the basket of vegetables from his own garden, and waved them on their way.

Angus saluted the doctor and started the team. "An interesting fellow," their driver informed them. "He's a bigwig of sorts. Wrote a book on invisible bugs—microbes, he calls them. Studied in Rome with some fellow who studied with some other fellow named Pasteur."

Thea's opinion of Angus dropped several degrees, but Dr. Ruggieri went up several notches in esteem. A prominent microbial specialist was on a higher social plane than a doctor who kept chickens in his dooryard and raised his own vegetables. Perhaps she might invite Signora Ruggieri to tea one afternoon. If there was a Signora Ruggieri. "Does he have a family?"

"No. He's a widower. Retired after his wife died, and came back to the island. He looks after us if there's an emergency. You'll be seeing a lot of him. He comes out to the dig a lot and he's up to the villa for supper almost every week. On a place this small, everybody gets to know everybody else pretty quickly."

Fanny asked the question most on her mind. "Are there any younger people we'll be meeting?"

"Naw. This side of the island there's nothing but the villagers—fishermen, a few farmers and winemakers and such—and those of us with the excavation."

Fanny's face fell. She looked so disappointed that Angus relented a little. "There are a couple of university fellows in our group. One of them's some kind of lord or something," he said, with a sly glance her way. "Being an American, I don't put much store in titles, myself. I call him Jonesy."

She digested this information glumly. The presence of a young lord would normally have excited her interest greatly: One named Jonesy didn't sound at all promising.

Fanny lapsed into a sulk. Lydia had written her several chatty letters from Cairo. It seemed that all the finest sprigs of England's landed families were wintering there, and willing to dance attendance on any young lady to whom they were introduced.

Dances and galas and luxurious barges floating along the Nile to Luxor and Aswan.

She stared out over the deserted landscape with deepening gloom. Oh, how she wished she were in Cairo with Lydia instead, having high tea with cream buns on the terrace at Shepheard's Hotel!

Col and Lewis were just leaving the house of Signora Calcaterra, the midwife, when an English-woman pulled up in a pony cart. Her features were regular and pleasant, if not actually pretty, and she was smartly dressed in a white shirtwaist piped in navy and a navy skirt. Her masses of soft coppery brown hair were piled atop her head and partially confined beneath a wide-brimmed white hat. A few waving strands had fallen loose to brush her cheek and the nape of her graceful neck.

The men went to meet her. Cynthia Morville was a valued member of Professor Fairchild's team, appreciated for her cheerful companionship as well as for her skills in restoring mosaics. She had worked with Carruthers on several projects in recent years, Col had learned.

"I've brought Mr. Adams's things," she said. "There is a suit and clean shirt among them for the laying-out." She bit her lip and blinked away tears. "It's so—so terrible!"

Lewis looked close to tears himself. He and the dead man had been about the same age. They had stayed up half the night talking of schools and mutual acquaintances, of sailing and foreign ports and dangerous escapades, of lost illusions and first loves and all the things that adventurous young men talked about together.

That had been only a few hours ago. It shocked him that Jethroe's story had ended so abruptly, that he had been cut down so suddenly like one of the lightning-blasted pines on the high ridge above. He pretended to sneeze as an excuse to draw out his handkerchief. With his face half-hidden, he went around to take out the basket of the dead man's belongings.

Col handed Mrs. Morville down from the cart, the fingers of his left hand splayed against her slim waist. A waft of light, flowery fragrance came to him. It was as delicately, as seductively ladylike as its wearer. Under other circumstances he might have been interested in pursuing their acquaintance more aggressively.

Cynthia had a ready smile, pleasant face, and an apparently soft disposition. A lithe and womanly figure, and a certain air of sexuality kept in check beneath her buttoned-up exterior, only added to her attractions. Col appreciated them all. From a polite distance.

He suspected that the widow was tired of her state, and ready to trade her freedom for a wedding ring. Visions of a cozy, rose-colored cottage dancing through a woman's head were enough to send him packing—for the woman's sake, more than his. Some men were born to wander the earth, unattached and unencumbered. He was definitely one of them. He suspected that the scars of his youth had left him unable to love anyone deeply.

Lately he had been wondering if there was something in the wind between the widow and the professor. Col had his own set of rules. He never knowingly poached in another man's territory, unless the man was uninterested himself, and he never encouraged false hopes.

"You should have sent one of the laborers in your stead," he said.

"I felt it only right that I should come. I didn't think he would have appreciated having his landlord paw through his belongings."

"*Bon giorno,* Signora Morville, Signore McCallum."

They turned at the voice. Dr. Ruggieri had come along the path to join them. His shoulders seemed weighted down by the cares of the world. "A sad happening," he said.

"Yes."

Ruggieri attempted a smile. "But now, with the arrival of the beautiful ladies, we must put on a good face. Their arrival will cheer us."

Cynthia looked surprised. "I didn't realize that we had visitors. The count?"

"Professor Fairchild's daughters arrived an hour ago," Col said. "I saw them down at the jetty when I brought the rowboat around."

"Oh dear. Rather unfortunate timing, with this fresh tragedy on our hands! I suppose Richard has been informed?"

Col nodded. She forced a smile. No one had seen fit to tell her of their arrival. A sparkle that might have been hurt or just a trick of the light glimmered in her eye.

Ruggieri's comfortable face settled in unhappy lines. "It is troubling to have another untimely death, following so close upon the tragic loss of Sir John Carruthers."

Cynthia Morville sighed. "Poor man. If he had followed your advice, he would still be alive today."

A strange expression crossed Ruggieri's features.

He looked suddenly stern. "I sincerely doubt it." He tipped his hat. "Good day, Signora, Signori."

Lewis looked after the doctor as he entered the midwife's house. "That was an odd thing to say, don't you think? What do you suppose he meant?"

Col frowned. "I don't know." But he intended to discover the answer.

Thea, Summer, and Fanny were tired and dusty by the time Angus halted the team on a rise. He pointed to the right, where the tops of strange turrets of dark lava stone rose above the trees like a gothic mirage.

"Is that the villa?" Thea asked, praying that it was not.

"No. That's the *castello*. It belongs to the Count DiCaesari."

Fanny perked up. "A count? What is he like? Is it a large family?"

"Couldn't say. Never met him." Angus started the team again. It was another mile or so before he paused again. "There it is, ladies, your new abode."

Summer sat up. Olive orchards filled the valley below, their wind-tossed leaves giving the illusion of a silver-green sea. Above them she caught glimpses of sprawling, whitewashed walls and varying rooflines, with rows of glazed tiles the rich red-brown of autumn leaves. It reminded her of paintings of ancient Rome.

"It's very large!" Thea's voice was breathless with relief. She'd been expecting something rustic: This was a proper villa.

"Yes." Angus was pleased with his surprise. He'd had a bit of fun along the way, by implying that the house was little more than a glorified peasant's cottage. That way, he figured, they would appreciate its benefits, instead of bemoaning how different it was from their estate in England.

He grinned at them. "It's called the Court of Three Sisters."

The coincidence fascinated Summer. "How did it get its name?"

"No one knows. The villagers say it has been called that since before their grandfathers' grandfathers' time. In Diocletian's day," he added, "it was the villa of a noble Roman. One Marcus Tullius Glaucus. He added on to an earlier domicile, and used it as a summer place at first. Later he moved here permanently with his entire family—brothers, sisters, in-laws of all sorts—to escape the corruption and terror in Rome, when the emperor purged the place of his enemies and rivals."

"How can you know all that?" Fanny asked doubtfully. "I believe you are making it up."

Angus shot her a look of disdain. "I know it because I worked for Sir John Carruthers and he purchased an early compilation of the entire library of Tullius Glaucus. For the last year I've been doing a new translation of the books into English—including hundreds of his scrolls, from his diaries and philosophy to his rents and taxes to the amount of cloth and pickled fish relish he and his family devoured with their daily meals. If you don't believe me, I'll show them to you."

Thea had to revise her opinion once more. Angus Gordon might know nothing of Louis Pasteur and his work, but he certainly knew his Latin and his Roman history. Martin was right, she thought with a tiny pang. She did judge people too quickly, and too much by external qualities.

Angus snapped the reins and the oxen plodded steadily on. They reached a wall of worn stucco that attached to a rambling building. A vine with enormous deep gold flowers spread along its length. Summer was surprised to glimpse the sea beyond the villa. There were no windows facing the road, but the wagon entered a stone-flagged courtyard through an arched opening.

It was dishearteningly shabby. Chickens scratched at the kernels strewn over the court, and two tiger cats lazed in the shade of a broken trellis. Overgrown boxwood outlined weed-choked gardens and the bottom of the tiled pond in the center sported nothing but dried leaves and a layer of dirt. More weeds poked up between the paving block.

Angus stepped down to help the ladies out. "Welcome to the Court of Three Sisters, ladies."

They were dumb with dismay. He knew how it must look to them. "The main section's been put to rights. The rest of the place is closed up."

He handed Thea down first, then lifted Summer out as if she were a babe in arms, despite her assurances that she could manage on her own. It irked her no end. When Fanny dismounted Angus tipped his hat back on his head.

"Go on through that gate while I take care of your luggage."

They passed through the arch and immediately their spirits perked up. The central portion of the house was larger than their home at Kingsmeade and built in the style of ancient Rome, two stories around the central atrium, open to the sky. It was like a private walled garden, Thea thought with approval. Certainly large enough for Summer to walk in each afternoon for her daily exercise.

The blue-tiled pond in the center was filled with clear water, reflecting the pearly clouds. On three sides the roofline extended to form a colonnaded loggia, which shaded the doors and windows cut into the thick walls. Although the gardens needed more plantings, there were flowers, shrubs, and an herb border, and birds hopped about in the branches of the fruit trees. In all, a pleasant place to while away an afternoon.

The far side of the atrium departed from tradition. Instead of a solid fourth wall, the ground-floor section of the building was transected by a wide double arch. It led out to a stone terrace surrounded by a low balustrade. Beyond they could glimpse silky blue sky and a glint of sapphire water.

"You could have a garden here," Fanny said to Summer.

Summer shook her head. "I've lost interest."

Thea frowned, remembering. Once upon a time Summer had longed to have a garden of her own. When that was discouraged she had crept out at dawn to try and clear a patch of ground, and had been found by a frantic Nana hours later, covered with dew and dirt.

Everyone had been horrified and Father feared that Summer would come down with pneumonia from sitting on the cold ground. At Thea's suggestion, the gardener had planted a little box for Summer, and set it on the wide sill of her window. Summer had ignored it completely, and the gardener had taken it away again. The memory disquieted Thea. If she lived to be a hundred years old and full of wisdom, she would never understand Summer.

They went out to the terrace. Fanny dropped into a chair, weary and disillusioned. They had come to the ends of the earth, it seemed. There would be no balls and afternoon garden parties. Summer ignored her younger sister's sighs of melancholy. Personally, she was enchanted. All the delays and hardships of the journey had been worth it.

She opened herself up to the atmosphere of the villa. An air of peace pervaded her. The timeless, ancient walls closed around them in protection and welcome. "We have seen the rise and fall of empires," they seemed to whisper to her. "You humans and your petty problems are as grains of sand, washed away in the sea of eternity." Summer ran her hand along the balustrade, and smiled.

As they were wondering which doorway to enter, a black-garbed woman came out of one, wiping her rawboned hands on her red-and-white apron. In halting English she introduced herself as Signora Perani, who cooked for the professor and looked after the house.

"Previously I have been with Signore Carruthers for several years. I came here from Turin to see to his meals and look after his household."

Thea expected the signora to be put out at having three more people under the villa's roof, but that was not the case.

"No, no," the housekeeper exclaimed. "Now that you have come at last, I will bring in my nieces, Zita and Pellegrina, from the village to do the heavy work. Giovanni Falluchi is to come and look after the gardens. After today I will only cook and oversee the others, and wait upon you and the professor at meals."

That seemed like quite a bit to three English-women who were used to servants jealously guarding the exclusivity of their special tasks. Why,

Fanny thought, Cook would no more wait upon them than Mrs. Croft would prepare meals or wash the floors.

They followed Signora Perani into the first door on the left. They entered, and found themselves in another world. They had stepped back in time. The room was large and cool, the floors tiled with unglazed terra-cotta bordered by a wide mosaic strip inset with designs of purple grapes and graceful vines. But it was the glory of the frescoed walls that struck the newcomers silent.

They were done in the garden style favored by wealthy Romans of the late empire. Lush foliage and branching trees, flowering shrubs and exotic ferns vied for attention. Bees gathered pollen from the hearts of huge poppies, and butterflies had been captured in midflutter. Cranes peered through stands of reeds on one wall, while frond-tailed birds roosted in trees and peacocks strolled along hidden pathways. In one corner a painted cat stalked a painted mouse.

It was all fascinating and foreign. Thea was overwhelmed. She noticed, gratefully, that not everything was strange to them. A humidor of tobacco and a meerschaum pipe rested on a low smoking cabinet between two wing chairs.

"It looks like Father's study at Kingsmeade," Fanny exclaimed.

Thea agreed. The long refectory table was littered with books, open or stacked, and all sorts of papers. Pieces of creamware pottery, painted with rust-colored swirls, nested in an open wooden box. Even that looked familiar: There was always something—a broken bit of statuary, a fragment of clay tablet or glass—on Father's desk. In such alien surroundings, it was good to see his familiar possessions. Things would not be so different here after all. She felt immediately better.

The signora showed them a large, empty room with the same tiled floor, which they were to furnish with items from the villa's storerooms, for use as a parlor. "The professor has his chambers above your bedrooms. You must tell Angus where to put each of your trunks. Meanwhile, I will set out a luncheon in the loggia."

The sisters began exploring. There was something exciting, almost illicit, about opening doors in a house that was not their own. They went along the corridor, peeking in one after the other before making their selections. Thea, as eldest, took the largest room. It was also the least ornate. It had been fitted with a wardrobe painted a pale green, a huge bed of dark wood, with a narrow table and chair beneath the large window. A geometric design in deep burgundy and bright blue ran along the top of the whitewashed walls. It matched the mosaic border of the floor, done in tiny squares of burgundy, white, and blue.

The gay colors, which would have seemed gaudy in England, perfectly suited the surroundings and the brilliant light. Summer had noticed how drab their garments had seemed once they'd reached the Mediterranean.

Fanny's room was next to Thea's, smaller and prettier. It had whitewashed pine furniture and was floored with blue tiles framed in a thin border of gold. The ceiling was painted blue with gold stars. Best of all, it had a faded fresco on one wall featuring a young girl drawing water from a spring. The blues and greens, rose, and ocher of the painting had mellowed over centuries but the details were quite clear.

Summer drew closer. "Look, the small amphora she is holding is made of the same cream-and-rust ware as the potsherds we just saw in Father's study."

"Perhaps she is one of the sisters," Fanny said eagerly. "See, the house on the hill behind her looks exactly like this one!"

Thea designated the third room for Summer, since it was nearest a door that opened directly into the courtyard, where they would take their meals. Despite its convenience Summer was dissatisfied with it. The walls were a deep oxblood and the floor an undersea of dark green and blue. The central design was a purple octopus with yellow suckers on its writhing arms. A lone window looked out on a shaded wing of the house.

"It's like a catacomb," Summer exclaimed. "It will be dark in here from sunrise to sunset." Something in her rebelled. She couldn't bear to sleep in such a confined space, and refused to have her trunks taken inside it. "There must be another room in this vast pile of stone."

The housekeeper had returned. "There is no other place suitable for a young lady of the house," she explained in her slow English.

Summer scarcely listened. She had gotten her bearings and was already moving down the corridor. "There is another room on the end."

"A storeroom, only, Signorina. Small, and plain."

Summer ignored the pain in her leg and back and pressed on. The last room was a good twenty feet past the others. The door was ajar. She pushed it wide with her hand and stepped inside. It was full of odds and ends of furniture of varying styles and periods, and had neither size nor beauty to recommend it.

There was one wide window on the end, letting in the golden light. It was so large that the wooden shutters had to be pulled back against the side walls. They were painted the same rich blue she'd seen in the village.

It wouldn't be too bad, once it was emptied, she decided.

There were no colorful murals, which was a disappointment, but the rest made up for that lack. The rough plaster walls were bright and fresh. The floor—at least what she could see of it for all the furniture and cartons—was of honey-colored wood, covered with an old Turkey carpet in shades of blue and rose. Even from the doorway she could hear the gentle whispering of the sea. It was perfect.

She scanned the piles of furniture stored there. It was a positive treasure trove. "Look, there is a bed behind the painted chest and a very nice wardrobe on the opposite wall. We could have the divan and chairs put in our sitting room, along with those tables. That old ladder-back chair doesn't match, but it could stay here. There wouldn't be much else to move out, except these cartons."

The housekeeper looked dismayed. "It is not as suitable as the other room," she said flatly. "You would not like to be here all alone and so far from the others."

"I assure you I am used to it. It would make a lovely bedroom and it can't have been disused for long. The walls have been whitewashed recently," she pointed out.

The signora nodded. "Sir John intended to use this as his study originally, but it proved too small."

Summer went to the rectangle open to the bright blue sky and leaned against the high sill. The view was breathtaking. She felt as if she were suspended in thin air. As far as her eye could see, there was nothing but sea and sky, with a darker line to mark their union at the distant horizon.

She poked her head out and looked straight down. The house was built on the side of a sheer cliff. At its foot waves lashed themselves into gouts of sparkling spray against the jumbled rocks.

"Do come back from that window," Thea said sharply. "It looks unsafe." She turned away to the corridor. "You need to lie down, Summer. You're pale as plaster. You'll be perfectly happy in the other room, and it will be much easier for you to get about."

"No," Summer announced firmly, "I have made up my mind. I will take this room."

Thea was tired and dusty from travel. She wanted a light meal and a long nap. She was in no mood to humor her sister's sudden whim. Her usually calm facade cracked and hot irritation leaked out.

"Don't be difficult! It would make a good deal more work for the servants, fetching and carrying."

Summer didn't turn away from the view. She couldn't. It held her mesmerized. After seeing this room with its sun and light she could not bear to be cooped up in the other. "I will do my own fetching and carrying. I have made up my mind. This will be my room."

Fanny was eager to explore the grounds and hoped they wouldn't start a long and drawn-out debate. It would only end with Summer moving into the storeroom anyway.

It was true. There was a stubborn streak in

Summer that surfaced only rarely; but when it did, it was formidable. Like the matter of Nana sleeping on the truckle bed in Summer's room. Once she decided that she no longer needed Nana in such close attendance, nothing they said could make Summer change her mind.

Thea might have tried to dissuade her sister further, but she saw that Summer was increasingly fatigued, even as she seemed increasingly overwrought. Such excitement could bode no good for her delicate health. Thea's own head was beginning to throb. Her hand trembled on the door and tears prickled her eyes. This whole trip had been ill-advised. Really, it would have been better if she'd stayed on alone at Kingsmeade, or gone to Aunt Leonie—dreaded thought—until Martin returned from his duties in Brazil.

Or if she had sailed to South America with him when he left.

That was the real problem, not Summer's sudden obstinacy. The tears that had only threatened now spilled over her lids for a variety of reasons, none of which she could remedy at present. Thea dashed them away quickly before anyone could notice.

"Very well. Perhaps Mr. Gordon will help. Otherwise you will have to wait until the village girls arrive. I have no intention of trying to move that heavy furniture for you."

Thea turned on her heel and went to her own chamber, closing the door softly. A bird hopped on the vine outside her open window and trilled a cheerful song. She closed the shutters. There were boxes and trunks and valises stacked along one wall, ready to unpack, but Thea's cool practicality had completely deserted her. She sat on the edge of the bed and stared blindly at the diamond-and-gold wedding band on her left ring finger. The three gems sparkled against her hand, no brighter than the silent tears that splashed among them.

After refreshments in the loggia, Thea and Fanny went to their rooms to nap. Their father would not be home for two more hours, Signora Perani told them.

Summer fought her tiredness and managed to keep it at bay when Angus volunteered to help the housekeeper clear out the storeroom. She couldn't remember when she had been so excited about anything. Her own room. Hers by choice, not necessity.

At Kingsmeade, to save her the effort of climbing two flights to the bedroom floor, a small salon had been converted to a bedchamber. It was convenient but had no view, and the pictures, draperies, and carpet had remained from its former use. It was like sleeping in a parlor, Summer had always thought. Even the narrow tester bed and dresser brought down to it had been purchased with the house. In that sense, she had never had a place that was exclusively her own.

Angus set the chest where she indicated and straightened up. "Where would you like the bed? You'd catch the breeze if it's beneath the window."

"Thank you, but I'd prefer it on that long wall." She wanted to be able to lean against the sill, to look out and down onto the sea. A view that demanded nothing of her but observation and enjoyment.

But she was being selfish. Summer eyed the wardrobe doubtfully. "It looks quite heavy."

"I can move it," he said scornfully, and put his shoulder to it. He wanted to impress this strange, prickly girl who read obscure translations of even more obscure Roman philosophers. The wardrobe was heavier than he expected, but Angus managed to shove it along the wall to the spot where Summer wanted it placed. As he slid it away a thick tapestry was revealed.

She went to examine it. The subject was familiar, the rape of Persephone. It depicted Demeter's daughter, only a moment earlier picking wildflowers with her attendants, suddenly being carried off to Hades by the lord of the underworld. The chariot of Dis was drawn by snorting black stallions and the vehicle itself had been woven from pure gold threads. The style was unusual, although she couldn't put her finger on just why. It certainly needed a good cleaning.

Angus joined her. "That's kind of pretty. It's a good thing you wanted to rearrange things."

He looked a little closer and goggled. It was one thing to read history, and quite another to see it depicted so boldly. The man in the chariot had swooped a beautiful girl up with one arm, and his hand was cupped possessively over her bare breast. From the leer on his face there was no doubt about what the captor had in mind for his fair captive. Angus wasn't sure if was all right for an unmarried woman—really, little more than a girl—to have a couple of half-naked gods romping on a tapestry in her bedroom. It would never be allowed in Amherst, he was sure.

He blushed and slid a glance at Summer. She didn't seem to mind. This was different, he guessed, since they were in a foreign country and she was a professor's daughter. You couldn't study the classics without running into statues and paintings of naked

people. He'd seen some at the Pompeii excavations
that had made his hair curl. Angus was almost twenty
and had thought that he was getting to be a man of
the world: the Pompeii frescoes had been quite a setback to that notion.

"Well, if there's nothing else?"

"No. Thank you." Summer was glad when he left.
She wanted to soak in the magical feeling of her new
room. And this wonderful tapestry was a bonus! She
tucked a loose thread from the edge back behind the
hanging and stopped in surprise. Her hand had
touched wood.

Summer pulled a corner of the tapestry aside with
difficulty. Its weight was surprising. Yes, there was
something behind it. It appeared to be part of the
solid wall, but was really a small, whitewashed door.
She was on the hinge side. She went to the other
edge, scarcely aware of the way her leg dragged
across the floor from fatigue. She had been presented
with a mystery, and meant to solve it.

She couldn't open the door. It seemed to be stuck
tight from long disuse. She looked at the hinges
again. They were in good repair, but two small
wedges of wood had been stuck between the door
and the jamb. She worked them out, breaking a nail
in the process. If she meant to sleep in this room, she
wanted to know what was on the other side.

It would serve her right, she thought, if after all
this effort it turned out to be just another door leading to the atrium. She pulled the handle and this
time the door opened easily. Sunlight spilled on her
arms and Summer pushed through. She stopped in
amazement.

Incredible! Where the walls of two wings of the
house formed a vee, a private terrace had been built.

The crumbling stucco walls were colored a warm ocher and had been gaily decorated. Their tops were bordered with maroon stripes, framing stylized rows of white birds against a blue sky. Above the floor was another border, this one enclosing curling blue-green waves tipped with white foam.

Summer turned slowly. It was no wonder that the door had been closed up and blocked. At the wide end of the terrace there were remains of what had once been a low balustrade. Now the pavement ended abruptly, with nothing to prevent an unwary trespasser from falling over the cliff. She inched her way carefully, keeping back from the edge.

Her heart pounded as she glanced over from a safe place near the wall. The view robbed her of breath. The cliff went straight down for hundreds of feet, to the teeth of the dark rocks below. Waves dashed themselves to diamonds among them, sending up glittering rainbow sprays. Suddenly Summer was dizzy, hurtling without warning into *Before*.

Rocks and spray and shining pools of water and . . .

No, no! She fought against it and this time succeeded. Inch by inch she stepped back until her pulse slowed and her breathing eased. Summer felt weak and drained. She turned her back to the drop. A raised garden bed was covered with dust and dried leaves. In the vee was a stone platform centered with a carved stone chair. It looked like a small throne and reminded her of something, a drawing, perhaps, in one of her father's many books. The paint at the base of the platform was flaking away, but there was enough to show a pattern of leaping dolphins.

She sat on the stone chair. It might have been made for her. The arms had been polished and worn smooth by touch, the seat slightly hollowed. It was surprisingly comfortable. She leaned back against the hard upright and looked out over the sea below, like a queen, surveying her watery kingdom. The heat of the sun-warmed stone seeped into her tired body. All the tension of the past weeks drained away.

Summer felt as if she had come home.

Doctor Paolo Ruggieri said good-bye to his unexpected visitor and looked at the clock. He'd been invited to the Court of Three Sisters this evening. There was still time to take his usual dip in the mineral baths. That always helped him think more clearly. If he hadn't been so tired he might not have given away so much of his disquiet about Carruthers's death.

He made his way down a path to a certain sheltered cove. It was part of his daily routine. He had retired to Ellysia, where his grandfather had been born, after severe arthritis and loneliness had ended his practice in Naples. The sea air and warmer weather helped some to ease his symptoms, but the real attraction that drew him back was the healing mud baths at the hot springs near Appolinaria.

The baths had been built in Roman times, although the reputation of the hot springs they enclosed had dwindled over the years. They were not the grand, sybaritic affairs that most people associated with the Romans, buildings with fine mosaics and formal pools, caldaria and tepidaria and fountains for taking the waters internally. No, these were quite primitive, merely a succession of stone walls built out into the sea, to enclose the vents of bubbling, sulfurous water.

At high tide when the moon was full, the waves washed completely over the walls, making them look like the ruins of a submerged city. In the 1400s, sailors stopping in search of fresh water had believed them to be the remains of the lost island of Atlantis.

Perhaps, the doctor thought, Ellysia had been a healing center in the ancient world, like the spas at Montecatini. That would explain the surprising extent of the temple ruins that Sir John Carruthers, and now Professor Fairchild, were excavating on the headland. The Romans understood the efficacy of the mineral waters such as those at Bath in Britain, or Germany's Baden Baden. Few of the island's inhabitants used these naturally heated bathing sites nowadays. That was fine with Dr. Ruggieri. He liked his privacy. And he needed to think.

He removed his hat, sandals, and robe and went into the first enclosure in his bathing costume. The slanting sun shone on his round, bald pate as he settled into the water and walked out from the shore. Until the English came he had bathed naked, as Appolinarians had for centuries. Since the English had come, bringing their women, he had modified his behavior.

Dr. Ruggieri lowered himself onto one of the seats built into the stone. The water lapped at his waist as he reached down for handfuls of thick, yellow mud and rubbed the slick stuff on his aching limbs. Ah, that felt good. The lowering sun streaked the horizon with phosphorescent orange and rose. His thoughts were not on the beauties of nature, however, but on the news he had received earlier today.

The letter that Signora Armstrong delivered to him had been sent from Naples. Its contents weighed heavily on his mind. If all had gone right, the letter should have reached him weeks ago, when Signore McCallum first came to the island, but it must have just missed the supply boat.

Odd, that. Mario knew how eagerly he'd been awaiting it.

Ruggieri sighed. He hardly knew what to do or where to turn. Perhaps if he tried to relax, the answer would come to him. The steam and chemical vapor rising from the water, the soft lapping of the waves against the walls, lulled him into a pleasant stupor. He was glad he'd come to the baths before going up to the villa. It gave him time to think things through one more time. He closed his eyes.

When his body adjusted to the temperature of the first bath he got up and moved to the next, where the water was much hotter. The water was also deeper here, up to his chest. The bubbling was more intense and so loud he couldn't hear the waves anymore. The heat was almost unbearable at first. He knew that in a few minutes it would seem comfortably warm and incredibly soothing. The minerals in this spring seemed especially efficacious for his arthritic condition.

His thoughts drifted back to the problem. He'd been suspicious from the start. Carruthers's symptoms had not been consistent with a systemic infection. They'd had all the hallmarks of poisoning. He'd been quite frank about it. Sir John—obstinate mule of an Englishman!—had laughed off his alarm. His condition had steadily improved over the next several days and he'd returned to almost full activity.

The following week, assured that all was well and feeling rather foolish over his alarms, Ruggieri had gone off to Lipari on the steamer, to attend the wedding of his cousin's youngest grandson. When he returned ten days later, Carruthers was dead.

It had been a terrible shock. The archaeologist's remains had been sent to Naples for embalming and return to England, but Ruggieri had excellent contacts in high places. Along with the formal papers, he had enclosed a letter written to a certain influential friend, asking for a quiet investigation. Today he'd gotten the results.

"Whether accidental or intentional," Francesco Crocci had written in his ornate, spidery script, "the conclusion is without a shadow of slightest doubt: The death of the estimable Sir John Carruthers was due to ingestion of a deadly, cumulative poison."

Crocci had promised to keep the results confidential until he heard from Ruggieri, but could hold them no longer than six weeks. Several had already passed. The doctor sighed. His main duty was clear. The poisoning must be reported to the proper authorities.

But first he must make very sure of his facts. It was possible that Carruthers had been taking some tonic that had an arsenic-like alkaloid in it. Although vigorous, Sir John had been getting on in years. A man of a certain age might resort to all sorts of chemist's potions to restore his hair, his energies. His virility. Had he been eyeing Mrs. Morville with the enthusiasm of a much younger man? If so, it was not impossible that he had taken the poison himself, albeit unknowingly.

That comforting theory, Ruggieri knew, would explain why Carruthers had dismissed the warning given him. He had been a man of pride. And what such man, infatuated with a much younger woman, would admit, even to a physician, that he was physicking himself with herbal tonics to restore flagging potency? Yes, it *was* possible.

But, Ruggieri decided, not probable. Carruthers had often hinted that he was on the brink of an astounding discovery. Not even Circe herself could have tempted him to take a virility potion if he thought it would kill him before he'd finished his work. The doctor understood that. Women, delightful as they are, were in one compartment of a scientist's life and his work in another. No, Sir John would have put his discoveries ahead of a pretty figure and fetching face.

Which brought Ruggieri back to his quandary. He had seen a case in Rome, early in his career, where a contessa had died in suspicious circumstances. Since she had been plain and much older than her philandering husband, he had been blamed for her death. Oh, not officially. Instead he and his young paramour had been accused, tried and convicted by hearsay and slander. It was said that they had paid the contessa's maid to poison her, in her nightly cordial.

Three years later the husband was a ruined man, awash in bitterness and alcohol. His paramour, thinking him guilty, had fled his arms, only to end up in a brothel, full of disease. The poor servant had hanged herself in an attic.

Much later, with four lives destroyed, the truth had come out: the contessa, hoping to restore her faded beauty, had obtained a concoction from an herb woman who lived upon her family's estates. It was the herb woman who had poisoned the contessa. Her husband had been wrongfully imprisoned for poaching on the contessa's forest lands, and died there, leaving behind his young wife and four fatherless children. So many lives destroyed because of lies and whispers.

The memories of that tragic affair still haunted Ruggieri. He had been one of the experts called in to assist with the inquiry into the contessa's death. The evidence had not convinced him, but although he had spoken up, in the end he had been overawed—*overwhelmed*—by the opinions of his superiors. He had never forgiven himself.

And for that reason, he must be careful now. The innocent must not suffer.

He sighed again and moved to the third bath, which was back near the edge of the water. There was no beach here. The relentless sea had undercut a rocky ledge and the enclosure butted up against it. The sulfur fumes were so strong that this bathing pool was nicknamed the Devil's Bath. He lowered himself in gingerly. Hot as Hades! Inch by inch he let himself sink deeper. When he was fully immersed the water came up to his neck. The fizz and pop of the bubbles tickled his mustache, and he had to hold a wet finger beneath his nose to keep from sneezing.

Ruggieri flexed his hands and fingers. Already he could tell that the stiffening in his joints was easing. The pain was almost gone. If he stayed long enough, he might be able to sleep half the night without waking in distress. If this thorny problem would let him.

The doctor came to a decision. After visiting with Professor Fairchild tonight, he would pay a visit to Signore Col McCallum. Several reasons pointed to him as the best choice: He seemed a man of good sense, he was not directly attached to the professor's group, and, perhaps most importantly, he was not associated with any of the others, and had been a thousand miles away when Carruthers was murdered. Yes, murdered.

He must not shirk that word, hard though it was to contemplate. He had no certain facts as to the identity of the murderer but he had suspicions. They were vague and he could not find the logic of them; but Ruggieri had not attained his sixty-three years without learning a certain wisdom. Part of that wisdom was to trust the voice of intuition, whether it whispered or shouted in his inner ear.

His friend in Naples had written that he would not make his findings public for six weeks. Unless they had reason to deem the poisoning the result of accidental ingestion, there would be a great scandal. The doctor did not think it was at all an accident. That was one of the things he wanted to consult about with Signore McCallum. The American could take up the investigation and he, Ruggieri, could return to his beloved gardens. He hoped to discover a crop that would become a staple of the island's inhabitants and ease their dependence on the fickle seasons and the sea. And he would name the new iris he was developing for his late wife. Those were proper pastimes for a retired physician, not making moral judgments and playing inquiry agent.

Making the decision was a relief. With Signore McCallum in charge, Ruggieri could go back to his books and his vegetables. Tonight he'd go up to the Court of Three Sisters to pay his respects to the English ladies. It would be very pleasant having them on the island for a few months.

He leaned his head back against the ledge and let his limbs float upward. He was weightless, like a babe in the womb, warm and completely relaxed. Dr. Ruggieri was so relaxed he didn't hear stealthy footsteps over the gurgling of the water or know that the sulfurous breath he drew in was his last on earth.

There was no time to struggle. The heavy rock struck him with great force, shattering his skull like a china teacup. He lost consciousness instantly. Then the same hand that had wielded the rock pushed and held his bloodied head under the fizzing, fume-laden bubbles until the job was done.

4

EXPLORATIONS

Notes from a lady's diary

I remember well that sultry evening when Col McCallum walked out to the terrace and into our lives. The moment he entered, the atmosphere was charged with the crackle of unseen forces, like the electric tension of a coming storm.

With his bright golden hair and dazzling smile he looked like a young god. A chill wind blew through me. It might have been premonition, or merely the breeze off the dark sea foaming against the rocky shore so far below.

Everyone seemed greatly intrigued by him. I was the only one who held back. I wanted to dislike him, but found myself drawn against my will.

Perhaps I sensed even then, in some subtle way, that he was the kind of man who made things happen. Once he entered our lives, it was inevitable that they would be—that we would be—changed forever.

Richard Fairchild returned to the villa a little before sundown. The formalities of the terrible accident had consumed most of the afternoon, and he was ready for a happy reunion.

His daughters were waiting, rather anxiously, on the loggia when they heard a trap pull into the outer courtyard. Fanny ran to the archway opening on the outer court.

"Papa is here!" she exclaimed, rushing out to meet him.

Thea came to stand in the doorway and looked out. Summer kept to her invalid chair beneath the lavender shadows of the loggia. She was in more pain than she could remember. Or perhaps it was only that she noticed it more. She felt more awake, more alive since she'd come to Ellysia. Everything seemed sharper, brighter, more intense here: the colors, scents and tastes, the glowing intensity of light and the velvety luminescence of the gathering twilight—but, especially, the pain.

A sable cat strolled over, one of the many felines who seemed to inhabit the villa. It turned its head to fix her with its mysterious green-gold stare, then curled up at her feet, purring.

Richard returned with Fanny, his arm around her shoulders as she rattled on a mile a minute about their journey, her new room, and the simply stunning bonnet that Thea had refused to let her purchase in Marseilles on the grounds that it was much too worldly for a girl just out of the schoolroom. Which opinion, of course, Fanny still disputed.

He pinched her chin, announcing that she had grown taller and even prettier since he'd seen her last. "I shall buy you any number of fetching bonnets once we return home," he promised.

Next he greeted his other two daughters warmly, commending Thea for her managing to get them all safely to Ellysia and for her good sense in leaving Nurse to the care of the convent sisters. His greeting to Summer was restrained due to the guilt he felt at seeing her pale face and obvious discomfort.

"The weather here is salubrious. Once you've rested you will be glad that you have made the effort," he added by way of reassurance.

"I am already glad," she said, surprising even herself.

Signora Perani bustled in announcing that supper was ready. Her nieces Zita and Pellegrina, both strong farm girls, had joined the villa's indoor staff, and her nephew Giovanni was to come and attend to the neglected gardens and look after the horses. The professor had made arrangements to have the use of a carriage and team belonging to the *castello*, as well as two hacks for his daughters to ride.

Such excitement! The signora was in her element. Now other rooms in the villa could be opened up for use, and perhaps there would be many feasts, as her uncle Salvatore had at his grand home in Messina. Inspired, and wanting to honor the professor's daughters, she had prepared a meal fit for a king. So much food!

Richard led his daughters off to a room they hadn't seen yet. It was on the far side of his study and at right angles to it, with a glimpse of yet another tiled courtyard leading off to the side.

Summer was limping badly and let herself fall

behind so the others wouldn't notice. This house, she thought, was like one of those clever lacquered Russian boxes that Martin had given her, all nested together. One of the cats padded along behind her like a small, lithe shadow. Thea had tried to keep Summer in bed until dinnertime, and all because of her earlier faint. There would be more skirmishes along the way, but at least she had won this one.

She entered the room set aside for dining, and promptly dubbed it the Aviary. The chamber had a vaulted ceiling painted a delicate blue, complete with clouds. The walls were stuccoed in palest spring green fading to lavender hills, and decorated with a frieze of orange- and lemon-colored lilies. The artist's whimsy had not stopped there. Colorful waterbirds stood near the banks of a turquoise river, spangled with leaping fish, and swallows soared and canaries darted on the ancient, invisible breeze.

"Utterly charming!" Thea exclaimed. Tall windows with wrought-iron railings framed a view of the blue, whitecapped swells stretching to the horizon. Beyond them was a sheer drop to the Tyrrhenian Sea.

How private and protected the villa was, Summer thought, with its blank walls facing the hills and fields, opening only to shielded inner courts or to the sea. Whoever had first built it must have had a great love for the sea. She could almost feel it. She *could* feel it. A deep, aching yearning that was so strong it was almost like . . . *Before.*

She thought again of her secret terrace and wondered who had built it and put the stone chair in place. She had no doubt that it was designed for, and most likely by, a woman. There was no proof of it, only an overwhelming certainty. What, or whom, had she waited for there, looking out over the endless blue?

Waiting. Praying. For fair weather? A ship? The return of a lover by sea?

"You are a long way off, Summer."

She started at her father's voice. "I was wondering about the people who built the villa. Who they were and how they lived and what their dreams were."

He was surprised and gratified. "You see, the journey has already done you good. You are beginning to think like an archaeologist." It was the highest compliment he could give.

Summer flushed with pleasure. She had read her father's philosophy books after devouring almost everything else in his library. She had sought answers there, and found more questions. As to the more practical aspects, she had always thought of her father's profession as dealing with *things*, with facts and objects and measurements, with pottery and carvings and ancient buildings.

For the first time she grasped that it was more than that, that the purpose of his work was to find the essence of the vanished people themselves. It intrigued her greatly.

Signora Perani brought them each a glass of the island wine, the color of cowslips, and they drank a toast to their reunion. No one mentioned the young man who'd fallen to his death.

Summer and Fanny tucked into the hearty meal of sliced cooked eggs, shredded goat meat stewed with onions and dumplings, and loaves of crusty fresh bread and sweet pale butter. The side dishes were purple-black Kalamata olives; a bowl of fava beans with garlic and rice; more rice steamed with bits of fish and zucchini; firm red tomatoes, sliced and served in pale green olive oil; and a third dish of savory rice formed into tiny balls, then stuffed and deep fried, which the signora called *arancini*—"little oranges."

Thea, however, was not delighted with the signora's feast. She considered it peasant food, unaware that the quantity of stewed kid they had just eaten would be more than any of the island's inhabitants ate in a year's time. She made a mental note to instruct the signora in foods more suitable to English palates. A nice roast of lamb or beef would have been quite unexceptional and infinitely more welcome.

The final course fortified her decision. To finish off, the signora had made a very special delicacy: fried pastry rolls with a creamy filling made from mashed chick peas, sugar, and cinnamon. Although both Fanny and Summer sampled them and pronounced the treats delicious, Thea could not bring herself to touch them.

Afterward Richard Fairchild beamed at his daughters over the remains of the dessert. "Well, this is cozy. I can imagine no greater joy than having my family gathered around me once more."

They all stared at him. His heartiness struck a false note. Normally he was a reserved man, rarely given to expressions of sentiment. His infrequent extravagant phrases were reserved for finds associated with his profession.

Fanny put into words what the others were too polite to point out. "You seem uncommonly glad to see us, Papa!"

He was taken aback. "What an outlandish thing to say. Of course I am delighted. Why—"

His pocket timepiece chimed the hour and Richard realized that it was later than he'd imagined. He should have brought the matter up earlier. He cleared his throat.

"You are tired from your travels, and no doubt looking forward to an early bed. Perhaps it was a bit precipitate of me to act without conferring with you first, but I have invited a few of my colleagues over this evening. There is someone I wanted particularly for you to meet."

His seemingly casual scrutiny took in their reactions, which were characteristic: Thea looked resigned, Summer disturbed, and Fanny pleased.

"Will there be many guests?" Thea asked, wondering if she were meant to provide them with refreshments and entertainment. How like a man to thrust a group of total strangers upon them on their first night at the villa, without so much as a warning!

"Seven or eight, if Dr. Ruggieri can get free. Angus Gordon told me you've already met my old friend. My associate, George Symington, along with his wife and daughter. Then there is Carruthers's godson. Lewis Forsythe, who is on leave from Cambridge and acting as my assistant. Unfortunately," Richard continued, "young Gavin Finch-Jones has gone off to Sicily for a few weeks." Fanny's face fell. She wouldn't get to meet "Jonesy" after all. "Last, but not least," Richard continued, "our mosaic specialist. We're very lucky to have her—quite a capable type of female and an asset to our little company, is Mrs. Morville."

That struck a distant bell in Thea's memory. "Morville? I seem to know the name, although I can't recall anyone to mind."

Richard concentrated on pouring out another glass of his favorite brandy. "Your husband may have known Lawton Morville. He was in the diplomatic service before leaving to devote his time to the study of antiquities. He died abroad some years ago."

Richard topped off the glass. "You will like Cynthia, I think. A very interesting and intelligent woman, I must say! I don't know what I would have done without her on the spot."

Cynthia? The bells in Thea's head clanged in alarm. She sent her father a keen look, but he refused to meet her eyes. A sudden fear that he had become entangled in the nets of a cunning husband-seeker took hold of her. She was very anxious to meet Mrs. Morville. Perhaps it was not too late to intervene.

Summer could have wept with exhaustion. She wasn't up to dealing with meeting new acquaintances; her pain was considerable, and the last thing she wanted was to have her deformity put on display before a group of perfect strangers.

Perhaps tomorrow, prepared in advance, she might face that hurdle more easily; but at the moment her nerves were worn paper thin. The lack of rest and the exertions of the day had taken their toll. She'd made the journey on pure willpower. Suddenly her energy was draining away like water in a sieve. Summer wanted desperately to curl up in her bed and fall asleep with the window open to the murmur of the sea.

She pushed back her chair. "If you don't mind, Father, I believe I will retire before their arrival."

Richard Fairchild tried to ignore her shadowed eyes. Summer must not fall into her old ways here. He would not have her immured in her room whenever visitors came by, like some mad relation locked away in a garret, as Leonie had said. What would people—what would Cynthia—think?

"Nonsense," he said. "It is far too early. If you

retired now you would only wake hours before dawn to toss and turn. They shan't stay long, I promise you."

His hearty reassurances rang as falsely in her ears as they did in his. There was no time for any more. They heard laugher—a woman's bell-like soprano and a deeper, masculine chuckle. Footsteps came almost up to the threshold and Signora Perani entered and announced the guests. Summer remained seated. The rest of the family rose and went to greet them with varying degrees of eagerness.

Fanny had formed a vague picture of what a female expert on an expedition would look like, especially one who had been described as capable and intelligent: serviceable garments and shoes of brown or navy, a simple hairdo and thick spectacles adorning an otherwise plain face. Cynthia Morville floated into the room in a gown of rose-petal silk and Brussels lace, and shattered Fanny's stereotype completely.

She came in breathlessly, including everyone in her warm smile. "It is my fault that we are so late, Richard! Do forgive me. I misplaced my best garnet earrings and worked myself into a state trying to find them, and to no avail."

Her smile flashed out again, directed at each of the sisters in turn. "I did so want to look my best to meet your daughters."

The professor hurried to the doorway, holding his hands out to take hers in his grasp. "My dear Cynthia, you look splendid! As you would in sackcloth and ashes."

He flushed, suddenly aware of three pairs of eyes taking in the little scene and turned to the young man beside her. "Forsythe, glad you could come!"

"The Symingtons will be along any minute." Lewis

nodded in Cynthia's direction. "Since we were both ready we drove up together in the gig."

Richard tore his gaze away from Mrs. Morville long enough to initiate introductions. "Cynthia, may I present my eldest daughter Thea, who is Mrs. Martin Armstrong."

The two women curtsied slightly and shook hands, eyeing each other as cautiously as two cats with one mouse. They exchanged polite murmurs.

Richard Fairchild beamed. He needn't have feared. It was all going swimmingly. "And here is Summer, of whom you've heard me speak. And of course, little Fanny."

His youngest daughter, who so loathed her given name, was mortified to be presented as "little Fanny" before such a sophisticated, fashionable woman and so good-looking a young man. She wished that she had worn her new blue frock with the silver knots instead of her simple yellow organza. Lewis Forsythe had melting golden eyes, curling brown hair, and a dashing air. It was too bad of Papa not to have given them any notice.

Forsythe bowed over Thea's hand and remarked that he had met her husband once, at a diplomatic reception in Paris. He welcomed Summer to Ellysia with the same gesture but made the unforgivable error, in her view, of fixing his eyes on her face as if it sat upon a shelf, with no body beneath it. It was the opposite of being stared at, but every bit as distressing for her. What Forsythe, and no doubt the rest of the polite world saw as proper etiquette, was to Summer a slap in the face, a refutation of herself as a person. She took an immediate dislike to him.

But she wasn't being quite fair, and knew it. He

from the outer courtyard, distinguished in his white shirt and dark clothes. Her father gestured toward the newcomer. "Ah, there you are, McCallum. Come, meet my daughters."

Lanterns had been lit and his face was momentarily highlighted in stark contrast, all sharp planes and empty hollows, like a mummer's mask. He stepped closer and was transformed by the mellow light into a tall god with chiseled features and thick hair spun from gold. He looked dangerously handsome, Summer thought, and wondered why that particular description had leapt to mind. As he closed the gap between them Summer heard a slight gasp behind her but didn't turn around. She imagined he often had that effect on susceptible females.

Col McCallum joined them without showing any change of expression. Yet he felt as if he had stepped onto solid ground to find it turning to quicksand beneath his feet. He recovered himself quickly.

"Good evening." His gaze raked over the party.

The women reacted to it in varying ways. Cynthia Morville greeted him with a smile, shifting her carriage subtly to expose her elegant line of throat and bosom. Candlelight was always kinder to her than daylight, and she was wise enough to know it.

Thea gave him a cool smile and a nod. Fanny was dazzled as he bowed to her.

Summer's reaction was a dull ache in the pit of her stomach. She had been trying to move away into the shadows. She hated to have her deformity on display but was trapped in a circle of light like a deer blinded by a poacher's beam. She looked away.

Years of being stared at had sharpened her perceptions. She was aware of the exact moment that his eyes moved from Fanny to her, hesitated at her ivory-handled cane, swept over her from head to toe, and then moved on.

He was not told about me, Summer realized. *He wasn't warned in advance that I am a cripple.*

She looked away, afraid that when his scrutiny returned to her, she would see either pity or revulsion. She turned and limped defiantly toward the terrace, head high, pretending not to care that her slipper dragged so audibly, whispering across the tiles.

The rest followed in a cloud of bright chatter, moving toward the courtyard archway that led out to the terrace. Signora Perani hovered nearby and Mrs. Morville addressed her.

"You may bring the refreshments out to the terrace. Ratafia for the young ladies, of course—"

She broke off as she realized her error. She had made the appalling error of acting as if she were the hostess. The signora raised her eyebrows and glanced pointedly from Mrs. Morville to Thea. There was an awkward pause.

Cynthia Morville was aghast at her lapse. "No doubt you will think me encroaching! You must forgive me, Mrs. Armstrong," she said hurriedly. "In the absence of another woman, I have been used to playing the hostess for Professor Fairchild from time to time. Now that you have come, of course, there will be no need for me to continue in the role."

It was a gracious speech and Thea responded in kind. What else could she do, with others present? *Used to playing the hostess, indeed!* Mrs. Morville took entirely too much upon herself. Thea was distinctly uneasy about the nature of the widow's relationship with her father. Surely he couldn't be thinking of marriage again, at his age?

Her misgivings were soon conquered. Her father

seemed more interested in what Col McCallum had to say about finds in Mexico than in Mrs. Morville's charms. Thea was left to conduct her own conversation with the widow. It was easier than she'd anticipated. They had several acquaintances in common, which helped somewhat, and the widow managed to include Fanny in her airy comments of London life.

Fanny was flattered to be spoken to as if she, too, were familiar with the glittering conversation and whispered scandals of the aristocracy. It was good practice, she imagined. She so wanted to have a London season when they returned to England, and Thea had promised to put in a word with Papa on her behalf.

She *must* have a London season, Fanny thought in an agony of longing. How else would she ever meet the man she was destined by fate to marry? This unknown stranger, whoever and wherever he might be, had not appeared in Kingsmeade, and she doubted she would find him among the severely limited company on the island.

Angus Gordon joined their party and took a seat near Col. He seemed distracted, and added little to the talk. His open American mannerisms were gone, replaced by quiet tension. Col hadn't anticipated a sparkling evening, but this was much worse than anything he could have imagined. He wished he hadn't come.

Glancing across the way, he saw that Cynthia Morville and Thea Armstrong were enjoying the get-together as little as he. Angus leaned close and spoke softly, but so that both Col and Richard could hear him.

"Dr. Ruggieri still hasn't returned home. Giovanni is going to ask after him in the village. I searched the road along the way, just in case he set out and came a cropper, but it's black as the devil's heart out there."

The professor shrugged. "Most likely he was called out to visit a patient, although it's unlike him not to send his regrets."

The housekeeper returned with decanters of brandy and sherry. Zita and Pellegrina brought more pastries, several glasses, and a stone pitcher of lemonade. Signora Perani made a point of setting it down on the table nearest Thea. There was no doubt at all in *her* mind as to which lady was the professor's hostess.

Col took one of the pastries as Zita came around with her tray. She flashed her dark eyes and smiled, telling him which of the pastries she had made herself and urging him to take another.

As she moved off he couldn't help contrasting the English women with the two village girls, so tanned and strong and bursting with health. The former were pale moonlit roses, fragile and tightly budded, Zita and Pellegrina like the sun-drenched, rich, extravagant bloom of peonies.

He turned his attention to Summer, sitting apart from the others. She didn't fit into his neat mental image. She had set an invisible and thorny barrier around her: *Touch me not.*

Upon first seeing her, he'd thought her to be a girl, perhaps a year or two older than Fanny. Her body was slight, perhaps a result of an illness or whatever had made her lame, but her contours were womanly. So were her too-wise eyes. Watching her face as she sat apart from the others, he saw an aloof and keen intelligence, coupled with an unworldliness that made him wonder about her.

Col was always interested in the history of lives,

past or present. It was one of the reasons he'd become an archaeologist. The blessing, the curse of wanting to *know*, and of one bit of knowledge leading, inevitably, to a need to know even more.

Summer saw him looking her way and averted her eyes, as if she hadn't seen him. She was in no mood for chitchat and even less to be on display. The very presence of someone as strong and vital as Mr. McCallum made her feel inconsequential. Weariness descended upon her like a transparent veil, wrapping Summer in its invisible cocoon. Although she could still see and be seen, everything seemed detached and muffled.

The discussion had turned to an impending visit from Richard's patron, Sir Horace Chriswell, who had agreed to underwrite their explorations. He was sailing the Mediterranean, his date of arrival unsure.

The conversation quickly bored Summer. Miss Symington's few comments had been rather entertaining—certainly meant to shock—but had been ill received by the others. The poetess had lapsed into silence. Although she replied to occasional questions addressed specifically to her, she then returned to her own thoughts.

Summer rose and slipped into the deeper shadows by the wall, alone. The sky was star-filled and curiously luminous, although there was no sign of the moon yet. The sea was a vast, inky blackness, like a chasm into the depths of the earth. She heard someone at her elbow and turned to find Col McCallum there.

He held out a glass of sherry to her, and she surprised herself by taking it. The stem of the glass was silky and cool to her touch. Her heart hammered uncomfortably against the bodice of her white lawn dress. She was unused to being in company at all. To be suddenly thrust into the midst of these sharp-eyed strangers, this handsome, perfect man, was cruel in the extreme. She used the sharp edge of her wit as both shield and weapon.

"If you felt obliged to come and draw me into the conversation, Mr. McCallum, I must tell you that your good manners are as praiseworthy as they are unnecessary. I came here to get away from the others."

"So did I."

He sat on the balustrade with his back to the wall and turned his gaze toward the sea. She was nonplussed. He certainly hadn't taken her words as a rebuff. The sable cat padded over and sat down beside Col. Summer realized they had the same eyes, gold one moment and green the next, depending on the light.

He spoke without turning his head. His voice, she noticed, was deep and low, like the murmur of the distant waves.

"What were you thinking of, when I so rudely interrupted your peace, Miss Fairchild?"

His frankness startled the answer out of her. "I was being a Roman. Trying to imagine what it was like two thousand years ago."

She ran her finger along the rim of the glass. "Do you suppose they ever guessed that someday, other people from foreign lands would stand on this terrace? And that they themselves would be nothing more than ashes and dust?"

"I doubt it. They had too high an opinion of themselves. Like us, they expected their empire would last forever."

He set his glass on the parapet, then rose and came

to her side. "You interest me. You have the soul of a scholar, or a poet, Miss Fairchild."

Summer deflected the compliment as if it were a blow. "Or the overactive imagination of a child."

He smiled. "How refreshing. A woman who doesn't like talking about herself."

She averted her face. He realized he had made her uncomfortable.

Summer was intensely aware of Col just behind her. Except for her father, she couldn't recall ever standing so close to a man before. His stillness was unnerving. She wasn't like other women her age, used to indulging in laughter and flirtatious banter with charming men. She had no conversation.

The wind was fresh on her suddenly heated cheeks and it pulled loose a strand of hair. Summer brushed it away. Just when she thought she couldn't stand the silence another moment, he spoke again. "Look," he commanded softly.

The same strange force that had made her accept the sherry made her turn the way he'd indicated.

Then, as she watched, scarcely breathing, the full moon rose. It lifted majestically from behind the bulk of Hades's black volcanic cone, like an enormous silver globe. Its effect on the view was incredible. The dark sea was suddenly alight, as if its surface were strewn with nets of scintillating diamonds. Summer felt as if she had been given a marvelous gift.

"*Oh!* Oh, thank you," she whispered.

"I can't take the credit." His voice was low and laughter filled. When she looked at him, Col was smiling. Summer drew in a breath. Yes, he was dangerous. He'd managed to breach the shell that surrounded her with a word, a gesture, a sense of wonder that she would never have associated with him. A strange, shared intimacy bound them together and held them for several long seconds.

Something changed. His smile vanished as their glances locked. It was like nothing Summer had ever experienced before. She felt vulnerable, her very soul stripped bare. She couldn't sustain the intensity. With a little gasp she turned away, breaking the fragile contact that had held her spellbound.

Col was fascinated. When she looked up at him her face had been transformed, illumined from some secret, inner source. It had vanished in an instant, like the snuffing of a bright candle. He knew that he had overstepped somehow. She had shuttered herself away in some remote, unreachable space within her. She was waiting for him to leave. He hesitated, for once unsure of himself, then moved back toward the main group.

He tossed back the rest of his brandy. Christ, what was he thinking of, engaging in moonlit tête-à-têtes with her? Summer Fairchild was an enigma. Highly intelligent, he surmised, yet innocent and unworldly. More girl than woman. No, he corrected himself: She was a woman, but untouched by life, like the heroine of a fairy tale, encased in glass and sleeping dreamlessly. Her passions were deep but still unstirred. He knew it instinctively, and those same, sure instincts warned him to keep his distance. Especially under the circumstances.

Summer watched him walk away, then closed her eyes and downed the sherry quickly. Her hand shook. She was glad that he'd left her and afraid that he might come back again. She didn't want him to return. He saw too much.

Retreating to a chair on the fringe of the group, she tried to follow the conversation. The talk was spirited and involved recent discoveries in the Greek islands. Fanny looked bored and sulky, but became animated when Col McCallum came to sit beside her.

It was an uncomfortable evening for Summer in every way. She felt vulnerable in her new situation, more aware of her deficiencies than ever before. When Col McCallum had looked at her she had wanted, so suddenly, so desperately, to be whole.

The moon rose higher and she grew tired of watching Fanny hang on Col McCallum's every word, and Cynthia Morville hanging upon her father's sleeve. She was inexperienced but she was not blind. Judging by the easy familiarity between the young widow and her father, and by his extraordinary eagerness for them all to embrace Mrs. Morville wholeheartedly, it appeared that there was more than met the eye. From what Summer could see, their relationship went beyond that of mere colleagues. She wondered if Father intended to marry again. A lump of ice formed in her midsection: more changes coming.

She glanced across the way and saw that Col McCallum had engaged Miss Symington and drawn her out of her solitude. Their heads were bent together in private conversation. As Summer watched she saw him take a glass from the tray that Zita held and present it to the poetess.

Perhaps taking social misfits under his wing was Mr. McCallum's specialty, Summer thought bitterly.

Suddenly it was all too much. She longed to escape. Summer looked around quickly. Thea would prevent her from leaving, if she could. Fortunately, Thea was engaged in a discussion with Lewis Forsythe at the moment. Fanny got up and crossed nearby. Summer rose and made her way toward her younger sister as quickly as her lameness would allow.

"My leg is aching abominably but I don't mean to break up the party. I'll just slip away to my room. Please make my excuses."

Fanny was easily persuaded. With two handsome and unattached males to dazzle, she had no desire to see the evening end prematurely. "Go quickly, before Thea notices."

Summer fled the terrace as quietly as possible. Col McCallum was seated facing the archway and she was acutely aware of him observing her as she made her escape. He knew she was fleeing like a coward. She could sense it. Summer could have wept with sheer frustration when she stumbled over a loose bit of pavement in her hurry.

Once safely away and in her own room, she changed into her nightshift and brushed out her hair. The day had been long and horrible and she wanted to blot it out. Summer rarely took any of the medication her doctor had given her for pain, but she desperately needed the relief. Surely she had earned it.

She poured herself a dose and swallowed the bitter fluid in a glass of water. Usually it relaxed her and sleep came within the hour. Instead her mattress felt like a stone, her pillow a block of wood. She tossed and turned, half expecting Thea to come and deliver an angry lecture on what Professor Fairchild's daughters owned to their guests. Summer was in no mood for it.

The secret terrace lured her from bed. After propping her pillows beneath the sheet and closing one of the huge shutters, she moved the tapestry aside, opened the little door, and went out.

It was all silver and shadow. She imagined herself in a dim, twilight world where the moon and stars were the only light that ever shone. She named it in her mind—*Persephone's garden*. The sanctuary of the queen of the underworld, who passed the winter months below the earth, waiting for spring and a return to the living world above.

The fancy pleased Summer. She was glad she'd run away from the visitors to her special haven. The sea soughed in the darkness. She couldn't tell where the starry sky ended and the waves began. There was no balustrade at the edge, she remembered. The terrace ended in midair, as if the people who had made this secret place were fairy creatures, able to walk as easily on moonlight as on the more substantial pavement.

The tranquillity and the medicine she'd taken earlier soothed her. Summer limped to the throne and sat upon it, canopied by the night. She tried to imagine what the villa had been like a hundred years ago, a thousand years ago. Perhaps the lilies painted on the salon wall had once grown in this very garden. It must have been very beautiful.

Summer had always loved flowers. She remembered when she'd wanted to have a small garden plot of her own at Kingsmeade, but Dr. Blackman had advised her father that it would be too strenuous for her to attempt. She had refused to sit out in the garden the rest of that year. "Biting off her nose to spite her face," as Thea had termed it.

Perhaps she would weed this garden and restore it to beauty. Since no one knew of its existence, no one could stop her this time. Summer smiled. It would be her secret.

She didn't know how long she'd been sitting there in a waking doze when she heard muted voices and laughter. A trick of acoustics brought the voice from the atrium over to her ears. The guests were saying their good-byes. It was safe to return to her room.

As she was getting up she heard voices again, this time harsh whispers of argument. One was a woman's, hissing a protest. The other rose slightly and she could distinguish its source: Col McCallum.

"What are you so afraid of? You've changed considerably since our last meeting," he said sharply. "You weren't so cold to me then. You begged me to take you away with me!"

Summer was appalled. She had no interest in overhearing any more of his sordid personal business. She went toward the door as quickly as she could, but tiredness and the laudanum made her clumsy. Once again the woman's whisper carried to her, urgent with emotion, but unintelligible.

Col's answer was low and intense. "Damn it, I think you at least owe me an explanation."

"I owe you nothing. What happened between us must be forgotten. It was a mistake from start to finish."

"Then at least let us say good-bye properly."

"Let go of me!"

A gasp and then silence, followed by heavy breathing, then quick footsteps, running away. Summer stopped, frozen in disbelief. That last cry had sounded very like Thea. Could it be? Summer recalled that gasp she'd overheard on his arrival. She stood as if she had grown roots, pushing down and down between the tiny cracks of the pavement, long after the other two left. It took great effort to wrench herself finally free.

Her imagination had been running away with her. Thea and Col McCallum? It was ridiculous. They'd just met this evening for the first time. Summer could have laughed at herself.

But as she returned to her room she quietly opened the door to the corridor and peeked out. Thea's door was closed.

Summer started to close her own door, then went hesitantly along the hallway, stopping before her sister's room. As she stood there in indecision, the sound of her muffled weeping came to her.

Her heart squeezed painfully within her chest. She must not jump to hasty conclusions. There could be a number of reasons for her sister's tears. Perhaps Thea was sad and missing Martin, or merely tired from weeks of travel, or even homesick for England. Summer remembered her saying, upon her return from St. Petersburg, that she was so glad to be on English soil, she never meant to leave it again.

Should she knock? It upset Summer to hear her sister in distress. Thea, always so calm and perfect. Thea, so proper and controlled. A model of womanly virtue, and yet, *Thea . . . and Col McCallum?*

No, it was impossible. It had been someone else. Perhaps Miss Symington? That would explain why the poetess had been so silent and strange earlier.

But a shadow of doubt would not be dismissed. Summer sighed. Everything had seemed so simple and straightforward back at Kingsmeade, free from the struggles and desires of the outside world. Earlier she had thought that everything was changing since their arrival on Ellysia. Now Summer wondered if that was really true, or if her whole image of the world, of the people nearest to her, was a hollow sham, built on false assumptions.

She stood outside Thea's door for a long time, bewildered and afraid. In those interminable, lonely minutes, listening to those muffled sobs, she took her first real steps along the path to adulthood. It was a painful journey, filled with doubts and shadows.

The chill of the night air grew more pronounced and she ached all over. After a while Summer turned and went quietly back to her bed.

The next day started off badly over breakfast. The table had been set out in the loggia to take advantage of the warm morning sun. Thea was as pale as her white linen day dress, but her cheeks sported two bright flags of color as she poured out fresh coffee. Summer was being obstinate and she was in no mood to humor her.

"How can you possibly consider going to examine the ruins today, when you were so exhausted yesterday that you fainted on the jetty, and then had to leave our guests without so much as a good-night?"

Summer set down her fork. "Is this about my health," she asked smartly, "or about my lack of proper etiquette? It sounds surprisingly like the latter to me."

Their father looked up from the papers he was perusing. "What? Do you mean that you aren't coming out to the excavations?" Richard was flabbergasted. "You have traveled for weeks in order to see them!"

Thea put her bone-china cup down so abruptly that it rattled in its delicate saucer. "That is exactly the problem. Summer is all done in from yesterday's exertions. Surely you can see that she needs to stay here and rest. We can't simply abandon her."

Fanny was outraged. "But I have my heart set on going!"

Lewis Forsythe had promised to show her around. He seemed nice enough, but the real lure was her hope that Mr. McCallum would be there, too. She wasn't sure exactly what his capacity was in regard to the excavations, but had overheard him saying his good-byes to her father last night, and adding that he would stop by the site if time allowed.

Fanny was in a fair way to developing a tendre for him. There was an air of rash excitement about him that intrigued her greatly, and made even the dashing Mr. Forsythe pale in comparison.

Summer had slept poorly and was heavy eyed. She slathered her toast with English marmalade from the stores that her father had brought out with him, and shot a look at her older sister. Outwardly Thea seemed unchanged. Her eyes were not reddened or puffy, but was there just a faint hint of distraction in their depths? Only someone who knew her well and was watching closely would notice, Summer thought . . . or someone who had heard Thea weeping in the night.

"I have letters to write," Thea was saying. "With all the traveling I have been very lax in keeping up my correspondence with Martin. Why, I don't remember writing to him since Naples!"

Summer looked up abruptly. She didn't recall her sister writing to her husband since before they'd left England. She took another bite of toast. Familiar foods were comforting at a time like this, although the signora had shaken her head over the odd ways of the English ladies. Precious eggs, squandered for breakfast! She had thrown her hands up in horror and surrender and vanished into the kitchen at their request, but the eggs had been cooked and served. The toast was too thickly sliced and underdone, but at least it was toast.

"Summer?"

She gave a start. While she'd been blocking out the previous night's events with inconsequential musings, her father had been appealing to her to break the impasse. He was used to being the ultimate authority. Thea's balking was an unpleasant surprise. When had she become so outspoken? It was unseemly in a daughter.

"Well?" he asked impatiently. "Do you wish to ride out this morning?"

"Please say you do," Fanny implored. "I should hate to stay cooped up in the villa all day just because *Thea* thinks that you are too tired to make the effort! I'm sure that you wouldn't mind staying here with the signora to look after you."

Summer was saved from answering Fanny's appeal. Cynthia Morville swept in, wearing a striped shirtwaist in blue and peach with a rolled collar edged in point lace.

"Perhaps I may be of help, Richard. If Mrs. Armstrong and Miss Fairchild wish to remain at the villa, I shall be delighted to take Fanny under my wing." She sent the girl a radiant smile. They had become quite friendly the previous evening. "I will take you up in the gig with me, if you like, and bring you back whenever you say. I am rather at odds and ends today."

The professor rose to greet her. "Excellent. I knew I could count on you, my dear Cynthia." He gave his daughters a look that said clearly, "Did I not tell you that she is a woman of great good sense?"

Thea felt her authority melting slowly, like butter in the sunshine. It was important that she retain her position for a variety of reasons. "How kind of you, Mrs. Morville. However, I believe that what Fanny says makes sense. Summer will not come to any harm with Signora Perani to look after her. I shall accompany Fanny to the site."

"As you wish."

Matters were quickly settled. Fanny and Thea went off to fetch their hats and gloves while Richard ordered the carriage. Mrs. Morville was alone with Summer. She took the other chair at right angles to the table.

"I do hope that you do not feel I am making light of . . . of the circumstances," the older woman said quickly. Her slender hand settled upon Summer's shoulder. "I am sure that you would like to recuperate after your long journey. It can't have been easy for you."

Summer was embarrassed. "It was no great hardship."

"How very brave of you," Cynthia said with a gentle smile, "and quite what I would expect from Richard's daughter. He has spoken of you often."

In what context? Summer would have liked to ask, but good manners prevented it. She sipped her coffee and didn't reply.

"You need not guard yourself from me," Cynthia continued. "Indeed, I hope we shall be friends. I believe that it is important that I be frank with you. Your father has told me that, aside from your injury, you also suffered a drastic memory loss. He felt obligated to tell me so as to spare us both from awkwardness, since we will be thrown so much together in the months ahead."

The woman's face and voice were sympathetic, yet wonderfully matter-of-fact, and without the unctuous pity that Summer so dreaded and loathed. She let go of her pride. She was grateful to her father for smoothing the way. It *was* a relief to have it out in the open.

"Yes," Summer said after a moment. "It is strange at times, and an innocent question by an acquaintance can have me at sixes and sevens. I have no recollection of anything earlier than my twelfth year. It's as if I sprang to life then for the first time, with no past. No joys, but I suppose I should be grateful that there are no sorrows, either. Nothing at all . . . before."

A shadow flickered in Cynthia's eyes and was gone in an instant. It was almost, Summer thought, as if the widow envied anyone who could forget the past. She was thinking of her husband, Summer realized with a flash of intuition.

She wanted to take Mrs. Morville's mind off the past. "I feel like Athena," she said, "springing forth from the head of Zeus, fully grown. Most appropriate for the daughter of a classical archaeologist!"

"No doubt you have some of her wisdom," Mrs. Morville said.

Fanny returned in a fetching bonnet and went off happily with Thea, leaving Mrs. Morville and her father to follow in the gig.

After they left, Summer was restless. No one had taken her own preferences into account. After weeks of confinement the thought of going out among the ruins sounded quite pleasant. She was irritated with herself for not speaking out more strongly.

She was in her father's study, looking for something to read, when she heard a sound from the outer courtyard. Surprised, she went out in time to see the signora leave with the donkey cart. No one had taken the housekeeper's plans into account, she realized, nor apprised the woman of theirs.

Summer had the house to herself. She went away to her room and out to her secret place. The breeze off the sea was brisk and cool. She wished she'd thought to take a wrap with her. Then discomfort faded away as the aura of the place enfolded her.

She had always been sensitive to atmosphere. At Kingsmeade there were certain rooms she felt cold and uneasy in, while her sisters noticed nothing wrong. One little-used salon at the back of the house had always made her skin crawl, and more than once she'd fancied that someone else had been in that room with her, when in fact she'd been quite alone. Then one day Summer had overheard Nana telling the parlormaid that a woman had been murdered in that same chamber, fifty years earlier. From then on Summer had avoided that parlor at all costs.

The terrace had a very different feeling. There was a strange serenity here. Strange, because it was colored with a strong sense of yearning. Summer wanted to understand what it meant. She sat on the scalloped throne again and opened herself to the past. In her mind's eye the frescoes were fresh and gay, the edges of the worn paving sharp and new. Again the impression came to her, stronger than before. She was no longer Summer Fairchild, a crippled Englishwoman far from home.

No, she was someone else not even remotely connected to her own past. Someone to whom this terrace was a familiar and everyday sight. Although her memory was intact, her personality was submerged, like a rock beneath an incoming tide. While remaining herself, she also *became* this stranger staring out to sea. Hands tightly clasped on the ends of the armrests until the edge cut into her fingers. The cold weight of a jeweled pectoral resting against her collarbone as she sat there. Praying. Waiting.

For what?

But the atmosphere faded, as if a cloud had passed over the sun. The light dimmed. She was only Summer Fairchild once again and she was tired to the bone. The stone throne felt like ice and she wondered how long she had been sitting there, alone . . . and waiting.

Although it was only ten o'clock in the morning, on what should have been a balmy spring day, the sun was white hot and pitiless. It reflected off the water of the Roman baths like liquid fire as Col knelt along their rim, dazzling his eyes.

He took off his hat and used it to cast a shadow over the edge of the rock-lined pool, hoping he wouldn't find what instinct told him he would. As soon as he'd heard of Ruggieri's fatal accident he'd ridden down to the village. The doctor's widowed sister was inconsolable: To have Paolo return after all these years, only to lose him so stupidly!

But Col feared that carelessness had not played the greater part in the tragedy. He'd paid an early visit to the doctor's home. Ruggieri had already been laid out by the midwife on his bed, with candles at head and feet and a black-and-silver rosary clasped in his cold hands.

Left alone to pay his respects, Col had played detective as well. Any trained archaeologist was used to looking for clues with an open mind. Parting the doctor's hair, he had probed gently and felt the long scalp gash. As clues went, it was a stunner. As far as Col could tell, the only way Ruggieri could have slipped and sustained the type of injury he'd suffered, was if he'd been standing on his head!

He'd felt very bad about Ruggieri's accident, and after viewing the man's body, Col felt sick. That blow to the late doctor's head had not been caused by a tragic slip and fall against the rocky ledge. It had come from a sharp-cornered piece of rock, wielded from above and behind.

Col dipped his hand into the hot, sulfurous water. This was where Ruggieri's body had been found by a village lad this morning. The volcanic rock was rough and sea worn. Together with the bright light, it made Col's task all the more difficult. The lip of the rock was clean. He widened his search.

After going over the ground inch by inch, he found the weapon, tossed casually away on a pile of boulders and stony rubble. The murderer had been careless. The sharp rock was still blotched with dried blood and stained threads of white hair.

Col put it in his saddlebag and rode back to the cottage. He didn't know whom to notify, because he didn't know whom to trust. Better to keep his own counsel a while longer.

The workroom of the house was cool and dim. The white walls looked a pale lavender blue, and the deep reds and greens of the rugs and pillows were muted to shades of umber and black. He felt the same inside. He threw himself down on the cushions of a sturdy armchair woven of dried vines. Reaching for one of Carruthers's journals, which he'd been scanning earlier, Col opened it to a certain place:

Ruggieri is getting old and suspicious, I fear. His warnings—ridiculous! It is sad, a tragedy to see a brilliant man and valued acquaintance slipping slowly into senility. It is my own clumsiness and subsequent neglect that has given me this infernal infection. In any case, I am improving steadily.

There were a few measurements below and notes to have the local carpenter make up some packing cases. Col frowned. The handwriting had started out strong, but grew thin and wavery toward the end. Two lines finished the entry for that day:

The heat oppresses dreadfully but I've accomplished a good deal. The excitement more than makes up for the weariness. Col will be speechless with amazement, as I was.
Very tired. I shall take a nap before writing up the day's reports.

Col closed the book with a snap. Those reports had never been written. Carruthers had died that very afternoon, in his sleep.

A SECOND VISIT WITH ANGELS

The chief angel came back to check on the youngest Fate, who was trying to make the leap from apprentice to journeyman. She was gradually getting the hang of it, weaving the threads together with more sureness of hand; but the pattern was emerging slowly and there were, the chief angel saw with a sigh, no new and unexpected combinations.

Hearing the music of the heavenly door open, the weaver looked up from her loom. "It's so jumbled." She sighed. "It looked so easy when you did it!"

She held out several loose threads. They lay like a colorful tassel in her golden palm. "No matter how I try to bring them together, they seem to have minds of their own, and just when I think I've gotten them back, they pull free again. And this one! . . ."

She held up the broken thread of Dr. Ruggieri. "I don't know what happened here. It was so sudden."

The chief angel regarded the tapestry with the wisdom and the patience culled from eons of experience. "You've forgotten to take free will into account. It's a common beginner's mistake."

She took the broken thread of Dr. Ruggieri's life and tossed it into the air, where it was caught by an angelic sunbeam and whisked away for return to the Source. One of the first rules of Heaven was that nothing was ever wasted.

"Did you think you'd caused that thread to break by pulling too tightly?" she said, smiling gently. "It was already ordained. Sometimes it is necessary for a particular thread to end, so that the new design can begin, or to put an old one into clearer focus. If you look at this Ellysian tapestry closely, you will see exactly what I mean."

The weaver wasn't sure, but she *thought* she did.

"Here," the chief Fate said, "let me help you get onto the right track. I usually find that this is the trickiest part."

Taking the thread of Col McCallum's life in one hand, she lifted those of the Fairchild sisters in the other. "Pick these up where the other ended. Bring them together here. Start by twining them together, first one and then another. It will get stronger as it goes."

"Oh, if only I could do it so easily! So perfectly!"

"You will. Now watch. You must weave them into one another's lives until only the most well-trained eye can detect the exact place where one ends and another begins."

Her graceful bronze hands wove a pattern that seemed to incorporate the heavenly light and the music of the stars with the flame of life from the mundane human filaments. A deft turn here, a skillful twist there, and the tapestry began to look quite different. New, and decidedly unique.

Really, the youngest angel thought, it was remarkable! She gazed at the chief angel with admiration. "How do you do it? How do you know?"

The chief Fate smiled. She recalled when she had asked just such questions herself, in the long, long ago. "It is the same for us as it is for them. We learn by doing—and by undoing, when necessary. Let their energy flow through you and, after a bit more practice, you sense the proper pattern emerging." She smiled enigmatically. "Don't try to force it. Some things *are* inevitable, you know."

5

THE GOLDEN CIRCLE

Notes from a lady's diary

*I thought the end of the world had come. In a
way it had. Although none of us realized it, from
that day forward we were all suddenly thrust
into a turbulent world of events, over which we
had no control.*

Signora Perani did not return from the village. Belatedly, Summer realized that the housekeeper had thought the entire household had gone on
to the excavation site.

Summer made her way to the kitchen and rum-
maged around, finally settling for bread, cheese, and
olives and a bottle of cold water. Then she escaped to
the terrace, feeling that she had done a daring deed.
In all her life, Summer couldn't recall ever foraging
for food herself, or having so unorthodox a meal.

She settled in a corner out of the hot sun, and watched the sea shift from blue to green to aqua, like the changeable taffeta of her favorite skirt. Two boats plied the water, the near one bright red with a curving prow, the other dark and blurred with distance.

She set the bottle down in the shade and spread her booty in her lap. Thea would be absolutely appalled, but Thea was not there to spoil this minor Eden. The sharp cheese and tangy olives were like forbidden fruit, and Summer ate them with gusto.

Afterward she went to her room and stripped to her shift for her daily nap. She couldn't sleep. The secret terrace called to her again. Summer sat up. Why not? There was no one to hover and advise. She was free, at least until Thea and Fanny returned, to do exactly as she pleased.

Summer lifted the tapestry in her bedchamber and opened the door to her concealed terrace. It had grown considerably hotter in the past half hour. The vine had unfurled huge umbrella-shaped leaves that laced across the small end of the vee and shaded the pavement, and the high walls protected it from the strongest sun. The tiles were still cool to her bare feet. She hadn't bothered to put her dress back on and wore only her shift, which made the heat tolerable.

She sat on the ledge rimming the bare garden. It would have been the perfect place for a fountain. In fact, she realized, there must have been one, once. The very center showed a bowl-shaped depression, and what she'd mistaken for the remnant of a slim tree trunk, was a stone pipe. She touched the dirt. It was hard as concrete. Picking up a twig, she brushed away the dust and debris and saw that it was a solid plastered surface, not the garden she'd thought it. It was too shallow to transplant flowers from the overgrown borders in the central court. That was a great disappointment. Then a gleam of gold caught her eye.

It seemed to be below the dusty surface, barely visible through a narrow crack. She forced the twig between the crack and prodded at it. The plaster crumbled. Another sharp dig revealed more gold. Perhaps twenty minutes more of persistent labor, and she had uncovered less than two square inches, but now she knew what she'd found: a mosaic that appeared to be edged in tiny squares of real gold.

Why on earth had it been covered up? Perhaps it was ruined by time and weather, and only portions remained. Summer intended to find out. It was far too soon to guess what the pattern was, but the precision of the inlaid stones, no larger than grains of rice, and the exquisite blend of colors told her she had found something of rare beauty.

Gradually she realized that her body was sweaty and her shift sticking to her skin. She sat up, noticing for the first time how stiff and sore her muscles had become. And how, for the first time in days, she had been completely unaware of the pain that was her daily companion.

It had been there, ignored as she focused on her task. Now it came back with a vengeance, augmented by the time she'd spent hunched over. She stumbled up, wincing, and wishing she had brought her cane out with her.

It was still hot, but not the terrible wilting heat of a short time ago. Then she looked up and noticed the sky was half filled with swift scudding clouds, and the shadows stretched almost all the way across the terrace. She'd been at her task longer than she'd imagined. All that work with such small results!

It should have daunted her but, without conscious decision, Summer had already committed herself to the work of uncovering the mosaic.

She pushed the damp hair back from her face. A few blossoms fell lifeless from the vine, and even the birds were stilled. That was quite enough for one day.

She rose and went back to her room to wash away the dust and sweat of her labors. She felt sore and tired, yet it was the tiredness of accomplishment. Excitement gave her a surge of energy. Dressing once more, she took up her sketchbook and decided to go back to the main terrace, which would be in shade now.

As she was about to leave her room, she glanced back at the tapestry of Persephone that hid the secret door. Every day, when Thea thought she was napping, Summer intended to be out in Persephone's garden, uncovering the mosaic in the dry fountain. She wondered what she would find, and why it had been hidden away.

Col was going back through Carruthers's journals in reverse chronology, when he heard Tonino talking to someone. A moment later the door opened and Angus Gordon entered. "I brought you those books you wanted. Find anything out in the village?"

Col took the books and set them on the table beside him. "The funeral will be Wednesday," he said.

He knew that wasn't what Angus had meant, but it was better not to tell him too much. Knowledge could bring danger. There had been too many deaths already. The question was, were they connected?

Angus picked up a terra-cotta ex-voto that Col had

found in the woods. It was shaped like a phallus. "What the heck is this?" His own specialty was ancient texts and linguistics.

"An offering to the gods from a man hoping to restore his flagging virility, or perhaps from a woman hoping to achieve pregnancy."

Angus set it down again. "I think a bouquet of flowers or one of those candles the Catholics light is more to my liking." He looked around the study, puzzled. "I still can't figure out why Carruthers moved here from the villa with his valet. Evidently his servant couldn't stand the come-down. That must've been the last straw that made him pack up and leave."

Col had risen to pour them each a glass of wine. He arrested his action in midmotion. "Do you mean Evans? I assumed that Carruthers's valet went back after his master's death."

"No siree. It was a week to the day after they moved down here to the cottage that he left. I could see he was in a royal snit about it, too."

That didn't sit right with Col. Evans had been with Carruthers for decades, and was completely loyal to him. Hadn't he followed him across veldt and tundra for the best part of twenty years? No, if Evans had gone away that could only mean one thing: that Carruthers had sent him. But where, and why? He'd have to follow up on that immediately; but first there were other matters at hand.

He finished pouring the wine and handed Angus a glass. "You saw Ruggieri yesterday. Did he act any different than usual? Say anything or do anything out of character?"

"I don't follow you."

"Was he excited? Worried? Afraid?"

Angus shrugged. "He was like he always was.

Friendly and courteous as a lord. When Mrs. Armstrong delivered his letters he thanked her as politely as you please, although you could tell he was eager to open them."

"Letters? From whom?"

Angus raked a hand through his shock of sandy hair. "From the count and some other doctor fellow. From Rome, I think."

That interested Col deeply. After talking with the doctor's sister, he'd been given permission to look over Ruggieri's papers and had searched the dead man's correspondence. Except for Count DiCaesari's, there hadn't been any recent letters among them. "Try to remember the name on the return address. It's important."

"Umberto something or other. Started with 'B.'" Angus paused with his hand on the door. "Are you coming out to the ruins? They're sinking a new test trench."

Col frowned. "No. I've got a site to check out. I might ride out to the Court of Three Sisters and visit the Fairchilds this evening."

Angus cast a knowing look. "Got an eye on that blond-headed filly?"

"Fanny Fairchild? God forbid! She is fresh out of the schoolroom, with not a thought in her head but the set of her bonnet."

"The other one's married. Not my cup of tea. Two much starch and vinegar."

Col laughed. "Your mixed metaphors are enough to make me queasy."

After Angus took his leave Col was glad the American hadn't made one of his jokes regarding Summer Fairchild. He found her the most intriguing of the three, and he felt protective of that knowledge.

If Thea realized it, she would do everything in her power to keep him away from her sister.

Col had been sifting ideas while the sun rose higher in the sky, until his mind was cluttered with their dust. Carruthers's death might not have anything to do with his discovery—whatever the hell *that* might be, Col concluded.

For all he knew, his godfather might have been murdered for more personal reasons. God knew, the old lion had a way of putting people's backs up at times. And Ruggieri's death might have been arranged because the doctor had known or guessed too much.

He rose from the table. His mind was reeling. Christ! He needed a ride to clear his head. Earlier Col had found one of the old maps that Carruthers had obtained, showing the position of an old settlement. He decided to head up the valley in search of the site and see what it looked like.

He packed a hamper with food in case he spent the rest of the day out and had Tonino put the gray mare between the shafts of the buggy. The site he meant to examine was the opposite direction from the temple complex that Richard Fairchild was excavating.

It didn't take him long to locate it. The sharp angles beneath the uneven terrain were obvious to his trained eye, although they were completely covered over. It looked as if another *villa rustica* had been here at one time, with extensive outbuildings. Nothing of major importance.

He intended to turn back, but found himself climbing higher along the track. It was then that he realized his true destination: He was heading for the

Court of Three Sisters. That amazed him. In the evening he could be sure of a discussion with Richard Fairchild over a glass of brandy or two, but with only the ladies present, he would be plied with nothing stronger than tepid conversation and pitchers of too-sweet lemonade.

Ah, well. It was a fine day for a ride. He regretted taking the buggy instead of his hack, and wondered why he'd done it. Horseback was his preferred mode of transportation. As a child he'd ridden bareback, imagining himself one of Arthur's knights galloping over the meadows, when the fine palfrey of his pretending had been nothing better than an old, sway-backed cob.

Uneasiness stirred. Playing knight in shining armor was what had gotten him involved with Thea Armstrong in the first place. Christ, if he'd known she was Richard Fairchild's daughter and that she would be staying with her father, wild horses couldn't have dragged him to the villa! That was one little escapade he'd be glad to forget.

It certainly wasn't because of her that he was riding up to the villa. She had made it clear that she had no intention of resuming their friendship, except on the most distant terms.

That was fine with Col. All he'd really wanted was an explanation. What a fool she'd made of him!

He knew a lot about females in general, but he didn't understand women like Thea Armstrong, warm one minute and cold the next. He much preferred the brazen but honest charms of the Lulitas of the world. A man knew exactly where he stood with them—and if he didn't, they never hesitated to tell him! Miss Fanny Fairchild, he suspected, had much more of the latter in her. The other one, now . . .

He tried to pigeonhole Summer Fairchild, and found that he could not. She was unlike anyone he'd met before. Certainly unlike her two sisters, neither a lively, naive girl nor a cool, cosmopolitan woman. Miss Fairchild was something more, and at the same time, less. Like a seed within its husk, a flower-to-be, lying dormant.

The villa came into sight and Col finally realized that instinct had been driving him toward it for a damned good reason. It came to him all at once. John Carruthers had been a man wedded to his scholarly pursuits, yet addicted to his luxuries. He never traveled without his own featherbed and linens, crystal, and china. When he'd traveled across Africa, he'd had his brass bathtub, a silken tent, and cases of old French brandy and Havana cigars carted along, over river and mountain, through jungle and savanna.

And he always took his valet along. Yet Carruthers had moved out of the comfortable Court of Three Sisters to the cottage, on the pretext that it was more convenient to his excavations. And then he'd sent his Evans off somewhere.

Col laughed aloud a second time. He couldn't believe how obtuse he'd been. Of course, he'd only heard about Evans leaving today. If he'd known about it sooner, he would have figured it out days ago.

Yes, it was beginning to make sense: Like all of his ilk, Carruthers was highly suspicious of his colleagues and jealous of his finds. There was only one reason that Carruthers would have given up his comforts to rough it in a peasant's cottage, and it had nothing to do with being close to the dig. It was to throw others off the scent of his great find. After all, he'd retained the lease to the Court of Three Sisters right up to his death.

Which meant that, whatever the find was, he had hidden it at the villa. Or, even more likely, he had *found* it at the villa.

And it was still there, Col thought. Waiting for him.

He gave the mare her head. He was delighted that Richard Fairchild had brought his family to Ellysia. It gave him the perfect excuse to spend time in, and around, the Court of Three Sisters. He would have to cultivate their acquaintance, especially that of Miss Fairchild, further.

Suddenly even the thought of over-sugared lemonade seemed tempting.

Fanny was bored, bored, bored! There was nothing to do. And no one was paying the least attention to her, not even Lewis Forsythe. Her lower lip stuck out in a pout that her family would have recognized as boding no good. Father and Mrs. Morville were too busy for her, and Thea was too enchanted with the size and splendor of the ruins to care about anyone else!

"Why, I never dreamed there was so much here," her elder sister had exclaimed. "Or that it was so lovely."

After that, armed with a book that Mrs. Morville had given her, Thea went off to look at the temple complex in more detail. And from her absorbed progress and the way she stopped at *everything* and looked up items in the reference book, Fanny feared they would remain at the site until dusk fell.

The temple ruins were much larger than she'd

imagined. Acres and acres of them. Walls and pavements, porches and columns, many intact, stretched from the edge of the meadow all the way to the cliffs. Their mellow stone, the color of old ivory, stood out gracefully against the trees. Lovely as they were, Fanny had had a surfeit of tumbled masonry.

If she'd known that Mr. McCallum was not going to be here she wouldn't have bothered to come to the excavation in the first place. Fanny kicked at a stone, scuffing the toe of her blue boots, which she positively *hated* and had only bought because Thea had insisted upon it. She wished she'd stayed at the villa with Summer. At least she could have played with the sable cat or curled up in a chaise with one of Mrs. Gaffney's famous gothic novels to pass the time. What a shame she hadn't thought to bring one with her.

Richard Fairchild eyed his youngest daughter with misgiving. There was work to be done and he didn't have time to cosset her. An idea occurred to him. "Perhaps you would care to help Mrs. Morville clean the mosaic?" he said doubtfully.

Cynthia was taken aback but managed to hide it. The last thing she needed on her hands was an amateur who had neither interest nor skill. The local laborers were bad enough, treating the tiny pieces of thousand-year-old treasures as if they were no more than chunks of gravel. Really, she was surprised that Richard even suggested it. She smiled at them both, smoothing over the awkwardness with years of practiced ease.

"Such dirty work, and very hard on one's hands," she noted gently. "I'm sure that Fanny would much rather wander around on her own and soak up the atmosphere until it's time for the noon meal. I thought we might have a picnic beneath the trees, or even down in the cove."

"A picnic!" Fanny was instantly diverted from her fit of sullens. "I should adore it."

All was settled happily, and Richard and Cynthia went off to attend to their work. Now that a treat was in store, Fanny was quite ready to be pleased. There was a grandeur to the standing columns and a certain melancholy to the fallen ones. As if a fairy castle had been destroyed by a giant's cruel hand. The imagery pleased her and she drifted through the arches of the main temple and down the other side to a grassy sward, away from Thea and possible lectures on the histories of a lot of dead Greeks and Romans.

While she had little interest in archaeology, Fanny did have an appreciation for a splendid view, and there were marvelous vistas on every hand. She noticed Signora Perani's nephew loading a cart with rubble to be carried away. With his dark good looks he was as handsome as the hero in the novel she'd left at the villa, and so shy that he had blushed when they were introduced.

He would be leaving his duties at the excavation site to tend the villa's neglected gardens for a week or two, and Fanny was glad of it. At least there would be someone her age to speak with—and speak with him she would, even if Thea did not approve. It would be, Fanny thought virtuously, a good way of improving her Italian, which was still quite rudimentary.

The cool sea breeze helped to counteract the fierce sun. She opened her parasol and strolled along toward the grove of trees lining the western edge of the complex. A narrow footpath led her through a dappled meadow dotted with wildflowers of every description. Wild iris and tiny pinks poked up everywhere along the way as she followed the path. Spying a familiar thatch of sandy-red hair ahead, she wandered toward it and found Angus sitting on a rock.

He was copying an inscription from a block of stone. He glanced up but kept on with his quick scribbling. Fanny felt a comment seemed called for. When he didn't speak, she offered one of her own.

"Why, I declare, I am glad I came to see the ruins. They are far more interesting than the Roman fort at Kingsmeade."

Angus rolled his eyes. "I don't know what you have in your little hamlet," he replied, "but it could never hold a candle to this."

He had work to do and he wanted to finish copying the inscription before breaking for the noon meal. Bending his head to the paper he continued with his task.

Fanny was miffed. She was *not* a child, and being the daughter of a distinguished professor of archaeology, she knew *something.*

She stepped closer and examined the script. "That is not Roman," she said casually, "nor does it appear to be Greek."

"Any idiot could see that," Angus retorted, and went on with his work. Entertaining silly chits, no matter who their fathers might be, was not on his list of duties.

Fanny was aghast at his appalling manners and turned him a cold shoulder. "I have never met any other Americans, Mr. Gordon, but if you are any example of the national nature, they are rude in the extreme!"

Angus threw back his head and laughed. For the first time he looked at Fanny as if she were something more than a doll in ladies' clothing. "Touché,

Miss Fanny Fairchild. I didn't think you had it in you."

She didn't deign to answer. Fanny took herself off as fast as injured dignity would allow, canting her parasol to block him from her view. If the earth opened and swallowed Angus Gordon up whole, she thought furiously, her chief emotion would be one of enormous satisfaction!

She had gone no more than ten yards when a deep groan seemed to come from directly beneath her feet. The air suddenly began to hum. It tickled the inside of her eardrums, making her dizzy. At first she didn't realize what was happening. Horses neighed, and dogs bayed eerily in the distance.

It stopped as quickly as it had begun, but Fanny still felt lightheaded. Something crashed through the bushes, frightening her. It was only Giovanni, the signora's nephew.

"Are you all right, Signorina?" he asked solicitously. "I was up on the hill and saw you down here alone. I was afraid you might be frightened by the tremor."

"I—it *was* rather alarming," she replied in faltering tones. "W-what exactly was it?"

Giovanni was impressed. He saw that the little signorina was as brave as she was beautiful. He smiled, flashing his strong white teeth against his olive skin. "Poseidon Earthshaker, striking the seabed with his mighty trident."

"I beg your pardon?"

"Forgive me. An old myth, you understand." He gestured toward Hades, visible through a gap in the trees. "These tremors, I have felt them all my life. They are harmless."

Fanny was relieved to hear it. "But what causes them?"

"The old volcano on Hades is restless. From time to time it shudders and the ground shivers beneath our feet, but it causes no harm, Signorina, except to the delicate nerves of the English ladies."

He lowered his voice conspiratorially. "Signora Morville, she does not like them at all, and Signora Symington took to her bed for two days after the first one she experienced, but Signorina Symington is full of courage, like you. She was not at all afraid."

He turned his head, listening. "I am needed at the trench, Signorina. I must leave you now."

His voice was so full of regret, his eyes so full of admiration that Fanny could not help but be charmed. He swept her a bow and went back up the meadow path in a strong, sure stride.

She watched him appreciatively until he was out of sight. Now *there* was someone who didn't think she was ignorant nor underfoot; and he had come all the way down to look for her and make sure she was not frightened out of her mind, unlike the others, who didn't even seem to realize that she'd wandered away.

Fanny smiled to herself, dimples peeping at the corners of her mouth. She was no longer lonely or bored. She and Giovanni were going to be friends.

Col reached the Court of Three Sisters and left his horse to graze outside the stuccoed walls. The place had an abandoned air. No one answered his hello, and he went through the courtyard to the terrace, expecting to find Signora Perani at her household tasks. Instead he found Summer, sitting in a chair with a sketchbook open in her lap and staring out to sea. Framed against the brilliant light, she looked fragile and insubstantial in her white organza dress. It made a poignant picture. If he were an artist, Col thought, he would have ignored the golden sunlight and painted the scene in shimmery blues and grays, with Summer Fairchild like an ethereal vision from the past.

A gull swooped through the air beyond the terrace, shattering his fanciful images. He stepped through the archway. "All alone, Miss Fairchild?"

She looked up sharply and dropped the charcoal that had lain idle between her fingers. Her heart sped up and skipped a beat. "You seem to have a talent for stating the obvious, Mr. McCallum!" She was upset that he'd been watching her without her knowledge: How long had he been there?

He was sorry he'd frightened her and thought of apologizing and taking his leave. A gentleman didn't call upon an unchaperoned lady. But then, he wasn't always a gentleman.

If he were a betting man, he'd lay odds that his visit with Miss Fairchild would be much more interesting without the constraint of the others. Surrounded by them, she tried to fade into the background. She wouldn't have that option without her family present.

Col crossed the terrace and picked up the fallen charcoal stick. "I can't imagine why they went off and left you alone, but since I've come all this way, I hope you won't ask me to leave, merely because you're unchaperoned."

"Highly improper of you, Mr. McCallum," she retorted. Her cheeks bloomed with color. "And incorrect, as well. I am perfectly content with my own company. In fact," she added pointedly, forgetting how she'd argued to accompany her sisters earlier, "I prefer it."

He strolled over and took the chair facing her. A twinkle lurked in his green eyes, like sunlight glinting off the waters below. "If you say things like that, Miss Fairchild, I'll begin to think that you are distinctly unsociable. What are you sketching?"

She faced him squarely. "Are you trying to distract me from how indecorous your being here is? It won't succeed. I wish you would leave."

"Do you?" He took her hand, ignoring her start of surprise. "If it's unseemly for us to be alone in the villa, let me take you for a carriage ride. It's too lovely an afternoon to spend all alone here, like a cloistered nun."

Summer tried to pull her hand away but he held it fast. She was furious. He was as horrid as Thea, treating her like a child, as if she had no voice, no choice, except to do what they ordained.

"Thank you, but I have no desire to go for a carriage ride. I prefer to remain here, immersed in my work—exactly like a cloistered nun—and that, Mr. McCallum, is no business of yours."

He released her hand. "Yes, that is what I would expect a proper young Englishwoman to say." His voice filled with challenge. "I am disappointed, Miss Fairchild. I thought you had more courage."

Her hands trembled as she fought to control her anger. Since she was unable to suddenly jump up and leave the room, she chose to ignore him. Picking up her sketchbook and charcoal, she began to shade in the side of a column.

Col took it from her gently. "That's very good," he murmured. "However, It might be easier to continue if you turned the picture right side up."

As he turned it over he examined her work, and was surprised by her skill. With a few strokes of her charcoal she'd caught the serenity of the terrace, the glittering restlessness of the sea below, and the stark cone of Hades rising up into the sky. There was just the suggestion of a single, square sail on the horizon but she hadn't finished the rest.

"You've a definite talent, Miss Fairchild."

He handed the sketchbook back. She batted it away angrily and it fell to the floor. Summer was on the verge of tears and far beyond the bounds of politeness. Her helplessness had never been driven home to her more stabbingly.

"Why are you harassing me, Mr. McCallum? Please go, and leave me in peace!"

He retrieved the sketchbook and set it on the table. What a strange, passionate creature she was! He wished that he could go away as easily as she imagined. Something held him. Perhaps, a cynic might say, it was the knowledge that somewhere in the villa he might find what Carruthers had hidden before he died.

Or perhaps it was the fear he sensed behind her fierce bravado. She interested him. She angered him. She touched him. But it was something that came from deep inside himself that kept Col from leaving.

Their gazes locked in a clash of wills. Summer wanted to look away and found she could not. The strange light in his eyes mesmerized her.

"Come with me for a drive along the cliffs on this fine afternoon," he said abruptly. "You needn't even speak to me unless you wish to."

She had spent the better part of the morning trying to persuade her family that she was well enough to visit the temple complex; now this dashing near stranger was asking her to accompany him as if it were the most natural thing in the world, as if she were not a cripple.

A wild surge of longing shuddered through her, like the first warm, compelling winds of spring. Freedom called. She struggled against it. "If I refuse, will you leave?"

He cocked his head. "No. As I see it, I have two choices. Either I can pull up a chair and spend the afternoon here on the terrace with you, or I can pick you up in my arms and carry you out to my carriage, kicking and screaming."

The ridiculous picture he'd conjured up broke through her defenses. She laughed, startling them both. "You are a very impetuous man, Mr. McCallum. I almost believe that you are really capable of such peculiar behavior."

His eyes darkened from sea green to the color of emeralds. "My dear Miss Fairchild, you may be sure of it!"

For a moment Summer felt as if all the air had gone out of her lungs. Suddenly she could almost feel what it would be like, to be held in his arms, with her head cradled on his shoulder and the rough cloth of his jacket rasping against her cheek. Yes, he was capable of doing it. A shiver sliced along her spine, frightening and delicious. She couldn't bear to be shut up inside the villa another moment, and yet . . .

She cleared her throat. "It does seem like a fine afternoon for a carriage drive."

He knew she was teetering on the brink. "I can understand your hesitation, Miss Fairchild," he said suavely. "No doubt you're concerned that Mrs. Armstrong would not approve."

He had taken a chance in reminding her of Thea, but it worked. The light in Summer's eyes was fired by rebellion. "I am an adult, Mr. McCallum. I do not require my sister's permission to take a carriage ride with you." She rose. "I'll fetch my hat."

Col swept her a bow. "I was sure that my eloquence would sway you."

Summer raised her eyebrows. "Eloquence? I should say, Mr. McCallum, that it was more the result of your intimidation."

"Ah, yes. I usually confuse the two."

"Perhaps I can give you instruction in discriminating between them," she said saucily.

She left him on the terrace and went to her room to get her bonnet, terribly conscious of her affliction as she walked away. What she was doing was mad, but she didn't care. Taking her white straw from the top shelf of her wardrobe, she tied the ribbons firmly beneath her chin.

A sense of urgency propelled her and she was afraid that something would occur to prevent her from driving out with Mr. McCallum. She felt as if she were making an escape. She was heartily tired of being told what she could and could not do, and the urge to kick over the traces would not be denied.

Col was surprised at how quickly she returned. He'd been prepared to cool his heels awhile. "Promptness is a virtue I have always admired in a woman."

Summer didn't tell him that her timely return was not due to innate punctuality as much as to the certain knowledge that she would lose her nerve if they didn't set out at once.

He escorted her out to the carriage and settled the vexing problem of how she would get into to it without embarrassing herself, by picking her up and depositing her in the seat. The tremor hit at that moment, but much more mildly than it had at the temple site. Summer felt a moment of dizziness, which she attributed to being held in Col McCallum's arms. He was so used to them that he ignored it.

Climbing up beside Summer, he gave the reins a gentle snap and the gray mare started off crisply. Once they were safely away from the villa he turned off on the track leading west.

"There's a pretty little cove along the coast with a stunning view. I think you'll be pleased with it. We'll have a picnic there before heading back."

Summer pursed her lips and touched the hamper with the toe of her shoe. She hadn't noticed it earlier. It gave her an unpleasant shock. "You were rather sure that you'd persuade me to come with you."

"Not at all, Miss Fairchild. I only hoped."

It was true. He realized it as he spoke the words. It had been in the back of his mind all along. That unsettled him. He turned his attention back to driving, for the track deteriorated quickly into a barely discernible path winding through the meadowland.

She sat back against the seat, flushed and disbelieving. She had learned that people sought out friendship for two reasons: Either they felt a genuine liking for the other person, or there was something to be gained from the relationship.

Mr. McCallum was not a fool. He'd already felt the lash of her tongue and she had nothing of value that he might want. Not a man like him.

Her flush deepened and her face grew hot with it. She was no fool either. He had no evil intentions, she was sure, nor did he have romance on his mind. But, given time, she would discover what it was that he wanted from her. Could it be something to do with Father's excavations? That was the most likely possibility.

He sensed her mental withdrawal. A quick glance caught her looking down at her hands clasped in her lap, a small frown forming between her winged eyebrows. "What is it?"

"Nothing."

Col cursed silently and wondered if she was in pain and trying to hide it from him. He wanted to ask, but couldn't. He'd made up his mind that he would treat her as a young woman, not as an invalid. But, damn it all to hell, it was unforgivably stupid of him to have taken her over this rough shortcut.

A glint of sunlight bounced off the horizon. They must be nearing the sea, Summer realized. She twisted the ribbon rosette on the back of one of her gloves, until it pulled loose and threatened to come off in her hand. Her reclusive life had left her awkward and suspicious. Perhaps, despite her worries, he had no ulterior motives. Summer tried to believe that, but was unable to convince herself. She wasn't like Fanny, drawing men to her like hummingbirds to a honeysuckle vine.

The carriage rolled along over a low hill covered with sea grass, and they descended and reached the beach. The sand was black near the cliffs, gradually paling to silvery gray where it met the sea. The water was incredibly clear and shaded from pale apple green through dazzling aqua to intense sapphire. The waves that lapped softly against the shore were edged with scallops of foam, as airy and delicate as the lace on Summer's deep collar and cuffs.

Col drew the carriage to a halt and swung her down. He did it so easily, so nonchalantly, that it seemed quite natural, not as if it were because she was lame. He grabbed a pillow from behind the seat, then took her arm with the same ease and guided her to a stone bench cut into the rock. He placed the carriage blanket on the black sand and set out the picnic food. He sat at her feet.

Summer realized that she was ravenous. The foods were strange but tempting, and she washed them down with two glasses of tart lemonade. Col watched her with amusement. The exercise and brisk air were doing her good. He handed her another napkin wrapped around a pastry.

"Will you ride out with me again, Miss Fairchild?"

Summer frowned slightly. She hadn't heard him. "What is that strange black rock in the sea?"

Col glanced at the irregular finger of basalt rising straight out of the water. "That? It's the remnant of some old volcanic formation. The islanders call it Persephone's Handmaiden."

She remembered the tapestry in her bedchamber. A strange coincidence? She eyed the oddly shaped rock. The top broke into two projections reaching skyward. With a little imagination it did resemble the figure of a woman with her arms stretched up in supplication.

"There must be a legend associated with it. Why Persephone?" she asked. "And why her handmaiden? It could as easily have been named for any of the other goddesses or minor deities."

"Most sources say that Persephone lived on the island of Sicily. That it was there that she was abducted by Dis while picking wildflowers, and carried off to the underworld. The Ellysians claim that it happened here, not on the main island. When her handmaiden ran to rescue her mistress, Dis turned the maiden to stone. According to the legend, she must remain so, until the island sinks into the sea from which it came."

"Not a very happy story," Summer commented.

"Few of the old ones are. Life was harder then."

She gave the rock another look. "Poor Cliete, to end up like that."

Col looked at her in puzzlement. "Yes, it's also called Cliete's Rock. You must have heard the legend somewhere."

A shadow passed over them. He'd been so engrossed he hadn't noticed the clouds piling up overhead. "It looks like rain. I'd better take you back."

He packed up the picnic things and returned them to the carriage. Summer was glad he'd invited her for a drive, and even more glad that she'd gone with him. It was against all the rules of middle-class society. She didn't care. Col McCallum was unlike anyone she had ever known. Indeed, how could he not be, when she had lived in her constricted little world, surrounded by servants and women?

She smiled, thinking of the nursery poem of the worm that lived within a walnut, boasting that his tiny shell was the whole wide world, and he its center. Unlike that silly creature, she had always known there was much more than her circumscribed existence: Her folly was that she had feared what was beyond, hiding away at Kingsmeade like an anchorite in the Sinai desert, when there was a universe of experience waiting beyond her door.

The wind picked up suddenly, sending a veil of sand and slivers of dried seaweed blowing across the strand. Summer blinked and closed her eyes against it.

Was that a voice calling her name? A woman's voice? She opened her eyes and looked around, expecting to find Thea marching along the sand in high dudgeon; she saw no one but Col, placing the blanket back in the carriage.

Summer sat tensely upon the stone, drawing her gloves between her hands. The bench seemed to radiate cold until she was enclosed in a chill, silver sphere.

The light scattering off the waves changed from warm gold to pewter and mist rose off the sea. The signet ring on her right index finger twisted around, digging into her hand. She pulled it off and enfolded it in her palm, feeling the solid, warm weight of it.

Someone called her name, and she turned to look farther down the beach. A woman came along the water's edge, laughing and half running through a spattering of giant raindrops. Her hair was pulled back to fall in tight ringlets over her shoulders and she was dressed in a most peculiar fashion. Her gown was dark blue with a pattern of embroidered gold bees, and the tight bodice above a snug golden belt was made open to the waist, revealing her breasts.

Oddly enough, Summer was not shocked. The bare-breasted gown seemed perfectly normal after that first startled moment. She strained her eyes. It was difficult to see in the strange, shifting light.

"You were right, sister," the woman called as she hurried toward Summer. The wind blew her hem about her bare ankles. "The rain didn't hold off as I wagered it would."

She drew so close Summer could have reached out and touched her arm. "We had better hurry," the woman said, "or I shall be frozen forever, like my namesake there."

Summer turned to Persephone's Handmaiden. The rock was taller, sharper in the wavering silver light. In the steaming mist the shadows moved over it, giving the semblance of a young woman with her arms raised over her head in the steps of a graceful dance. Summer struggled for a name. It came to her slowly, as if from a long distance. *"Cliete?"*

"Yes. Is something wrong? You look so pale and ill."

But even as the woman spoke she was becoming silvery and transparent. Summer could see the contours of the coast taking shape through the outline of her body and the design of bees on her gown faded into the tiny pebbles strewn over the coarse sand.

The light warmed and grew brighter, as if the sun had come out from behind a dark cloud. In an instant the phantom fog—the laughing woman—vanished. Summer was on the beach, alone, with Col McCallum coming toward her from the other direction.

He drew in a quick breath when he saw the pallor of her face and damned his impetuosity. He'd completely misread the situation, thinking that Thea was too protective and Summer too used to being cosseted. Thea was right, her sister really wasn't ready for an outing so soon after their arrival.

Col set the basket down and went to kneel beside her. "You're ill!"

"No." She fought to recover from the little episode, unsure as to exactly what had just occurred. Her chest ached with a sense of loss. Had she been dreaming? Her head felt muffled and filled with cobwebs, her tongue thick. There was something she was forgetting. Oh, yes! Panic swelled within her.

"My ring! I've dropped my ring!"

"I'll find it." Col was relieved to see her color return. Perhaps she had only suffered a moment of faintness. He didn't want to embarrass her by referring to it, and dropped down to his knees to look for the ring.

He searched the sand by her feet without any luck, and scraped away the loose grains with his hands. Nothing but dry pebbles, dank seaweed, and sharp bits of broken shell. He sat back on his heels.

"Are you sure you were wearing it?"

"Oh, yes. I have to wear it always . . . " She trailed off in alarm. Her thoughts were still fuzzy and full of gaps. It was almost like *Before*, when things merged until she couldn't tell what was real and what was dream or shattered memory.

Col stretched his arm beneath the bench. He was rewarded for his labors. His fingertips touched and grasped a thin circle of metal and a carved stone. "I've got it. It's wedged toward the back."

How the hell had it gotten back there? he wondered. It took a hard yank to pry it away but it finally came free. He pulled out a gold ring set with an oval of translucent, peach-colored carnelian.

"No harm done to it," he announced, turning it over in his palm.

The intaglio carving was exquisite, with the design of a leaping dolphin cut deeply into the surface. The gold of the ring was worked in an ancient style. Possibly Minoan, he decided. It looked as if it might be used as a seal for impressing into soft wax or clay. Intriguing items of the past often surfaced in little shops all over this area, from the Mediterranean to the Aegean and the coast of Asia Minor.

The undocumented removal of antiquities was a shame. Ancient trade routes could be divined by noting the trail of export items found in situ. Those removed by enterprising looters lost immeasurably in their historical value. It was one of the most frustrating aspects of his work. At times, piecing together knowledge of the ancient world was like trying to put a library back together, with nothing but a few scraps of paper and scattered words.

Grains of sand clung to the surface of the stone and he brushed them away. "An interesting piece of jewelry. Is it an original work or a copy?"

"I don't know." She stared at the ring with a slight, puzzled frown.

He polished it with his handkerchief, then took Summer's hand in his and started to slip the jewel on her ring finger. It was much too large for it, he realized.

"It goes here," she said, taking it from him. She slid it on her right index finger. It fit perfectly.

Col looked back at the bench, brushing the sand from his knees.

It was a good three feet from the front edge of the bench to the cliff face behind it. "How the devil did it get back there?"

Summer didn't know. And she certainly didn't know why she had told Col that she'd lost her ring, either. Perhaps exhaustion had addled her brains. Perhaps her worst secret fears were coming true, and she was going mad. It didn't make any sense.

She touched the carnelian stone with the finger of her other hand. It was lovely and cool, and as familiar as the contours of her own face in the mirror.

But that was impossible; Summer hadn't been wearing any jewelry—and she had never seen this particular ring before in her life.

6

POSEIDON SHRUGS

Notes from a lady's diary

One summer Mrs. Croft planted nasturtium seeds outside the kitchen door. Tiny green stems came up within two days of each other, seemingly identical with their twin leaves. Although she nipped and watered and fed the sprouts, some grew tall and sturdy, others thin and frail. Some never grew at all. In the end she had eight little plants as the fruit of her toil.

I thought that people were like plants. Those who grew and flourished went from seed to seedling, sprout to leafy plant, according to some inbred timetable. Each stage a further progression of the last. We aren't, though. I learned that on Ellysia.

No, human beings have more kinship with insects, dreaming away in our cocoon stage and bursting forth one day as butterflies. That is how it was for me. I kept myself in seclusion, sequestered from Life, but Life would not let me be. Tardy though I was, I became a woman. I was terrified at my exposure. Frightened, because I knew I could never again retreat to the safety of my drab cocoon again. And, oh! astounded with my wings! Their color and sweep! Their power! Their fragile, fleeting beauty!

No, I was not a seedling, growing to an inner pattern; nor was I an insect, counting out the slow days of maturation. One day I was a girl, the next a woman. And it was neither the light of the sun nor the rhythm of days that changed me.

It was Col McCallum.

Col kept his promise to have Summer back at the villa well before the others returned. She was very quiet on the return trip. He glanced over at her. "Tired, Miss Fairchild?"

"No. Just thinking."

She couldn't very well discuss the odd matter of the ring with him. The whole episode had left her disquieted.

Summer blushed. She was a very poor liar, having never practiced this necessary social art. He was still watching her. "They must be weighty thoughts indeed, to take your attention away from such a splendid panorama."

They had taken another route back. They were skirting the upper rim of the cliffs, approaching the villa from a direction she'd never been before. The tiled roofs and flowering trees, representing man's attempts to civilize the land, were visible on one hand, with the shimmering sea and the formidable peak of Hades rising from it in the distance. Untamable. Unknowable. The volcanic cone was so dark against the bright sky that it appeared to absorb the light, and its summit was wreathed with a soot-streaked cloud. A shiver ran through her.

"How strange," she said, to turn the subject, "that this island should be a paradise of flowers and the other so remote and barren."

He reined in. "Stranger still, when you know their history. In the past they were one island."

She looked at him in disbelief. "Surely it isn't possible."

"There are ancient maps still in existence to prove the story. The combined island was named Ellysia then, and it was an important source of obsidian to the ancients, long before Carthage rose. Then tragedy struck."

Col pointed to the sweeping semicircle of bay. It was so perfect it might have been scooped out by a giant's spoon.

"There is part of the evidence. The bay, and all the way across to the shores of Hades, was once the caldera of a volcano much larger than the one you see. Bigger than Etna on Sicily, some legends say, although I doubt it." He saw he'd captured her complete interest. "Haven't you been told the legend of Ellysia and Hades?"

She shook her head, laughing in that sudden way she had that illuminated her otherwise solemn face. "My education has been neglected in the area of obscure Mediterranean legends. It is up to you to rectify it, sir."

He caught the spirit of it. "Very well, although I draw the line at 'once upon a time.' The Ellysians on this end of the island were devout, and followed the prescribed rituals—perhaps at the very site your father is excavating. The others, living at the far end, offended Poseidon by refusing to sacrifice a sacred bull to him. The god retaliated by sending a fountain of flame and smoke in the sky, followed by a rain of stones and fire."

His voice was hypnotic. As Summer listened she could see it happening in her mind's eye. He continued: "The blasphemous islanders tried to save themselves by sacrificing all the bulls they could get their shaking hands upon, but it was too late. Poseidon struck the island with his trident. The earth shook and sulfurous vapors rose from cracks in the shattered ground.

"The sky grew dark and the people wailed and prayed. The mountain exploded. The sea rose up in a great tidal wave and blackness fell, lasting for seven days and nights. They thought it was the end of the world."

"For them it was," she whispered. The scenes he described were so terrible and vivid she felt as if she'd witnessed them herself. She felt the heat of the blast upon her face and the burn of the acrid fumes inside her lungs. She almost thought she could hear their screams, then realized it was only the cry of sea gulls.

"When the sun rose on the eighth day," Col continued, "the volcano was gone and the island was rent in two. All the inhabitants had been swept away to their deaths."

"Even the good ones? That seems very hard." Her eyes twinkled. "And if it were true and everyone died, then how is it that we know the legend today?"

Col groaned in mock dismay but his eyes were

filled with laughter. "I told you that you had the mind of a scholar, Miss Fairchild, but I did hope that you had just the smallest bit of poet in you as well."

"Imagination and logic are two sides of the same coin, Mr. McCallum. But I thank you for sharing the legend with me."

He put one finger beneath her chin and tilted her face to his. "And I, Miss Fairchild," he said softly, "thank you for your companionship."

The warmth in his eyes dazzled her. Her heart literally skipped a beat. Was he flirting with her? Or merely taking a liberty? She clasped her hands more tightly in her lap and turned away. Summer had no more idea of how a lady was supposed to respond to something like this than she did of how to fly. It seemed her education lacked considerably more than a knowledge of obscure legends.

Col saw that he'd erred. She was as skittish as a doe, dashing for cover at the most innocent of gestures. He snapped the reins and the carriage started forward.

Summer tried very hard not to think of the way her insides had melted when he'd touched her. She castigated herself for being such a ninny. If she'd continued going to the assemblies with Thea and Fanny she might have learned to accept such matters with ease. Or would at least know the proper response. However, her one and only outing to a subscription dance with her sisters had been more than enough. Overhearing two young sprigs commiserate that their mothers were insisting they dance attendance on that "pitiful crippled girl," had taken care of that.

Being called a cripple hadn't bothered her. Her lameness was a fact of life; but she could never forgive them for thinking her pitiful.

She lapsed back into her earlier reverie, turning the carnelian ring around her finger as if it were a magic talisman. She had known somehow that it was wedged there behind the bench. A ring she had never seen, in a place she had never been before.

If not for the band with its carnelian insignia, Summer would have thought she was suffering hallucinations; yet Col McCallum saw it too, so it wasn't a product of her imagination. But *how?*

By the time they arrived at the villa she had worked it out carefully in her mind. Somehow, she had glimpsed the ring without it fully registering. The vision of the woman on the beach, which she'd had when he'd gone to the carriage, had been a sort of waking dream, the kind that seems unbelievably real.

Yes, that was it. Like that incident a few years ago when Fanny was recovering from a fever, and had wakened the household in the middle of the night, insisting that a pink pony had been cropping grass in her bedchamber. It had taken several minutes for Fanny to be fully convinced. They had teased her about it for days afterward.

Summer didn't have a fever for an excuse, but it was true that she'd slept poorly the previous night. Nana had often fallen asleep during Sunday services when her rheumatic complaints interfered with her sleep. After a few healthy snores and several sharp nudges from Mrs. Croft, she would snort and jolt awake, vowing that she had been so the entire time. Poor Nana. Summer hoped she would soon recover from her accident.

Thinking of more mundane things as they drove up to the villa helped settle her nerves. By the time they pulled into the outer courtyard, Summer had completely convinced herself that her theory was correct. There was nothing mysterious about her finding the ring, except the mystery of its age and origin.

Col jumped out and came around to assist her. He lifted her down matter-of-factly. She was grateful to him again for not making a fuss or treating her like a helpless invalid. His strength amazed her.

When he set her on her feet his hands were still about her waist. She looked up at him to find him staring at her with a small frown between his eyes. Her eyes were usually keen but guarded. At the moment they were open and vulnerable, and there were shadows beneath them. A short ride, a quick picnic on the beach, and she was exhausted.

"You should have told me you were tired."

"I'm not," she protested. It was a lie. She was ready to drop in her tracks.

The weeks of travel had been an ordeal but she had gone on sheer excitement and willpower, not wanting to make things any worse for Thea and Fanny, afraid that if she fell ill she would delay or abort the journey for them all. She had even kept to her hated invalid chair in order to conserve her energy. After arrival on Ellysia, she had remained keyed up through their installment at the villa and the reunion with their father. Today, for the first time, she had relaxed enough to let down her guard. Beneath the thin veneer of resolve that had kept her going, there was nothing. Nothing at all.

He saw it. Damn them for not taking better care of her! He saved a few choice curses for himself. If he hadn't been so selfish in insisting that she accompany him, she wouldn't be ready to drop now.

"Come, you're exhausted."

He put his arm around her for support. It seemed

the most natural thing in the world. She jerked back as if she'd been burned. They were both embarrassed. Summer turned awkwardly. "Would you care for some refreshments, Mr. McCallum?"

"Thank you, but I must get back." He covered her hand with his. "Will you ride out with me again?"

Prudence dictated caution. She threw them both to the winds. "I should like that. Very much."

Col smiled down at her. Lifting her hand to his lips, he bowed and kissed her fingertips. Before she could react he relinquished them. "So should I. And I shall hold you to your word."

He left, taking Summer's breath away with him. Or so it seemed. Her heart was pounding as if she'd climbed one of the island's cliffs. Her hand, her arm, her entire body tingled with sensation. Her mind was dazzled, as if a great ball of light had exploded inside her head. She listened for the sounds of his carriage driving away and went slowly down the hall to her room.

She didn't recall getting there, yet here she was, standing before her dressing table like a woman in a trance. The oval glass reflected her face, rosy and glowing, despite the shadows beneath her eyes. Summer scarcely recognized herself. And all because Col McCallum had kissed her hand.

She pressed her fingers against her heated cheeks. It was inconceivable that she had broken every rule of propriety by going out alone with him once—and she had agreed to do it again. She hoped, oh! so very much, that it would be soon.

Carefully removing the signet ring, she placed it in a box of alabaster and scented wood beside her opal-and-turquoise earrings and her pearl set.

Something fell from the folds of her skirt. She

stooped down to pick it up. A spray of tiny purple flowers, no more than two inches long, that had been caught in her sash. Each floret was shaped like a miniature lily, petals curving back to expose a delicate lavender throat. They were from the picnic site. She had seen them growing beside the bench.

Summer lifted the lid of the box again and tucked the spray inside, a souvenir of a most exhilarating afternoon.

Thea drove the gig away from the excavation site with Fanny. Their father had run into a problem and intended to stay late. The fleeting alarm caused by the tremor had been superseded in her mind by the tragic news of Dr. Ruggieri's death.

"I believe it would be for the best if we avoid mentioning anything to Summer about poor Dr. Ruggieri," she declared as they came through the meadow. "I will tell the servants not to speak of it in her presence. We don't want her going off on one of her bad spells."

"Oh, I wouldn't dream of it!" Fanny responded, hiding her disappointment that she wouldn't be able to share the news with Summer. As if she were likely to be upset over the death of an elderly man she didn't know and had met only once. And who had been just as likely to die in his bed from old age! Fanny thought in exasperation. But then, Thea had a most unnerving way of being right.

Fanny wanted to ask about Giovanni and find out when he was coming to tend the gardens, but thought better of it. She searched for another topic.

"I wonder why Mr. McCallum wasn't there?" she said idly. She'd looked forward to seeing him and had been chagrined by his absence, but somehow that seemed more removed now.

Thea jerked the reins and the horse reared slightly in protest. It was only the work of a few seconds to settle the beast, but it left her shaken.

"Under ordinary circumstances men like Mr. McCallum would not even enter our social sphere," she snapped. "If you are so bold as to go setting your cap after a man, I would advise you to turn your interests toward Mr. Forsythe, who is well connected and seems a perfect gentleman!"

Fanny eyed her askance. "Why, you don't like Mr. McCallum, do you? How amazing! He seemed perfectly unexceptionable to me."

Thea flicked the whip out over the horse and accidentally touched its ear. The startled creature broke into an unwieldy gallop, and by the time Thea brought it under control Fanny had already forgotten her question and gone on to other things.

Thea would have been shocked to know that Fanny's thoughts had wandered to the handsome young man she'd seen at the excavation. Fanny intended to learn more about Giovanni.

Summer was lying on a chaise with a book at her side, and didn't hear the gig arrive. The book lay open but unread. Since returning from Cliete's Rock her mind had been occupied with two subjects: Col McCallum and the strange vision she'd had of the woman coming toward her.

She had eventually dismissed the vision as a trick of the light or a dim memory surfacing and superimposing its images over the landscape of the sheltered beach. Mr. McCallum was more difficult to dismiss.

He invaded her thoughts as he'd invaded her privacy earlier and, just as persistently, refused to leave.

Summer was no fool. She knew that her inexperience made her vulnerable to his flattering attentions. She tried to be sorry that she'd let down her guard enough to let him coerce her into the carriage ride, but wasn't enough of a hypocrite to make a good job of it.

Since returning, she'd been alternately restless and dreamy. Excitement quivered through her body, along with a dull but not unpleasant burning that filled her chest until she feared her heart would burst with it. It made her jumpy and dissatisfied.

Her sketchbook was on the floor beside the chaise but she had as little interest in her art as she had in the book. Summer didn't know exactly what it was that she wanted, but she did know that she *wanted*. That she felt yearningly, achingly incomplete.

With nothing to compare it to, she mistook the giddy, early stages of infatuation for something more dire. Summer feared that she was losing her mind, when she was really only in danger of losing her innocent, untouched heart.

The sound of footsteps echoed and she looked up to find her sisters coming through the archway to the terrace. The moment of truth was upon her. A blush of guilt added color to her face. Should she admit that she had gone for a carriage ride with Mr. McCallum?

Thea uttered a small cry and went to Summer's side. "Your eyes are positively glassy! Have you been in the sun too long?" She tsked at her flush, and placed a cool hand on Summer's forehead.

"You have the fever! Oh, I knew I shouldn't have left you. All the excitement yesterday was too much for you. Thank God I made you stay home today. Indeed, you must spend the next several days resting. No, don't even attempt to argue," she said when Summer opened her mouth to protest. "I won't hear anything to the contrary!"

Summer leaned back against the cushions. The decision had been made for her. If she told Thea that she'd been out for a drive, Thea would blame the activity for her "fever," which Summer realized was a mild touch of sunburn.

Thea would surely put a stop to any further outings. Summer couldn't risk it. She hoped . . . she *wanted* very much to spend another afternoon in Col McCallum's company. Soon.

Thea was outraged when she learned that Summer had been alone, without any of the servants to look after her. Even the boy who looked after the horses had strayed from his post, lured no doubt by the sunny afternoon and the absence of his employers.

"This cannot be allowed," she said ominously. "I shall have a talk with the signora immediately upon her return."

Panic fluttered in Summer's midsection. "Please don't. What you mistake for fever is color from all this warm, fresh air. I am not an invalid. The last thing I want is to have the servants hovering over me." She saw that she wasn't convincing Thea. A burst of inspiration came. "It irritates my nerves," she said quickly. "I found the solitude and quiet refreshing. Indeed, I feel quite restored."

Thea accepted her explanation, but with reservations, and sent Fanny to fetch some cool water to bathe Summer's forehead. Summer was forced to endure it.

Later Pellegrina came up from the village with a

basket of cheeses, and set out a light repast for the ladies. They took it on the terrace: The view of sunlight and sparkling sea hadn't lost its novelty. After the horrid winter they'd endured, Summer didn't think it ever would. "I'm glad we came," she said suddenly.

Thea rubbed her temples. Her head was beginning to ache, and she was used to afternoon tea at this time of day, not peasant food! She pushed away the dish of pungent cheese.

Summer dripped olive oil on crusty bread hot from the oven, as she'd seen Zita do, and blurted out the thought foremost in her mind. "What do you think of Mr. McCallum?"

Thea sat up straighter. First Fanny, and now Summer! "I don't think anything of him," she said coolly. "Indeed, why should I? I don't believe I exchanged ten words with him all evening. I was much too busy playing hostess."

That was true. Summer let out the breath she'd been holding. Relief made her giddy. How silly she'd been to entertain the idea, for even a minute, that it had been Thea talking to Col McCallum last night! Why, Thea—correct, proper, perfect Thea—was the last woman on earth ever to become involved with another man! How shocked she would be to know that she was suspected, for even a moment, of having committed so great an indiscretion.

Summer dabbed at her mouth with her napkin to hide her smile. No, and she couldn't imagine an impetuous man like Mr. McCallum laying siege to someone like Thea, so opposite to him in every way. Her sister was looking very pale. "Would you like one of my headache powders? Or perhaps some of Dr. Finlay's Restorative Elixir?"

"Yes, that might be wise," Thea said, surprising them both.

She rationalized that she wouldn't be able to care for her sisters if she didn't look after her own health. The chaperonage of two young ladies, one flighty and the other an invalid, was more of a charge than she'd realized. "A little elixir and a short nap should put me to rights. Don't get up, I know where to find it."

She glided across the terrace like a serene goddess, in total control of her universe. The bottle of Dr. Finlay's patented remedy was on top of Summer's night table. Pouring out a scant ounce into a glass, Thea took it back to her room. But when she reached her chamber all her self-possession vanished. It was not her head that was heavy, but her heart. Seeing Col McCallum had brought back an overwhelming weight of memories. If Martin learned somehow that Col was here . . . it didn't bear thinking of!

She flung herself upon the bed and buried her face in her hands. Dear God, she would never have come if she'd had any idea that he was here! The last she'd heard he had gone off to Africa, searching for King Solomon's mines. If only he'd stayed there!

She had come to Ellysia to think things over and get her life sorted out, away from all distractions. Running into him so unexpectedly had rocked her to her core. She hadn't forgotten any of it. Images flooded back.

Paris . . . the D'Arcys' cotillion . . . a fountain of champagne punch . . . gold and glitter and jewels . . . Martin's angry words . . . and then Col standing there in evening clothes, like a knight in dark armor, his bright hair forming a halo in the candlelight.

Pride and folly had led her on. She had rushed headlong to Col's hotel and nothing had been the same since. That winter season in Paris had been a turning point in her life, and she had chosen the wrong fork in the road. Why had she been so foolish?

She stretched out on her bed and stared up at the frieze of grapes that ringed the room. Although the island basked in balmy spring weather, it was harvest time in Brazil, where Martin was.

And she was here alone in her celibate bed, harvesting the results of her mistakes. Oh, God! She'd been such a blind fool!

She rolled over and buried her face in the pillow, soaking the soft linen case with her tears.

The following day the three sisters were all restless and preoccupied. Fanny was eager to go back to the temple ruins, in hopes of seeing the handsome Giovanni again. She couldn't get him out of her thoughts.

Thea's reflections kept curving back to Martin and to Col McCallum and Paris. She was too unsettled to stay cooped up with her own problems any longer, and agreed that there was still much to see. "I'll order the carriage."

Summer looked up from her sketchbook. She'd learned that Mr. McCallum avoided the site of her father's excavations, and was torn. She was anxious to see the remains of the great center of ancient worship, yet hoped that Col might come to the villa again. He was very much upon her mind. In fact, she found it difficult to think of anything else.

"I believe I'll rest another day. Perhaps by tomorrow."

Thea hesitated. Today was a feast day and the servants had gone into the village to take part. Summer had spent yesterday alone without any problems.

Surely there was no harm in leaving her alone again, for a few short hours. "Very well."

She went out but Fanny leaned over the back of Summer's chair, examining her drawing. "Why, that's the same type of writing that Angus Gordon was copying yesterday."

Summer glanced at the picture forming on the blank page. She'd intended to do a study of the sable cat sleeping on a cushion near the balustrade. Instead she had drawn a woman holding a feathered fan so large it obscured most of her upper body. The figure was sitting on the stone bench in the cove where Col had found the ring. A small frown formed between Summer's brows. "There is no writing."

"There." Fanny pointed. "In her crown."

Yes, Summer realized with a shock, there was indeed an inscription. It was the shape and design of it that startled her: a plain band, set with a centered oval. In her mind's eye she saw the oval made of peach-colored carnelian, for it was a duplicate of the ring she'd found. The very ring that she wore tucked in her bodice, hung on a blue silk ribbon.

Thea returned. "Fanny, get your hat and gloves. The carriage is ready."

After they left Summer stared at the drawing until it blurred before her eyes. The air silvered and grew bright and the roof of the terrace dissolved into hard, blue sky. The balustrade vanished, too, and a small gilt chair formed out of the air before her, while the sharp volcanic cone of Hades rose higher as she watched in fear.

The ginger cat came awake and jumped to its feet, back arched and hissing. It leapt forward, mewling weirdly, then shot off toward the courtyard in a blur of dusky fur. The gilt chair vanished in an instant and the terrace reverted to its former state. Summer struggled up, heart pounding and limbs wooden and shaking. She was terrified.

First the vision on the beach, and now this! She rose and made her way out to the court. The cat was crouching in a weedy flowerbed, but turned tail and whisked away when it saw her.

Summer stumbled to a chair in the shade of the loggia, sick with fear. She was losing her mind. Even the cat sensed it.

Suddenly she wished she weren't alone in the old, rambling villa. She wanted noise and voices and laughter, all the reassuring sounds of everyday life. As if in answer, she heard a woman's soft chuckle from the far side of the wall. Zita must have stayed behind.

Rising, she went in search of her. It took a moment for Summer to figure out her bearings. She went through two rooms that opened into one another and expected to find the maid, but instead came up to a blank wall. It didn't matter. Just knowing that Zita was in the house helped calm her shattered nerves.

Summer was about to turn back when she noticed the door. The wall fresco of farmers in a field had been extended to cover it. She opened it and found a corridor with colorful turquoise and yellow tiles. Why, she'd never seen this part of the house. She followed it.

A rising sense of excitement overcame her natural caution. She decided to explore this older section of the house. She had never done anything on her own like this, but the opportunity was priceless. Thea would be fit to be tied if she found out, but then, Thea was gone. There was no one to tell Summer not to go poking about. That was a good part of her enjoyment. This was a wonderful adventure, trying something she had never done before, alone and unassisted. The freedom was as heady as last evening's sherry.

Summer went through an enclosed yard that might have once housed the stables. The next section held some kind of press and a quantity of empty barrels, but she couldn't tell if they had been used to hold wine or oil. A vine, old and woody, splayed out against a crumbling wall. The structure didn't look safe, so she avoided it and turned through an open door.

The villa was like a maze, and it went on forever. A large room, in bad repair, opened to yet another small court with a loggia and two doors of pale gray, sun-bleached wood. The yard was paved with brown hexagonal tiles that made her think of honeycomb. Summer took the nearest door and found herself in a room filled with empty crates and cobwebs. A scuttling sound from behind them sent her back the way she'd come.

The ginger cat came bounding out behind her, and sat in the sunlight, staring up at her. Summer laughed. "Naughty cat! You gave me a fright."

The cat only grinned at her, then licked its paw and purred. When Summer started off again the cat followed, then darted ahead and vanished amid a welter of terra-cotta pots. He seemed to have no fear of her now.

No one had explored here in many a long day, Summer noted. A thin layer of sandy dirt covered the pavement and her footsteps were the only tracks in the dust. She went to the other door, framed by hanging clay pots filled with the brittle wisps of plants long dead.

It swung open with a loud creak. Inside it was dark as a tunnel. Then she realized that the door didn't lead into a room, but to a small landing and a narrow flight of stairs. They appeared to be hewn from the living rock, and went down into a cool dimness showing a source of light on the far end. They echoed faintly with the whisper of waves.

The cat came up silently and paused beside her, peering down the dark stairway. Summer wondered where it led. The walls were stuccoed and faint traces of crude designs remained. Each tread was high but shallow in depth. The cat leapt down them in bright, bouncy springs, and vanished.

Summer wanted to follow. The urge to discover where the stairs led was almost irresistible, but her fear was just as strong.

She struggled against frustration: The everyday actions that others took for granted were such great obstacles to her. She cursed the affliction that had fostered her curiosity, while denying her the means to satisfy it. But this time, instead of turning back, she was determined to find a way. Perhaps if she took her time and inched her way down, step by step.

Even to think of doing it was a wonder to her. She had lived her days in the shadow of Nana's strictures and dire forebodings. But Nana, poor dear, was far away in Naples at the convent. And she, Summer, stood at the top of a mysterious stairway, leading to—to who knew *what* marvelous adventures?

She took a cautious step down. The stone was worn from countless footsteps, but the surface was coarse and rough. It would keep her from slipping. She took another step. The light was rather faint just ahead, before brightening somewhere below. She hesitated, imagining the scold she would get from Thea if her older sister learned of this little adventure.

While Summer stood at the head of the steep flight, debating her ability to get down them without falling, she heard an ominous sound. A low distant rumble that grew louder quite suddenly. Where on earth was it coming from?

Little bits of stucco rained down on her head and plaster dust rose at the same time in a feathery cloud. She coughed and felt the rumbling transmitted up through her feet. She stared in disbelief. The solid floor was no longer solid. It moved in ripples as if it were the back of a living creature.

As she fought to maintain balance, a clay pot fell from the wall beside her, smashing into a thousand pieces. The dried twigs skittered across the pavement with a weird, whispering sound. The air trembled and shook. The next second the ground jumped away from beneath her. Summer gasped and grabbed for the edge of the doorway but was helpless to save herself. She pitched forward down the stairs.

As she fell a terrible roar assaulted her ears, like the bellow of a monstrous bull. In her infinite terror, she hardly registered the pain as her body ricocheted off the walls. Her head struck the support beam near the bottom. Colored light flared in her head, violent reds, brilliant blues, and blinding, incandescent yellow that pierced her brain like a knife.

Then the lights were quenched and Summer's world went completely black and still.

When the tremor struck, Fanny was walking listlessly along a row of columns that had once defined a great enclosure. She was hot and tired and had not seen Giovanni, except at a distance, though she hoped their paths might eventually cross.

Suddenly her ears tickled and then hummed. This time she knew it for what it was, which didn't lessen her fright. She started to run to where she'd last seen her father. The earth jumped beneath her feet and she almost fell. Scrambling up, she tried to maintain her footing but the ground rolled sickeningly, like the waves of the sea.

A man shouted, "Earthquake!" At the same time she heard her father's voice. *"Fanny? Thea?"*

"Over here, Papa!" The shaking stopped but she was in complete panic, not knowing which way to run. As she stood there, frozen, the ground began to move again, even more violently. Screaming in fright, she reached for one of the temple columns in an attempt to keep herself erect. A body hurtled at her, knocking her to the ground.

Fanny found herself sprawled flat on her back with a warm body lying protectively over her. She clung to it for dear life.

The ground heaved and shook amid the thuds and groan of nature's rampage. They were rattled about together like dried peas in a jar.

It ended as abruptly as it had started. Suddenly she was free and a handsome olive-skinned young man bent over her. "Giovanni!"

His skin had paled to the color of cream and his thick lashes shaded eyes like dark amber, filled with concern. "Signorina, are you injured?"

She struggled to sit up and regain propriety. Her skirts were tangled about her legs and her bonnet sitting askew over one eye. "Only bruised from being knocked down so roughly!"

"A thousand pardons, Signorina," he said, helping her to her feet. "I had no choice, as you see."

Fanny gasped. They were some yards from where she had been standing when the earthquake hit. The column she'd reached for only moments earlier now lay in three pieces, the stone drums that formed it torn apart and scattered over the landscape by the violent quake. She burst into tears and buried her face in her hands.

Giovanni feared she would faint, and put his arm around her gingerly for support. "Do not be afraid. Ah, no! Do not weep. It is over now. You are safe with me, *cara!*"

Fanny scarcely took in his torrent of mingled Italian and English. She was shaking uncontrollably with the knowledge of how close she had come to sudden death. A small aftershock made her shriek in alarm. Giovanni realized the poor signorina was hysterical with fear. It was up to him to calm her, he knew. He was forced to hold her sweet little body against his even more tightly, to keep her from coming to harm. She grasped his shirt and clung to him, sobbing against his chest.

That was how her father found them, and he was not pleased. The rest of his party had sustained nothing more than aggravation and a few moments of general fright. "Giovanni, what the devil is all this? Fanny, control yourself!"

Her rescuer gently unpried her hands from his white cotton blouse. "The signorina has suffered a terrible shock."

"Oh, yes, and, Papa . . . he saved my life!"

She gave Giovanni a brilliant smile, which was not lost on Richard Fairchild. Nor was the stunned look of admiration on the younger man's face. It drove all thought of their close call from his mind and replaced it with anger. Deaths, earthquakes, and now a daughter and the gardener—that was all he needed! He'd put a stop to it, fast.

"Nonsense! It was merely a small quake. They are quite common in the Mediterranean. It is a wonder we haven't had one here before."

Fanny pointed mutely to the broken column. Richard's florid coloring drained away, leaving him pasty and suddenly older. "I see that I judged too hastily. Remarkable. This column has stood here since before the birth of Christ, and now . . ."

He dabbed his brow with a folded handkerchief, then put his arm around Fanny's shoulders. "I am greatly in your debt, Giovanni. My daughter is very precious to me. You may be sure that my greatest wish is to keep her from any harm."

Fanny didn't hear the coded message, male to male, that was in her father's last sentence. Giovanni did. His lashes swept down to hide his eyes. "Fortunately, all is well and the signorina is safe. I will return to my duties."

He gave her a stiff little bow, another to the professor, and went rapidly past the fallen column and along the worn footpath. Fanny watched until he was out of sight and sighed. She brushed away the dust and bits of twigs from her skirt. Her pliant mind had already recovered from the fright. How fortunate that she had worn her blue driving dress, which showed her fair coloring to best advantage.

"Giovanni might have been killed, yet he risked his life to save me. He is very brave," she said, and took her father's arm.

"Yes. The local peasants have a deserved reputation for doing what needs to be done."

He could not have stated his position more baldly. Fanny bit her lip. How positively *archaic* of Papa to carry on about the difference in station between the Fairchilds and a young villager like Giovanni. Of course he was not on the same social or educational level, but he was so brave, so handsome.

"Ah, there is Thea now. I think that you should both return to the villa. The trembling seemed confined to this area, however Summer will be concerned for your safety."

Fanny was hardly listening. She was remembering the warm look in Giovanni's eyes, and the feeling of his hard young body against hers.

Col McCallum was in the little garden behind the cottage when the earthquake began. The neighing of the horses had brought him outside and he was halfway to the stable when the ground shifted beneath him. The beasts shrieked in terror and he managed to get the stalls open before they kicked them, and themselves, to splinters.

Tonino came running up the road at the same time, and helped him calm the animals once the tremor subsided. The mare shivered, whickering as he comforted her. They led them out to the meadow, where they would be fairly safe if another quake followed the first. He wondered if Summer Fairchild was at the villa, alone.

The village appeared to be intact and there were enough people at the excavation site to deal with the aftermath of the quake, but the Court of Three Sisters lay at the opposite end of the island. True, the villa had survived without major damage for many years, but it was the oldest inhabited building on

Ellysia. There was no telling if the walls had maintained their integrity. His disquiet grew. He had to get up there immediately.

He ran his hand over the gelding's flanks and nose until it was soothed and quiet. "Saddle him for me. I'm going up to the villa," he said to Tonino.

He went back to the cottage for his riding boots. The plaster had cracked on the south wall. The only other damage seemed to be a few smashed pots. Then he saw that, by damnable luck, his brass inkstand had overturned, spilling its contents over the table. Some had splashed on Carruthers's notes and the packet from Dr. Ruggieri's house. Cursing, Col quickly blotted up what he could and put the package away in a secure place.

He wished that he'd been able to finish going through them before the quake had struck. What he was looking for was bound to be in them somewhere. Why else had Ruggieri hidden them in his desk behind a very clever sliding panel?

When he came out Tonino had the gelding ready to ride. Col mounted in a swift motion and headed out across country for the Court of Three Sisters. With every second his sense of urgency grew.

Col glimpsed the Court of Three Sisters as he came over the hill just to the west of it. He was relieved that the walls he could see seemed to be intact. A few tiles were gone from one part of the roof but it still held up. He hoped the damage had been confined to that, but as he rode through to the outer courtyard he heard someone cry out his name.

"Col, thank God you've come!"

Thea came rushing out, pale and frantic. Her hair

and the shoulders of her white dress were dusted with minute flakes of plaster and paint. "Oh, do hurry!"

He swung down and looped the reins around a post. "Is anyone injured? Where are your sisters?"

"Fanny is in the loggia—" Her voice broke. "I can't find Summer! She's not in her room. There's no trace of her anywhere."

A cold hand gripped Col's heart. "Christ! Are there any walls or ceilings down?"

"No, at least, I don't know. We were at the temple site when the earthquake occurred. We came here immediately, because we'd left my sister alone for the afternoon. If anything has happened to Summer I shall never forgive myself!"

He went past her toward the entry. "Have you looked in the old section?"

Thea stared at him blankly. "Why, no. Summer wouldn't have gone there."

A slight aftershock shook the ground. More tiles slid off the roof, shattering over the pavement. Col caught Thea as she tripped. "Get Fanny and go outside. Stay out in the open, do you understand? I'll find Summer."

He ran inside, not waiting to see if Thea obeyed. The place was a rabbit warren of rooms, atriums, and courtyards. He went through to the unused section, calling for Summer. If she'd wandered there she might have been hit by falling debris and knocked unconscious. Or worse.

The ginger cat sat in an open doorway, winking up at him, then rose and disappeared into the unused area. Col followed.

*   *   *

Summer dreamed. She was in her favorite room, reclining on a divan while Cliete plucked at her new lyre. The new frieze of lilies and griffins had delighted her, as she knew it would.

Cliete set down her lyre. She had been very restless all day. She went to the family altar and picked up the chamois bag that held her sister's divining sticks. The tiny sticks, carved ivory in the shape of bones, revealed the future to those who knew how to interpret their patterns.

On impulse she shook the bag and upended it. She looked at the sticks and froze.

There was something about Cliete's utter stillness that struck fear into Summer's heart. "What is it?"

There was no answer. Cliete might have been turned to stone. Summer rose from the divan and ran to her sister's side. The divining sticks formed a pattern she had never seen before, but the symbols engraved upon them spelled it out in terrible clarity.

Terror. Chaos. Death.

Destruction on a massive scale.

Summer steadied herself by grasping the edge of the altar. Even as she touched it the ground began to tremble and shake. Cliete gasped beside her.

The painted goddess on the altar held her twin snakes aloft, still wearing her golden circlet and sure, knowing smile. Then she teetered and tipped forward to shatter in the offering bowl. The air was filled with shrieks and prayers.

Pieces of colorful faience mingled with the purple iris and tiny pink orchids that had filled the broken bowl. Cliete cried out again in primal fear. Summer reached for her sister, but the floor shook so hard it seemed to shimmer like water. They were both knocked off their feet.

A bronze mirror clattered across the tiles, ringing like a cracked bell.

Great fissures zigzagged up the walls and the ceiling buckled, showering them with debris. Summer screamed and screamed, but no sound came out of her mouth. The screaming went on deep, deep inside.

She kept on screaming because she knew that if she stopped, everything would stop for her, for Cliete.

Forever.

Col found the open door leading to one of the old wings. He looked up and saw Thea, white faced, in the doorway. "I said get outside! Where's Fanny?"

"Out beyond the walls. I have to look for Summer, this is all my fault!"

"Since when did you gain the power to create earthquakes?" Col snapped. He had no time to listen to her recriminations. He started toward the door. "Leave it to me. I'll find her."

"Summer would never go there," Thea protested from a few yards behind him. Her voice held doubt. The only possible alternative was that her sister had vanished into thin air.

Col didn't bother to answer. He had already picked up Summer's trail. "She's been through here. See that? The hem of her skirt has dragged a trail through the accumulation of dust."

He went on and Thea followed at a distance, ready to bolt at the first sign of danger. "I don't understand. This is very unlike her! I can't imagine what she could have been doing here."

Col could. "The same thing I would do. She's been exploring."

The concept of investigating an unused, shabby area was foreign to Thea's tidy nature. "But there is nothing here, and the place is filthy. I'm sure no one has gone this way in years!"

"That's part of its charm."

He covered the pavement in long strides and she had no choice but to retreat, or follow. When Col reached the stairs she stopped short in alarm just as Summer's tracks stopped abruptly at the top of the steep steps. Thea peered around him. The tomblike staircase and the darkness below appalled her.

"She can't have gone that way. She'd never have been able to negotiate them."

Col turned a look on Thea that made her blood turn to ice. "Wait here. Don't come down unless I call for you."

He paused only long enough to see that she would comply, then hurried down the stairs. The sound of his bootheels echoed hollowly, bouncing off the stone. Halfway down the steps curved sharply to the left. It was dark and he almost stepped on Summer's hand. She was lying on her side, wedged into the curve with one arm flung out. In her white dress she looked like a crumpled flower.

Col knelt and felt for a pulse. It was strong and regular. He was encouraged, but when he slid his hand behind her head it was sticky with blood. "Summer? *Summer!*"

There was no response. He felt for obvious broken bones and found none. Her skin was cool, though, and he feared she was in shock, but his touch roused her. Summer struggled to sit up. "Cliete?"

Relief flooded through Col. She was awake, but certainly not out of the woods. Even in the half-light he saw how vague and dazed her eyes looked. "It's

Col McCallum," he said in the same low, soothing tones he had used to calm the mare. "You'll be fine. Just stay quiet."

He stripped off his jacket and wrapped it around her upper body. She stiffened when he lifted her in his arms, then went limp with her head against his shoulder. Col carried her up the stairs.

When she saw her sister, Thea's face went as white as Summer's dress. "Oh, dear God in Heaven! Is . . . is she? . . ."

"She's alive, but she's taken a bad thump to the head. She's in shock but I don't think there are any internal injuries."

Summer moved her head against his arm and her lashes fluttered. "There, I think she's starting to come around. Show me to her room."

He followed Thea through the house, carrying his burden easily. Summer's room was full of bright light and the tapestry on the wall rippled slightly from the fitful breeze. He put her down on her bed and pulled the lace-edged quilt up to her chin. Thea started to close the shutters, but as she drew them shut Summer opened her eyes.

"No, don't! I must be able to watch!"

"Watch for what?" Col asked, but Summer's eyes snapped closed again. After a moment she turned on her side. One hand came out to rest against the pillow, her fingers clenched around some small object.

Col gently covered her hand with his, and pried her fingers away. A carved cylinder, cracked and yellowed, lay nestled in the hollow of her palm. She'd held it so tightly that its shape was impressed upon her skin. He nudged it over with his fingertip and frowned in surprise.

It looked like a tiny ivory bone.

*   *   *

Silence. The shuffle of a shoe sole on the floor and the creak of wood. Summer fought through layers of wet, suffocating wool. Her head ached dully. What had happened? Where was Cliete? She was in a strange room. The walls were plain and the closed shutters created a murky twilight. A servant's quarters? But no, even her lowest servant lived in beautiful surroundings.

She tried to concentrate. Remnants of reality broke through, mingling with the residue of dream. She looked over and recognized Thea sitting in a wooden chair beside the bed, half dozing. Summer leaned up on one elbow. She was in her bedchamber at the Court of Three Sisters, then. But where was Cliete? Was she safe?

She must have spoken aloud without realizing it. Thea jumped up, still groggy, and looked over at her sister in concern. "Who is Cliete?"

Summer started to answer but already the threads of the dream had grown thin and fragile as cobwebs. The more she tried to grasp at them, the more quickly they melted away, and soon there was nothing at all. She stared at Thea.

"Cliete?" she said slowly. "I don't know anyone by that name." She sank back against the pillow. "My head aches dreadfully."

Thea bit her lip. She had heard Summer murmur that name several times over the past hour. "You suffered a fall."

Summer leaned back against the pillow to ease the pounding. "It must have been quite a fall, from the size of the pounding in my skull."

"There was a minor earthquake," Thea explained

hurriedly. "The islands are subject to them from time to time. Mr. McCallum thinks that it struck as you were at the top, pitching you forward down the stairwell."

Summer tried to think back. The last thing she could recall was having lunch with Thea on the terrace. After that, try as she could, she couldn't remember a single thing. It wasn't an impassable barrier, like *Before*. It was a void, completely empty. "I can't remember. And I certainly don't remember any stairway."

Thea rose and took a turn about the room, searching for exactly the right words. Her initial relief had metamorphosed into exasperated anger. She blamed herself mostly, but part of the fault was Summer's. She could be so difficult at times.

"You gave me a terrible fright. We found you in one of the older sections of the villa. You were quite lucky that Mr. McCallum came by. He was able to discover the way you'd gone. You might have lain there for hours before Fanny and I found you. I shudder to think of it!"

There was a note in her sister's voice that Summer knew too well. "I seem to have put everyone to a good deal of trouble."

"I wouldn't phrase it so strongly," Thea replied, although it was apparent that that was exactly what she thought. She came back to the bedside and poured out a draught of thick brown liquid. "Here. This will soon have you to rights."

When Summer obeyed her sister sat down again and took her hand. "My dear, you have given us quite a fright. The entire household is in a tizzy. What on earth were you thinking of, to go wandering through the unused portions of the villa, alone."

Summer's brow knotted. "I don't know."

That only silenced Thea a moment. "I believe that I do. I shall be frank. It was very thoughtless of you. You had no business going off 'exploring,' as Col—as Mr. McCallum phrased it. It would be different perhaps, if—" She broke off for a few seconds and then resumed. "I don't mean to distress you further, but you must take into account the lamentable fact that you are . . ."

Summer sat up again, pushing a damp lock of hair from her forehead. "Lame? Crippled?"

Thea looked away. "I knew that you would snap at me! I intended to say that you are not physically up to climbing over the clutter and debris without causing hurt to yourself."

Silence was Summer's only response. There was nothing she could say to refute the accusations. If Thea said she'd been exploring the villa, that was what she had been doing. Thea was always right. That was the most infuriating thing about her.

The medicine that Summer had taken was having a rapid effect. She had difficulty focusing her eyes and her brain was fast filling up with soft, gray cotton.

Thea stifled a sigh. Summer was scowling at her in that hard, intense way of hers. If she thought she could avoid a lecture by glowering so, she would learn it would do her no good. "Perhaps I should not have raised the matter, but I would be neglecting my duty to you, and to Father, if I did not let you know that I feel your actions were heedless and ill advised."

Before Summer could reply there was a soft tap at the door. Thea answered it, opening the door a few inches. Col McCallum's voice filtered in to Summer and she closed her eyes against the wedge of bright light from the corridor. It cut through her brain like a scythe.

"I heard voices."

"Yes. Summer has regained consciousness again, and except for an aching head, she is quite her old self," Thea said wryly. "A few more hours abed and she will be as good as new."

"That's excellent news. I'm very glad to hear it. The signora has prepared some refreshments. She thought you might be feeling peckish."

"I cannot leave my sister alone."

"Very well, then. I'll stay with her."

"You cannot be serious! It would be totally inappropriate for you to enter her bedchamber while I went off to dine."

"Nonsense! Do you think I mean to ravish her while you sit out in the loggia a few yards away, eating potted figs?"

The sound of his voice was soothing. Summer had no strength to talk to him, or to Thea, or anyone at all. She didn't even have the strength to listen to them argue. Pulling the quilt up to her chin, she rolled over with her back to the door and pretended to be asleep.

Their voices were low, rising and falling like the surf. Within seconds Summer was asleep once more.

In the days immediately following the earthquake things returned to normal. While upsetting, the tremor had done little damage, except to one already ruined pillar at the temple site. And, of course, to the Fairchild sisters' nerves. Their father assured them that the earthquakes were rarely so strong, and that often a year or two passed between one and the next.

His nonchalance soothed their fears. Summer had come to no real harm, and her accident was generally considered more an error of her own judgment and physical infirmity than of the quake itself. Additionally, Richard Fairchild saw no reason to make her uncomfortable by bringing up any reminder of deformity. God only knew, she had enough of a burden living with it, without his adding to it.

Only Fanny, who had come close to disaster herself, made an especial effort to show her sympathy. Summer was touched. Also relieved that she hadn't been subjected to more lectures on her folly.

The whole episode had left her terribly disheartened. The trip to Ellysia had opened doors for Summer, to experiences she had never imagined. And since circumstances had removed her most zealous guardian from the scene, she had begun to look forward to the daunting yet exciting prospect of greater freedom. How often she'd chafed at Nana's endless strictures to avoid exertion or watch her step! It seemed that she should have heeded her old nurse's dire warnings. The one time in her life that Summer had taken the opportunity to act independently, it had ended in near disaster.

Fanny enjoyed retelling her dramatic rescue to anyone who would listen. She daydreamed of Giovanni constantly. The only cloud on her bright horizon was that she had made several trips to the excavations and had only seen him once more. The warm admiration in his eyes on that occasion had been enough to fuel further gauzy fantasies.

Even Thea, a worrier of the first order, was reassured at the way everyone dismissed the earthquake. "This house," Signora Perani reminded her, "has

stood upon this height for two thousand years and is
still standing."

Summer was the only who didn't rebound from
the episode. She kept to herself. She refused to
leave the villa, and retired more and more to her
room, except for meals. Her world increasingly
revolved around her secret garden, and her
strangely disturbing dreams.

It wasn't that those dreams were frightening, or
even unpleasant. Upon wakening she could not
remember much of them at all, but it seemed to her
that the earthquake and her fall had shaken loose
something inside her. Barriers had tumbled down,
and doors had opened, although only in sleep thus
far. She did not recognize them as the boundaries of
memory and reality, and feared that she was skirting
the periphery of a terrible, barren land, with good
reason.

She saw and heard things that weren't actually
there. The shifting dreamscapes merged increasingly
with remnants of *Before*.

And with something else, something both foreign
and familiar, that was not memory, not *Before*, but
. . . *Other*.

She began to fear that she was truly going mad.

7

VISIONS

From Colin McCallum's letter to the late John Carruthers

    ... *and am greatly intrigued by your mysterious hints of an amazing discovery. You are right, of course, that I am ready to return to what I'd planned as my life's work. I can think of nothing better than to begin with you and your marvelous find. I've some business to clear up in Marseilles, but I plan to reach Naples the first week in March, and hope to be on Ellysia shortly thereafter.*

    Meanwhile, I hope you are enjoying the tins of cocoa I sent you from South America. I believe that you are as addicted to your nightly cup of chocolate as you are to those foul cigars on which you dote. I'll bring you a

fresh supply from Havana so that you may light up of an evening, and think kind thoughts of
Your affectionate godson,
Col

The day before Dr. Ruggieri's funeral dawned unseasonably hot and fierce. The wind was like a blast from hell. The Fairchild women stayed closed up in the villa. The earthquake and Summer's accident had rubbed Thea's nerves raw. Even the snip of Giovanni's shears from the outer courtyard, where he was working on the neglected gardens, set her teeth on edge.

With the excuse of having letters to write, Thea left the terrace and went to the sitting room to search for pen nibs, leaving Summer to her book and Fanny curled up in a chair with the cat on her lap. She had been trying to think of a name for it that pleased her, but there were far too many to choose from.

No sooner had Thea gone than Fanny yanked on the side of her skirt, startling the creature. It jumped down, gave her a reproachful look, and stalked off toward the courtyard in a kittenish version of high indignation.

"Come back," Fanny exclaimed, rising to follow it out.

Her ruse wasn't even necessary. Summer was busy with one of her own. The propped-up book was an excuse to hide her daydreams of Col McCallum. He had captured her thoughts and even if she really tried, which, of course, she hadn't, there was no way of escaping. Summer was terribly aware of her lack of worldly experience. She knew that she mustn't read anything into his actions other than a friendly and casual interest, and feared making a laughing-stock of herself.

Fanny had no such worries. She knew quite well her effect upon susceptible young men, and upon Giovanni, in particular. By the time she reached the courtyard she'd forgotten the cat completely. Giovanni was bent over the fountain that he'd cleaned earlier, and was priming it at the moment. The siphoning worked and the water bubbled out suddenly. As he joined the pipe to the fountain the water splashed over him, dousing his clothes.

A moment later the fountain was gurgling happily, filling the air with a fine spray spangled with rainbows. It surrounded his healthy young body like a glittering aura.

Fanny clapped her hands together in delight. Giovanni turned in surprise. He hadn't heard her join him.

"How very clever of you!" she told him. "And how very beautiful it is!"

He bowed. "No more beautiful than you, Signorina."

They both blushed at his daring. He gestured around the garden. "I do this for you. To make a lovely setting for one so angelic."

Under any other circumstances she would have scolded a young man for such impertinence in speaking to her in such a manner; but with Giovanni standing there, so darkly handsome and with his wet clothes molded to his well-muscled physique, she was too awed to do anything but stare.

He came to her and knelt at her feet, one hand over his heart. "Forgive me, Signorina. I have offended you. I would rather cut out my tongue than speak any words that cause you to disdain me, as you have every right!"

"Oh, no!" Fanny exclaimed, encompassing all of his utterances. She was not in the least offended. How could she be, when Giovanni looked at her as if she were his sun, his moon, his stars. "But do get up before someone sees us and—and misunderstands the circumstances."

She glanced around quickly. The shutters of Thea's room were closed against the sun and the splash of the restored fountain would cover their conversation. "I—that is—if you don't mind . . . I will sit here and watch you work awhile. I . . . I am quite interested in gardens," she said, suddenly realizing that she meant it.

Giovanni gave her a look that would have fused glass. For the next two hours he worked like a man possessed, while she sat in the shade of the loggia and watched. As he weeded and transplanted, Giovanni talked to her of raised beds and weeds and watering, of lilies and roses and flowering shrubs.

At first Fanny was bewildered. She didn't understand that Giovanni's soft words, couched in terms of the garden, were really spoken in the language of blooming young love. His voice was hypnotic as he talked of the legends of the plants and trees: of Narcissus, who'd fallen in love with his beautiful reflection; of Daphne, who'd fled Apollo's unwanted advances and was changed by the virgin goddess, Diana, into the bay laurel that crowned the sun god's hair; of Dis and Demeter and the abduction of Persephone.

She listened and watched until she heard Thea calling for her, and realized that she had passed a good deal of the afternoon in Giovanni's gentle company. Certainly in England, Fanny thought, as she slipped away to her room, she would never let a young man entertain her with the amorous intrigues of ancient gods and goddesses. Really, the myths as he recited them were *much* more interesting than the edited versions her former governess had related!

Not that she understood quite everything. Perhaps it was her schoolgirl Italian that was at fault, and Fanny decided that she would practice the language with Giovanni at every opportunity. Meanwhile, perhaps she should ask Thea about the parts of those myths that she didn't understand.

Unaware of what an uproar such questions might cause, she went blithely inside. Fortunately for all concerned, she was sidetracked by the news that Summer had spotted hummingbirds in the vine along one side of the terrace, and she forgot Giovanni's stories for the moment.

Richard returned to the Court of Three Sisters earlier than usual, with a definite spring in his step. "You look as if you've had a very good day," Thea commented as they sat down to supper in the lily room. Summer had felt well enough to join them for the meal.

"Does it show?" Their father smiled a curious, self-satisfied smile. "We've encountered the inner precinct of an early temple beneath the rubble. I hope you will all stop by the site on the way home from the funeral tomorrow. It might prove interesting."

Fanny was all agog. "Do you expect to find a great treasure, Papa?"

He laughed. "Are you imagining gold and jewels, my dear? I am thinking more of mosaics and bronze statuary. But all in all, I must say that I am quite satisfied with the way everything is progressing."

Another smile flickered over his features. He looked younger and more carefree than any of them remembered. Realizing that they were all staring at him, he picked up his napkin and shook it out without looking at them. "You may ring the bell, Thea."

The food the servants brought out was as foreign to English palates as on the previous days. Thea's nose crinkled in distaste as Zita brought a dish around. "What is this, if you please?"

The girl smiled and shrugged. She didn't understand English, and, from the look on Signora Armstrong's face, she was glad of it.

Fanny spoke up: *"Funghi trifolati.* Mushrooms with anchovies, garlic, and lemon." She peered into the bowl that Pellegrina uncovered and set before her father. "With *stracciatella*—'rag soup' with eggs and noodles—to follow."

"Rag soup!" It almost destroyed Thea's appetite.

Fanny accepted a serving of the *funghi trifolati*, not without misgivings. But when in Rome . . .

Thea worked her way valiantly through the veal knuckle in sauce, planning a stern talk with her father's housekeeper. She inquired as to the other main dish, which appeared to be a sort of thick stew, and blanched when Fanny explained that it was one of the signora's specialties, *cervello al burro nero*, braised brains in black butter sauce.

Thea's fork clattered to her plate. Her stomach rebelled and she put her napkin to her lips, struggling to quell an attack of nausea. She was furious. It was evident that Signora Perani had no intention of following her well-meant suggestions. Very well, then, her "suggestions" would become *orders*.

She realized that Summer was giving Fanny a very

odd look, and belatedly realized why. "Your Italian seems to have undergone considerable improvement in the past few days!"

"Thank you. I have been practicing. It is much easier to learn a language when one is surrounded by people who speak that language," Fanny replied airily.

Their father took another helping of the *cervello*. "There is nothing like a hearty meal to top off a hard day's work."

Thea saw her little talk with the signora as one more failed dream.

The sun set quickly in these latitudes, and the breeze off the sea was chill this evening. The family repaired to the sitting room. Summer was aching from her labors with the mosaic, and retired to her room. Not long after, Fanny drifted off to look for a book, then took a seat on the divan.

Thea took one of the brocade armchairs, and her father the other. The chairs were rather old, but seemed ridiculously young to him, in their ancient surroundings. The lamps were lit and cast a cozy light across the divan and other extra furnishings that had been removed from Summer's room. The chairs were arranged around a small table, and a narrow bookcase that Carruthers had left behind had been filled with the selection of books the women had brought with them.

"It's getting quite homelike," he said, looking around with approval. "The place certainly needs a woman's touch."

Thea looked up sharply. Something in his tone had sent a chill down her spine. She recovered herself quickly. "Well, Father, now that I am here, you will not need to concern yourself with housekeeping details. I shall look after everything for you."

Apparently that was not the exact answer he'd expected. He went to the side chest, where several glasses and decanters were arrayed, and poured himself a glass of port. It glowed like a garnet in the lamplight and the sight seemed to concentrate all his attention. After a moment he tipped the wine glass back and took a deep draught.

"Yes, I suppose you are right. But in September Martin will return from his duties abroad and you will be back in England, waiting for his ship to sail into port, which is as it should be. Things will go on here in your absence, however. There is so much to be done!"

"I thought that you meant to return to England at the end of the season."

Richard poured himself another drink. "Ellysia's mild climate makes for an extended season," he replied. "The expense of travel must be considered, of course, but it is not my main concern." He swirled the liquid around in his glass. "It would be a waste of valuable time to travel home for a few short weeks and then make the return journey again. I could put the time to better use by writing up my notes."

He glanced up and saw the shock on her face as she anticipated his next remarks. "I could spend ten years with these excavations and barely scratch the surface," he continued hastily. "Indeed, I could spend ten lifetimes!"

Fanny looked up at that. "Ten years! But Papa, what of my London season?"

"We will cross that bridge when we come to it."

Fanny burst into tears and fled the room. The professor frowned after her. "You warned me that Fanny was becoming a rare handful, Thea, and I see that you were right in your conclusion."

"Yes, she should have been sent away to school to learn how to conduct herself in adult company."

Richard sat down beside her, fumbling for his pipe. This was exactly the opening that he required. "I realize that I have put quite a heavy responsibility upon your young shoulders, expecting you to look after the household and your sisters as well. You have been an absolute jewel, my dear, to put up with my impositions. It was unconscionable of me. After all, you have your own obligations."

Thea flushed at his praise. "You know that I am glad to spare you in any way I can."

"And that," he continued quickly, as if she hadn't spoken, "is what gave me a most excellent idea this afternoon!"

Thea's heart sank. Signora Perani and the maid had been cleaning out some of the unused rooms all afternoon. She knew what he was going to say before he said it, and she resented it deeply. Richard went blithely on.

"Currently, Mrs. Morville is ensconced in a house in the village, with the mayor's mother-in-law and her spinster sister. Cramped and uncomfortable, to say the least. Meanwhile, here we are with this great empty villa."

He made a show of tamping tobacco into his pipe, anticipating, perhaps, that his daughter would take the initiative. It was a forlorn hope. Thea sat upright, staring straight ahead. Richard braced himself.

"Well, what do you say to inviting Cynthia to join our little house party? We have room here and to spare, so that would not be a problem. I'm sure you would welcome another woman to talk with in the evenings. She is well informed on a number of interesting topics."

Thea bristled with barely concealed hostility. "I am sure that Mrs. Morville is quite comfortable in her present situation."

Her whole world was falling apart. She fought against the tears and the panic. Much as she loved and respected her father, she was fighting for her own future. She had planned it so carefully in her mind, and now it was going all awry.

Thea had been certain that this trip would enable her to take up her proper place in the family once more, just as if she had never left home. When Martin returned, and it became known that they weren't living together, it would not cause any comment that could sabotage either his career or her reputation. It would be thought that she was staying on at Kingsmeade awhile to chaperon Fanny and see her launched into society. After that, there were any number of excuses that could be made acceptable to the polite world.

It was plain, however, that Mrs. Morville had plans of her own.

Thea's fingers knotted together, as they did when she was anxious. If the widow succeeded in insinuating her way into the midst of the family, there would be no getting rid of her. All the signs were there. Cynthia Morville would soon become indispensable to her father, and inevitably she would became a permanent part of his life.

Not that Thea begrudged her father taking a wife. He had been alone for years and certainly deserved happiness. He was a strong, vigorous man and she had often wondered why he'd never remarried. There had certainly been enough caps set at him.

Thea bit her lower lip. But once he took a wife, or even a well-chaperoned fiancée, there would be no need for her to stay on at all. She had no idea where she would go or what she would do then. A married woman, living apart from her husband, had no place in proper society.

Once word of her separation from Martin got around, things were bound to leak out. She would be ruined. No respectable people would have her under their roofs. The scandal would make it impossible for her to stay at Kingsmeade—only think of what it would do to her father's position, or Fanny's chances for an eligible marriage! And, despite her estrangement from Martin, Thea hoped that his career would continue its meteoric rise. It was his whole life. It meant everything to him.

She suddenly realized that her father was still waiting for her response. Her lips were stiff as she answered.

"I do hope you will reconsider, Father. As good as Mrs. Morville may be in a crisis, she is still almost a stranger to us. You see how Fanny is acting, and you know how Summer can be. To be thrown into such intimacy at such short acquaintance would be a great strain upon everyone and—"

There came a terrible clatter from out in the courtyard, followed by a shout. Thea jumped up. "What on earth?"

Signora Perani entered the sitting room, wiping her hands on her apron. Her dark eyes slid in Thea's direction and then away.

"Signore, Angelo has come from the village with an oxcart piled high with Signora Morville's trunks and belongings. Where do you wish them to be put?"

Richard turned to his daughter a bit sheepishly. He shouldn't have left his little talk with Thea until the last moment, and he could see that she was offended.

He'd imagined that Thea would be grateful to have another female for company, but saw that he'd been mistaken.

He tried to placate her. "You must discuss that with my eldest daughter. I will leave it to Mrs. Armstrong to direct their placement."

White faced, Thea looked from her father to the housekeeper. She understood why he'd ordered other rooms cleaned. "It might be just as well if Mrs. Morville selects her own room. I wouldn't deign to choose for her."

She gathered her skirts and fled to the privacy of her own chamber. Richard frowned after her. Now, what had brought *that* on? Women were strange creatures, he thought with a sigh. There was no understanding even the best of them.

He gave the signora her instructions and went to meet his guest. Perhaps he'd handled it badly by not speaking up sooner, but he'd had more serious matters to attend to lately. By the time he reached the central courtyard he'd dismissed Thea's uncharacteristic reaction as a case of nerves. Females were known to be prone to them.

He went forward to greet Mrs. Morville with his hands outstretched and a smile on his lips. "Cynthia, my dear. Welcome! I hope you will be much more comfortable here with us."

She thanked him prettily and let him remove her cloak and escort her into the sitting room. One quick glance showed her it was deserted. She nibbled her bottom lip. Oh, dear! It seemed that Richard was the only one who did welcome her presence at the Court of Three Sisters.

She straightened her shoulders and took the chair that Thea had just vacated. At thirty years of age, she had already faced many adversities, and triumphed over them. She didn't see any reason that she wouldn't this time, either. A bit of diplomacy, a pair of helping hands, and deference to the ladies of the house would soon set things to rights.

Fanny had been in the shadows of the loggia and had heard snatches of her father's conversation with Thea, and witnessed Mrs. Morville's arrival. The nuances had gone completely over her head. Since anyone over the age of thirty seemed old to her, she had not thought of possible romantic entanglements between her father and the widow.

It was nothing to her if he invited a dozen Mrs. Morvilles, as long as they took no interest in her own affairs. There was certainly room to house them, and to spare, especially if she and Thea had gone back to London for her debut as she'd expected! A crystal tear etched its way down her cheek and splashed upon her hand.

Giovanni materialized out of the darkness. It was he who had taught her the names of the dishes she'd had at supper this evening. Her heavy spirits lightened at seeing him and she made a halfhearted attempt to dash away her tears.

He took her hand in his. "Do you weep, my goddess? Ah, yes! I see the tears. Tell me the name of this villain who has wounded your heart, *bellissima*, and he shall know my wrath!"

Her mouth quivered into a smile at his sweet fierceness. She was touched by it. And poor Papa! What would he say if he could hear Giovanni championing her, without even knowing the cause of her distress?

"It is nothing," she told Giovanni bravely. "I am only sad because I will not be going back to England. We are to stay on Ellysia for years and years!"

The last words came out on a sad little hiccough as her great disappointment came crashing down to crush her spirits again. Giovanni's reaction was quite opposite. He gripped her hand so tightly it almost cut off her circulation.

"Is this true, *carissima?* Ah, I am the happiest man in all the world! My every prayer has been answered."

She blinked away her tears. Why, Giovanni's eyes were filled with light from the reflected stars. She had thought his praises were on the order of the extravagant compliments with which her pretty ears had been filled at every assembly she'd attended since putting her hair up; but no, this was something different. Giovanni meant every word he said. That both humbled and exhilarated her. It also frightened her just the tiniest bit. "You are hurting my hand," she whispered.

At once he was contrite. He loosened his grasp amid a torrent of apologies. Despite her mild alarm at his intensity, she stayed and talked with him until the moon rose over the walls of the courtyard. He was unlike anyone she'd ever met before, and the uniqueness of their setting carried her away. The moonlight and starshine worked their eternal magic, conjuring up sudden romance in two young and untried hearts.

By the time Fanny entered the house again it was growing late, and she'd almost forgotten her pique over her lost London season.

She tiptoed to her chamber, not noticing the housekeeper standing inside the archway of the darkened lily room.

Signora Perani was displeased. *Ai-yai-yai!* There was trouble brewing. She was responsible for Giovanni and didn't want him making sheep's eyes at

her employer's daughter; but how could a simple
peasant lad ignore the wiles of such a forward young
beauty? Nothing good would come of it. The signora
determined to have a talk with her sister about that
boy, as soon as possible!

The house soon grew quiet. At the far end of the
hallway Summer lay awake in her bed, staring at the
night sky through her open window. With the shutters thrown wide and the shadows of the room as
lavender blue as the heavens beyond, it gave the illusion that she was floating through fields of stars. At
any moment she might fly out that window and soar
on the warm night wind.

Stars . . . floating. A wisp of memory tantalized
her. It seemed urgent that she remember it, but the
more she tried the more elusive it became. Summer
stopped trying to force it, and an image took shape in
her mind. It had the same haunting quality as her
visions of *Before*, yet she recognized that it was something else. It must be a remnant of a dream, she
thought.

Instantly the scene grew more real, drawing her in
until she was a part of it. The tiles were smooth
beneath the thin leather of her sandals and the air
was filled with heavy incenselike perfume. She was
standing somewhere in silvery starlight, feeling the
warm breeze play over her face and throat. Where
was she? It reminded her of her secret terrace, yet she
knew it was not. Still, it was familiar.

Although she was caught within the setting, a part
of her was removed. An onlooker. That part of
Summer knew that she had never been in this particular place in her waking life.

A tinkle of tiny bells and a soft click-click made
her turn. She saw a slender woman with masses of

dark, curly hair and black, kohl-rimmed eyes. The woman was standing before a table where a dish of incense burned, thin smoke rising to mingle with the night.

As Summer watched, the woman raised her hands, and the bells that wreathed her wrists sounded softly. She tilted her cupped palms over the table, and sticks of carved ivory tumbled from her hands.

Summer smiled. Ah, yes. Cliete.

The scene faded until there was nothing but the wide window, framing a thousand scintillating stars. She yawned and surrendered to overwhelming sleepiness. But just as she was sinking into it, Summer jolted awake again.

She sat up, pushing the heavy hair back from her temples. It had happened again. She felt a rush of fear.

Who—and *what*—was Cliete?

The day of Dr. Ruggieri's funeral, Col unearthed the first important clue to Carruthers's discovery. It happened as he was sorting papers at the desk. He removed the humidor of cigars that the old lion was so addicted to and set them away on a shelf. The sight of them bothered him. That was odd, because he'd rarely seen Carruthers smoke one. His mentor was a generous man, but not with his Havanas. He had usually saved them until he was alone for the night, claiming that they made him think better as he went over his notes.

Col had found a fresh blotter and replaced the one ruined when the inkstand had tipped over in the earthquake. As he was tossing it into the discard basket, he realized that the old blotter felt rather thick.

In fact, it was really two sheets that were stuck together. Col was always thorough. He didn't want to overlook anything in his search. He peeled the sheets apart with great care. Amid a welter of scratches and blotches were a few lines of writing, crossing one another at angles. They had been formed by blotting, and the words ran backwards.

As a schoolboy, like many another youth, Col had spent time when he should have been translating Latin and Greek, in more interesting ways, such as writing left-handed, or backward. He'd never guessed it would come in handy in adulthood.

It was hard to make out. He took the blotter to the window. The bright sunshine turned the crisp hair on his arms to gold as he read. ". . . jealousy. I feel it bears watching . . ." The second was even more difficult to decipher because the thick ink had been absorbed by the blotting paper into fuzzy little squiggles. Only fragments of these sentences were legible, but use of a mirror made them easier to read: ". . . the most fabulous treasure . . . my life's crowning achievement. I have carefully hidden the sketches and the   map   ."

Intriguing bits of information, but from their positions on the blotter he imagined that they were from two different notes. If only Carruthers hadn't been so damned secretive! But then, Carruthers had always been a man who savored the dramatic moment. No doubt the old lion had been waiting to spring his surprise upon an astonished world, Col included.

He groaned. Whatever his godfather had hidden, it would be in the devil of a place to find, that was for certain! But now Col had one more important piece of information: Somewhere, and God only knew where, there was a map that would lead him to this "treasure." It was up to Col to find it. He owed the old man that.

The church bells began to toll down in the village and he checked his watch. No time to continue his search for the map. If he didn't hurry he'd be late for Dr. Ruggieri's funeral service.

A short time later he rode into Appolinaria. No damage had been sustained in the village, outside of a few broken cups and dishes. As he entered the street fronting the harbor, he spied Angus's red hair, rising like a beacon above the dark shawls of the village women.

The slow tolling of the bells and the heavy scent of incense welcomed the mourners into the little white-washed church. They entered with bowed heads to pay their last respects to Dr. Ruggieri.

Everyone from the village was there, as well as the members of the archaeological team. Lewis, and the others staying in the village, had come on foot. Col saw Professor Fairchild standing outside the door with Mrs. Morville and went over to greet them. He noticed right away that Richard was laboring under some great excitement, and trying to hide it.

"I trust that Miss Fairchild is recovering well from her accident?"

"Yes," Richard said, "but she is still a bit shaken up. She insisted on coming to the funeral, however."

Removing his hat, Col followed them in through the carved wooden doors. The temperature dropped ten degrees within the thick walls that shut out the heat of the day. The interior of the church was vastly different from the outside, filled from floor to roof with golden splendor. Pure beeswax tapers burned in gold candelabra and lamps of pierced brass lit the nave, their candles sending flickering shadows over the floor and walls and the dark beams of the high, arched ceiling. Gold stars had been painted overhead on a field of azure, and they shone with reflected light.

Summer sat with her sisters, enthralled by the beauty and atmosphere of the church. She felt a deep and abiding peace tinged with awe. The altar, beneath a lamp of ruby glass, was covered in heavy linen and rich, hand-made lace. An enormous fresco of saints with long Byzantine faces rose behind the altar, beneath a gilded figure of the risen Christ.

There must have been two dozen gilt-haloed figures clustered at the bottom of the fresco. Summer could identify Mary and Joseph, St. John, Moses with the Ten Commandments, and St. Agnes with her lamb. She wished that she knew the others. The church at Kingsmeade had been severe in its Norman restraint although its carved altar screen was renowned throughout England. She much preferred this white stucco church, with its gilded glory.

All the painted faces of the fresco seemed filled with immeasurable sorrow, as they stared down at Dr. Ruggieri's simple coffin. It was covered with a black cloth embroidered in silver thread, and six huge white candles in tall brass holders surrounded the catafalque like an honor guard of angels with fiery swords.

Col was taken with the interior as well. Unlike Summer, he'd seen many of its kind, but there was something special in the air here. Perhaps sacred was the word he wanted. It was a powerful Presence that reached out to welcome the most weary and callused heart.

A man of Celtic blood, like Col, could not dig

through the rubble of vanished and once-mighty civilizations and touch the past without developing a sixth sense about the mysteries of life. He'd known this sense of Presence at Delphi, and at the wall in Jerusalem that was a remnant of David's great temple. He had sensed it among the ruins of quiet cloisters and in ancient Celtic groves where druids had worshiped, and in whispering catacombs beneath Rome. Looking up at the altar, he wondered if such places gained their atmosphere from generations of worshipful prayer, or if the sites were originally chosen for their wellspring of peace and spiritual strength.

He found a seat near the back where he had a clear view of the three Fairchild women sitting together. Time and again his eyes were drawn to Summer. She had taken off her dark jacket, worn out of respect for the funeral. Although her high collar and wide hat hid her from his view, now and then she turned her head to whisper a remark to Fanny. Framed between her sisters, she seemed ethereally fragile, like a tiny flame that burned too brightly, consuming itself.

A sharp stab of apprehension caught him unaware. He drew in a deep breath and pulled his inner defenses around himself like a barricade. He must not get drawn into Summer Fairchild's life. She was his best entree into the Court of Three Sisters, and she must remain only that, a means to an end.

He scanned the assembly looking for something—anything—to take his mind away from her, and from the fact that her father was his chief suspect in Carruthers's death. The most important question to ask in solving a murder was that of who stood to gain the most. Seen in that light, who had better motive than Richard Fairchild, coming out from the relative obscurity of scholarly research and into the golden arena of a major discovery? Lasting fame, an assured place in history. That was the greatest prize for those of a certain temperament. Men had died to achieve it.

And men had killed for less.

Col was fairly certain that the two deaths were linked, especially in view of the missing letter that Thea had delivered to Ruggieri the afternoon of the doctor's "accident." Ruggieri's sister had supplied the names of the late doctor's Roman correspondents. He hadn't expressed his suspicions to anyone—yet; perhaps it was time to try. Yes, Col decided, he would set a trap, and use himself as bait.

But not until he got closer to solving the damnable mystery of what it was that Carruthers had found. At least he had a hint of what to look for now: not more diaries, but drawings of some sort. And, of course, the map that would lead him to them. If he could only find it!

Where the hell had Carruthers hidden that map?

Mrs. Morville shot him a look and Col wondered if he'd spoken out loud. No, it was Lewis Forsythe who'd caught her attention. The young assistant was holding forth on some topic, but stopped as the haunting strains of the Dies Irae filled the nave.

Summer was more tired than she realized. The funeral mass was long, but the interment in the churchyard mercifully short. The sun shone with infernal brilliance, as if mocking the sorrow of the occasion. The colors of the flowers seemed brighter, the cheerful birdsong at odds with the setting. She bowed her head as the prayers for the dead were spo-

ken. It made her sad, for she had taken an immediate
liking to Dr. Ruggieri.

"Requiescat in pace." The priest sprinkled the
coffin with holy water and the pallbearers lowered it
down into the earth on ropes. Each of the village
mourners took a handful of dirt and tossed it into the
grave. Then the sexton shoveled the rest until the coffin was covered. Soon there was nothing but a
mound of scarred earth and a scattering of flowers to
mark the spot.

Paolo Ruggieri, a son of the village, had now
become a part of it forever.

After the burial the mourners repaired to Dr.
Ruggieri's house for the wake reception, hosted by
his brother, a retired government official, who'd
sailed over from Lipari. The open rooms were soon
filled with people, but the villagers preferred to con-
gregate in the sunny courtyard beneath the trees,
while the visitors seemed more content within the sitting room and library.

Col could barely shoulder his way in. The house
still smelled of garlic sausage and leather and
lemon, but it had the sad, stale scent of a house no
longer lived in. It was poignant to see the shelves
already bare of the doctor's books and possessions,
and Col hoped the brother was taking them back to
Lipari with him, and that they would find a good
home.

Col found the Fairchild sisters grouped together
near the empty fireplace. He had no chance to talk
to Summer alone, but he overheard Thea trying to
convince her sister to return to the villa and rest after
the exertions of the morning.

Summer set down the cup of tea she'd been holding. "I intend to see the excavations today and noth-

ing short of iron shackles will stop me." Her mouth was smiling, but her eyes looked very determined.

Thea rose, standing very straight. "Very well. But you must not blame me if you are sadly out of frame for the rest of the week because you insist on overtaxing your strength."

Col leaned over the back of Summer's chair. Her hair brushed his cheek like a cloud. It smelled of lilacs, bringing him a swift memory of his childhood home. "Good girl," he said softly. "Don't let them swaddle you in wool until you smother."

Thea heard and shot him a look that was as sharp and cold as an icicle. Col grinned and turned away. She was too well bred to give him an earful in company, but he was sure he'd hear from her on the subject at the first opportunity.

As he was leaving, Lewis Forsythe bumped into him, sloshing wine on the faded carpet. "Are you coming up to watch us remove the slabs this afternoon? We believe that we may have found the temple treasury. There's been a good deal of progress on the main building of the complex in the past few days, the nasty temper tantrums of Poseidon Earthshaker notwithstanding."

"Don't tempt the ancient gods with your impudence," Col said, sipping a glass of the same yellow wine he'd shared with the doctor on his arrival. "Some of the villagers think they are still here and very much alive."

"So far the only things we've dug up are cold stone and bronze, but I'll keep a look out for the old boys and girls."

Forsythe went away, whistling. Col watched Lewis's rather unsteady progress. He seemed a nice young chap, handsome and idealistic, with the whole world at his feet, and with his reputation still to make in his chosen field. It only took one major discovery to put a man on the map of history. Fame and honors followed, along with the interest of wealthy patrons to back other projects. Col stroked his jaw. How far would young Lewis go in order to succeed?

How far would any of them, himself included? It would be nice to see the McCallum name noted for something wonderful, instead of for the old, painful scandal.

He tossed back his wine. Time to seek out Miss Fairchild from among the guests, and cement his growing acquaintanceship with her. He hoped he hadn't lost his touch.

The sun reflected off the stone columns was blinding, but a canopy had been set up along the grove of trees to shield the ladies from the worst of it. Col was surprised to see Cynthia Morville out in the heat. She wore light gloves and a wide hat to protect her from sunburn, but the glare off the pavement was intense. Then he realized that she was concerned for the safety of her Poseidon pavement, in case the slabs fell, and was directing the workmen in emergency preparations. Her dedication was admirable.

He came up past the pit where the stone slabs were ready to be winched upright; unfortunately, one of the ropes had become too frayed to proceed and it was necessary to redo the rigging. Col recognized a familiar face.

"Whitney Vance, by all that's holy! You're the last man I expected to find in this forgotten spot!"

The other man looked up quickly. He was tall and

wide shouldered, a graceful giant with elegant posture and thick, curly brown hair. He should have had the face of a god; Whitney Vance had been cursed instead with a large head and decidedly homely features. The juxtaposition was like a cruel jest. In repose, his face looked heavy and threatening. Illuminated with a smile, as it was now, it became transformed.

Col was delighted to see his friend. Whitney was one of the kindest and most genuine people he'd ever had the good fortune to know, and he was an architect of great skill and artistry.

"Col! I've been reading up on your adventures. The last I heard from you, you were on your way to Peru!"

"And so I would have been. Carruthers called me back."

Whitney's unattractive features settled into lines of sympathy. He offered Col his hand. "The news reached me in Palermo last week, where I was visiting with Count DiCaesari. I was truly sorry to hear of it."

He looked over to where the laborers were putting new ropes around one end of the slab. "I came over to help out with this. Fairchild sent a message to the count last week that he was on to something. DiCaesari is on his way by private yacht, along with the contessa, a half-dozen guests, and enough baggage for an army. Since I pack lightly I decided to catch the first boat and come on ahead."

Col's every sense went on alert. He acted nonchalantly as Whitney went on. "The count was leery that things might go wrong and everything beneath the slabs would be smashed to powder. I offered my expertise, and came in this morning. As you can see, it's not going as well as I'd hoped."

"I won't keep you at this critical juncture," Col said quickly. "We'll talk later."

"I look forward to it." The giant's dark eyes warmed with affection. "Damn, but it's good seeing you again!" *I only wish that Alistair were here.*

The unspoken words hung between them, shining with unshed tears. Col went on his way. Whitney and Alistair had been best friends, despite the disparity in their ages. Perhaps it was the architect's talents that had made him old beyond his years, but Col suspected it was the burden of his face and the rejection it caused that made Whitney so gentle and so wise. Col had never heard him utter a harsh word to anyone.

Skirting the area, Col went off toward the canopy. Mrs. Symington, unlike Cynthia Morville, had sought shelter with her daughter. She was conversing with Thea Armstrong, who answered the woman's dull comments with the ease and appearance of interest that would do any diplomat proud. The fair Fanny was talking to Lewis Forsythe, while surreptitiously scanning the area for something, or more likely, Col thought, *someone* else.

He spied Summer off in a corner, fanning herself with a piece of peach-colored silk on an ebony stick. For once, Thea wasn't hovering over her like a shepherd with a sick sheep. Rosalind Symington was a few feet away with her back to the rest, looking sullen and unhappy. She looked up suddenly and saw Col watching Summer. She smiled briefly and turned away. A moment later Rosalind went off with her sure, mannish stride, trailing the smoke from her cigarillo behind her like a scarf of gray chiffon.

Col grinned. A very astute woman, Miss Symington! He would have to cultivate her acquaintance in the future. He slipped around through the trees and came up behind Summer. Her cheeks were a deeper shade of peach than her fan, and she looked hot and uncomfortable. She wore a white lawn blouse with a deep lace collar that cascaded past her elbows in the latest style, almost like a short cape. No wonder she looked ready to melt, he thought critically. If she wouldn't favor those caped gowns that were so fashionable yet so impractical in a hot climate, she'd feel a lot better. He had no patience for female vanity. Given a choice of comfort or fashion, there would be no contest on his part.

Hiding his exasperation at this feminine weakness, which he wouldn't have expected in her, he smiled down at Summer.

"Believe it or not, it's much cooler on the far side of the complex, where the sea breeze is fresher." He kept his voice soft so the others wouldn't overhear. "Would you care to take a little stroll, Miss Fairchild?"

She looked up from beneath her winged brows. Her forehead was damp, her clothes were sticking to her, and the stays of her boned undergarment were digging into her ribs. Let him see her limp: At the moment it was one of the least important things on her mind.

"If you could guarantee me a cool breeze, Mr. McCallum, I would cheerfully jump into the boiling caldera on Hades!"

"That would defeat your purpose." He took her hands and pulled her to her feet. Summer glanced down at the far end of the canopy, but Thea was still busy with Mrs. Symington. Col led her around a jumble of red lava rock and along a grassy verge until they were safely out of sight. "Where shall we start?"

"Let us pretend to be pilgrims of the ancient world," she suggested, "and follow the path they would have taken."

Col raised his eyebrows. Summer Fairchild never ceased to surprise him. "Very well. Shall we be Greeks or Romans, classical or preclassical?"

Summer laughed. "I'm not a scholar, Mr. McCallum."

"No? Perhaps you should be. You have all the prerequisites—curiosity, keen intelligence, and here, literally at your feet, you have the opportunity. It would be a shame to waste it."

Summer flushed. "You will think me extremely ignorant. My only knowledge of ancient civilizations comes from the books that I occasionally took from my father's study."

Col turned to her. "Is that so? Rather strange for a daughter of a professor of antiquities."

"My interest in such things was greatly discouraged," she replied shortly. She lifted her face to the breeze. It blew fresh and invigorating off the sea, just as he'd promised, cooling her heated cheeks.

Col began their tour in the great open courtyard, lined on three sides with stone columns thirty feet high. Shallow steps ran the length of each side and they went up them. They were shaded by the overhang that once held up a roof. Beyond them were some of the few intact walls of the complex. They passed through a wide doorway almost fifteen feet high and entered a rectangular chamber, now open to the cloudless sky.

A frieze went around the top of the walls, alternating squares of geometric design, with medallions centered with sheaves of various grains tied with ribbons. "The temple of Demeter, goddess of grain and the fruits of the earth," he explained. Part of the floor showed the same red stone blocks that formed the Via Sacra, the Sacred Way, but almost half of it was covered with marble slabs.

"Brought over from the mainland," Col told her. "They're a much later addition by the Romans. The lower floor is much earlier, and is probably Greek."

Summer listened with interest as they moved through to other rooms. The temple complex was extensive. Larger, in fact, than the entire village of Kingsmeade. A city of worshipers. And nothing was left but a few ruined columns and the great floor beyond. It was movingly beautiful, and brought a subtle glow to her face.

Col was pleased at her reaction. This was his favorite of the standing ruins. "You say you are untrained, Miss Fairchild, yet I see that you have an inborn appreciation of excellence."

"This appears to be much older than other parts," she murmured, embarrassed at this proof of her ignorance.

"You have a good eye. I suspect there are even older remains on this island. This temple is Greek, built shortly after Pericles achieved leadership of the Athenians. The great pyramids of Egypt were about two thousand years old then. Your ancestors and mine, Miss Fairchild, were still wearing animal skins and living in withy huts."

She laughed at that, but felt the great weight of time upon her shoulders. Running her fingers along the fluted grooves of a column, she thought of the workers and artisans who had dressed this very stone. The temple they had built had lasted over two millennia, yet not even their names were known. What buildings of her own people would still be standing two thousand years in the future? Would there be any remains of the great British Empire or, like imperial Rome and ancient Carthage, would there be only fallen stones and puzzles left behind for scholars to argue over?

Col had noticed her growing fascination, and he recognized the farseeing look that came into her eyes. She was doing something he had done hundreds of times in hundreds of different places. She was imagining what it had been like more than two thousand years earlier. Throwing herself back in time.

She was doing even more than that. Summer was opening up to the atmosphere of the days when this had been a thriving place, filled with worshipers and acolytes. It filled her, as if she were an empty vessel. Images flashed before her.

A procession of young girls, their hair garlanded with wildflowers. Suppliants bearing baskets of grain and gold, amphorae of wine and olives, jars of unguents and precious perfumed oils. Temple dancers, swirling between the columns, their colorful scarves as diaphanous as their garments.

Sounds came to her also, muted but real. Lyre and tambour, flute and panpipes, borne on the shimmering air. A woman beckoned to her to join in the procession. Summer felt a burst of joy. She took a step forward—

"Careful!" Col exclaimed, catching her as she fell forward. Summer blinked and the illusion vanished. She cried out in alarm, grasping his arm for balance. She had almost stepped into a pit where several paving blocks were missing. He had saved her from a nasty fall.

He looked at her with concern. She was pale and shaken. "The sun must have blinded you."

"Yes." How could she tell him that it had not been an inability to see, but the ability to see too much? To see things that weren't there? She put the back of her hand to her forehead and closed her eyes. The dancers and musicians had seemed so real! Even now she could still hear faint echoes of the jingling bells and smell the lingering scent of incense.

Col put his arm around her waist to support her. Her eyes were wide and dark with emotion, and not quite focused.

"Here, let's get you out of the afternoon heat. You look ready to swoon."

He assisted her into the shade of an intact wall, where a stone bench lined one side. The shadows were deep lavender in contrast to the brilliance of the light. There was a fair view over the shallow valley and out to the hills beyond. He stripped off his jacket and put it down on the dusty bench.

"Sit down. Don't try to talk yet."

Leaning forward, she buried her face in her hands. She was trembling all over. It had been years since she'd experienced these waking dreams . . . no, *spells*. Now they were coming in clusters, vivid and disturbingly real. She was mortified that one had occurred in Col's presence.

They sat awhile in the shade and gradually her trembling abated. The breeze lifted the hair from the nape of her neck, cooling her feverish skin. "I'm sorry," she said. "I don't know what came over me."

Col thought that she did. "What did you see?" he asked softly. "You did see something, didn't you?"

Summer was too stunned to reply. He looked

away, out over the valley. "It happens sometimes, you know. It happened to me. Only once."

She glanced over at him. His face was in profile to her, his brow furrowed. He paused and his eyes took on a distant look. "I was on the plain at Thermopylae. The sun was in my eyes, but for the span of a few heartbeats I saw the glint of armor and heard the clash of battle, the war cries and the groans of dying men. Then it was gone."

For a moment his first words had brought hope; then reality intruded. It wasn't the same. He had been dazzled by sunlight and his imagination had supplied the rest. He had always been aware of who he was and where he was in actuality.

"I saw nothing unusual," she lied, afraid of what he might think of her: For whatever Col McCallum had seen at Thermopylae, it was nothing like the vivid experience she had just had, where the present vanished as if it had never been, and she was thrust, unwillingly, into an unknown and alien world. And this time, that world had mingled with the realm of dreams, for she had seen a woman dancing along the Sacred Way, and recognized her:

Cliete.

The breeze had turned so chill that gooseflesh stood out along her arms; but Summer saw the beads of sweat along his hairline, and noticed Mrs. Morville across the way, fanning herself with a sheaf of papers. The sun was as brazen as before. The chill had come from within herself, a physical embodiment of her deepening fear. Something was dreadfully wrong with her.

She rose abruptly and started walking away from him. Col followed and took her arm in his. Neither spoke.

They came at right angles to an area covered with tender shoots of the new grasses and myriad wildflowers. There were thick clusters of white and yellow, and others in every tint of pink and blue and lavender imaginable. Even in her misery, Summer noticed enough to be astonished. They grew so thickly in places that they seemed to form patterns, like the Persian carpet in her father's study. They were interspersed with delicate dried stalks of last year's crop.

It was only when she felt the hardness of the ground that she realized they were traversing a wide pathway of sunken blocks. The paving was carved from blocks of a rough, red material that rasped at the thin leather soles of her shoes.

"Lava stone," Col said conversationally. "Easy to work with and readily available." He kept up an easy flow of idle chatter. Whatever had happened to her a few minutes ago, it was plain that she didn't want him to mention it again. For a moment he'd been startled, had almost been sure . . .

He sighed. No use dwelling on it. "To be proper pilgrims, we should have started at the other end of this," he added. "This is the other end of the Sacred Way, the avenue that led the worshipers to the temple precincts. Come, I'll show you how they came up to it."

He took her elbow and escorted her along the flower-strewn road. Summer imagined that it had looked much the same once upon a time, but the flowers would have been scattered by attendants and worshipers of the old gods. They went several yards, with Col accommodating his long stride to her halting one. Summer stopped short when she saw where they were headed.

"But the road goes straight over the cliff!"

"In a manner of speaking."

He led her away from the maze of walls to where narrow stairs rose in zigzag flights from the strand at the base of the cliff. The sun was bright and the wind was strong, bringing the mingled scents of pine trees and the sea.

"I should have brought you here first," he said. "Do you see the steps carved into the cliff face? At the far end, below us, is where the pilgrims began their climb to the temple."

Summer's hair whipped loose from her chignon. She tried to restrain it. "It's so steep and the wind is strong. It must have been terribly difficult. How did they manage to climb up to the shrine without meeting disaster?"

"Not all of them did. The villagers' name for this place roughly translates to Pilgrim's Plunge."

She shuddered. An image, this time from memory, came to the fore. A white-and-black seabird swooping down the cliff face: a bird that was really a man, falling to his death. Her breath caught in her throat.

"The man who fell . . . this . . . this is the place it occurred."

Col shaded his eyes. "No. It didn't happen on the temple grounds. He was several hundred yards away from us, down there to the left, when he slipped. I'd still like to know what the devil he was doing there."

His last remark was more to himself than to her. Summer turned to look at the columns a short distance away. "No," she said, shaking visibly. "It was from this very spot. I recognize it now."

He swung around sharply. "What do you mean?"

"I . . . I saw him fall. We were on the boat coming from Naples when it happened. At first I didn't realize what I had seen." She twisted her hands together. "I—I thought I'd spotted a large bird flying off the top of the cliff. It was later that I realized the cliffs were much higher than I'd imagined. It must have been his white shirt I saw—"

He caught her wrist. "Are you sure?"

"Yes!"

Col's face was grim. He gripped her shoulders. "Listen to me, Miss Fairchild. This is terribly important. Don't repeat that to anyone else. Not anyone!"

"I think that I may already have done so."

His face was suddenly etched in severe lines, as if his strong cheekbones and jaw had been hewn from granite. "To whom?"

The change in him frightened her. "It may have been in a gathering. I—I don't recall."

"Try! It's vital that you remember!"

Summer closed her eyes and tried to concentrate. The smell of the sea became stronger, the sun grew hotter upon her face. High summer. Memories flooded in . . .

The sound of waves dashing to spray upon the rocks and the piercing cry of a seabird. No, not a bird at all. She looked in time to see something white and black, hurtling down from the cliff. Except this time, she was looking down upon it from above.

Without warning, the inner door of her memory opened and Summer was plunged down into the sucking, spiraling, whirlpool of *Before*.

A Third Angelic Lesson

The assistant angel had promised to come by and see how the tapestry was coming along. The apprentice hoped she would keep her word: She did so want to become a full-fledged Fate!

She stood back and examined her work. Yes, it was taking form. The colors were there, weaving together merrily. But it needed . . . it needed . . .

"Gold," the assistant angel said, coming up behind her. "It always helps to throw in a little gold."

The youngest Fate took strands of purest light, spun from the essence of the suns. Eagerly she wove it into her tapestry to see what effect it would have. She stepped back and cocked her head. It was exciting, yes, and disturbing.

"Yes, I see now. Gold changes everything."

8

THE GLINT OF GOLD

From Richard Fairchild's excavation journal

. . . and I am certain that I have located the treasury of the temple of Demeter. The spot lies some hundred yards from the entrance, inside the two remaining walls. I plan to direct the removal of the slabs that formed the ancient roof tomorrow, but the removal must be delayed until after Dr. Ruggieri's funeral.

If there are great finds tomorrow, and I feel in my bones that there will be, then I will have vindicated the faith that Sir Horace and Count DiCaesari showed earlier, in giving the concession to me rather than to Carruthers. I will have proved myself to them, to my colleagues, and to posterity.

Fanny was bored. Lewis had left her since they were attempting to lift the slabs. They'd been at it for ages, and she had nothing to do except wish that she were back at the villa, talking with Giovanni. Suddenly the team of oxen lurched forward and a great shout went up from the workers. Even Mrs. Symington ceased her prattling and turned her head. Winches groaned and the ropes strained, then sang through their pulleys as the hitched teams lurched forward and gathered strength. The great slab lifted up and away. It looked as easy as taking the lid off a candy box.

The slab thudded down to the earth as the tension was released, and the archaeologists darted forward to the gaping hole. The cry went up, "Gold! Gold!"

The voice was so hoarse with excitement it was impossible to tell to whom it belonged. It couldn't be Papa, Fanny thought, for he would never be so undignified.

Mrs. Symington bolted out of her chair as if she'd taken a physic. *"Gold?"*

Thea found herself rising, too, although she certainly hadn't intended to do so. What was there about precious metals and ancient, buried treasures that made even the most blasé person's blood thrill at its discovery? Perhaps, she rationalized, she was only reacting to the excitement that filled the air. All attempts to move the other slabs were halted as everyone crowded around the site. There was nothing to do but go down and find out for themselves what all the fuss was about.

She turned to address Fanny, and saw that her hoydenish sister was already halfway down the rise in a flurry of petticoats. Only Mrs. Symington's bulk kept her from scuttling off as quickly. Rosalind came back from the path she'd been wandering, her wild strawberry blond hair springing out from the combs and pins whose futile duty was to confine it. She eyed the scene below, with workers running to and fro like frenzied ants scurrying around a dropped lozenge of barley sugar. She stopped with arms akimbo.

"What is all this?"

"I believe they have found a treasure," Thea replied. "We seem to be the only two who haven't run down to discover exactly what it might be."

Rosalind dropped her cigarillo stub in the dirt and ground it out beneath the sole of her expensive French boot. "Ordinarily I shun doing anything that everyone else considers de rigueur. However in this case, I believe I might be induced to contravene my principles and accompany you."

This was said with a wry smile that barely touched her world-weary eyes, and an eagerness reined in by iron control.

Thea smiled back. "And I, you." It was strange: She had taken Miss Symington, with her odd manners and thick miasma of burnt tobacco, in dislike at their prior meeting; but the poetess's frankness and humor, combined with an air of almost desperate aloneness, touched a chord in Thea's heart. Life had not been kind to Rosalind Symington, she guessed; and being a woman of letters—and of brilliance—had done nothing to enhance her state. Thea determined to cultivate Miss Symington's acquaintance.

They arrived at the site just as an "Oooh!" went up from the onlookers. Thea stepped through an opening in the crowd but was halted by the press of bodies. Recognizing her, the laborers shifted to allow her to a closer view. Rosalind came in her wake. Thea stopped short in amazement and heard her companion gasp. Gold indeed!

In the half-exposed chamber, shafts of sunlight

struck a mellow glow that only one substance on earth could impart. More gold than the eyes could take in at first sight. It was like Aladdin's cave, or the cavern of Ali Baba.

There were superb vessels of thin beaten gold—kraters and rhytons of gold and rock crystal, empty-eyed masks of gold and enamel, chairs and tables covered with thin sheets of the priceless metal and studded with semiprecious jewels, vast pottery jars spilling with gold coins and chains, statues of marble, of gold and gilded wood, stacked like logs.

Richard Fairchild stood down inside the dim treasury, which was illuminated by the sun reflecting off the polished golden surfaces. Never in his life had he expected to find such a trove!

He was pummeled by two strong and conflicting emotions: The first was the joy of the discoverer—seeing things that no man had seen in thousands of years. He heard the cheers of his team and the laborers from the village and felt his heart near to bursting with pride. His other reaction caught him by surprise. Suddenly he understood the jealousy of the Nibelungs in the old Norse sagas for their gold. Like those mythical dwarves who forged their hoarded gold into fabulous artifacts and hid them away, he found himself wishing he could hide his own fantastic treasure away from the world, at least for a little while, while he studied the objects and gloated over them.

Common sense righted itself. The first thing to do was to post a guard from among his own people. Forsythe and Symington could stand the first night watch, and he would stand the next himself, with Angus Gordon. He would take no chances until the golden artifacts could be catalogued and removed to safety. Richard knew, too well, how gold madness could strike men, turning honest workers into thieves, sailors into smugglers . . . yes, and brother against brother.

He rubbed his jaw. The safest place for some of the smaller, hence more portable objects, would be at the villa. He would oversee their removal before the larger items were moved.

Up above, Fanny was awestruck at the extent and beauty of the glittering treasure. One golden coffer was as full as it could be of gold bracelets, jeweled tunic pins, and necklaces. Oh, and that diadem set with red stones! How magnificent! She was sure it had been worn by a queen, and wondered if her father would let her try it on.

The hush that prevailed after the initial outcry was soon broken. Whispers, laughter, growing louder with excitement until the scene reminded Thea of the Tower of Babel. She realized suddenly that she hadn't seen Summer anywhere. Guilt flooded her. Oh, dear! Looking back to where the canopy stood, she saw that Summer's chair was empty. Where could she have gone?

It was then that she saw a figure come over the rise along the Sacred Way, carrying something cradled against his chest. As it drew nearer she recognized Col first, then it dawned upon her that the fluttering white in his arms was the collar of her sister's blouse.

No one could hear her cry out above the noise. Without thinking, Thea gathered her skirts and ran toward them. She saw Summer, still as death, her face as pale as the ghostly little flowers that bloomed at the base of the old columns and steps. A terrible fear blew through Thea like a blast of winter wind.

"What is wrong with her? What have you done to her?"

"Nothing, damn it!" He was pale with anxiety but his eyes hardened at Thea's assumption. "She fainted from the heat! When she came to, she was hysterical."

Summer cried out and Thea reached for her. "Get my father," she told Col.

He held Summer against his chest more tightly. "No. You fetch him. I'll carry her to the carriage. She needs to be out of this damnable sun."

For a span of several seconds a silent battle raged between them. He shook his head angrily. "Why would you think I would harm a hair of her head?" He pitched his voice low, so that only she could hear it. "You should know me better than that, after spending an entire night with me in Paris!"

She blenched. "It is cruel of you to remind me of that night! Cruel beyond words!"

"At the moment, your sister's health is more important than your pride. I'll take her to my cottage. It's cool there, and it's close. You can come with me, or not."

The impasse ended with Col turning on his heel to take Summer off to the carriage. A voice hailed them. Fanny and Cynthia Morville came hurrying up in alarm, with Rosalind behind them. Col explained his intentions.

"Heatstroke," Mrs. Morville said, summing up Summer's pallor in the light of her experience in hot climes. "She needs immediate action and I believe the drive to the cottage would be injurious. I think . . . yes, bring her to the treasury. It's dark and cool inside, and if we get the crowd to disperse we can loosen her clothing a bit."

Within a few short minutes, Summer was lowered

to her father in the vault of the ancient treasury. He settled her onto the cold stone floor, hoping it would help to ease her symptoms. Cynthia and Thea clambered down, sent Richard out, and began to loosen her collar and wrist bands. Her skin should have felt hot and dry to the touch, but it was damp and clammy. Thea knelt beside her sister, chafing her hands.

Cold. So cold. Summer was terrified. It had crept into her bones and numbed them so that she could hardly move. It was difficult to breathe, but that might have been from the fear that gripped her. Mama! Mama!

His face loomed up before her. She would never forget his face . . . cold . . . blue . . . the crabs had nibbled at his white, bloodless flesh and the little shreds floated in feathery strips, like ghastly seaweed.

The tide pool vanished. She found herself wedged into a cleft in the cold rock, shaking with fear. Time was running out of sequence now. Earlier the sound of the carriage had awakened her and brought her down to the water's edge. She had been lying in the grassy circle of the rocks on the headland, more than half-asleep, when she heard it. She'd jumped up, started running. . . . Running . . . running . . . running, and not getting anywhere . . .

Or was that the dream? She kept mixing things up. Bits and pieces all jumbled together any which way. It was impossible to sort them out now.

She did remember falling. She had been watching the carriage, afraid that if she looked away it would vanish and she would never find it again. Somehow she'd gone too close to the cliff's edge . . . it all came back. The sickening feeling when her foot met air instead of solid ground . . . the desperate, scrambling, screaming, grabbing, falling . . . falling.

"She's coming around," Thea said in relief. "Look! Her eyelids are fluttering."

Suddenly Summer opened her eyes. Her pupils were so widely dilated that her eyes looked like jet. It was dark as night after the blazing sunlight. Summer turned her head an inch or two. Above the blackness was a square of hard blue sky, but so far away she knew it was hopeless. She groaned and closed her eyes.

Somewhere above her her mother waited for her . . . No, Mama was dead. It must be Cliete, then. Yes. She could smell the incense and the sandalwood oil her sister favored. But she remembered now. Cliete was dead, too. The beam had struck her when the walls collapsed.

Water dripped nearby. A drop splashed upon her cheek. The tide was coming in. How high would it rise?

The square of light and blue sky began to shrink and recede. Despair flowed through her veins like poison, paralyzing her. Summer knew that she could never reach it now, no one would ever see her lying alone in the darkness. There was no one left to hear her cries. She would never be found, except by those greedy, scrabbling crabs. . . .

Thea leaned over Summer and wiped the tear that had fallen from her eye to her sister's face. "Summer?"

At the touch of Thea's chilled fingers Summer's face contorted with terror. The stone-lined chamber echoed with her screams.

* * *

Col was overruled. Mrs. Symington produced a bottle of "nerve" medicine from her purse, which he suspected was laudanum, and Summer was dosed liberally with it. She was quieted, covered with cool cloths, and removed to her own villa by the ladies, while Col stood by in impotent rage. It was ridiculous to take her all the rough way back, when she could be made perfectly comfortable in his own bed at the cottage! If she came to any harm from their insistence, he would . . .

Would *what?* He had no say in what they did with her. She was not related to him in any way. He was powerless to intervene, and it filled him with furious helplessness. Col couldn't remember the last time he'd been so angry. He wanted to punch something until his knuckles ached.

A hand came down on his shoulder and he turned reflexively, like a boxer. Whitney Vance's homely face looked down at him. The architect's wide mouth split in a grin. "Don't do it, Col. It would be unseemly, since I'm your elder. And I'm larger than you."

Col laughed shortly and relaxed. "Older by a year, and taller by two inches. Neither would be enough to save you if I'd a mind to put your lights out, and you know it." He shielded his eyes against the glare for a last sight of the Fairchilds' carriage. "By God, I can't believe they're hauling that poor girl off as if she were a sack of flour!"

The idea forming in the back of Whitney's mind grew more solid. "Not exactly a girl, Col. I saw her, and I would say she's definitely a woman."

The answering fire in Col's eye told Whitney that he'd struck a nerve. He didn't say anything. Col kicked a rock and watched it bounce away down the hill. "Physically, yes. But she's as innocent as they come." He scowled. "Do you know the fairy tale of the princess on the glass hill? That's Summer Fairchild. They hem her in, keep her isolated. Untouched and untouchable."

That interested Whitney very much. "She seems to have touched you," he ventured softly.

"Don't be a damned fool! I feel sorry for her, that's all. She's entitled to a life, a real life of her own."

The carriage was gone, not even a plume of dust to show its passing. The other man touched Col's arm. "Since there's nothing you can do about it, come look at the treasure."

From the look on Col's face, his friend could tell that he'd forgotten about the discovery. Yes, there was something going on, whether Col realized it or not. Whitney smiled.

As they walked along toward the half-buried temple, he decided to learn more of the situation. "This Miss Fairchild you've befriended. Why is her family so protective of her?"

Col stopped. "Of course, you wouldn't know. You never saw her walk." He started again. "She suffered an accident in childhood. It left her with a limp. As far as I can see, that's the only result of it. She's overly conscious of it, though, and shuns company. I'm not sure how much is her family's doing, and how much her own choice."

Whitney could understand that. He was strong and healthy as an ox, but a face like his, a face that frightened children or made them point and giggle, was a handicap in its own way. At least he had been compensated by his skills in architecture.

And, he thought wryly, it kept him from being

besieged with endless dinner invitations from match-making mamas hoping to marry off their daughters. Like Col, Whitney had long accustomed himself to a future alone. It didn't stop him from looking at a pretty face and wondering what life might have been like under differing circumstances.

They were almost at the treasury. "Who was the lovely blond sprite in blue?" he asked, keeping his voice carefully neutral.

Col was no fool. He laughed. "That was Miss Fanny Fairchild."

"Ah."

"A spoiled little baggage," Col continued care-lessly, "but kind-hearted if what her sister says is true. Miss Fanny is causing quite a stir with those big blue eyes of hers. From what I've seen, she can't decide if she should make sheep's eyes at the hand-some young gardener, or confine her flirtations to young Forsythe."

Whitney was grateful for the veiled warning. "With a face like that," he said airily, "she'll land her-self a prince."

They had reached the edge of the hole, which had once been the ground floor of this particular temple. The gawkers had moved away, sent about their work by their employer. Richard was inside, and invited them to view the discovery at firsthand.

Whitney descended first, concerned that his weight would collapse the remaining slabs. They held firm, as they had for centuries. Col jumped lightly down. The site was amazing from above, even more so at close range.

His long-neglected training came to the fore. Scanning the piled statues, the helter-skelter furni-ture placement, he realized that this was no ordinary storeroom. "It appears that these goods were hidden away in great haste."

Richard was irked. "What makes you draw that conclusion?"

"The general disarray." Col knelt by two miniature gold figures, no longer than his hand, and touched them gently. "And these." He had identified them by their symbols as Demeter, with her crescent sickle and sheaf of golden wheat, and her daughter, Persephone, holding a carved garnet pomegranate in her perfect golden hand. Valuable and sacred artifacts. "If there were not some great urgency, why would the priestesses have left these effigies of their goddesses so carelessly arranged and face down upon the floor?"

The professor was chagrined that he hadn't seen it himself. While McCallum had envisioned the past, he himself had been blinded by visions of glory. The knowledge was bitter as gall. He recovered quickly. "Yes, a very good surmise. I was examining the same theory myself."

They looked about until Angus returned to help Richard with the initial inventory. After Col climbed out the professor addressed Whitney. "I take it that you and Mr. McCallum have been acquainted for some time?"

The other man looked at him blankly for a moment. "Col? I was at Oxford with his brother, Alistair. You may have heard of him—he was in charge of the excavation at Ilykion when he died. A great loss to the academic world, and to his friends and family."

Vance's comments had an earthshaking effect upon Richard. Things fell into place for him with a resounding thud. "Alistair? Do you mean the late Lord FitzRoy?"

"Why, yes, now that you mention it, although I always think of him as Alistair McCallum. I'd known him for many years before he unexpectedly came into the title."

Vance was unaware of the impact of his words upon the professor. "He didn't take it very seriously. From his letters, the notion of being called Lord FitzRoy was more of a jest than an honor, I'm afraid." He was looking up past the ruined columns of the temple of Demeter and into the distance, as if looking back through time. "He passed on within a year of inheriting."

He reached up and levered himself up from the treasury. Richard clambered out after him, stunned and disbelieving. The full ramifications hit him when he was on solid ground once more. He'd just shown off a fortune in gold to a man he suspected of being a common thief—at the very least of it, an accomplice.

All the old anger and humiliation came back. One day he was the discoverer of the only existing statue by the great Praxiteles; the next merely a man who claimed to have found it. Without the Venus of Ilykion he had nothing to back it up. He'd been a laughingstock instead of a legend. For a few minutes, Richard was lost in the memories of that devastating disappointment. Then Richard spotted the architect and Col walking away together, and went charging after them. He gained ground quickly and was less than ten feet when he called out, "FitzRoy!"

Col stiffened, then turned slowly.

Richard's hands doubled into fists. "So, you do acknowledge your identity!"

There were white lines around Col's mouth. He'd been found out. He had inherited the title upon Alistair's death; and with it, he'd also inherited a mountain of debt run up by his distant cousin's excesses.

The name FitzRoy had unhappy memories associated with it. He used it for official purposes, and on his books of exotic travel and adventure, minus the title, as a means of maintaining anonymity. He faced Fairchild.

"When I'm traveling I prefer to use McCallum, my family name."

"Yes. I can see why you would be loath to use the title your brother dishonored," Richard snarled.

He was upset that he hadn't made the connection sooner, but there was little resemblance between the athletic man facing him now, and the vaguely remembered stripling who'd visited his brother at Ilykion. "You must have a nose for treasure, FitzRoy, or McCallum, or whatever you call yourself. But a thief by any name is still a thief!"

Col bristled with outrage. "By God, I'll—!"

Whitney Vance posed himself between them, using a wide shoulder to block Col. There was blood in the air, and he wouldn't have it. "Get a grip on yourself and apologize, Fairchild."

"Apologize to the man who helped his brother abscond with the Venus of Ilykion? The man who caused a scandal so grave it almost ruined my career?"

Col pushed past his friend and faced his adversary. "You will eat those words, if I have to shove them down your damned craw!"

Richard wasn't a cowardly man, but what he saw in Col's eyes sent him back a step. "I stand by what I said! Your brother stole that statue and you damn well know it. Everyone knew FitzRoy was on the verge of bankruptcy! But selling the Venus to a private collector would have been more than enough to pay off the creditors."

"You are mad!"

"Not I," Richard said, his face contorted with all the pent-up frustration. "The most important thing I'd ever found, till now, was taken by Alistair, before it had even been examined! And I realized later that the only way he could have spirited it away from the site was with your help. It was brilliant. Who would have suspected a schoolboy?"

Col's face flushed red, then white with the heat of his anger. "Alistair never stole that statue!"

"Then why did he kill himself?" Richard attacked. "That was as clear an admission of guilt as I've ever seen!"

"He killed himself because the newspapers hounded him to it. Because, through your vile stories, people turned their backs on him. He knew that nothing he could do or say would ever clear his name, and he was too proud to live with it!"

"Too guilty, I say!"

Col lunged at him. His hands wrapped around Richard's throat, squeezing with deadly power. Whitney through himself into the fray. It ended with Richard on the ground, gasping, and Col held back by the giant's strong arms.

"Col, damn it, think of that poor girl you've befriended, if not of yourself."

A few deep breaths and Col was in control again. By God, he could have killed Fairchild for the terrible things he'd said! The urge was still in him, but he mastered it. He'd had years of learning to do so.

Forsythe came running over and helped the professor to his feet. He looked shaken. "What in God's name—"

"Never mind," Whitney snapped. "Come, Col. I'll ride back with you to your place."

Richard massaged his bruised throat. "Stay away from here," he said hoarsely. "And stay away from the villa. If I catch you anywhere near my daughters, I swear I'll shoot you like a dog!"

Col sent him a blazing look. "Get this straight, Fairchild. If I have a mind to do it, nothing you can say or do will stop me!"

Col and Whitney Vance went into the village. There was a small taverna on the harbor that served simple food and excellent wine. They found an outside table, nodding to the village regulars nearby, and ordered a meal. The food was cooked to perfection, the wine like nectar of the gods, but it was all dust and vinegar in Col's mouth. He hadn't thought that the old scandal had the power to hurt him anymore, but found the wound of Alistair's disgrace and death as deep and raw as ever.

"You knew him, Whitney. Alistair was a man of honor, incapable of deceit in any form. A gunshot may have killed him in the end, but it was despair over the scandal that pulled the trigger."

He slapped his open hand on the table. The bottle and glasses jumped like live things. "I thought it was all buried with him! That he could be remembered now for his scholarly accomplishments. To hear Fairchild rake it up, slandering Alistair's name after all these years! By God, I wish you'd have let me throttle the bastard!"

Whitney had never felt so awkward and helpless. "I never knew exactly how or why he died, if that's any comfort. The word was evidently confined to archaeological circles."

Col looked out over the harbor. The water glistened with iridescence, like the scales of a great blue fish. "He was set up, Whitney. Someone purposely destroyed him." His eyes met his friend's squarely. "If I ever find out who that person is, I'll kill him."

"Do you mean to stay on now that Fairchild knows your relationship to Alistair?"

A grim smile twisted Col's lips. "Nothing will make me leave. Not until I discover who murdered Carruthers. Yes," he said, seeing the other man's surprise. "Carruthers was murdered."

He knocked back his wine, leaving Vance puzzled. He'd conducted the last part of the conversation in Italian.

Vance leaned forward. "Be careful what you say. They'll hear you."

Col's smile widened but his eyes were cold as death. He reverted to English. "I certainly hope so. The only way to flush the villain out is to set a trap, and you see, *I'm the bait.* Just spread word that I've uncovered something in one of Carruthers's diaries."

"You cannot stay in your room forever," Thea told Summer.

There was no answer. Summer kept her back turned, her eyes closed, although she was wide awake. It had been more than twenty-four hours since she'd been drugged and brought back to the villa. Since awakening, she had refused to speak or leave the snug cocoon of her bed. It was foolish, she knew. Retreating from the world would not stay her headlong plunge into madness. But inside the familiar walls, rolled up beneath the light quilt, she could cling to the illusion of safety. Of sanity.

"Summer, you are being very rude." Thea's voice trembled. "What must Mrs. Morville think?"

Poor Thea, Summer thought, mistakenly supposing that any concern over breaches of etiquette would rouse her from her despair. She held herself very still. *Go away! Leave me in peace!*

After a moment she heard her sister's footsteps, followed by the sound of the door closing. Summer stayed hunched beneath the quilt until she was sure that Thea was gone. Then she rose and silently slid the tiny bolt across to lock the door. It was a flimsy affair and wouldn't hold against any real pressure, but at least it would give her enough time to get back in bed and pull the covers up over her head.

She went to the window and looked out. It was safe to view the outside world from here. Only from here. After she'd awakened again yesterday she had been near hysteria to find the room dark and the shutters closed. Once they were opened to the sky, she had retreated to the safe womb of her imagination, in search of comfort.

Even that was a risk. It was all too easy to fall from daydreams into dreams, from dreams to nightmares. The last one had been terrifying, although she couldn't recall it now. Something about crabs. She shivered as fear crawled through her, little snakes of icy terror, sinking their cold fangs deep into her soul. Summer returned to her bed.

She didn't know why she felt such dread. It had grown worse since the earthquake. That had been frightening but she had suffered no real harm. The bruises and scrapes had faded and healed quickly, but she realized, too late, that there was other, hidden damage.

She burrowed deeper in the blankets, shivering. Hiding. The trembling earth had shaken something loose inside her. The dust of shattered memories swirled through her mind and the dark shadow of *Before* hovered over her like an evil cloud.

Summer pulled the pillow over her head and prayed for deep, dreamless sleep.

The following day, as Richard prepared to leave the villa, he saw Giovanni carry in a basket of stone fragments with Cynthia Morville leading the way. "Why, what is this?"

"I'm putting together a shattered mosaic," she replied with a twinkle in her eye. "It's rather delicate, so I thought it would be best to do it here. I believe it to be the work of the same artisan who designed the dolphin mosaic we uncovered last week. If so, it is a major find."

"That's usually the kind of task that comes after the digging season is finished."

She flushed. "You've found me out. I should have known that I couldn't pull the wool over your eyes." She favored Richard Fairchild with a glance from beneath her thick eyelashes. "Shall I confide in you, then?"

"You may always confide in me," he said, with such warmth that even Giovanni noticed.

Cynthia smiled and hurried to elaborate. "My intentions are quite honorable. From something Fanny said . . . well, I'm afraid that your daughters will soon be heartily bored with sitting by, while everyone else is involved with the dig in some way. Ellysia is not exactly brimming with the social life they are accustomed to enjoying in England!"

"I'm beginning to realize that," he said ruefully.

"Yes, well. I thought that perhaps Miss Fairchild and her sister might develop an interest in helping me put the pieces together. It would assist my work greatly, and would also make the time pass more quickly for them."

"Very thoughtful of you," Richard told her. "And very clever." He had discussed the coolness of Thea's reception with Cynthia, as much out of embarrassment as a need to explain Thea's reaction. This was a stroke of brilliance, he thought: There wasn't a shadow of doubt in his mind that it was a carefully planned step to further her friendship with the three Fairchild women.

"Will you be coming to the site later?"

"Of course. Only let me set my plan into action." They grinned like conspirators.

"Let me know what comes of it," he told her, and went out. Cynthia was a rare treasure. He hoped his daughters would soon come to value her as much as he did.

In the sitting room later, Fanny watched Cynthia Morville set out broken bits of pavement on a long table. She lined them up according to the colors of the stones and dusted off her hands.

"Do you like puzzles, Fanny? Perhaps you might be willing to help me. There are hundreds of fragments to sort."

Fanny's eyes widened. It seemed a hopeless task. Some of the pieces were the size of shoe buttons, the individual tiles even smaller—and all of them appeared to be composed of combinations of white, blue, and green. Not only would it be tedious, she was sure that handling the rough and broken edges would be hard on the delicate skin of her hands.

"I'm afraid that I would not be much use to you. I am hopeless at puzzles. Perhaps Summer might help out when she awakens. She has nothing better to do."

That sounded ungracious, Fanny thought, blushing. She was glad her sisters hadn't been present to overhear her. "I mean, perhaps Summer might find it interesting. She has a knack for games and puzzles, you know . . . and . . . and I have decided to spend more time working on the gardens."

Thea entered and Fanny gave a guilty start. "Is Summer feeling more the thing?" she asked brightly.

"Yes. I left her writing another letter to send to Nana when the next boat leaves for Naples. She will be able to join us for dinner tonight."

"I hope you don't mind me setting these things out here," Cynthia said. "I hoped that I might be able to induce Summer to help me sort through them. Perhaps it would give her something to do while she is recuperating."

"How thoughtful of you." Thea brushed a strand of hair from her forehead. "Fanny, would you be so good as to see if the signora is ready for us?"

Fanny was about to protest when her sister sent her a look laden with meaning. She took herself off with alacrity. When they were alone, Thea addressed Mrs. Morville. "I wanted to speak to you in privacy." Her fingers twisted together tightly as she faced her unpleasant task. "You have been so good, so very kind and helpful. Why, I don't know what I would have done when—"

Oh, dear. This was not going well. Thea took a deep breath. "I am afraid that I owe you an apology, Mrs. Morville. I haven't been a good hostess since your arrival. I . . . I should have seen that you were made comfortable and your things properly bestowed in your room."

A gleam of appreciation lit the widow's eyes. She guessed, quite accurately, how difficult the apology was for Thea to make; more than that, she realized how mortified Thea was at thinking she had not done her duty to her father's guest.

"Earthquakes and funerals are more than enough to rattle anyone." She tactfully omitted Summer's hysterical outburst of the previous day. "Let us be frank, my dear Mrs. Armstrong. We have gotten off on the wrong foot and the fault is mine, for usurping your place as hostess that first evening we met, albeit in complete innocence."

"No, no! I assure you—"

"Please, let me finish." She put her hand on Thea's sleeve. "I understand your misgivings and feel it is only fair, to all parties concerned, to dispel them. You are concerned for your father."

Thea was struck dumb with shock at Mrs. Morville's directness, and could only stare at her in horror. The widow went on, choosing her words carefully. "My being here is very much your father's idea. He thought that you might need . . . respite . . . from the care of your sisters. And of course, I am very glad to assist you in any way possible."

Thea was abashed. How she had misjudged the case! Martin had always told her that she jumped too often to the wrong conclusion, and then doubled the problem by not bringing it out into the light for examination. "You have been an enormous comfort to me. I cannot thank you enough."

"It is my pleasure." Mrs. Morville looked down at the mosaics spread out on the table and nudged one gently. "I admire Richard Fairchild greatly. He and I are colleagues, and, inevitably, we have become friends as well. We share our work in common—my late husband excavated with your father in the past, so we have known each other for some time."

Tears welled in her gray eyes, threatening to spill over. She dabbed at them with a fine lace handkerchief. "We have also another bond. We both lost our spouses the same . . . the same year. But our relationship is purely platonic, and shall always remain so."

She lifted her chin, although her eyes swam with unshed tears. "After my husband passed on I never thought of marrying again. You may think it very odd, perhaps unwomanly of me, but the focus of my life is my work, and the mosaics that I restore."

Although she felt utterly abashed, Thea found her tongue. "Oh, but I admire you greatly for making your mark in the world in your profession! Really, I don't know why you are telling me this, Mrs. Morville! My father is an adult. It is certainly neither my position, nor my intention, to judge his friendships. Nor to interfere with them."

She was aware of how stilted she sounded. Her complexion went from white to red. "I am sure there is no need for us to be discussing the matter in this way."

"Ah, now, there you are wrong. There is every need." Mrs. Morville smiled warmly. "I cannot tell you how delighted I am that you traveled to Ellysia with your sisters. Unfortunately, I have no husband to provide for me and must make my own way in the world. Although I am very circumspect, there is always the question of protecting one's reputation from cruel gossip."

Thea's flush darkened, but Cynthia Morville's words were not a gibe at her. "As the only woman on the team, I have been very lonely for female companionship. We shall be constantly thrown in one another's company in the next months. My dear Mrs. Armstrong, I sincerely hope that you and I can become friends."

All Thea's former reserve vanished like smoke up a chimney. She felt foolish for her jealous suspicions, and greatly relieved. Taking Cynthia Morville's hands in hers, she smiled back. "I think I should like that . . . very much."

Fanny returned to announce that their afternoon meal was ready, and the two older women went out to the terrace in great amity. The table was set with silver and china decorated in a rich Oriental pattern. A centerpiece of flowers in a crystal vase added an elegant note.

Mrs. Morville took a seat to one side of her hostess and unfolded the linen napkin in her lap. She couldn't help wondering what other luxuries Richard's daughters had brought with them in their many trunks. She was heartily sick of the tiny room she'd taken in the village, and of sharing meals with her landlady's family. This was much more the thing.

And she couldn't help congratulating herself on how well her little tête-à-tête with Thea had gone. She'd smoothed over the unpleasantness of their initial meeting, and turned what could have been a liability into a decided advantage.

Cynthia Morville sipped her glass of fruit punch and sighed. She was glad it was over. It was always better to clear the air. And it hadn't been as bad as she'd feared. Well, now that all that was out of the way, she and Thea Armstrong would soon become bosom companions. It *was* nice to have a female companion with which to share one's innermost feelings, and she was sure that Thea felt the same.

An enigmatic smile that might have done justice to an Etruscan sculpture lifted the corners of her mouth. Everything was going according to plan.

On the second morning Summer woke up and looked at the window. Someone—Thea, no doubt—had tiptoed in and closed the shutters while she was still asleep. Thin lines of pearly light filtered through the gaps between them. It must be almost dawn. The enclosed space stifled her. It was dark as a tomb, she thought with a shiver.

Summer rose and bolted her door. She had no desire to join the others. but felt compelled to go out to her private terrace instead. In her haste she grabbed the latch of the hidden door too hard, and the old leather broke off in her hand. She hoped that the heavy tapestry would be enough to keep the door closed.

It was cool outside, the sky scarcely lighter than the sea; but the heavy air and cloudless expanse promised another sultry day. She took a deep breath and felt it fill her lungs. Much as she wanted to stay alone in her room, Summer knew she could not indulge herself that way. Her refuge was turning into her prison, robbing her of air and freedom. Closing her in with shards of memories that could not—would not—leave her in peace.

She went to the low wall that separated the disused fountain from the terrace and sat down. The stone was cold but she welcomed it. She needed a shock to clear her head. Muddled thoughts and left-over dreams chased one another through it. Seaweed and water, tiny ivory bones, a carriage riding off . . .

She pushed back her hair. None of it made any sense and none of it seemed frightening, yet she was still afraid. Deathly afraid. That was one of the reasons she knew that she was losing her mind. They'd blamed it on the heat, but she knew.

Idly, she picked up the piece of wood she'd been using to remove the stucco from the mosaic and wedged it in a crack. The end caught and she pried it up, not even thinking of what she was doing as she pondered her problems.

Col McCallum hadn't come to inquire after her. She was glad of it. How could she face him after her hysterical collapse?

He was everything that she was not: quick and sure and strong in mind and body.

She gave the stick a vicious jab, and a great section of stucco came loose, pitching her forward. Bracing her hands, she kept herself from tumbling ignominiously over the low ledge and into the abandoned fountain. Her hands were badly scraped. Tears stung her eyes but she dashed them away with the back of her arm.

The section had broken away to reveal a stunning fragment of the mosaic. It was part of a peacock's tail, rendered in tiny stones. The artist's skill and the early light gave the blue-and-green eyes of the tail a splendid iridescence. It looked so real, so vivid, that she had to touch it, to reassure herself that it was not a fan of real feathers.

The work went beyond artistic skill and into the realm of genius. Summer was amazed. Who had covered it up, and why?

More of the stucco was loose now. Taking the stick, she worked at the edges, levering up segments of stucco as big as her hand with every try. The edge of a lake or pond was revealed. Summer set herself to enlarging the area. More work uncovered shimmering mosaic fish, gold and silver and particolored, with long, veil-like fins swirling gracefully beneath the surface. Above them floated strange blue water lilies that she recognized as Egyptian lotus flowers.

The task became an obsession. Suddenly it was the most important thing in the world to uncover the rest of the mosaic. It appeared to be edged with lengths of entwined ribbons and flowers. As she was attempting to remove a particularly resistant piece, she heard pounding. Thea was knocking at the door of her bedchamber. She looked up. Good God, how long had she been at it? The sky was bright with golden light.

Dropping the stick, she ran inside and pulled the tapestry in place, praying it would stay that way. There was nothing for it but to let Thea in, before she roused the help to break down the door. Summer realized that her hands were raw and streaked with dirt. She grabbed a hand towel and dipped it into her water pitcher, then wiped her face quickly, and wrapped the damp cloth around her hands.

"I'm coming," she said, just as the little bolt jolted out of its holder and the door swung inward. Thea stood on the threshold with the signorina behind her. They were both surprised by the quiet domestic scene. They had begun to fear the worst.

"I prefer *not* to have an audience when I bathe," Summer said quietly, pretending to be in the midst of washing.

The housekeeper tactfully retreated. Thea stood firm. She had been badly frightened, and was furious. "Why didn't you answer?"

"I did, but you were so busy pounding that you didn't hear me."

"Are you coming to breakfast this morning?"

Summer saw the tapestry move slightly in the draft. She had to get Thea out before she noticed it, too. "Very well."

Thea smiled her relief. "Father will be pleased. I'll leave you to your ablutions."

The moment she was gone, Summer dragged a straight-backed chair across the room and stood it against the tapestry. It was sturdy enough to hold it in place. It seemed very important that no one find the secret terrace and the mosaic she was uncovering. Not yet.

Summer spent the rest of the morning doing a scale rendering of the atrium with pen and India ink. Later she wandered to the outer court to see Giovanni's progress with the flower beds, and found Fanny ensconced on a bench in a corner, watching. Her cheeks looked flushed with sun. She jumped up when she saw Summer.

"Isn't it beautiful? Giovanni is going to let me help him choose the plants for the inner court, and he plans to train the vines up over the loggia, as the Romans did." She held out a pair of thick cotton gloves. "He said I must wear these to protect my hands."

"I didn't know you were interested in gardens." Summer plucked a pink flower from a tree and floated it in the fountain.

"Well," Fanny said brightly, "there is nothing much else for me to do. Thea and the signora see to the house and you have your drawing, but I am left with too much time on my hands."

A few days ago Summer would have taken her

words at face value, but the feelings that Col McCallum stirred in her had made her aware of other undercurrents. Was Fanny developing a tendresse for the gardener? Thea would be mortified!

She watched Giovanni for a few minutes. He seemed totally intent upon his work. Too intent, she decided, for a young man in the presence of an extremely pretty and lively young woman. But perhaps Giovanni's heart was already given to one of the village girls.

She certainly hoped so.

Summer left them to the gardens and went back inside. As she did so, Giovanni glanced up at Fanny. Their eyes met and they smiled without a need for words.

The signora came out from another door leading off the loggia. "Giovanni! What are you about, to be making eyes at the English signorina! If she does not know her station, then you must! Go down to the village and fetch me a pullet for tonight's dinner from Signora Liotta. A nice, fat one, mind you."

The young man flushed with embarrassment. He knew, as his aunt did not, that Fanny had understood every word. She had turned away, pretending to observe one of the tiny canaries hopping about in the branches of the almond tree, but he had seen her lovely lip quiver.

"There is a fine, fat pullet scratching corn in the kitchen garden," he said stiffly. "I will wring its neck for you."

"No! That one is for the laying of eggs, not the stew pot. Enough of your excuses. Be off with you."

He left, sullen and mortified. Fanny was still staring at the bird, her color high. She was deeply offended by the signora's strictures, as well as by her harsh treatment of Giovanni; but worst of all was the image of Giovanni's strong, brown hands wringing the neck of a hapless chicken. Somehow it did not fit her heroic image of him. She was sure she could not eat a mouthful of supper, be it ever so good!

Later that afternoon Cynthia Morville came back from the dig to find Summer at the worktable she'd set up. A good portion of the small tiles that she'd brought to sort had been removed from the basket and fitted together like pieces of a puzzle.

"Clever girl! Why, you've made quite a good job of it."

Summer jumped. The sable cat, which she'd named Pandora, leapt up in startlement and darted from the room. Summer put a hand over her fluttering heart. She'd been so immersed in her task that she hadn't realized she was no longer alone. She set down the fragment she'd been about to place.

"Yes, and even Fanny has agreed to help, now that she can see what the design will be."

Cynthia was puzzled until she saw the drawing that Summer had made. Using the larger fragments, she had figured out by the curve of leaf or petal, a sound approximation of the original design. She had drawn it out on a heavy sheet of paper, with the assembled parts in place, and dotted lines to show where the missing tiles would go. She was using the sketch as a pattern to fit the pieces. It formed a motif of scalloped seashells and leaping dolphins, vaguely similar to the one in her secret garden, but framed in a basket-weave border.

"How ingenious of you to make out the design."

"It wasn't difficult. It's a repeating motif, and once

I'd worked out the first, the rest fell into place. Now it is only a matter of sorting the colors and setting them in place. The tedious part was drawing the initial layout of the design."

"But you must have been at it for hours!" The woman's voice lowered in concern. "I do hope that you haven't worn yourself out."

"Not in the least," Summer said, trying not to bridle. She knew that Mrs. Morville's intentions were good. She set a fragment into the mosaic pattern. A perfect fit.

"I am not the invalid my family would have you believe," she said, "my . . . heatstroke . . . notwithstanding. If left up to them, I would sit in an invalid chair with a lap rug over my knees and do nothing more taxing than turn the pages of a book.

"And," she added, looking back at the mosaic with satisfaction, "it is about time that I did something useful!"

"Not only useful, but essential. Thank you."

They smiled at one another in easy harmony. For all her saying that she didn't care if her father was interested in Mrs. Morville, Summer hadn't been as indifferent to the idea as she'd pretended. In fact, at times she'd been put off by the woman's unflagging politeness. It was plain that Mrs. Morville, knowing her presence might cause friction, had gone out of her way to make everyone comfortable.

Richard heard them talking as he came in, and joined them. He looked at Summer's work approvingly. "What an excellent idea! I'm surprised that we didn't think of that ourselves."

Summer felt her color rising in direct proportion to her pleasure. She was unused to hearing compliments from her father. "I have more time on my hands than either of you," she said quickly.

As always, her father was uncomfortable with any reference to her lameness. He picked up her sketch-book lying open nearby and examined the architectural drawing she'd done of the atrium earlier. Summer was pleased with it, and glad that she'd taken the care to render it to scale.

"Why, this is very good." He showed it to Cynthia. "By Jove, just look at the texture and detail!"

The widow murmured her appreciation. "Very nice. Almost professional in quality."

"Quite professional, I would say."

Summer pinked with pleasure as they turned the pages, absorbed in her work. When they'd finished her father set the sketchbook back in place.

"Well, well, Summer. I didn't realize that you had become so accomplished at drafting." An idea came to him. The brain, he often thought, was like any muscle in the body. There was nothing like work and the satisfaction of doing it properly to keep one's mind active and fit. If she had something to occupy her, Summer might be less prone to her morbid dreams.

"Perhaps you might like to come out to the excavations and do some scale renderings. We have so much work that I'm afraid Cynthia cannot keep up with it."

Summer threw a quick glance at the other woman. Mrs. Morville's complexion grew flushed with mortification. "Really, Richard, I had no idea that you thought me so inefficient. Perhaps I should spend less time on the mosaic and more on—"

His fingers touched her sleeve. "My dear, I didn't mean to imply anything of the kind. I merely meant that your talents could be put to better use, if Summer would spend a few hours each week doing drawings at the site. If they are as good as this, they could be included in my published reports, which would save additional time."

He gave his daughter a doubtful look. "But of course, it would be too taxing for you."

Summer could hardly believe her ears. In her heart of hearts she had dreamed, but never put into words, her thoughts of becoming an illustrator. That hope had seemed so fragile and remote that she had never voiced it to her family. How could she when, until this journey to Ellysia, she had been actively discouraged from any activity more strenuous than a walk in the garden at Kingsmeade? How far away that all seemed now.

To be honest, she had barely acknowledged it to herself. The very idea seemed as remote as the moon. She was almost afraid to move or breathe. To have her drawings included in one of her father's reports would be a giant step in the direction of achieving her nebulous goals; but she saw the opportunity slipping away before she'd had time to grasp it.

"Oh, no! I should enjoy it very much, Father." She looked questioningly at Cynthia. "If, that is, it wouldn't be an imposition?"

Mrs. Morville took Summer's hand in hers. "An imposition?" She laughed. "Why, it would be a boon! To speak truth, I *have* been a bit overwhelmed with work, and could use an assistant. And, my dear, I should enjoy your company very much. But I warn you, your father is a hard taskmaster!"

The look she exchanged with Richard was not unnoticed by his daughter. Although Mrs. Morville had been piqued by his undiplomatic phrasing earlier, there was warmth and shared understanding in their eyes. They put their heads together, talking animatedly about the day's work. Summer felt like an intruder.

They didn't seem to notice when she slipped away.

Dinner was a pleasant affair. As the dessert course was served, Cynthia announced the new plan to Thea, who was appalled. "Whatever can you be thinking of? Father, surely this is most ill advised! Why, it is only a few days since Summer was overcome with heat!"

"Yes," he admitted. "The thought occurred to me afterward. Perhaps it was not a wise suggestion on my part."

Summer listened to them, aghast, as they put forth more arguments. Her father was wavering. It was evident that the plan had been doomed to failure before it had a chance to be put into action. Suddenly it was all too much. Summer rose, knocking her water goblet over. She leaned her hands on the linen tablecloth for support, for she was shaking with rage.

"Oh, is that how it is to be? 'Poor Summer,' unable to do anything but create a scene? 'Poor Summer,' come out of your room, and do absolutely *nothing!* Is that it?"

All her pent-up frustrations boiled over and she could not keep them in. She was shivering as if with an ague. For the first time she had been promised an opportunity. She had seen something real within her grasp, only to have it yanked away as if she were an inept child. And even a child was allowed the chance to try to walk, even if it meant a few spills and bruises. Summer choked on a sob. She couldn't bear it!

"Now, dear, you're getting overwrought." Thea started to rise but Summer lifted her head and quelled her with a look.

"Don't 'now Summer' me. And stop trying to coddle me! I don't want it, and I don't want your two-faced pity. Oh, yes! I can jaunt all over the world, from Kingsmeade to Ellysia if it suits someone else's goals, but I am not to be allowed to contribute to the effort in any way. How vilely unfair!"

In the shocked silence she looked from one face to the next. "Is it my health you are so worried about, or the fact that I might embarrass you again by having one of my 'spells'? Yes, we all know that's what happened the other day, but you all tiptoe around it, as if it were some dread disease! Or as if the truth would send me off the edge of sanity. If you think I am insane, why don't you just lock me up in a room and throw me crusts of bread from time to time?"

Richard threw down his napkin. "That is enough!"

"It certainly is!" She pushed herself away from the table angrily and started for her room. No one came running after her.

She was in such a white heat that she found herself standing in the sitting room instead. Backtracking, she found the corridor to the bedchambers, went inside her room and closed the door, leaning her forehead against it. She was shaking.

When it ceased, she was stiff and aching. She couldn't tell how long she had stood there. It might have been minutes or hours. All the fury and defiance went out of her, leaving her weak and drained.

It was no wonder they'd been shocked by her behavior. It shocked her, as well. She'd acted the fool! She had gone up like a rocket, because they treated her like a child, and then had acted as if she were a spoiled three-year-old throwing a temper tantrum, like the red-faced little boy they'd seen in the train station at Marseilles, screaming and drumming his heels.

Summer poured water from the pitcher into the basin and bathed her face. The mirror reflected her image, pale and wide-eyed as a wraith. Her hair had come loose in wisps around her ears. She smoothed it back and tucked in the combs more securely. She owed them all an apology.

There wasn't a sound as she opened her door and slipped out into the corridor. They would be in the sitting room by now. Her father had given up the custom of a lonely glass of port in the dining room, to sip it surrounded by the ladies while they talked over the events of the day.

It wasn't until she reached the sitting room that she realized it was empty. They must have gone to the terrace instead. As she was turning to go out, Summer halted in disbelief. "Oh, *no!*"

She'd left her drawings on the worktable. The bottle of India ink had been knocked over, leaving a black swath across the paper. Summer was near tears. She opened the cover, staining her hands and sending an arc of wet, black dots across her skirt and bodice.

The ink had soaked all the way through the drawings. They were ruined, almost completely obliterated. All that work, for nothing! She could never recapture the effects of the sketches. It made her sick at heart.

The others had heard her cry of alarm and followed her into the sitting room. Her father came up behind her. "What the devil!" Thea joined him, white as bread in the lamplight. Fanny stood with her hands pressed to her mouth. Cynthia put an arm about Fanny's shoulders comfortingly.

"My drawings are ruined!" Summer exclaimed in distress. "I was sure that I'd put the stopper back in tightly!"

No one said anything in response to Summer. They all saw the splotches on her hands, the line of splatters across the front of her dress.

Their odd behavior puzzled her. Why were they looking at her so oddly? As if . . . as if she had done it herself!

"The cat must have knocked it over," she said defiantly.

"Yes, of course," Cynthia said with her quiet good manners.

But Summer saw that no one believed her. No one at all. She turned and fled, aware of the ghastly silence behind her.

9

FAR SEEING

Notes from a lady's diary

At times, when I try to remember, I catch glimpses of my past. Vivid and three-dimensional, like those photographs viewed through a stereopticon. But there are times when, perhaps, I try too hard. When I go rushing past my childhood, far into the past, and into memories that are not mine.

When that happens I understand my family's fears of me. They must know, as I do, that it is more than imagination.

That I am losing my mind.

    Cynthia Morville announced at breakfast that she would spend the day at the villa, ostensibly to write up her field notes; but Summer suspected it was because of her outburst the previous evening, and their unspoken belief that she had spilled the ink herself, out of spite. Father must think that she was on the verge of mental collapse and that Thea might need assistance, Summer concluded. They must all be of the same mind. It was mortifying.

Worst of all was the sharp anxiety within Summer that dulled everything else: *Had* she poured the ink over her sketchbook? Could she have done it and then forgotten it, wiped it completely away? It seemed hideously possible. After all, she *had* managed to forget twelve entire years.

They were still on their first cup of coffee when Lewis Forsythe came in and found them at the breakfast table. He offered apologies for the timing of his arrival, but there was an eager gleam in his eyes as he announced the reason for his visit.

"There's an enormous yacht putting in to the harbor, sir. The *Stormy Petrel*, flying the British flag. I thought you'd want to be informed."

Richard Fairchild waved the young man to a vacant seat and Thea poured Forsythe a cup of coffee. "I've been expecting it," the professor acknowledged. "As you've probably guessed, it belongs to Sir Horace Chriswell, who is funding part of our excavations."

Thea was startled. Her housewifely instincts were in turmoil. "But I've made no preparations for guests! I'll have to find suitable rooms, get them swept and furnished, linens and additional servants. Oh, dear!"

Her father pushed back his chair and rose. Why did women always have to make a fuss over such things? "Most likely Sir Horace will stay aboard his yacht. From what I have heard, it is outfitted like a palace. He will tour the various sites, but I doubt he'll linger in Ellysian waters for very long. After

all, he is used to all the luxuries and likes to sur-
round himself with a host of glittering company."
Female company. "He'll find things a bit dull here,
I daresay."

Lewis ran a finger around his collar, as if it had
suddenly shrunk. "From the looks of it, sir, he's
brought plenty of both with him."

"The devil you say!"

Thea looked unhappy. At the very least, she
would be expected to host a dinner party or two.
How like a man not even to mention that such a visit
was imminent!

Fanny's reaction was excitement. She had heard of
Sir Horace, of course. He was known for extravagant
parties and entertainments. She *so* hoped she might
be invited aboard his yacht.

For Summer, content in her relative isolation, the
news was unsettling. The arrival of Sir Horace and
his friends was like the advent of the serpent in Eden.
She immediately began thinking of excuses to avoid
the social agenda that she knew Thea was already
composing.

Lewis finished his coffee under the professor's
impatient eye. Before his empty cup had even
touched the saucer, Richard was back with his hat
and notebook, eager to impress his financial
backer.

The two men set off for the harbor on horseback.
The day was fresh and fair, the sun mild, and the air
permeated with the scent of lilacs and lilies. When
they reached the village a curious crowd had gathered by the jetty. The throng parted to let them
through.

Fairchild's jaw dropped when he saw Horace
Chriswell's mode of transportation lying at anchor at

the center of the harbor. Lewis had not exaggerated. The vessel *was* enormous. It looked less a yacht than a ship of the British Royal Navy.

Children laughed and skipped along the sand, waiting to see what entertainment the day would provide, while their elders argued whether the *Stormy Petrel* was truly the personal possession of a wealthy man, or an official delegation of the British Crown. Even the supply steamer would look like a rowboat beside this sleek white giant.

George Symington came up to greet Richard. "Sir Horace's yacht is causing quite a sensation. They have never seen anything like it in their lives."

The professor's mouth stretched into a wry smile. "Wait until they have a look at Sir Horace himself."

They didn't have to wait long. A tender put out from the yacht, and as it drew near a murmur went through the onlookers. A rotund man stood in the bow like a figurehead. Lewis strained his eyes for a better look. "Who on earth is that?"

Richard Fairchild gave a short laugh and leaned closer to his companions. "King Horace coming to review his troops. And from the look of it, he is bringing half his court with him."

The second man was glancing back toward the yacht and his face was hidden from them. The archaeologist and his assistant went down the jetty to greet the new arrivals. Meanwhile, several others had come out on deck of the yacht: two men in summer suits, one with a military air; five ladies, one quite young, and all dressed in the height of fashion.

Within a few minutes the tender was moored and Horace Chriswell clambered out. A murmur went up from the villagers. Lewis tried not to stare. Sir

Horace was almost as wide as he was tall. He must have been standing on something in the bow, for his legs were short and thick. He was dressed with extreme care, and the finicky neatness of his pomaded hair and curly beard proclaimed his vanity as clearly as if he'd worn a sign.

Sir Horace started up the jetty in quick, jerky little strides, like a bird pecking for corn. Richard didn't know the man with him, a tall fellow with a lean, athletic build, a neat mustache, and waving brown hair worn long, like a poet's.

"Well, well, Fairchild. How are things coming along, eh? Have you any wondrous discoveries to announce? I have promised Count DiCaesari, here, and my friends that you would have fabulous treasures!"

He introduced the men. Richard was impressed. So this was DiCaesari who owned most of Ellysia, including the excavation site. The count had gracious manners and an air of elegance, coupled with extreme reserve. His speech was lightly accented and as stiff as his handshake. "I trust you have been having a good season, Professor Fairchild?"

"You will not be disappointed, Count DiCaesari. The temple complex is much larger than originally thought, and several layers deep. We've uncovered some exquisite mosaics. The workmanship is fabulous. Unlike anything I've seen elsewhere."

Sir Horace's face darkened. He hadn't paid out good money in order for Fairchild to locate old mosaics. If he wanted mosaics, damn it, he could buy them!

"And," Richard went on smoothly, "we uncovered the treasury of an earlier temple a few days ago— intact. It is an important discovery. I vow there are more wondrous gold artifacts in it than in the Valley of the Kings."

"By Jove!" Sir Horace turned a look of vindication on the nobleman. "Didn't I tell you that Fairchild was our man? I knew I was right to go with him. I'm never wrong at choosing my subordinates. It's all a matter of instinct!"

He was unaware of the insult he'd dealt, but the count flushed with embarrassment at the gaffe. He gave Richard a little shrug of understanding between gentlemen. "We must excuse him," DiCaesari's expression said, "since he knows no better, not having our good fortune in breeding."

Sir Horace didn't care. He was a self-made man. He'd had no formal schooling himself and the lack of it—or rather, others' knowledge of his lack—rankled him. After all, he had got almost everything else he had ever coveted.

It had taken him twenty-five years to work his way up from an anonymous seller of hot pies in the streets of London, to the owner of a bakery, and then a string of tea shops all across the land. Then he'd gone on to make a fortune on the Exchange. With an eye to the future he had made many generous endowments to Queen Victoria's favorite charities.

The years of effort, the careful cultivation of friends in the right places, even putting up with the sneers had all been worth it. According to Horace's good friend, the prime minister, a lifetime peerage was in the offing. He removed his monocle and polished it with a special cloth from an inner pocket. This discovery, followed by the donation of several items to the British Museum, would clinch it. Half the articles recovered were to be his. If the Italians complained, like the

Greeks had over Elgin's marbles, he'd buy them off.

The count favored Richard with a bow. "We shall be delighted to see what you have accomplished, Professor Fairchild. The mosaics intrigue me greatly." His expression suddenly turned grave. "Sad news about Carruthers. I'm sure he would have been delighted to know his suspicions of the site were correct."

"Yes. There are few who can match his stature in our mutual profession. He will be sadly missed."

Chriswell popped his monocle back in place and looked at the professor. "My good man, if Carruthers were here, it would beyond a doubt be he, and not you, who would be rocketed into the firmament along with Petrie, Schliemann, Layard, and their ilk. Now it is *your* name that will go down in the history books."

Richard was so furious he didn't trust himself to reply.

He took the two men up to the complex and gave them an abbreviated tour. Sir Horace was unhappy that most of the golden hoard had been crated up for protection, but Richard promised they would see it later. DiCaesari was amazed at what had lain hidden beneath the tall grass and rubble on the headland in the shadow of a few ruined columns and walls. It pleased him that the accomplishments of his ancestors would not go unrecognized.

Their tour finished, the count announced that he intended to go on to the *castello* to see that everything was ready for Sir Horace and the others who would be staying there with him. The contessa was a bit under the weather and would rest aboard the yacht until she could be assured that the *castello* was aired and made comfortable, he explained.

Sir Horace had been thinking rapidly. He bounced on his toes, like an excited child, and announced that he would arrange an alfresco party to celebrate the good news. He'd thought of holding it aboard the yacht, but had decided to have it at the temple complex instead. The members of the excavation team and their families were to be invited, as well as local dignitaries.

Although there was important work to be done, Richard understood it to be a command performance. He would be glad to see the last of Sir Horace, and hoped his stay would be short.

Later, as he returned to his duties, the professor was thoughtful. Chriswell was a wealthy boor, with no feeling for history. To be named in the same breath as Layard and Petrie was an honor, but Richard had no high opinion of Schliemann's scientific techniques, despite the golden hoard the wealthy German had found.

But the little man had put his finger on the importance of the find, and his comments regarding Richard's own place, had Carruthers lived, were valid. While Sir Horace worshiped wealth and position, discovery and knowledge were the twin gods in Richard's personal pantheon. If he made a brilliant breakthrough here, those deities would reward him with their greatest gift: His name would indeed go down in history. He would be immortal.

Sir Horace was uncomfortably right—there were men who would kill for that honor.

After breakfast Summer retired to her room on the pretext of taking a rest, but instead she went out to her secret terrace and worked feverishly at uncovering the mosaic she'd discovered. She retrieved her stick and knife from the clay pot in the corner and began. The trick was to sweep the dirt and debris away without breaking the thin layer of plaster. She clambered over the low surround and sat inside.

If she was too hasty it crumbled and got into the cracks of the mosaic beneath, where the grout was missing. The next step was to slide a piece of thin metal she'd found in one of the storerooms under the plaster, and pry it gently away. Usually she could only get a few inches at a time, but once or twice page-sized sheets had cracked and broken free.

Hoping it would reveal more of the subject, she began her task in another spot. The very act of doing physical labor eased her mind and soothed her bruised spirits. There was a pleasure in seeing things take form, like the pleasure Thea took in her sewing, or Fanny in the court gardens, although that, she knew, was largely due to Giovanni's handsome presence.

She'd been remiss with Fanny, Summer thought suddenly. She would try to spend more time with her. She considered enlisting her younger sister in her project, but dismissed it almost immediately. Fanny had no discretion, and a tongue that ran on wheels. The secret would soon be out, and Summer wasn't ready to admit the others into her private little world. For one thing, they'd be sure to put a stop to her work on the mosaic altogether.

Her stick wedged beneath the plaster and a large section broke away. A doe's face looked up at her, all dark, startled eyes. Delighted, she pried up another piece. It was as easy to remove as the previous one.

Although the plaster looked smooth, it was coarse and crumbly beneath the finish, as if it had been done in slipshod haste.

Summer wondered more and more why anyone would cover up a work of such beauty. She sat back to wipe her forehead with her sleeve. An awful notion struck her. Could it be that the center was ruined, or that it had never been finished at all? That all her hours of effort would produce nothing more than an exquisite border around a huge patch of rough mortar?

She silenced her qualms. Deep in her heart she knew that there was something fabulous waiting to be discovered here. Summer even dreamed about it in her sleep, although upon waking she could recall none of the details. Little by little she found herself planning her day around the times when she could slip away to work at clearing it.

The task was more than busywork, it had become her obsession. It was a test of her commitment, and when she finished, it would be a testament of personal achievement. Proof that she could accomplish something of worth with her life, if she would only be granted the opportunity!

After ten minutes of effort she'd only managed to clear a section three inches wide. It was difficult reaching over the stone edging and her back and leg ached from the strain. Summer sat back upon her heels and wiped her brow with the back of her arm. Her family would think she had lost her mind entirely, if they could see her now, sitting amid the dust and leaf mold, in the center of an abandoned fountain!

Her face sobered. She would never have done such a thing at Kingsmeade, nor would she have been allowed to. With Nana, bless her dear heart, hovering like a hen with one chick, and the other servants almost as bad, Summer would never have thought of it. Much less attempted it. She was glad they'd come to Ellysia.

Although the vine checkered the terrace with shade, blazing light pierced through between the leaves. She closed her eyes against the brightness of the azure sky showing between the leaves. At first the hot Mediterranean sun had felt harsh and alien. Now it was a benison. Heat radiated from the air and from the stucco beneath her back, seeping through her like warm honey.

She smiled and went back to work. It went much more quickly. Large patches of plaster broke off and her excitement grew. A section of flower-strewn meadow and a woman's foot and ankle were revealed, with a gauzy shawl or perhaps a length of ribbon curling past them. The hunch she'd been nurturing grew. Could this be Persephone, dancing in the meadow with her handmaidens, unaware that Dis was thundering up out of the earth to carry her away?

Yes, there was something that looked like the edge of his chariot wheel. She pried at it but the plaster was too hard. Forcing it might damage the mosaic. She mustn't take the chance. Moving to another area, she was able to uncover more flowers and a delicate border that was probably the hem of a woman's skirt.

A soft sound caught her attention and she sat up to find that the sable cat had joined her. It sprawled on its side in the sun, licking its paws. There wasn't a spot or stain on the velvety pink pads, as there must have been if the cat had knocked over the bottle of

India ink. Summer reached out and tickled the furry little tummy.

The cat took that as an invitation and jumped into her lap, where it made itself quite at home, purring loudly. Summer felt immediately better. They said that animals had a sixth sense about people who were disturbed, but Pandora treated her normally. Small comfort, but she would take any she could get.

An hour or more had passed. She had best join the others before they came looking for her. Perhaps she would see if Fanny wanted to dig up some of the wildflowers growing outside the villa's walls, to plant in the gardens. Giovanni had taken the donkey cart and gone out to the meadow near the temple complex earlier, where there were banks of lemon yellow lilies. He planned to put them along one wall of the outer courtyard to add a splash of sunshine.

Summer left the cat to doze and went back to her room, where she washed hurriedly and redressed her hair.

Zita came out to the terrace, where Thea was writing letters, with a note sent up from the excavation site, along with a letter that Sir Horace had picked up in Naples for delivery to them. "Oh, it is from Nana! She must be feeling much better to be able to write to us already." Thea set the letters aside and opened the note.

"From my father," Thea said as Cynthia came out to join her. "Count DiCaesari has returned to Ellysia this morning with Sir Horace Chriswell."

"Ah, yes," Zita added. "The entire village is elated. It has been five years since the count has come back to his ancestral home." Her black eyes danced with excitement. "It is whispered that he and the contessa are expected to remain for several weeks."

There would be great doings at the *castello*, Zita prophesied. That meant there would be servants needed there. Pellegrina could save up for her dowry, and Zita's young man could earn enough to take them to Naples for their honeymoon to meet his family.

The count and contessa's arrival created ripples in the quiet pond that was the Court of Three Sisters. Fanny hoped aloud that there would be invitations to dine and other entertainments. Thea privately acknowledged that an infusion of fresh personalities would enhance their social circle. While she enjoyed Cynthia Morville's company, she had spent entirely too much time with her sisters in the preceding weeks.

Mrs. Symington seemed to have no interests other than her husband and her endless knitting, which she took with her everywhere, like Madame DeFarge. Thea could imagine the two dowagers as kindred souls, sitting before the guillotine, their needles flying, as royal heads rolled. As for Miss Symington, she found the poetess, with her acerbic tongue and air of cultivated ennui, to be almost as taxing.

"We are invited to an early supper given by Sir Horace," Thea announced after reading the rest of the note. "How very odd! It is to be at the excavation site."

Cynthia Morville raised her eyebrows. "How very like Sir Horace, you mean. He is known for his eccentricities, but also for his lavish entertainments. I am sure we should enjoy it greatly."

Thea scratched out a note of acceptance and looked around for Zita, but the maid had left the room. Fanny entered and her sister explained, and handed the reply to her. "Please take this to the messenger. I shall go tell Summer of the invitation. Perhaps it will get her out of the doldrums."

Fanny hurried out of the room, making a face. She wasn't a servant to be sent on errands. Not when she needed to go through her wardrobe and decide which outfit to wear to meet Sir Horace, and to dress her hair again in a more mature fashion and—

She stopped dead in her tracks. Giovanni stood in the outer court, his face dark as thunder. Fanny hurried to him. "What is wrong?"

"I am to report to the foreman at the excavation site. I am no longer to care for the gardens."

"Oh, Giovanni!"

Her cry of distress wrung his romantic heart. She was dressed in pink and rose and with her golden hair, he thought that she was as fresh, as breathtakingly beautiful, as the dawn sky. He was smitten with her. His mouth went dry and his tongue seemed too thick and unwieldy for the delicate words he longed to say to her.

Fanny's reaction was almost as strong. Since he'd rescued her during the earthquake, he had never been far from her thoughts. Within the walls of the villa, built by generations long dead, he was so beautiful and masculine, so vital and alive that he took her breath away.

Giovanni reached out and caught her hand between his. "How can I see you, if we are to be separated?" he said in low, impassioned tones. "Now that I am no longer to work at the villa, I will have no excuse to come here, and I think I will die if I do not see your sweet face and hear your lovely voice every day! You have stolen my heart, *carissima.*"

Fanny's equally romantic heart was thrilled at his

ardor. Then dismay set in. "We must meet. You must find a way!"

"Ah, my princess. My queen." He kissed her fingertips.

A shadow fell over them like a raven's wing. Signora Perani stood just inside the courtyard arch. "Santa Maria! Giovanni, have you lost your mind, to be making up to one of the young ladies of the house?"

She came up to him and cuffed his ear, as she had done a dozen times before. The young man blushed a fiery red beneath his tan, embarrassed that his aunt treated him like a child in front of this . . . this *goddess.*

Fanny was equally appalled. "How dare you strike him!"

The housekeeper turned her dark eyes on Fanny. "It is nothing to what your father would do to him, Signorina, if he saw this foolish boy kissing your hands. Eh, he would be glad to get off with a mere boxing of his ears, I tell you!"

Giovanni was more insulted at being called a boy in front of his inamorata than he was at being slapped in the face. Fanny drew herself up in the same haughty way that she has seen Thea use to such quelling effect.

"You have mistaken the situation," she said curtly. "Giovanni has delivered a message from my father."

It didn't have the same results. Signora Perani was undaunted.

"Ah, no. It is you, Signorina, who have made the mistake. And you will bring much trouble down upon my nephew by your lack of decorum. He needs the money that working for the professor brings in, to help his widowed mother. Yes, and to set aside for the bride price, when he takes Natalia Vico as his wife!"

"His wife!"

Fanny turned accusing eyes upon Giovanni. Tears shimmered against her blue eyes, making them look twice as bright.

Her voice broke the spell that bound Giovanni. He was her slave. He would have swum across to Hades and walked over boiling lava in the volcano's caldera for her, if she had asked him. And he had no intention of marrying the Vico girl, now or ever. He said this, in no uncertain terms.

Signora Perani glowered. "All the village knows that you call upon Natalia and have taken her bride gifts. Your own mother has told me this as well. She will make you a fine wife, that one. You will have many healthy sons."

Giovanni flushed to the roots of his hair. "Your information is incorrect," he said stiffly. "My mother is building cloud castles. I am not courting Natalia Vico, or any of the village girls. My heart is already given away to another."

His aunt cuffed him again. "Simpleton! Be off with you! And if the professor discovers you are setting your eyes too high, he is likely to put them out!"

Since the respect due an elder kept him from retorting, Giovanni turned from his aunt abruptly, bowed low to Fanny, then walked away.

His blood was so roiled by his aunt's interference, his eyes so blinded by a vision of the beautiful Signorina Fairchild, that he almost tripped over one of the cats lolling in the atrium. It yowled, hissed, and darted off in a blur of yellow fur.

Fanny wrung her hands in dismay. She couldn't bear to see him leave. Giovanni looked back over his shoulder. When he saw her still there, a look of such worship and longing shone in his eyes that she was dazzled by it. She sent him a smile that could have melted candles and his face was suddenly illuminated from within.

He rode off in the donkey cart. If not the most heroic mode of transportation, it was ameliorated by his own physical beauty. Fanny watched him until he was lost to sight, and spent the next few minutes thinking of Montagues and Capulets, and giving all for love.

She hoped the signora wouldn't carry tales to her father.

The novelty of the invitation soon drew Fanny out of her daydreaming. She didn't think that Giovanni would begrudge her a few hours of happiness in the midst of their mutual misery at being parted, and perhaps they might snatch a few moments alone.

It cheered her to think that at last she would have a chance in real company to wear some of the lovely afternoon gowns she'd bought in London. It was a waste wearing them with no better audience than her sisters and Papa. Summer had no notions at all of fashion, and Thea's were so old-fashioned they bordered on the gothic. As for her father, his idea of a well-dressed female was someone in a tunic and toga.

At least Mrs. Morville understood. While her wardrobe was limited and the color subdued, the fabrics were quite good and she had a definite flair. Fanny offered to dress Mrs. Morville's hair more becomingly. In return the widow volunteered to lend Fanny a pair of pearl-and-lapis lazuli earrings.

"They bring out the sapphire color of your eyes beautifully," she said admiringly. Fanny blushed and glanced at the mirror again. The dark blue stones did show her off to advantage, and made her feel very grown-up.

There was quite a commotion as the ladies readied themselves for their engagement. Fanny felt quite sophisticated in pale blue embroidered all over with tiny forget-me-nots while Cynthia was elegant in yellow with openwork panels. Thea had chosen a gown of soft rose embroidered with pale green. If they were a bouquet of blossoming English womanhood, the thorn was Summer. She refused to go.

Summer was afraid that she couldn't see the spot where Jethroe Adams had fallen to his death without provoking one of her peculiar visions. She wished now that she had answered Col McCallum's question about what she had seen; but even though she wanted very much to talk with him again, she was not ready to face the invisible procession along the Via Sacra, or let loose memories of the tide pool that haunted her, waking and sleeping.

She couldn't explain in any way that Thea would understand. Indeed, an explanation would only make them more certain that her mind was becoming unhinged. There was only one excuse she could fall back on, and she did.

"I have no desire to dine with total strangers, who can have as little interest in meeting me as I do in meeting them. I shall remain here with the signora and Zita."

What Thea saw as her sister's stubbornness exasperated her beyond all measure. "Without Count DiCaesari's permission and the financial assistance of Sir Horace, this expensive expedition could not have been launched. It would not do for us, *any* of us, to offend them."

Summer saw there was nothing for it. She would have to rely on Thea's fear that she would be difficult, and that the best course of action was to leave her at home. "I doubt they will miss me, unless they find watching a cripple stumble over the ruins a form of high entertainment."

It didn't work. Thea was so angry that all the color drained from her face. "People would not be so conscious of your limp if you did not throw it in their faces at every opportunity! For once think of Father, and not yourself!"

Bright color flared in Summer's face but she would not back down. "I am thinking of him. If I felt my presence would help or that my absence would hinder him in any way, you may be sure I would make the effort. As it is, I see the only outcome would be an exhausting day, where I would possibly embarrass everyone concerned with another fainting spell."

Tears of contrition sprang to Thea's eyes and she put her hand out beseechingly to her sister. "Forgive me! I did not mean to be so harsh! You are right of course . . . how—how could I have forgotten?" She rubbed her temples. "I have been under such strain these past few months that I can scarcely think and . . . oh!"

To Summer's astonishment, her elder sister broke into sobs and turned to flee the room. She tripped over a hassock and clutched at a table to keep from falling. Summer went to her side. "What is it?" She could not ever remember Thea losing her composure so absolutely. It was frightening.

Putting her arms around Thea, she helped her to

the settee. "Something is dreadfully wrong. I have suspected it for some time now. Will you tell me what it is and how I may help you?"

Thea could only sob like a brokenhearted child. Cynthia heard and came to the door of the room. Summer shook her head, warning her not to intrude, and the widow went away at once. Thea wept until her eyes were swollen.

"Martin . . . Martin has left me. . . ."

Summer was nonplussed. "He is a diplomat. He had no choice, although I am sure he would much rather have—"

"*No!* Martin has *left* me. Our marriage is over in everything but name."

"*What?*" That was inconceivable to Summer.

She remembered the way Martin had looked back at Thea as he drove away from Kingsmeade before leaving for Brazil. Although her brother-in-law was not a sentimental man—far from it!—he had seemed to her to be a man deeply in love with his wife. But Summer was out of her depth now, and thoroughly ashamed. How foolish and blind she had been, wrapped up in her own selfishness, while Thea had carried this great burden in silent agony.

She cradled Thea in her arms. "Oh, my dear! I didn't know. All those letters you've written to him . . ."

Thea sat up and dabbed her eyes with her lace handkerchief, fighting for control of her emotions. "And never sent. I hadn't the courage, and I had a deal too much pride to let him know how this has . . . has *devastated* me!"

Without warning Fanny popped into the room, all smiles and golden curls. "The carriage is ready. We must hurry or we shall be late." The stiffness of her sisters' posture and Thea's reddened eyes registered upon her. Her own grew wide in alarm.

"What has happened? Not Father?" A world of love and fear was in her trembling voice.

For Thea that was like a call to arms. Someone needed her and she responded. Rising, she crumpled her tearstained handkerchief in her palm. "Everything is fine," she said in her usual brisk tones. "I'm sorry we frightened you. Summer was kindly removing a speck from my eye." Her chin lifted bravely. "I am ready now."

The change in her was miraculous, Summer thought in considerable awe. She had not expected Thea to be so strong, nor such an accomplished actress. A pang filled her heart. They were sisters, yet they knew so little of one another. It was enlightening knowledge, and it was very humbling.

She put her hand on Thea's arm. "If you like I will come with you."

Thea smiled, blinking another sting of tears away, and put her own hand over her sister's. Summer was growing up. Or had grown up, while she had barely noticed. "There is no time for you to change," she said softly, "and you need to rest. Don't worry, I—that is, my eye is all right now. I shall manage."

And she would. They both knew that it was true.

Cynthia came in, tying a fetching bonnet over her hair. "Giovanni says the horse is getting impatient."

Giovanni? Fanny was instantly diverted. Coming into the room she had sensed something dark and tragic, but it had only been her imagination. She went tripping lightly out to the courtyard. Mrs. Morville had exquisite taste. She had made a very good choice in suggesting the blue earrings, Fanny thought happily. They did make her eyes seem large and even bluer. She wondered if Giovanni would notice.

The villa was silent, dreaming its ancient dreams. The servants had left shortly after the carriage, for it was another feast day in the village. Summer thought of repairing to her secret terrace, to continue her work of uncovering the mosaic, but the balmy air had seduced her to idleness.

Excusing herself by noting she'd already uncovered three square feet of the masterpiece and was aching in every limb, she decided to indulge herself with a few chapters of a much-loved book. She was sprawled on some plump cushions with her well-thumbed volume of *Jane Eyre*.

Novels were her secret vice. Although Father did not approve of them in general, he had let her have a subscription to not one but two lending libraries. Their groom at Kingsmeade had made both regular stops on his weekly errands. The copy of *Jane Eyre* had been a birthday gift from Thea.

She let the book fall open in her lap, unread. Poor Thea. Life was not turning out like a romantic novel for her. Yet Summer was sure that there was some mistake. Why would Martin leave Thea, perfect Thea? The more she thought of it, the more she was sure there was an explanation. Perhaps Martin was angry that Thea had not gone with him. Again Summer pictured his face as he turned back for one last glimpse of his wife. No, there was no anger there. Only loneliness and great longing. It was a puzzle to which she had no key. Summer tried to read again. She loved the story of gentle, fairylike

Jane who had tamed Mr. Rochester with her inner
beauty. But whenever Summer tried to picture the
novel's hero, his face was constantly blotted out by
that of Col McCallum. She sighed and set the book
aside. Well, then, she could lie here all afternoon,
looking out at the sea and pretending she was living
back in ancient times, or she could get to work on
the mosaic again.

With everyone gone this was a perfect opportunity, and she really should take advantage of it. For
once, it wouldn't matter how grimy she got. It was a
trial to keep herself always in good repair, in case
someone came looking for her. By locking her chamber door she gave herself just enough time to strip
off her gloves, get inside, and wipe the perspiration
from her face with a dry towel. But this afternoon
they would be gone for many hours. That decided
her.

She changed into the old gown that she wore for
working, and which she kept hidden in a bandbox at
the back of the wardrobe shelf. Out of habit she
closed the door to her room and slid the tiny bolt
into place. Pushing back the tapestry, she went out
to the terrace. Heat rose from the pavement in shimmering waves, the sea was mirror bright.
Fortunately, the vine cast shade over the mosaic at
this time of day.

Summer realized suddenly that she was happy.
Truly, deeply, happy. How had she ever stood her life
at Kingsmeade, with nothing to look forward to but
afternoon tea? There were so many things to do on
Ellysia that interested her, from this secret project to
Mrs. Morville's restorations to—yes, admit it! To
Col McCallum's visits. It surprised her that he hadn't
come by to inquire after her welfare. It was the usual

thing to do, and it seemed unlike him not to have done so.

A drop of sweat trickled into her eyes and she wiped it away. The sun was growing fierce. Staying much longer would be courting a nasty burn on any exposed skin. It was time to call a halt. Summer rolled over and levered herself up.

It was easier to make out the design forming from a standing position. Another pair of slender legs, in a lily-strewn meadow, had been revealed by the afternoon's work. She was more sure than ever that it was going to show Persephone and her handmaidens. Or Cliete.

The earth shook beneath her feet and she ducked as something hurtled down at her, like a falling stone block. Then the projectile wavered and vanished. The ground was as solid as it ever was. She had only stood up too fast, she told herself, and got dizzy.

She was relieved. For a horrible moment she'd imagined that she was about to fall into one of her imaginary scenes. An idea arose in her brain, persistent and unwelcome, that the shaking ground and falling block were as valid memories as the dreadful tide pool. She pushed it away quickly.

Time to go in. Summer started for the door. Her damp hair hung in ringlets around her face. Pulling back the strands that had come free from her nape, she accidentally scratched her cheek with a bit of stucco clinging to the side of her hand.

Her bedchamber seemed dim as a cave in comparison to the glare out on the terrace. Summer poured water from the pitcher into the matching basin on the little table she used for a washstand. She dipped the cloth in and held it to her throat. It felt wonderful against her heated skin, but seemed to evaporate almost immediately. Perhaps she should strip down to her shift.

Her hands were on the second button from the top when she heard a footstep in the corridor. Summer listened. Had one of the servants returned? She glanced at the clock. It was far too early for them. She realized that she'd been hearing sounds of movement for several minutes; since she was so used to a houseful of people she hadn't noticed it until now.

A door opened. A few seconds later it closed again. Silence. Then the squeak of Fanny's door—she recognized it, because its hinges needed oiling.

Another pause. Another squeak. Fanny's door closed. Soft footfalls coming closer. Summer's heart jumped up into her throat. There was no reason for anyone from the household to go through the place in such a furtive manner. Her mouth was dry as old wool.

What was that? She pricked her ears. There it was again. A light footstep, barely audible, coming toward her own door. She stumbled back and hit her washstand.

The china pitcher chinked softly against the basin. Summer gasped and held her breath. To her it seemed to clang like a suit of armor, but she knew it was fear that heightened her senses. Had it actually been loud enough to have been heard on the other side of the door? As she watched, the handle turned, but the little bolt held firm. Summer stood rooted to the ground, her hand pressed against her heart.

Someone was in the house. Someone who shouldn't be there. It seemed as if she stood there for hours, waiting. Listening. And someone on the far side of the door was doing the same. She was sure of it.

After an eternity she heard a soft rustle and the sound of careful footfalls, moving away. Summer was frozen. She didn't know what to do. How she longed for a keyhole to peek through, but the old-fashioned door had none.

Pressing her eye to the tiny crack between the door and jamb she tried to look out. All that was visible was a section of featureless wall. Now she was in a quandary. There was no way out except through the door and down the corridor leading to the courtyard. She was trapped.

She had no weapon, and certainly was not fleet enough to evade any intruder. It was a damnable situation. Were those footsteps coming this way again, more stealthily than before? With the flimsy bolt she couldn't chance it. Summer escaped through the hidden door and went into the place she had come to call Persephone's garden.

Moving with awkward haste, she crossed to the throne and sat on the ground on the far side of it, where she would be least visible from the doorway. Tired and shivering, she waited there until she was stiff and hungry, and time lost all meaning.

Gradually the stones soaked up heat, but the lingering warmth was soporific. She'd worked hard and fatigue caught up with her. Summer sat with her back to the throne, nodding and fighting the urge to fall asleep. She was afraid she couldn't keep her eyes open any longer.

Perhaps the intruder had gone. She crept quickly back to her bedchamber and listened at the door. As she leaned against it the bolt wobbled in the shaft.

"Miss Fairchild?"

She jumped back in alarm, then drew in a deep breath. *Col McCallum.* So he was the intruder. She

felt very foolish and opened the door. He stood looking down at her through narrowed eyes. "What on
earth have you been doing?"

She found her voice. It came out hoarse and tight.
"I might ask you the same."

Col favored her with his most charming smile.
"Looking for you, of course."

"You might have tried calling out, rather than
making yourself free of the house and frightening me
half to death!"

"I apologize for doing so, but I have been calling
for you. I knew you were here alone. I saw the others at the temple site. When you didn't answer I
became concerned. I was afraid you'd taken another
tumble."

Her indignation died out in a rush of breath. He
certainly had a point there. Five minutes! Was that all
it had been? It had seemed like a lifetime. She was
mortified. "That was kind of you. I expected that you
would be off with the rest, being wined and dined by
Sir Horace and his friends."

So, she didn't know of his altercation with her
father. Well, that was just as well. "I had other fish to
fry." Col looked her up and down. "What in God's
name *have* you been doing, cleaning out the grates?"

"I beg your pardon?"

He walked over and swung her around by the
shoulders until she caught her reflection in the looking glass. His meaning was painfully clear. With
streaks of dirt across her face and her hair in disarray, she looked like a chimney sweep. Her hand fluttered up to her hair. It was no use. She tilted her chin
up with an expression that Thea would have recognized instantly.

"Had I known I would be receiving company this

afternoon," she said pointedly, "I would have been better prepared."

He broke into a grin. "I should certainly hope so. You look like the kind of relative one keeps locked up in a garret, like Mr. Rochester's mad wife."

His reference to *Jane Eyre* unsettled her, following so closely upon her foolish daydreams, and her fears for her sanity. Summer had had enough. "You found your way in, Mr. McCallum. I'm sure you can find your way out again."

"What, aren't you going to invite me to stay awhile?"

"No. It would be totally inappropriate, and it is late. I intend to freshen up before my family returns."

His ready laugh rang out. "It would take a bit more than freshening up, my dear Miss Fairchild. What *have* you been up to?"

She was startled but recovered quickly. "Having nothing better to occupy my time, I decided to do some more exploring."

He'd registered that flash of something in her eyes. "And have you made any spectacular finds?" The treasure that Sir John Carruthers hid, for instance?

He didn't say it aloud, but she was aware of a subtle change in him. "More cobwebs and more spiders than I care to think about."

He relaxed fractionally. "Good. Then you won't mind leaving it for another day. There's to be an interesting spectacle in the village this afternoon. The annual Blessing of the Blossoms. I thought you might like to see it. It begins with a procession from the church to a small shrine in the hills, where blossoms from all the trees and flowers are brought, along with shoots of new growth from the fields. I think you might enjoy it."

He'd snared her attention. Pellegrina had told the sisters about the ceremony, but neither Thea nor Fanny had been interested. Summer had thought it sounded colorful and fascinating. There was a Roman Catholic church near Kingsmeade, but she couldn't imagine its sober parishioners marching through the high street with plaster saints and satin banners, strewing flowers in their wake.

But there was no way to reach the shrine by carriage, only a steep footpath wound up to it from behind the church. Summer knew she could never negotiate the climb. She made an airy gesture of dismissal. "I've seen the shrine from a distance. I don't care to see it at closer hand."

A single line creased Col's brow. "Don't lie to me. Or, for that matter, to yourself."

"Oh," she replied with cool sarcasm, "and are you able to see into my mind, Mr. McCallum, and know my thoughts better than I do myself?"

Col took her chin between his fingers and forced her to look up at him. "Your thoughts are very easy to read, Miss Fairchild. For all you keep your features so carefully schooled, your eloquent eyes give you away." He smiled at her. "Every time!"

Summer was embarrassed. How much could he really see in her eyes when he looked into them so intently? Did he know how his presence excited and confused her? Startled and a little afraid, she lowered her lashes to shield herself from his penetrating gaze.

He chuckled softly. "So, you do have secrets to hide. I wonder . . ."

Her heart beat a little faster. For a moment she almost believed that he could read her mind and see the sorrows and yearnings buried there. He relinquished her chin abruptly.

"But we're digressing. If it's the long walk and steep ascent that concern you, there is another place from which to view the ceremony that is accessible by carriage." He saw her hesitation and knew she meant to refuse. "You really should take advantage of my offer," he said, rather sharply, "instead of holing up in the villa like a frightened rabbit hiding in its burrow."

She sent him a withering look. "At the risk of being as rude as yourself, Mr. McCallum, may I remind you that my actions are none of your business?"

He lounged against the door frame, a sardonic smile tilting one corner of his mouth. "Now that's much better! Genteel sweetness sets my teeth on edge. I much prefer a woman with a little pepper on her tongue."

She blushed furiously. His voice took a tone that changed his teasing words into something entirely different in meaning. How *did* he manage to invest everything he said with undercurrents of intimacy? "You are a horrid man, Mr. McCallum! You take a positive delight in embarrassing me."

"Perhaps it's because you look so becoming with your cheeks all pink and rosy. You may be as rude as you like in return, Miss Fairchild. But I can guarantee that it won't stop me. I'll continue to ask you impertinent questions until you stop hiding from me, and the world at large, inside these walls."

"I am not hiding!"

He came intimidatingly closer. "Aren't you?"

When he looked at her with that odd light in his eyes, Summer found that she lost all objectivity. She backed up, he came forward. She bumped into the corner of the room. Col leaned in, planting both hands on the wall, on either side of her head.

"Walls can be wonderful things, Miss Fairchild. They give shelter, support, and protection. But as you can see, they also form a trap."

His nearness, his deep masculine scent, overwhelmed her. She felt helpless, and that frightened her. It also made her exceedingly angry. "Why are you doing this?" Her voice quavered. "Why won't you just go away and leave me in peace?"

"Because you are an intelligent and interesting woman, far too young to lock yourself away, as I pointed out before, like a cloistered nun."

He cupped her chin in his hand and touched the corner of her mouth with his thumb. Her soft mouth trembled and he fought the sudden urge to lean down and kiss her. The impulse came out of nowhere, so acute, so intense that it took all his command to control it.

"You were never meant to be a nun, my dear. I can tell you that for certain."

A shiver ran through Summer. His eyes were green and troubled as a stormy sea, arousing strange currents in her blood. She marshaled her courage and pushed his hand away. "From your vast experience of women?"

Unexpectedly, that made him laugh. "As you say, Miss Fairchild."

His sangfroid annoyed her. "I find you insufferable! I wish you would go away."

"Do you?" He looked at her with interest, his eyes showing bright with the laughter they held. "What an original you are. No other woman has ever told me that."

"Perhaps they didn't have the courage!" Almost instantly she saw the trap she'd fallen into.

"And you do?" he said. "There was a time, Miss

Fairchild, when I thought so, but I'm rapidly revising my opinion. If you did, you wouldn't hesitate to take another drive with me."

Her face changed. One moment it mirrored her every emotion; the next it was a plaster mask, stiff and impenetrable. Col felt a sharp pang of remorse. He knew he'd hurt her. And he knew he would hurt her again, if need be. It was inevitable.

He caught her hands in his. "I respect bravery. Tell me, was I wrong to think you have it?"

He pulled her toward him until they were almost touching. Summer had no power to resist. Her breasts brushed against his jacket and a thrill of panic ran through her. Or so she thought. She was unused to repartee with a handsome man and afraid of making a fool of herself in front of him; but she was even more afraid of seeing him turn around and walk out the door, because she feared he wouldn't come back again.

"I suppose I could have no objection to a drive. The ceremony does sound quite intriguing."

He laughed and kissed her fingertips before letting her go. "I've a picnic basket packed. I hope you like cold chicken."

Summer shot him a shrewd look. "Were you so sure of me? Again?"

Col's face sobered. "Not at all. You are a very special kind of woman, Miss Fairchild. Only a fool would take you for granted."

She smiled suddenly, with a shy brilliance that lit up her eyes and brought fresh color to her cheeks.

Summer fetched her shawl and hat, and he escorted her out to the carriage. She knew that she should never have agreed to his foolish scheme, yet she hadn't wanted to look like a coward in his eyes.

Col's thoughts were running in similar lines. He had discovered that pride was the one spur Miss Fairchild responded to most strongly: a very useful piece of information.

As they drove away from the villa, Summer's muscles were aching and sore from all the unaccustomed exercise. They cut past a grove of trees and down a narrow, steep-sided ravine overhung with thick, leafy branches. It was like plunging into the heart of the underworld, Summer thought. She was relieved when they came out into sunshine a few minutes later.

They were in a shady copse, with a clear view of the shrine atop a sunny hill opposite. An ideal place to see and be seen. To make it perfect, a zephyr played lightly over their faces, bringing the fresh scent of flowers with it.

Col helped her down by the simple expedient of taking her firmly about the waist and lifting her to the ground. His sudden nearness filled her with unfamiliar sensations, not all of them pleasant. It made her feel protected, yet incredibly vulnerable. She was glad when he released her. For a moment they were still close to one another. She glanced up and found him watching her intently.

To be the focus of that sudden, fierce scrutiny was more than she could bear. Summer stepped away.

Col pretended not to notice. He spread the carriage rug for her to sit on. He sat beside her, aware of her soft eau de toilette, but not that she'd put it on with him in mind, or the effort of will she was making to appear relaxed. She doubted that she had ever been so aware of another human being. She tried not to think about it.

They were about thirty yards from the shrine. Summer had only seen it from afar, and had expected a sort of madonna, or an icon of the Virgin like the one in the village church. The two columns that had appeared to be of white stone were a gray volcanic rock on closer examination. They framed a sort of rude natural altar of black lava on which reposed a chunk of red volcanic stone that roughly resembled a woman. It appeared to be a product of natural weathering and not the hand of man.

Above the stone, a triangle of fired brick was crowned with the face of a woman, sculpted from marble. On her head was a coronet fashioned from a sheaf of wheat. "Why, it looks like a pagan altar," she said to Col.

"It is, or was. But like most such places, over time its use was usurped by Christian worship. The Blessing of the Blossoms is really a transmogrification of an ancient rite to Demeter, which was supposed to ensure good crops."

He thought it better not to describe the rites more fully, and was glad she didn't ask him to. Fortunately for modesty's sake, her attention was already distracted.

"Look, here they come now!" Summer had spotted the start of the procession leaving the church and leaned forward eagerly. Voices were raised in song, and snatches of melody wafted on the air.

The entire village had turned out for the event. Three boys in white led the procession, one carrying a tall crucifix. Next was a double line of the youngest children, with baskets of flower petals, which they sprinkled like fragrant confetti with every step. The priest came after them, swinging a pierced brass censer on a long chain. Clouds of incense wafted from it with every swing. Within a few moments the breeze brought its rich, oriental scent, redolent of sandalwood and spices, to Summer and Col.

The congregation came after the priest. They wore their traditional feast-day garments, the women in white blouses with dark red skirts and fringed green aprons, the men in tight trousers of the same red, with white tunics sashed in green. The children of the village were dressed all in white and their feet were bare. All had floral garlands around their necks, and the women and girls had chaplets of red and white blossoms.

Next came the religious societies with tasseled silk banners like colorful sails, each one embroidered with the picture of a saint. The strongest young men of the village carried a heavy litter, decked with all manner of flowers and covered with a fabric that glittered like cloth of gold. Atop it rode a statue of the Virgin Mary, crowned with a wreath of flowers and fitted with a white satin cape.

As they mounted the hillside their hymn grew louder. It was a joyous song, unlike the solemn Latin chants Summer had heard in the church, and augmented by the jingle of small instruments that looked like tambourines. She was utterly enchanted.

A sense of shifting light disoriented her. A new scene took form. Young girls in white, dancing up the hillside to the shrine, women gowned in blue, followed by priestesses in ornate headdresses . . . no, no! Not here. Not now!

Summer struggled against it and won. The vision faded and the villagers were back where they had been a moment earlier. She closed her eyes in gratitude.

Col's hand covered hers, warm and solid and comforting. "It happened again, didn't it?"

Her eyes opened and she stared at him. "I have no idea of what you are talking about."

He released her and she felt suddenly adrift, like a bit of wood tossed on the surface of a wide and empty sea. "I do understand what is happening," he told her quietly, "although I've never had a real experience with it."

She started to shiver. He knew that she had hallucinations, that she was going mad. And yet, he wasn't horrified as her family always was when they discovered she'd been "seeing things" again.

"I already told you what I saw once at Thermopylae." He turned toward Summer until their eyes met. "What I didn't tell you was that I was with two other men. They saw and heard nothing. They claimed it was a mirage, or that I'd gotten a touch of sunstroke. But I knew. It was as real as you are, standing here beside me."

His eyes darkened with emotion. "For an instant I had seen the past. However, it wasn't really the past. In that brief moment the past and present merged, became one, and I was blessed with the ability to see it."

Summer was amazed at his reconstruction of the phenomenon. "But how could that happen and why?"

He took her hand again and held it loosely in his strong clasp. Instantly she was safe and anchored in reality. Col looked out over the hill. "I can't explain it, Miss Fairchild. The intricacies of the human mind are in the realm of the physician and the philosopher. I am neither."

His wide smile creased his face. "But I am a Scot by blood. We of Celtic stock grow up with 'ghosties' and 'sightings' and 'things that go bump in the night.' While we have no monopoly on such things, they are as much a part of our lives as porridge and haggis."

She returned his smile tenfold. It all made sense when he explained it. "Then I'm not losing my mind. There is a reason for the 'spells' that have plagued me." Summer shook her head in wonderment.

"Tell me," Col asked, "have you any Celts hiding in the foliage of your family tree?"

"My mother's grandfather was a Welshman."

He tilted his head. "Ah, then that will explain your talent."

"You make it sound so prosaic! Like having a natural inclination for drawing, or the ability to sing on key!"

"To me, it is. Let me tell you why. My grandmother had 'the sight' and people came from miles around to consult with her in matters of urgency. My mother's gift was different, and manifested itself in homely ways. For instance, she always knew the day my father would return in his ship, after weeks at sea. Time after time she would put up a hearty meal and go down to the strand just as he sailed over the horizon. I never knew her to be wrong."

Summer mulled that over. "You call it a gift, Mr. McCallum, and believe that is what you have given me. You see, I always thought of it as a curse. The next step but one to madness." She bit her lower lip. "For as long as I can remember, I have tried to fight it."

"That in itself can cause difficulties, I suppose. I can't imagine trying not to see or hear."

She sighed as if a huge load had been taken from her. "Thank you."

He could tell that he'd given her much to think

over. "We'll discuss this again, if you like. But I'm sure you would rather watch the ceremony than play question-and-answer with me."

Turning her attention to the procession, she watched the Blessing of the Blossoms unfold. All the while she was singing inside. She wasn't losing her mind. It was as ordinary an occurrence to him as the rising and setting of the sun.

If she lived to be a hundred she would never forget what he had done for her this day.

Which was why, perhaps, she let him kiss her later, when he returned her to the villa. He didn't ask her permission.

One moment they were standing inside the inner court, where the trees were opening their flowers to the sun, shaking hands. The next she was in his arms with her chin tilted up and his mouth warm and tender upon hers. She couldn't think, she couldn't move. She could only feel his heart beating against hers until their rhythms mingled, and his lips as they pressed against hers, growing ever more possessive and hungry.

Then one of the cats jumped down from the roof of the loggia to the garden wall, startling them both. The ginger cat blinked at them in an enigmatic feline smile, and sat down to wash his paws. An awkward silence ensued.

Col was more than a little surprised by his precipitate action. The kiss had not been planned. The urge had come upon him, swift as a lightning flash, and he had given in to it. He didn't know whether to be glad or sorry that the cat had shattered the spell.

Summer was unaware of his confused feelings. Her own were compounded of astonishment and giddy delight. Her cheeks felt hot and her blood still tingled as if it were filled with tiny, golden sparks.

Col looked down at her face, so open now and full of light. So very vulnerable. It wrenched his heart to see it. He shouldn't have given in to his need. She didn't understand.

There was a feyness about her that almost frightened him. Something unworldly . . . almost *other*worldly about Summer.

A heaviness filled his chest like a weight of molten lead. She looked so fragile, like a paper lantern lit by a candle. The wrong man could destroy her.

And he was definitely the wrong man.

He lifted her hand with infinite regret, pressed his mouth against her soft skin, and left her standing alone in the Court of Three Sisters.

10

LOVERS

Notes from a lady's diary

The turning points in life, I find, often come like angels in disguise, unheralded and unrecognized.

It is only now than I can look back at my own objectively. I imagine my life as a map, tracing my way from the present to the past and I say, yes, this is where I stepped off the beaten path. This was the last quiet moment, before my life changed forever.

Sir Horace's party *was* a great success. Fanny had imagined a rustic luncheon, served alfresco at the ruins, but it was more like a royal tea party. He certainly traveled in the style and comfort of a reigning monarch.

By the time she and Thea arrived at the temple site a section of it had been transformed to something from the Arabian Nights. The interior of a ruined temple had been hung with bolts of sheer white fabric and strings of fairy lights were garlanded between the soaring columns, although they would not be lit until sunset. Fanny loved paper lanterns, and these were either blue or white, and cleverly pleated to fold flat for storage. She could hardly wait for nightfall.

Best of all was the look on Lewis Forsythe's face when he handed her down from the carriage. Although she was too young and inexperienced to identify the mix of awe, humility, and yearning in his expression, Fanny was feminine enough to know that she'd affected him like a bombshell. Why, she'd fairly dazzled him.

Glancing at her reflection in the glass of the carriage lantern, she saw that her cheeks were filled with roses and eyes were bluer than Mrs. Morville's lapis earrings swinging elegantly from her earlobes. She *was* in good looks today, if she did say so herself.

"This way, lovely ladies," Sir Horace said, coming to escort them to the table. The count joined them. "I regret that my wife and daughter cannot be with us this evening. They send their infinite regrets."

A number of gilded tables and chairs had been brought up from the salons of the enormous yacht and placed upon the Poseidon mosaic in the center of the temple. Fine porcelain and heavy silver graced the tables. Crystal wineglasses and goblets shone like diamonds in the sunlight. Fanny was enchanted.

Thea was taken aback. "All these chair legs scraping across the Poseidon mosaic! It is in need of restoration, and parts are sure to be scratched and gouged. I am sure that neither Father nor Mrs. Morville is responsible for the choice of setting."

Fanny's mouth formed a little O. "Goodness, I never thought of that. Why, that explains why Papa looks so stiff and formal. Poor Mrs. Morville is not her usual self, either. I thought perhaps she had the headache."

Soon, however, she was caught up in the spirit of the occasion, and began to enjoy herself immensely. It had made her feel quite grown-up to be in such splendid company. She looked around for the dashing Mr. McCallum, but he was not among the guests.

Fanny was seated beside Lord Lindell, a charming viscount, who was handsome and attentive, although many of his remarks went over her head. She smiled and nodded, pretending to understand. Even though he was quite old—thirty-five or forty, she guessed— she found him intriguing.

Thea was seated beside Count DiCaesari. The countess was still unable to join the festivities after the strain of travel. In addition to the Symingtons, there was a thin man whose name Fanny hadn't caught, a Miss Ottenberger, Colonel Bream, and Whitney Vance.

Fanny was rather frightened of the architect, who sat across from her at the table. Although his manner was quiet and gentle, his size and homeliness did nothing to recommend him to her. She spied Giovanni in the distance, bringing the donkey cart up from the village. His beauty was such a contrast to Mr. Vance that she found herself staring at him.

Whitney saw it. He was keenly aware that Fanny was unable to look at him squarely. It was a situation to which he'd become accustomed, although never resigned. Familiarity did not lessen the hurt, but he had learned to hide his feelings early in life, unlike Fanny. He found his eyes drawn to her time and again. She was full of life and sparkling with excitement and good humor.

He didn't like to see the attention that Lindell was giving to her, though. The man was a rakehell and scoundrel, for all his suave ways. Whitney appointed himself unofficial guardian of Miss Fanny Fairchild, and determined to keep an eye out for her any time Lord Lindell was around.

The beautiful Lady Hamlyn sat on one side of the architect. On the other side of the table were her mother—a Mrs. Ketteridge—Captain Jennings, until recently of the Horse Guard, with his pretty little wife, and Signora Croccetti, a sophisticated woman who was a cousin of the count's and acted as secretary to the absent contessa. Angus Gordon, Mrs. Morville, and Lewis Forsythe completed the party.

Fanny's attempt at worldly airs regressed into frank awe when a procession of liveried servants began to serve the meal. When her glass was filled with champagne she felt very grand indeed. It was too bad that Summer had not felt up to attending. Really, their sojourn on Ellysia was proving to be most enjoyable!

She was already planning her next letter to her friend in Egypt. Tea on the terrace at Shepheard's Hotel in Cairo was all very well, Fanny thought in satisfaction, but she sincerely doubted that Lydia could top *this!*

*   *   *

Dusk settled softly. Through his open window, Col could see the lanterns of the party glowing through the trees like fireflies, and outlining the temple of Poseidon. Damned fools, they'd ruin that mosaic if they weren't careful; and people of Sir Horace's ilk rarely were. The world was theirs, to use and discard, bought and paid for with the combination of wealth and powerful connections. He'd thought better of Fairchild than to allow it. It sickened him.

He had other things on his mind, and turned away from the window. He'd spent the evening going through Carruthers's books and papers. The old lion, he thought wryly, had been more of a pack rat. Col had seen their burrows in America, as full as they could hold of everything the tiny creatures came across, from pieces of twine to carved buttons. Evidently the same spirit had motivated his late mentor: Carruthers seemed to have kept every scrap of paper he encountered, no matter how small or how useless.

It made his job damnably difficult, but Col knew that he was definitely on the right trail. Whatever Carruthers had found, it had been at the Court of Three Sisters. And it was still there.

He had also come across a reference to the missing Venus of Ilykion as well. Like everything else, it had been written in the cryptic way Carruthers had, using abbreviations and setting down random thoughts out of sequence, which made them the very devil for Col to figure out. It was almost like trying to break a code; but once he put himself in the way of thinking like Carruthers it had begun to make sense.

Definitely Venus rising. Believe it tracks Athens to Rome to Cairo. Sent E. sniffing on the prowl.

Damn! Can't find anything without E. Pen nibs,
cigars, new razor strop.

Message to Col. Pattern forming. Frost on win-
dow. Not clear, but close. Dull day. Fairchild
ambitious. S. solid, but uninspired.

Map safe. Moving to cottage, A.M. *Will discuss*
V. of I. with C. at earliest."

"'Map safe' *where,* damn it?" The rest was clear
enough, even the part about Evans. He'd been
Carruthers's batman in the army, and was as much
trusted comrade as servant. The old lion had sent his
valet off on the trail of the person or persons who'd
sold the Venus from place to place, tracking it back
to its source. When Evans returned—*if* Evans
returned, which Col didn't really doubt—the matter
might be solved once and for all. Alistair would be
vindicated.

Damn it, he needed to conduct a thorough search
of the Court of Three Sisters, and that would take
time—and daring, since Fairchild had forbidden him
entrance there.

Col put the notebook away, smiling ironically. He
could still gain admittance to the villa, even if the
gates were locked against him.

Summer Fairchild was his key.

Richard Fairchild stood outside the temple of
Poseidon and surveyed the site. The evening was
winding down and the guests were preparing for
departure. There had been music beneath the stars
and impromptu dancing at Lady Hamlyn's suggestion. She was beautiful but calculating, Richard felt.
Not the type of woman he admired. Nor was Miss

Symington, for that matter. She had spent the latter part of the evening flitting among the temple ruins like a wraith in her flowing white costume.

He couldn't wait for them all to leave, and was concerned over possible damage to the mosaic. Cynthia had been livid over the use it had been put to, but he'd managed to calm her down. The land, and everything on it, belonged to DiCaesari, without government restriction. He could raze the place if he desired, although, thank God, he was an educated man, aware of the history of the place.

Sir Horace was a wealthy vulgarian, but his money funded the explorations. If he pulled out, Richard knew he could never expand the operation properly, or even keep it going more than a season. His personal resources did not extend to that.

Although the politics of funding was a familiar burden, Richard had chafed at the time lost from work today. The rains would be coming soon. The island, though partially arid, was prone to torrential downpours every spring, when the winds shifted for periods of up to four weeks. The storms resulting were so severe they were known to strip the blossoms and leaves from the trees, and could obliterate the crops. The same rains would flood his test pits and trenches, undermining the ruins. He would have to have them filled in before the wet season, so time was of the essence.

Angus came by with the remains of a champagne punch in his glass. Richard glared at him. Everyone else was having a good time of it, while he was left to worry about the details.

His expression softened when Cynthia came up with two more glasses of punch and handed him one.

"You look like a man in desperate need of champagne. I thought I would come to the rescue."

He thanked her and took a swallow, scarcely tasting it. As she turned to leave, he caught her hand in his. "I don't know what I would do without you. You have made such a difference in my life, Cynthia."

She smiled at the warmth in his eyes. He had never looked more handsome to her. She gave his hand a gentle squeeze. "As you have made a difference in mine, Richard. How fortunate that soon neither of us will have to do without the other!"

If there hadn't been dozens of spectators around, he would have pulled her into his arms and kissed her. "I cannot wait much longer, my love. Having you under the same roof is exquisite torture! I could hardly close my eyes all night."

Cynthia looked up at him through her lashes and laughed softly. "You will make me blush like a schoolgirl with such talk! I must prepare Thea. I think she will take it well." She sighed. "Two more months until the English parson reaches Naples. Not all that long—"

"It is an eternity to me!"

She fingered a button on his shirt. "You need not wait," she said huskily. "I already think of myself as your wife."

He drew in a long hiss of breath, unable to believe his ears. He had hoped for this, but never dared to ask. Cynthia's voice was so low it was barely audible. "I long to be with you, Richard. We have both been alone for so many years. I am so desperately tired of being alone, and I love you so much!"

Raising her hand to his lips, he kissed her fingers one by one. "There would be nothing wrong in it. We are pledged to one another before God. We would be husband and wife in everything but name. And once the parson arrives that will be taken care of, my darling. But are you sure?"

She laughed shakily. "Oh, yes. I have thought of nothing else for days."

He kissed her hand again. "I cannot wait until tonight. You have made me very happy, my dear, and very humble."

Sir Horace joined them, oblivious to the atmosphere of privacy with which they'd cloaked themselves. "Ah, there you are, Fairchild. DiCaesari and I have come to a decision. We want the rest of the gold artifacts removed from the treasury and brought up to the *castello*, as soon as possible, for safekeeping."

Richard went rigid with surprise. "Surely that is not necessary," Cynthia exclaimed.

Sir Horace was not pleased to have his orders challenged by a woman. "The gold articles are priceless. It would be too easy for them to be smuggled off the island aboard one of the fishing boats, then they could go anywhere to be sold—Spain, France, Italy, Africa. We mustn't chance it."

Richard fumed. More time lost. "I don't see any advantage to moving them, as long as we can post a sufficient guard."

"We don't have the manpower for it. The count tells me there is plenty of room in the old wine cellars. They are practically dungeons, according to him. Once there I will share the responsibility for the artifacts with him. You will be able to return to your excavations without concerning yourself over their safety."

"Very well. I will see that the artifacts are delivered to you as soon as may be."

"Excellent."

Sir Horace asked Cynthia to come with him and assist Signora Croccetti with a minor problem. They went off together, leaving the archaeologist to glare after them.

Sir Horace's timing was certainly poor, Richard thought angrily, aware that he would be forced to stay later than he'd planned. He seemed to be in a damnable hurry to take possession of the artifacts. Almost as if Chriswell didn't trust him with them.

An old anxiety cropped up. He wondered if Sir Horace had been sending him a message regarding the old scandal in Ilykion. If his wife hadn't sworn that he was with her that night . . . A sheen of sweat broke out on his brow. Damn it, was he never to be free of it?

He waved Angus down. "Where is the donkey cart? It was supposed to be brought up to the treasury. I want the ten smaller packing cases transported to the *castello*—tonight."

That would keep Sir Horace and the count up late, also, he thought with satisfaction. If they meant to remain on Ellysia for some time, it was best if the rules were set down from the start: The nobleman would have to understand that an archaeologist was a scholar and a professional man, not some flunky to do his bidding!

Angus glanced around. "The cart was by the grove the last time I noticed. Perhaps Giovanni has taken it down to the village. I will ask Lewis."

Later, as Richard saw the cartons off under guard, Cynthia came up beside him and slipped her arm through his. She didn't have to say a word. It was all there in the soft press of her body against his. A surge of desire swept through him, carrying the anger away. He was suddenly as eager as a man twenty years younger. This was the night he had waited for. Tonight she would be his.

As they went down to his carriage, Richard was so elated that he would scarcely have cared if Sir Horace carried off the entire temple complex, block by block.

Fanny returned to the villa with Thea in high excitement. She had enjoyed the time of her young and rather sheltered life. The delightful supper party had ended with an invitation to a sailing party.

She bounced into Summer's room with all the enviable energy of a sixteen-year-old who had just enjoyed her first taste of success. She found her sister at the wide window, leaning against the sill and looking out to sea.

"You should have come with us, Summer! It was the best party. Sir Horace is a funny little man, and says the drollest things! And Lady Hamlyn is *so* very beautiful and *so* elegantly dressed! Why, I daresay her rose silk slippers alone cost more than my entire wardrobe!"

She plopped herself down on the edge of the bed in a froth of petticoats. It was her first great social triumph, and it had made her as giddy as the champagne punch Sir Horace had poured so freely. It was probably a good thing that Thea had come along and taken the glass away. Spoilsport.

At least Thea had waited until no one was looking to remove the punch cup and hiss a warning in her ear. Fanny didn't think she could have got over the embarrassment of it otherwise. "I sat beside Lord Lindell, and he was most entertaining! It almost made up for having to look across the table at Mr. Vance. What a frightening creature he is, to be sure."

"Don't be cruel, Fanny. Everyone speaks highly of him."

"Oh, I am sure he is well enough, but I could hardly bear to exchange a word with him! It was a splendid party!" She chattered on, not noticing that Summer was listening with half an ear. "You missed the most marvelous time! Even though it *was* very hot, especially after the champagne punch."

"Thea let you drink champagne punch?" Summer raised her eyebrows, roused from her self-absorption. "I almost wish that I had gone, just to see that with my own eyes. She must have been suffering from heatstroke."

Fanny colored. "It was just a little glass," she said. "Please don't bring it up with Thea, or she will feel she wasn't doing her job of chaperon. Then she will stick to me like a burr the next time, and I am much too grown up for that!"

Summer let her rattle on awhile about the luncheon. It *had* been hard on a young girl like Fanny, having her social life so restricted.

Although Fanny's evening had gone so well, there was one dark cloud on her horizon. She steadfastly tried to ignore it, but it hovered on the edge of her pleasure, casting a long shadow. She'd known that Giovanni would be at the site, and had dressed with that in mind, just in case he did have an eye toward that village girl the signora had mentioned. She had wanted to look so utterly fetching that all thought of Natalia, her unseen rival for his attentions, was completely eclipsed.

Giovanni was exactly like her idea of a hero from a storybook. She had dazzled Lewis Forsythe, which was extremely enjoyable, but he hadn't looked at her with the same intensity that Giovanni did, as if she were the sun and moon rolled into one. That was far more intoxicating than mere champagne to a girl fresh from the schoolroom.

She dimpled and smiled at her sister. "Perhaps when we are guests of Sir Horace the next time, you will agree to be my chaperon instead of Thea. *Do* say you will, lovely, dear, dear Summer!"

Summer laughed. "I should be every bit as onerous a chaperon as Thea. I would guard you like a dragon, never letting the young swains within a hundred yards of you, be they ever so rich and handsome. But you are safe. I doubt Sir Horace plans to outdo his luncheon party. He is known to be a will-o'-the-wisp, flitting here and there and everywhere."

"Now, there you are wrong. That's what I've come to tell you." Fanny clasped her hands together eagerly.

"Sir Horace is staying on the entire season. He will be at the *castello* with his party, guests of the count. He is planning so many delightful things—dinner parties and musical evenings. A yachting trip to Hades, to see the volcano. Even a ball, once the contessa is recovered from her indisposition."

Fanny's ecstasies were Summer's nightmares. So much for peace and quiet. Sinking down against her pillow, she put her hands to her head in a gesture of horror that was only half-mocking.

"When are all these *treats* to begin?"

"The day after tomorrow we are invited to sail all around the island aboard Sir Horace's yacht. I am looking forward to it tremendously!"

This, Summer felt, was surprising in someone who had made the Channel crossing, and the trip from Naples, face down in a bunk with a basin next to her. There was no way she could avoid all of the festivities herself; however a sailing party was one for which she could safely send her regrets.

But Fanny was still listing events. "We are to have everyone to dine Tuesday evening, and on Wednesday we shall go over to the *castello* for an informal evening of games and cards, and then to a dinner party Sunday evening." Fanny could hardly contain herself. "My first grown-up dinner party! Won't it be heavenly?"

"I believe I'll send my regrets."

Fanny was shocked. "But you can't mean it! Why, *everyone* will be there. Even Mr. McCallum."

A tiny sigh escaped Summer. Her mouth still burned where he had kissed her. She felt her cheeks flush with heat at the memory. Despite her denial to Fanny she knew that, as surely as the sun rose and set, she would go to the *castello*. She would go against reason and inclination, damning herself for such weakness.

But she would go all the same, because Col McCallum would be there.

Thea did not come to Summer's room after the party at the temple site, and she avoided the opportunity for any tête-à-têtes with Summer the next morning. She was ashamed of the way she had broken down before her, and more ashamed that she'd let Summer know how things stood in her marriage. It wasn't difficult to avoid any private conversations with one another, for although she was unaware of it, Summer was avoiding her as well.

Mrs. Morville looked heavy-eyed and contented, but she was full of plans over breakfast, which kept everyone busy. "I have wanted to explore the *castello* since I first set eyes upon it. Surely you are as intrigued, Miss Fairchild? It looks like a gothic castle, sure to be haunted by a 'gray lady', or a 'lady in white.'"

Fanny was delighted at the prospect, but a chill slithered up Summer's spine. If she were as sensitive to atmosphere as Col would have her believe, she might "see" more than she bargained for.

They began talking over the previous night's entertainment and the guest list for their dinner party. Summer noticed one name was not mentioned. "Will Mr. McCallum be invited to our dinner party, or would that make an uneven number?"

Thea exchanged glances with Cynthia. "Mr. McCallum will not be invited. He and Father have had a falling-out of sorts."

"How can that be?" Summer was distressed.

"There was a problem in the past," Thea explained. "Something to do with Mr. McCallum's brother."

"How unjust," Fanny responded indignantly. "It is unfair to blame him for something that occurred between two other people. And very unlike Father, I must say."

Cynthia shrugged and looked wryly at her hostess. "A mutiny is brewing. I believe it is better all around if we tell the truth of the matter." She regarded Summer and Fanny sympathetically. "I see that his winning ways have charmed you as well as the rest of us, but your Mr. McCallum is not what he seems. Indeed, it was only recently that your father divined Mr. McCallum's true identity."

Fanny was confused. "Is he in disguise?"

"Not exactly," Thea replied. "Perhaps I had better take up the narrative. You see, many years ago, when he was a student on holiday in Greece, Mr. McCallum visited his brother, who was working on a project with Father. They made a wonderful discovery. An extremely beautiful and valuable statue made of gold. It disappeared from Alistair McCallum's custody and was never seen again."

"There is reason," Cynthia added gently, "to believe that the two brothers conspired to spirit the priceless artifact away and sell it to a private collector of antiquities."

Summer roused herself. "I do not believe it!" she said flatly. "I believe that he would take anything he wanted quite openly, but he isn't a thief!"

Her sudden vehemence startled the others. Summer couldn't restrain herself. He had no more taken the statue than she had.

"I would give my oath that Mr. McCallum would never involve himself in such a discreditable scheme," she said in a low, impassioned tone. "He is a man of honor, and his respect for the study of ancient times rivals Father's. He would *never* stand to let a piece of history be tucked in an antiquarian's vault, and lost to the world, in order to profit from it personally!"

"Your defense of him does you credit," Mrs. Morville replied, "however, you scarcely know the man. And they do say that rogues are often charming."

Summer sent Thea a beseeching look. "Surely you don't believe him capable of such a thing?"

Her sister looked acutely uncomfortable. "I don't know. If he was a mere schoolboy at the time, it is possible that he may have helped his brother without realizing the consequences of his action, and repented later."

"No." Summer was confused. Had her partiality

for him blinded her to Col's true character? "I will not believe what you say of Mr. McCallum unless I hear it is true from his own lips."

"That is unlikely under the circumstances," Thea said sharply. "He is no longer welcome beneath this roof, and we must comply with Father's decision."

Cynthia sent Summer a sympathetic smile. "No doubt this is a terrible shock to you. It is always upsetting to realize that one has been taken in by an engaging rake, such as Col McCallum. For that matter," she added, "it is inaccurate to address him as Mr. McCallum. He is more properly called Lord FitzRoy. He inherited the title many years ago, upon his brother's death. There is no fortune, for he comes from a long line of profligates. I believe he is nothing but a common adventurer."

They went back to their lists but Summer was unable to concentrate. FitzRoy. She knew the name from somewhere, but could not place it. It was a struggle to keep the others from knowing what a deep shock their revelations had been. Years of practice at hiding her feelings had made her a better actress than any of them guessed.

She wanted very much to see her erstwhile companion and ask him to explain himself. Summer was sure that he would have a good reason for his actions.

Fanny rose quietly, the discussion of Col's character half forgotten. She had spied Giovanni in the courtyard, trying to attract her attention. She slipped away before anyone noticed that she was gone.

Giovanni gave a sigh of relief as Fanny came out into the courtyard. "Let us go outside these walls," he told her in a low voice. "I must speak to you in private—something terrible has happened!"

Her hand flew to her heart as she followed him out through the front gate. "Is it—is it my father?"

"Yes, alas . . . !"

She started to weep. "I knew it! I have been so worried. Bring the carriage around. I must fetch my sisters!"

"No! What have they to do with us? I want to be alone with you, *carissima.*"

A suspicion formed in Fanny's head that they were talking at cross-purposes. "Then my father has not met with an accident?"

He stared at her. "What are you saying? I have not come to speak of your father, but of our future!"

"But you said that something terrible had happened to him," she said indignantly.

He clutched her hand in his. "Not *to* him, *bellissima,* but to us *because* of him." His face grew grave. "I am being sent away, to work aboard the yacht of his friend, Sir Horace! My mother says that my uncle arranged this, so that I might save up enough money to secure my future, but I know it is your father's doing. He means to keep us apart. We must fly away together, to Naples or Sorrento. Sicily, if you like. It does not matter to me, as long as you are happy. My friend Giuseppe owes me a great favor. He will arrange passage for us on one of the fishing boats."

Fanny looked at him as if he'd lost his mind. "But I don't want to fly away with you!"

"Of course not. You are concerned that we cannot manage without your dowry. Fear not, my love, I am young and strong. I can support you with the strength of my arms. Come with me!"

She pulled back. "You cannot be serious."

"I am! And I can provide for you. Listen! I shall rent out a small shop like my cousin has in Messina, only in the poorer section of town, where things are not so costly. I shall sell fish or vegetables in the stalls below—I have not decided which as yet—and we will live above the shop."

Fanny's mind boggled at his romantic fantasy of two lovers living above a fish shop. She didn't know what to say. "I could not elope," she managed. "The scandal would ruin my father. And I don't know the first thing about keeping house. Why, I cannot cook or mend. Nor do I have the inclination to learn!"

Giovanni was frustrated by this setback. Of course, she was right. "Then we will return to Elyssia after we are married. We can live with my mother. The house is small but only my brother and his wife live with her, along with their two children. What will one more matter? And you can help Bianca with the children. There is one more on the way, and never enough time to do all that must be done. In return, she can teach you what you need to know."

Even as he was speaking, Giovanni began to have doubts of his own. The possibilities that had seemed so right in his mind sounded totally impractical when brought into the clear light of day. He could not imagine Fanny—his beloved, beautiful Fanny—making tortellini under his mother's watchful, disapproving eye. Nor could he imagine her gutting fish or stuffing a goat's entrails.

A gulf seemed to open at their feet, deeper than any gorge. He had always imagined his wife filling the house with wonderful smells of baking foods from the kitchen. Sewing tiny garments for their children, making him a fringed shirt to wear on special feast days. Entertaining the wives of his friends.

The scales fell from his eyes. Had there ever been two such star-crossed lovers? Giovanni saw that he had been too presumptuous. It was not to be. Fanny must remain a goddess, worshiped from afar. "You are as wise as you are beautiful," he told her. "I see that now. You are too far above me. I was a fool to aspire to so much as kissing your delicate hand."

He turned away before she could marshal her wits, and ran off through the olive grove. When he reached the fork in the footpath, he took the one that led behind the village. A tantalizing odor wafted from the nearest house. His stomach rumbled. Giovanni glanced over and saw Natalia Vico framed in an open window as she rolled out dough.

She looked up and saw him, and waved with flour-dusted hands. "Come in, we are making chick-pea pastries for my cousin's feast day, and the first batch is out, fresh from the oven."

Giovanni hesitated only a moment, then he turned off the path and went past the chickens scratching in the dust, and into the Vico home. Goddesses were all very well to worship, but not to live with. He took the pastry that Natalia handed him and stuffed it into his mouth.

A wise man recognized his fate.

Cynthia looked up as Fanny rejoined them but didn't comment on her hectic flush. She addressed Summer instead: "You are not very enthusiastic over the coming dinner party."

"No. I dislike meeting strangers, especially whole groups of them! I don't relish being goggled at as if I were a freak on display at a country fair."

Mrs. Morville smiled deprecatingly. "I doubt that they will be standing in line to stare at you. You have an exaggerated notion of your ability to interest people like Sir Horace and the fair Lady Helen . . . "

Summer jerked as if she'd been slapped, but Cynthia went on without pausing. "I assure you that they are far too wrapped up in themselves to concern themselves unduly with you. I have never known a more self-important, self-centered man, nor a vainer, more empty-headed woman."

It was Summer's turn to laugh. "You make them sound so dreadful that I shall have to find another excuse, then."

Thea joined in. "No doubt they will be more entertaining than Mrs. Symington and her bag of knitting. She carries it about with her like a lapdog."

Almost as if her thinking of them had conjured them up, Mrs. Symington and her daughter came to call, the one with her infernal yarn and needles, and the other with her sphinxlike pronouncements and air of veiled tragedy.

Cynthia excused herself in advance from a dull afternoon by saying that she had promised to be at the site within the hour. Mrs. Symington was offended. Despite her daughter's renown, she did not approve of women having careers, or abandoning guests on such a pretext. Fanny had slipped away earlier, leaving her two sisters to entertain their callers. Summer was envious. She would much rather have been uncovering her mosaic than listening to the vapid comments that passed for conversation.

Rosalind Symington was so restless and uncommunicative that everyone wondered why she had bothered to come along. She was eccentric enough that mere courtesy was not deemed to be sufficient reason. Seeing the frantic looks Thea sent her way, Summer felt compelled to come to the rescue.

She invited Rosalind to enjoy the view from the balustrade, and they strolled over to it, followed by one of the purring tabbies. The vines shielded them, but the sea looked hard and bright as glass under a blazing sky. Hades shimmered beneath a dense, dark cloud. There had been a small tremor in the night, so slight that most people had slept right through it. Summer tried to find common ground for conversation. The cat perched on the balustrade, licking its paws.

"Tell me, Miss Symington, whose poetry has influenced your own writing?"

For answer, Rosalind looked across at her mother and quoted softly: "'What Soft—Cherubic Creatures—These Gentlewomen are—One would as soon assault a Plush—Or violate a Star—'"

Summer smiled at the aptness of the lines. "'Such Dimity Convictions—A Horror so refined—Of freckled Human Nature—'" It summed them up completely.

Rosalind looked at her keenly. "You are familiar with Emily Dickinson's work. I shouldn't be surprised. Do you like Poe? The Americans interest me. They are not afraid of darkness, nor do they necessarily find it ennobling. And they know pain. It imbues their words and rhythms."

She looked off into the sunlight, squinting against it as if welcoming the stab of brightness. "My lover left me," she said abruptly.

Summer was tongue-tied. She hadn't expected the conversation to change so bizarrely, nor was she worldly enough to deal with it easily. "I am most sincerely sorry."

Rosalind acknowledged that with a little nod. She was still staring out to sea. "Thank you. And would you be as sorry if I told you that she left me to go back to her husband? An artist of no real talent, with hands like Smithfield hams, who beats her senseless every time he's drunk!"

Her words were meant to shock, and they did. Summer knew of such things from her reading, but confronting them in real life was something else. She paused before answering, to get the words right. "Yes. I should be sincerely sorry for anyone who is suffering deeply for the sake of a loved one."

The poetess took a deep, shuddering breath. "Col is right about you. You are a breath of fresh spring air in a stale drawing room. He wants to see you again. Will you meet with him?"

It was Summer's turn to catch her breath. She felt dizzy with relief. He would be able to explain everything to her. She was certain it was all a big misunderstanding. Glancing at the others, she saw they were far enough away not to have overheard.

"Yes. When?"

"Tomorrow morning. When your sisters leave to go sailing with Sir Horace. He'll be waiting for you at the top of the sea stairs. He said you would know what he means."

A huge warmth built up in Summer's chest, then burst outward along her limbs until it enclosed her from toes to crown. She felt as if she could explode with sheer joy. It was a struggle to keep her voice even.

"I will be there."

"Good." The poetess glanced at Summer. "I wouldn't have imagined you and Col McCallum together. Have you been lovers long?"

"We're . . . we're *not!*"

A sharp little laugh, like breaking glass filled the air. "Lovers aren't born in the flesh, but in the soul. It is only a matter of time."

Rosalind turned with one of her brusque movements. "Don't let them see your face. It's glowing like the heart of a flame."

She walked away. Summer was left standing there alone at the balustrade. How could she bear the passing hours until morning?

She put her hands to her cheeks. They radiated heat. But that seemed only natural. Col wanted to see her again! She felt as if she'd opened the lid of a small, black box and found the sun inside.

Col checked his watch. Two more hours till sunrise. He poured himself a cup of coffee and flipped through the pages ahead randomly. It was difficult to concentrate. Another notation caught his eye:

Despite panic, no problem with the map. F. went to court with eye to moving in. Stood right over it without realizing it. Blind fool! Couldn't find it in a hundred years!

Col's heart sped up. Yes, the great discovery was at the Court of Three Sisters and Fairchild had stood right over it. Stood right over *what*, damn it all?

Well, he would know the answer to that soon. He put the journal away and went outside. The sky was dark but luminous and the air soft and warm. Spring was melting into summer.

Summer. It was no good fooling himself. Carruthers's mysterious find wasn't the only thing that drew him to the Court of Three Sisters. It was Summer Fairchild.

He sighed and leaned back against the stucco wall of the house. Summer. Even her name evoked something inside him that he couldn't identify. It was akin to the restless, unnameable urge that comes with the changing leaves and the poignant winds of autumn. He had never known its like before.

It was ridiculous even to think of her in that way. Her nature was as pristine as his was jaded. Something darker separated them. Col had suspected for some time that Richard Fairchild had a hand in orchestrating the scandal that had ruined his brother. It seemed so clear in retrospect: As Alistair's sun had set, Fairchild's had risen. If the professor hadn't proved himself by taking over at Ilykion, he might have remained an obscure archaeologist laboring in the shadows of a more famous man.

And then there were the suspicious circumstances of Carruthers's death, followed so shortly by that of Dr. Ruggieri.

The hitch in his theory was Fairchild's sudden withdrawal from fieldwork. Of course, he knew that was a result of the double tragedy of Mrs. Fairchild's death and the accident that had caused Summer's limp. But ten years was a long time to stay away— unless it was guilt that had kept Richard Fairchild in England.

Col checked the sky. It was beginning to lighten imperceptibly and he had a long way to go. The Court of Three Sisters was a little over a quarter of an hour away by carriage, and the same if one took the footpath through the orchards. It was less than that by rowboat from the cove below the cottage to the villa's sea stairs, but much too conspicuous, for the fishing fleet passed it every morning. He would have to take the long way around, skirting the cliffs and then down the ravine to the strand below the Court of Three Sisters.

By the time the sky turned from gray to a fresh rose, he was at the foot of the sea stair leading up to the abandoned section of the Fairchilds' villa. As he went up them silently, he thought of the way he'd described Summer to Whitney Vance—like the fairytale princess on the glass hill—and here he was, climbing up to meet her. The only problem being that he was not a pure and noble knight bent on winning the lady's hand.

Another black mark against his soul, he thought, and began his ascent.

It was dark inside the hollow of the cliff that held the sea stairs. Col came to a place where the steps split into two directions. He hadn't noticed that on the day of the earthquake, but then he'd been in a rush to get Summer to safety.

He paused and listened, trying to get his bearings. The sea was muffled and its echo seemed to come from all around. He wasn't sure which branch to take. He took the right-hand one and went up, feeling his way along the stone walls until he reached daylight. He'd definitely chosen wrong. Instead of the unused courtyard, he was on a narrow ledge on the cliff face, with the sea straight down a hundred feet.

He debated going back, then opted to continue to the top. It was only another two yards or so. The footing was secure although the steps were small. The outer half of the staircase had sheared off in some past earthquake. Presently he emerged on an open terrace, with walls on two sides and a sheer drop on the other. He stepped up and stopped short.

Summer's sleep had been deep, but plagued by dreams. Cliete and . . . what was the other woman's name? The one whose eyes she seemed to look out of, yet all the while retaining her own identity?

The household wouldn't rise for two more hours. She dressed, tossed a light wrap over her shoulders against the early chill, and went out into Persephone's garden. The sea was gray and smooth as polished silver, the line where it met the horizon blurred and blended until it was impossible to say where one ended and the other began. That was how she felt in her dreams and visions of Cliete. Where did Summer Fairchild end, and the other woman begin?

She didn't feel like working, and went to the stone throne. It was strange that it felt cool in the warmest sunshine, and warm even in the night. Summer sat in it, and felt her consciousness expand to hold the other. She . . . *they* . . . were waiting.

Waiting for *him*.

Her heart skipped a beat and then began to pound. A figure materialized at the edge of the terrace. For a moment she saw a man with dark hair, curled and pomaded. His chest was bare except for a jeweled collar, and an inlaid dagger was thrust into the waistband of his kiltlike skirt.

Then he merged with another shape and became

Col McCallum. But for a moment they had been one and the same man. Her racing heart slowed. For a moment she'd been plunged back into time. Summer had the premonition that if she ever went back too far, she would be caught and held by it. Trapped forever inside a world that was not hers—and that no longer existed.

Col stepped onto the terrace, startled to find Summer sitting there on a stone bench. At first he hadn't recognized her. She'd looked . . . *different*. Then the sun was just above the horizon, filling the air with luminous, pearly light.

He hadn't expected to find anyone stirring yet. It was much too early. "Did I frighten you?"

Summer held a finger to her lips. "Shhh. The walls are thick, but voices carry."

She wasn't sure at first that he was real. He'd appeared like a mirage from the edge of the cliff, where the balustrade had once been. Rising, she went to the edge. The path couldn't be seen; but by leaning forward and craning her neck awkwardly she could make out the edge of the stairs. They were so narrow and steep they seemed scarcely wide enough for a child to climb.

Her surprise was more that he had managed to navigate them, than that Col was standing in her secret garden. She became aware that, all the time she'd worked at uncovering the mosaic, in the back of her mind, he had always been her first intended audience. It was his face, more than other, that she had wanted to see filled with admiration and wonder.

At the moment there was only wonder.

"You are much too early," she whispered. "They won't be leaving until ten o'clock."

He was thinking furiously. "I needed to talk to you, to explain."

Col followed her gaze to a rectangular area, surrounded by a low stone enclosure.

"I've found something," Summer said softly. "I've been working on it for ages, although why anyone would take the trouble to cover such a wonderful thing over with plaster, is more than I can say."

Her words galvanized him. Col moved quickly to the dried fountain. What he'd thought was unfilled space was actually covered over with a thick coat of plaster. As he drew closer he made out the margins of lands floating in a wide blue sea. What the hell? His heart gave a great leap. Could it be?

He was afraid to breathe. He'd spent the past weeks searching for something John Carruthers had hidden from view, and she had already found it!

But when he reached the edge of the low wall he stooped down. The light was deceiving. What he'd mistaken for a map was only a festive scene. The parts that had appeared to be coastlines on a map were only the twisted fabric of a nymph's gown. The tilework was so fine he could almost touch the garment and feel the caress of diaphanous silk. His imagined ocean was only a swirling mosaic sky.

It was a masterpiece, but it had nothing to do with the map that Carruthers had hidden. Col's disappointment was out of all proportion. If he hadn't felt so bad about it, he would have laughed at himself for even thinking that something so large could be that precious, elusive map.

Summer came up beside him. It was urgent that

she know his side of things, yet she was afraid that someone would hear their voices and come to investigate. "We can't talk here. Can we take the sea stairs down? I think I can manage it."

He sat back on his heels. He'd hoped to do some quiet exploring of the old section of the house while the family was still abed. Then, if he'd found nothing suggestive, he'd planned to convince Summer to let him look through the rest of the villa. That plan was sabotaged by his error in choosing his route.

He nodded and led her to the stairs. Col went first, assisting her onto the top of the steps. She was able to negotiate the upper section with his help, but the darkened tunnel utterly defeated her. Summer misstepped, and fell against the wall.

She tried to stifle her cry. "My back!"

He scooped Summer up into his arms and carried her down the sea stairs. They passed through the dark tunnel that was the cliff, and came out in a small cove.

He set her down gently and probed at her shoulder where it was covered with rock dust. Summer jerked away, wincing. "It's nothing," she said quickly. "Merely a bruise."

He accepted her answer and sat beside her. Summer examined her surroundings. With the sun coming up the water was clear aquamarine, shading to a deep and vibrant blue-green. At the base of the cliff a shallow, natural cave was half covered by luxuriant vines, rich with bright red blossoms. It was a place of eerie beauty. Summer felt the hair prickle at the nape of her neck.

With a start she noticed a misshapen, blind-eyed face peering out through the leaves. Her heart jumped in her chest and she clasped a hand to her bodice. She almost gasped, but at the last second she laughed shakily instead. The cave was a sort of grotto, and the voyeur only a statue much scarred by time and the elements. She wondered what god or goddess had once claimed this cove as sanctuary.

"Will you tell me about your past?" she blurted without preamble. "I know that you had a brother, Alistair. And I know that he was blamed for something. I would like to hear it in your own words."

He hadn't meant to go into it, but the story poured out of him. It was like lancing a wound. All the vile purulence drained from his soul as he spoke of Alistair, his despair and the drastic way he'd chosen to protect his younger brother.

She put her hand on Col's arm. "It wasn't your fault. He wasn't thinking clearly, or he would have known that his death would only be harder on you than any hint of disgrace."

Col dug at the sand with a stick of driftwood. "You didn't know him. Alistair was a black-and-white person. There was nothing in between. He was happy or despondent, eager or so lethargic he retreated to his books like a hermit to his cell. He'd spoken to me that morning of hiring an inquiry agent to look into the matter. He was cheerful and sure that he could prove his innocence."

The stick dug deeply into the sand. "By sunset he was dead." A startled crab poked out of the trench Col had made, and scuttled away. "I left Alistair long enough to go down to order dinner to be brought up to our room. While I was gone he put a bullet to his head. I found him."

Her heart wept for him. She could see the young boy he had been peering out through Col's eyes, still lost and bewildered and dreadfully hurt. "I am so very sorry."

He didn't answer. They sat side by side while the waves dashed themselves to lace against the shore. The sky was smeared with purple and red. She hoped it didn't remind him of the blood.

After a while she began to shiver from the cold sand and the chill air. "I had better go back."

She started to rise, gave a small cry, and fell back against the sand. Col jumped to his feet. "It's nothing," she said sharply. "I'm stiff and sore from working on the mosaic."

"You've pulled a muscle," he told her. "Well, there's a cure for it right at hand."

He lifted her gingerly and her wrap trailed behind her like a train. Summer thought he meant to carry her up the stairs, but Col headed straight for the water. "Where are you going?" she asked warily.

"Something that should probably have been done long ago. I'm surprised you haven't tried it yet. These waters are known for their curative powers. You'll be much better for a dip in them."

"No!" Her voice was shrill. "I want to go back to the villa."

Col strode into the water with her, and the spray of the waves spangled their hair and eyelashes with diamonds. Summer tasted salt on her lips. He was laughing as he carried her into the sea. Summer was nearly in tears.

He smiled down at her as he splashed in past his waist. "This is a section of one of the private baths that belonged to the villa."

Summer was panic-stricken. The hem of her skirts was trailing in the sea and she felt the weight of them pulling on her. "Put me down, I said!"

"Very well."

He let her go suddenly, and she fell into the shimmering green water. It was surprisingly warm. She splashed about, attempting to head back to shore, and stumbled.

She came up sputtering and gasping and he caught her behind the neck with his arm. "Stop struggling and enjoy the waters. You'll find them very soothing."

"My clothes are pulling me down!" She floundered again and took in a gulp of pungent saltwater.

As she coughed and spluttered, he realized it was the heavy folds of her cloak pulling her off balance. He undid the single large button that held it in front and pulled it free.

"Up you go. The mineral salts will support your weight easily, if you stop thrashing about like a trout in a barrel."

It was true. She found herself floating two yards away from him in the bobbing waves, buoyed upright. It didn't make her any happier with the situation. Then she looked down into the water, and realized that her shirtwaist had become almost transparent. She crossed her arms over her chest protectively and tried to immerse herself to her neck. It was impossible to sink far enough beneath it. Summer bit her lip. She was hot with fury.

"I will never forgive you for this. Never!"

Col started to laugh, but the laughter caught like a bubble in his throat. Her hair had come loose and was plastered to her head, but the rest of it floated out over the lapping ripples like the lace of her shawl. He became aware, just as she had, that her lawn shirtwaist had turned as sheer as net.

Her shoulders gleamed like pearl beneath the

clinging fabric. The sweet upper curve of her breasts was visible just beneath the water and he felt a pull in his loins. She looked so angry and so beautiful, she took his breath away. He tried to ignore it, but failed. Reason told him to back off. Instead, Col found himself moving toward her through the water.

"Do you believe in mermaids, Miss Fairchild? You look like one, you know." He reached out his hand and cupped her face. It seemed the most natural thing in the world. The moment his skin touched hers something changed. The pull in his loins grew harder, stronger. Col knew then that he wanted her, had wanted her for a long time.

That he intended to have her.

Summer felt her heart stop, then slowly begin again in double time. The expression in his eyes was so intense she wanted to tear hers away. She couldn't. Col's thumb smoothed along her jaw, traced the corner of her mouth and the outline of her full lower lip. The anger melted out of her, replaced by another, unfamiliar heat.

He was so close that the wet fabric of his shirt brushed the tips of her breasts. She gasped and closed her eyes as he threaded his fingers through her hair, while his other hand cradled her cheek. Slowly and with great sureness, he brought his mouth down on hers.

At first his lips were gentle, persuasive. Their touch was sweetly seductive but quickly grew hard and fierce. She was spellbound, held fast by his practiced kisses, by the erotic play of warm water and cool wind against her skin, by the rush of longing that left her disoriented and gasping. As soft as it began, this was nothing like the first kiss he'd given her. That had been an end to something, this promised a beginning.

She grasped his wrist, meaning to make him stop or slow his sensual assault; instead she clung to it, feeling the corded strength of his arm and digging her nails into his skin. The kiss went on. She was an innocent and he was an experienced lover. She had no hope of dissuading him, and no desire to do so. It was so marvelous, so wonderful that she wanted it to continue forever.

He nibbled at her upper lip and ran the tip of his tongue over its contours until she sighed against his mouth. He wanted to deepen the kiss but held back. The denial was exquisite torture. He wanted her so badly it filled him with pain, yet he wanted even more to prolong the sensations. For himself, and especially for Summer.

His hand slipped beneath the water and touched her breast lightly. She stiffened, but he distracted her with his kisses. He slid his palm over her nipple, rubbing it slowly until it grew hard and erect. She moaned softly and moved closer, arching against him. His blood took fire. He had guessed at her buried passion, but not the extent of it. He jerked her collar open and slid his hand inside until they were flesh to flesh. She shivered with pleasure, and wild joy raced through him.

"I've always known it would come to this," he murmured against her mouth. "You knew it too, Summer, didn't you?"

"No. Yes!" It was true. From that first night when she'd seen him, she had been drawn to him. She took his hand and put it against her other breast. He toyed with the nipple until she moaned again.

His tongue probed at her lips and she opened them

to him. He teased her gently, then slipped inside, savoring the honeyed warmth of her mouth. As he plunged deeper, she wound her arms around his neck, forcing her breasts against his chest. Col groaned.

The situation had progressed so far that the outcome was inevitable. She was warm and willing, and the knowledge was a goad to his need. Perhaps that was what drew him to her, this innocence coupled with the hungers of a wanton.

He slid one arm around her waist, pulling her against him. Her skirts were tangled around their legs like seaweed. They were too much of a barrier, and he tugged at them, pulling them up and away. His fingers brushed the bare skin of her outer thigh and they both shuddered at the touch. Summer had convinced herself that this was a dream. A wonderful, passionate dream, and she refused to awaken from it.

When his fingers came to rest on her inner thigh she didn't protest. How could she, when his mouth covered hers and their breaths mingled? When she had lost awareness of the universe and everything in it? Everything that was not Col. She clung to him for strength, for sanity. Then his hand smoothed up her thigh and reached between her legs.

She was so startled she almost fell backward. He reached his other arm around to support her and saved her from another dunking. His hand closed over something odd beneath the deep ruffle at the back of her neckband. It took a few seconds to realize that it was her shoulder blade. His fingers splayed against her spine. He felt the line of scar tissue beneath the wet fabric, like a wide satin ribbon, and the erratic curves that shouldn't have been there at all.

He was suddenly sick with shame. Dear God, he hadn't dreamed the extent of her injuries. His fingers traced that wavering scar and he knew that she had almost died from her injuries. It was a miracle that she'd survived. That she could walk at all.

He pulled away. He was a fool and a villain. A wave of guilt and tenderness washed over him, and a wild, fierce possessiveness. She had been injured enough by life. He could never do anything that would harm her, in any way.

Summer felt the change in him before she saw it. From the moment he first touched her scar and her crooked shoulder blade, to the very second he realized how crippled she was. She had led him to believe it was nothing more than a limp. She had always known that no man could really love her, so misshapen and scarred. Her eyes met his, wide and stricken.

He released her and set her gently away. "Summer, I'm sorry."

Tears of utter desolation filled her eyes. She had wanted him to love her; and in her desperation she had been willing to give him anything he asked. It was plain from the look on his face that she had nothing he wanted. Not now, when he knew the truth.

She didn't wait for what he had to say next. She pushed him back with all the strength of her despair and he went down in the shallows. Gathering her skirts up over her legs, she slogged through the water to the shore without looking over her shoulder.

By the time Col righted himself she had reached the stairs. Ignoring the pain, no longer caring how ungraceful she looked, Summer scrambled up the chiseled steps.

Col lunged after her. "Summer! Wait!"

God damn it! She was closing the door behind her. He came splashing up through the water and reached it in time to hear the bolt of the sea stairs gate ram home. *"Summer!"*

He pounded on the door and peered through the tiny grille, but all he saw was the dripping hem of her skirts vanish up the wet steps. Christ, he hoped she wouldn't fall again.

Cursing, he turned and made his way back down to the shore. Although the sun still shone, a squall was moving in from the west. Lightning flashed in the dark clouds, no angrier than the emotions that shot through him. He picked up a stone and threw it into the waves with all his might.

What a goddamned fool he'd been! He hadn't known! Not about the extent of her injuries. Nor about the way she would feel in his arms, making him forget everything but his desire for her. Not about the way she would respond to his ardor. And not the way he really felt about her.

It was like a tiny flame in the center of dry wood. It hadn't grown gradually. The flame had doubled, tripled, and suddenly burst into a conflagration. There was an inferno of heat building up in him. Rage, sorrow, tenderness, passion, all wound up into a terrible, throbbing need.

He had never understood the need of some men to possess a woman completely on a permanent basis. A light flirtation, a few romantic moments leading to hours or days or weeks of sensual pleasures, and then a quick parting with no strings and hard feelings on either side had always been enough for him before.

The feelings Summer roused in him were something entirely different.

Col hefted another rock and flung it into the sea. He wanted to possess her, not just physically, but body, mind, and soul. He wanted that because it was the only way he knew to protect her. From hurt, from pain, from life. He knew that he would be afraid for her every moment that they were apart.

That might be a lifetime of fear. He doubted that she'd see or speak to him again willingly. She had a terrifying pride. She would never forgive him for exposing her injuries—hadn't she said that earlier?

And, he thought, smashing his fist into the palm of his other hand, he would never forgive himself.

11

History Repeats

From Col McCallum's notes

I remember a time when I was a boy and Carruthers fell ill. I was afraid that he was dying. He laughed at my tears. "Don't worry, you young scamp! I've many years ahead of me. A fortune-teller prophesied it. And even if something went wrong and I lost my allotted span, why, I'd come back to haunt you!"

I thought he meant as a ghost. At the time I wasn't sure that angels really existed.

Summer did not join her family for breakfast. Fanny went in search of her sister and discovered her still huddled in bed. Her eyes were heavy and rimmed in red, and the shutters were closed against the light. "Poor dear! Are you ill?"

"Only a sleepless night," Summer responded,

trying to keep the quaver from her voice. "I shall catch up on it while you are off with Sir Horace. By suppertime I shall be fully recovered, and you may tell me all about your day."

Fanny bustled off, full of hot tea to prevent queasiness at sea. She was sure that the tea, accompanied by a quantity of biscuits and soothing thoughts, would do the trick for her.

Summer rolled over to face the wall again. It would be a relief to be utterly alone, so she could sob her heart out. If she lived a hundred years she would never forget the shame of that terrible moment when Col had rejected her.

He had been willing enough at first, as so had Summer—the more fool she, she thought bitterly. She had secretly endowed him with every heroic virtue. One kiss and she had forgotten her ugliness, borne away by romantic dreams. The reality had been so very different. One touch of her mangled body and he had pulled back, as if burned. The humiliation was devastating.

She curled up in a ball of misery. Then she wept all the tears she had kept back for years, great floods of them; and she wept for the happy future she would never have, as closed and barred to her as *Before*.

When Fanny had a close look at the imposing yacht, she was awed by its sheer size. It hadn't seemed nearly so large from up on the heights.

"Why, it's enormous," she whispered to Thea as they went down the jetty where a tender waited.

"Don't gawk, darling," her sister chided, "or they will consider you farouche. And if the breeze picks up, mind you, watch your skirts!"

There was a darkling glint in Fanny's eye. She was weary of Thea's constant scolds and reminders. "I am not a child. You may be sure I won't do anything to embarrass you." She hadn't gone off to live over a fishmonger's shop with Giovanni, for instance!

"See that you don't. And keep to my side. I don't want you tumbling overboard."

That was so unfair and uncalled for that Fanny determined to spend as much time as possible at the opposite end of the yacht from her sister.

It was a beautiful craft with long, elegant lines, a sleek white hull with a narrow royal blue stripe, and brass fittings polished to the shine and luster of gold. There was little time to admire it, for they were escorted up the gangplank by a uniformed man splendid in white and royal blue and yards of gold braid. Fanny almost mistook him for some glittering military personage who was a guest aboard the yacht; fortunately, she spied another man in the identical uniform passing around a tray of drinks, and realized that both were servants aboard the yacht.

A dimple peeked out at the corner of her mouth. What a faux pas that might have been! She stifled a giggle. How Thea would have stared if she'd known! However, it did serve to remind Fanny that her sister was far more conversant with the social niceties than she was herself.

It was a perfect day for a yachting party, with clear skies and a fresh, warm breeze off the water. The count again expressed regrets that his wife was not yet recovered from the rigors of their journey from Palermo, explaining that his daughter, Emiliana, had elected to stay and keep her company.

"Emiliana looks forward to meeting you both, and is delighted, Miss Fanny, to know there is a young lady near her own age with whom she can visit. My daughter has just passed her seventeenth birthday."

"I shall look forward to making her acquaintance," Fanny replied enthusiastically.

She was in a dither of excitement. Sir Horace pinched her cheeks and called her a pretty minx, and the handsome Viscount Lindell seemed captivated. He listened to her gravely, although there was an odd little smile at the corners of his wide mouth, and she wasn't at all used to his cynical witticisms. Nor was Fanny sure if he realized how close he stood to her at the rail.

She was afraid to call attention to herself and more afraid of offending him, by imagining an impropriety where none was intended. Gathering her courage, she shifted an inch. Then another. He didn't seem to notice at all, and she was greatly relieved; but a few minutes later she felt his arm pressing against hers. It must be the rocking of the boat, she decided.

Surely no gentleman would purposely crowd against a lady in such a manner. Fanny knew that Lord Lindell must be a gentleman. After all, he was a peer of the realm.

She bit her lower lip. Whatever was one supposed to do in such a situation? For the first time she felt the weight of her inexperience. If only Papa and Mrs. Morville had come along! She glanced around for Thea, but her sister was engaged in earnest conversation with their host. Oh, dear!

The situation made her acutely uncomfortable.

Lord Lindell smiled. "Have you had your fill of

gazing at the water? I assure you there will be plenty of time to enjoy it during the afternoon. Are you feeling peckish? Yes? Come, let us find a place to sit out of the wind."

He took her arm and led her to a chair next to Lady Hamlyn. His attentions continued, and Fanny found them both flattering and alarming. She could never be quite sure if he was laughing at her or with her. He plied her with delicacies from the buffet that had been set up until her stomach rebelled. Oh, dear! If she felt like this already, what would she do once they cast off? Fanny took in a deep breath and concentrated on the horizon.

As the yacht pulled away from the harbor and into the open sea, its motion began to affect Fanny. She soon lost interest in everything but her rebelling stomach. Attempts to quell her growing queasiness proved futile. She stumbled toward the stern, hoping not to disgrace herself in front of the other passengers.

She found the gangway and stood wavering, wondering if she should chance going below or stay near the rail. As she swayed a sailor came up to her. "Are you all right, miss?" His accent was that of a Londoner.

"I—I don't know . . ." She pitched forward and he put his arm around her waist to support her.

"Here, miss. Let me help you down below."

"Unhand her, you scoundrel!" Lord Lindell had spotted them and misread the circumstances completely. He grasped the sailor by the shoulder and spun him around. The man didn't even see it coming. The force of the blow and the roll of the yacht conspired to throw him back against the rail. His head struck it and he went down as if he'd been poleaxed.

His eyes rolled up in his head and then his lids fluttered down over them.

Fanny shrieked hysterically. "Oh, oh, oh!" she wailed. "You have *killed* him!"

Lord Lindell tried to pull her away. "I hope I may have done so. If not, I shall finish the job!"

Thea had come running at the sound of Fanny's cries. "What has happened?"

Lord Lindell drew himself up to his full height. "This man tried to drag your sister down the gangway. Fortunately I saw it and intervened."

Sir Horace and the others had heard the altercation and were coming along the deck toward them. Fanny looked up, her face paler than the sailor's shirt. "You are mistaken, my lord. I . . . was overcome . . . he . . . caught me as I fell . . . and—"

She could say no more. Fanny buried her face in her hands as her stomach heaved and rolled like the sea. She was going to be sick in front of everyone.

Thea withered the viscount with one of her stony glances. "I thank you for your good intentions, Lord Lindell, however unnecessary they have proved to be. You need not bother yourself further."

She helped Fanny to her feet. The girl had gone from white to a sickly, greenish hue. Fanny squared her chin bravely. "I thank you for . . . coming to my aid, my lord . . . and I hope this . . . poor fellow . . . will not suffer further . . . for my sake."

Thea was gratified. Fanny, young as she was and ill into the bargain, had handled the affair just as she ought.

Waves of heat swept over Fanny and her ears buzzed. At any moment she was going to lose her breakfast all over the polished deck. Fine beads of perspiration broke out on her forehead.

Suddenly she felt a strong arm around her shoulders, so strong that if she let her knees buckle, as they wanted to do, she would still be held erect. "What the lady needs is fewer people standing about," a deep voice announced. "Come, Miss Fanny. I'll walk you to the bow."

She felt so dizzy and ill she could scarcely keep her eyes open, but that same strong arm propelled her along the deck until she felt the cool breeze on her face. She gulped, took a breath, and held on to the rail for dear life.

"Can you open your eyes? Good. Look straight at the church steeple until we are back in the harbor. Never fear, we'll have you on solid land in a wink."

Fanny nodded, unable to trust herself to speak. The biscuits had risen from her midsection to somewhere in the vicinity of her throat, where they had lodged like a brick. Between the hard feel of the railing against her palms and the strength of her companion she thought she could manage to keep her breakfast down.

"Good girl," her rescuer encouraged. "You'll do."

She glanced up and saw Whitney Vance smiling down at her. She felt dreadful, but was not so ill she didn't register how a smile transformed his craggy features. "Thank you," she managed. "You are very kind."

He only smiled and held her firmly against the rocking of the vessel. It took forever to turn the ship about and return to the harbor, but Whitney Vance stayed at her side the entire time.

Thea watched them. Fanny was safe with Mr. Vance. What a good man he was! Oh, if only her own problems were so easily solved. Lord Lindell was furious with the way she'd spoken to him. Crossing swords with him would do Martin no good. Lindell had friends in high places of the diplomatic service.

Thea put a hand to her temple. It seemed that she managed to sabotage her husband's future at every careless turn. *Oh, Martin!*

Her host joined her. "I didn't realize that your sister was such a poor sailor. How fortunate that we were not far out to sea when she became indisposed."

"It is kind of you, Sir Horace, to turn the yacht back when you had just gotten under way."

"Nonsense." He turned the conversation away from Fanny and to various social events. Their talk seemed to take bizarre twists and turns, as he recalled seeing Thea and Martin at several balls and official functions. "In Vienna, was it not?"

He leaned forward, the tips of his little gnome ears pink from too much sun and champagne. "That little episode?"

She was alarmed. Which episode?

Before she could speak he'd gone on. "No, not Vienna," Sir Horace said softly. "I recall hearing about it afterward." He fixed her with a keen gaze. "Ah, I remember. It was Paris!"

Thea's heart gave a sharp lurch in her chest. Dear God, did he know what a fool she'd made of herself in the French capital? The same calm manner that had served Fanny so well stood Thea in good stead.

"Paris?" she replied calmly. "Which episode might that be? I am sure Paris is rife with them!"

"Ah, all discretion on me now, are you? Well, a lady's reputation is nothing to bandy about, is it? I should tell you that there is not much that goes on in certain circles that doesn't come to my ears." He waggled a finger at her. "I have my ways, Mrs. Armstrong."

Thea was undone. She felt ready to sink through the deck and cool her heated face in the azure waters of the bay. If her folly had come to Sir Horace's notice that meant it was already common knowledge. It was only fair that she should suffer for it, but so unjust that Martin should be condemned as well. She struggled for composure.

"Too many times, Sir Horace, the innocent are dragged down with the guilty. I will not go into the circumstances, however, but only say that—"

"Tut, tut. You need not issue any caveats to me, my dear Mrs. Armstrong. If your husband accidentally discovered a certain highborn lady lurking in a clothes cupboard with one of the footmen, and managed to get them away to safety before her jealous husband came on the scene, you may be sure I did not hear the story from him."

Just as Thea almost collapsed in relief, Sir Horace favored her with an odd little smile. "Martin Armstrong is the last man to destroy a lady's reputation."

A sick rush of despair raced through her. She suspected that he did know of her own little episode, and was merely baiting her. Training and rigid discipline kept her from revealing her panic. Her lips felt as if they'd been carved from wood. She forced herself to smile.

"Yes. My husband is the most gallant of men."

"And ambitious."

She nodded, not trusting her voice. Sir Horace snapped his fingers and a servant produced two glasses of chilled champagne for them. Thea had had enough already, but was too unnerved to refuse. She curled her fingers around the stem of the cut crystal and prayed her hands wouldn't tremble and betray her.

Sir Horace proposed a toast. "To your husband, and to a most distinguished career." He swallowed a healthy mouthful. "I might be persuaded to put in a word for him. You would do everything in your power to advance his career, would you not? Host his parties, flatter the right politicians, put up with hopeless bores at shooting parties and so forth?"

She was wary. "Of course."

"You are an intelligent woman, as well as a beautiful one, Mrs. Armstrong. A combination that has often changed the course of history. Your husband is most fortunate. With your assistance he could go very far indeed." His tiny eyes were bright as boot buttons. His diminutive, perfectly formed fingers rested lightly on her arm.

Thea didn't care for the tone of the conversation, nor where it seemed headed. "I have no great hopes of becoming a fashionable political hostess," she said evenly. "Especially when Martin's duties call him to far-off ports. However I look forward to entertaining his guests during the little season, when my husband returns from Brazil."

"A wise move on your part. I always say that the most stimulating dinner parties are those given by the wives of young up-and-comers. An ambitious woman," he said in smooth, insinuating tones, "would go even farther. Perhaps greatly advancing her husband's ascent by forming a special friendship, even for a night or two, with a man of wealth and power. And, of course, with the consent of her spouse."

With a dull certainty she read the greedy invitation in his eyes. Thea clasped her hands together in her lap so tightly that her gold-and-diamond band bit deeply into her fingers. She wanted to strike him for his insult. Instead she used words as shield and as sword.

"I know my husband, sir! He is of an entirely different breed. Martin would rather labor at the bottom of the darkest, foulest coal mine that you own than to see his wife play the whore for his gain!"

Sir Horace was taken aback. "Blunt speech for the wife of a diplomat." Unexpectedly, he chuckled. "Yes, that is exactly my impression of Mr. Martin Armstrong. I am delighted that you confirm it so boldly. He has a fine champion in you, madam."

Having shot her bolt, Thea was speechless. Sir Horace rose. "And now, if you will excuse me, I have been neglecting my other guests. I am glad that we had this little talk, Mrs. Armstrong. My felicitations to your husband."

As he strolled away Thea found herself shaking from head to foot. She felt besmirched. What an odious, odious man! And she had handled it so badly.

She picked up her champagne and finished it off in one draught, then rose and walked quickly to the rail where she could gather her disordered thoughts. Thea pretended to admire the view of sapphire water and foaming waves, but all her thoughts had gone inward, into the familiar, dark tunnel of hopeless regret.

Now she had done it! One good word from her host would have made Martin's career. The opposite was equally true. And that was how one was usually blackballed, not publicly, with an outcry, but with a subtle word, a pale, lukewarm recommendation, an infinitesimal but telling pause.

Martin was ruined! He would be banished to some dreary outpost or, even worse, be recalled to London to fill some negligible position where he would live out his days, never rising further, always wondering what he had done wrong or whom he had offended.

A great fish broke out of the sea, startling her with an explosion of sound and light. The sun shone off its wonderful scales, shimmering silver and blue and gold. Then it plunged back into the waves, and was lost from sight. Thea sighed. If there were anyone she wished at the bottom of the sea more than the abominable Sir Horace, it was her wretched self!

Fanny's voice drew Thea out of her reverie. She was neglecting her duties sadly. She rose and went to the bow.

"Ah, here is Mrs. Armstrong, now."

Whitney Vance rose and gave up his seat to her. They had entered the harbor and the water was as still as glass. Fanny looked much improved. By the time she was set down on the jetty, her color had returned. It deepened into a blush as she looked for Mr. Vance. He was speaking to one of the sailors, but smiled warmly when he caught her eye.

"Oh, Thea," Fanny whispered, "he is the nicest man! So easy to talk to, and not at all pretentious despite his fame. I am ashamed to think that I avoided him at the dinner party because I thought him ugly. Why, he is really a very attractive man!"

Thea blinked. Was Fanny growing up at last?

"You'll never guess. He knows Martin! They grew up not five miles from one another."

That gave Thea hope. Whitney was the younger brother of Norbert Vance, who headed the Foreign Office. While all it would take was a single negative remark or sly insinuation from Sir Horace to end Martin's career, the right word from Norbert Vance would make him. Thea determined to further her acquaintance with the architect. She must make a good impression upon Mr. Vance, to counteract any harmful seeds that Sir Horace might sow.

The architect approached them. "No more sailing parties for you, Miss Fanny. You must recruit your energies for your return to London. How else will you have the strength for attending the theater and dancing till dawn, then rising an hour later for the rides and shopping and Venetian breakfasts that fill a beautiful young lady's days?"

If he hadn't seemed so genuine, Thea would have deflected his gentle teasing.

Fanny trilled a light laugh. "I assure you, Mr. Vance, that I am fortunate to do any of those in a month's time. We lead a retired life at Kingsmeade, in the country."

He bowed slightly. "London's loss is Kingsmeade's gain."

While Fanny blushed to the roots of her hair, he turned his attention to Thea with the ease of good breeding. "Fanny—your sister," he corrected himself hastily, "mentioned that your husband is Martin Armstrong. I hold him in the highest esteem. To say that he came to the rescue of a shy, sickly lad, and took me under his wing, is to put it mildly. We first met when I was in the process of being flogged half to death by upperclassmen. Although Martin had never set eyes on me before, he waded right in and thrashed the lot of them."

A flash of light shone in Whitney's eyes as they crinkled at the corners. "I thought he was an angel, sent from God."

Like Fanny, Thea found herself coming under the spell of this man's disarming manner. He seemed to think nothing of revealing things that other men would carry with them to the grave, and he did so with grace and humor.

She found him very comfortable to be with, and the two sisters were glad to accept his offer of driving them back to the villa in his hired carriage. As they drove away, Fanny chattered on and on about what a lovely outing it had been, despite its premature ending. Thea agreed.

If only Martin were as easy to talk with, she thought wistfully, their lives might have run an entirely different course.

It was much later when Richard returned home. The women were in the sitting room, for it had turned colder after sunset. Instead of joining them immediately, he went to his study and poured himself a glass of brandy. Half the day had been spent cleaning up in the aftermath of Sir Horace's party.

As it was, there were hardly enough hours in the day. He had to move quickly if he meant to succeed. This project was the culmination of all his dreams, and he had barely scratched the surface.

He removed the stacks of papers off the trunk beside his desk. He'd been using it for extra table space. Opening the trunk, he removed a large wooden box, where he'd put the two small gold statues from the treasury for safekeeping. The box had originally held cigars, but as there was a full humidor atop his desk, there was no reason to open this box.

A quite clever hiding place, he congratulated himself, as he pried out the nail that held the lid fast. No one would expect two such precious artifacts as the golden statues of Demeter and Persephone to be hidden in a lowly cigar box.

*   *   *

The clock was striking ten and the tea tray had just been brought in for the ladies. Thea poured, adding lemon to Cynthia's cup and sugar to Fanny's. She was about to pour out a cup for Summer when their father came into the room. He didn't say a word at first, but stood just outside the main circle of lamp-light.

A feathery insect fluttered around the clear globe, then flew up to lose itself in the shadows along the ceiling.

Fanny saw him first. "Papa? What is wrong?"

He held out the box to Thea. She looked at him questioningly. "Open it," he said hoarsely. "It is where I put the statues of Demeter and Persephone for safekeeping."

Thea lifted the lid. Inside, nestled in packing material where he had placed the statues, were two smooth black stones.

Thea was aghast. "Gone! But who could have taken them?"

"When did you last see them?" Fanny asked.

"The night of the find. I wrapped them up and hid them away in my trunk."

Cynthia rose at once and went to Richard's side. "So, it has happened again!"

He looked up sharply. "What do you mean?"

"I cannot believe that this is a coincidence. No, Richard, it is part of a plot to discredit you. He must not get away with it this time!"

"A plot?" Thea was alarmed. Who would try to harm her father?

Fanny's question was more basic. *"Who* is *he?"* she asked.

Summer said nothing at all. Her face looked tired and pinched.

Richard frowned. "Do you recall everyone who has been here these past two days?"

"The servants, of course. Mrs. and Miss Symington came to call," Thea said, ticking the names off on her fingers. "Angus brought up more of the mosaic pieces to be assembled. Giovanni delivered your note regarding Sir Horace's party. As we were leaving Miss Symington came back to drop off a collection of poems."

"Did any of them have the opportunity to go through my things?"

"I don't believe so."

"And no one else came by?" Richard's gaze raked the room.

Summer shrank back in her chair. No one but Col McCallum. She remembered, with a sinking heart, how she'd heard him walking about, opening and closing doors. No, he couldn't have done it. He would never have stolen the statues.

"Who couldn't have done it?" her father demanded, spinning to face her.

Summer went very still. She must have spoken aloud without realizing it. Doubt stabbed her. What did she really know of Col? She remembered now he had come up to the terrace at dawn, too early and not in the place he'd designated for their meeting. Had he been looking for other treasures? She began to shiver. Her whole universe was destroyed. She was lost in a cold, black void where the strained faces of the others seemed far, far away, like distant stars.

They came toward her, their mouths moving, yet she heard no sound except the rushing in her ears.

When she tried to speak nothing came out. She had been floating in the space between the planets so long she had lost her voice. It was frozen, like her heart.

Fanny stared at her and Thea ran to kneel at her side. Taking Summer's cold hands in hers, she chafed them until her sister responded. "Who came to the villa, Summer? Was it Col McCallum?"

"Yes," Summer whispered in a voice as cold as death.

The moon rose in a hazy night sky, spilling diffuse light over the island. The Court of Three Sisters was dark and still, but all its occupants remained awake while the hours crept by.

Fanny heard a door creak. It sounded like Thea's. Perhaps she was unable to sleep, too. After a while Fanny got up and put on her dressing gown. She needed company. There were too many whispering shadows in the corners of her room.

She padded barefoot to her elder sister's chamber. The door was shut fast. Fanny started to knock, then thought better of it. If Thea were sleeping she didn't want to disturb her. The creak might have come from anywhere in the old house. The place was full of sounds tonight.

She wondered what time it was. It must be late, judging from the slant of moonlight. It made everything appear in gray and black, like one of Summer's ink-wash drawings. As if there were no color in a world gone bleak, and never would be.

The courtyard was silvered with moonlight but reminded her of Giovanni and her earlier foolishness. The thought of Whitney Vance came to her. She wished that he could steady all of them against the theft of the statues, as he had done for her aboard the yacht.

The terrace beckoned and she went to sit awhile on the chaise. Afterward she couldn't remember how much time had passed while she remembered the day's events. The walls had absorbed the day's heat and radiated it back to her. Fanny yawned and closed her eyes. She was leaning back in the chaise, cozy and half dozing, when she heard something that set her hair on end: a low sound, half moan and half despairing sigh.

Fanny froze in place, expecting that some foul specter had roused itself from an ancient grave. Certainly there was nothing human about it. Shivering, she shrank back against the chaise as if she would meld with its cushions. A figure moved out of the darkness.

"Papa! How you startled me!"

Richard turned to his youngest daughter. His face was puzzled and blank, as if he wasn't quite sure who she was. "Fanny?" he said at last.

She rose. "Yes, Papa?"

He stared at her in the silver-gray light. "Go to bed child. It's late."

"Yes, Papa."

His demeanor frightened her. Even his face looked changed. She shivered as she walked past him. The world was upside down. Her beloved father seemed like a total stranger.

As Fanny started for her room she stopped short. What was that in his hand? It looked like a gun. She wheeled around for a better look. The moon glinted off the brandy snifter in his left hand.

Fanny sighed and went back to bed. It had only been an illusion.

*   *   *

Col was dreaming. He knew it was a dream, because Carruthers was sitting on the floor beside him, and he knew Carruthers was dead. Evidently no one had informed him of it. The old lion leaned down. "Get up, you lazy young cub. I don't have all night."

"I'm tired, damn it. You've left me a mess to untangle. You and your cryptic notes!"

Carruthers laughed. "If I'd made it any clearer, someone else would have found it by now. I saved it for you. You and Kallista."

Col wiped a hand over his eyes. "Who the hell is Kallista?"

Another chuckle. "That girl. You remember."

"I'm not sure. . . ."

"That's because there've been too many of them for you to keep proper track of! I mean the one who is a priestess in the temple of Persephone. It's been a while, but surely you can still recall her."

"Damn it, why do you always have to speak in riddles?"

The old lion grinned. "Life is a riddle, Col. Never forget it."

Carruthers got up and went toward the door. Col raised himself up on one elbow. "Where the hell are you going this time?"

Carruthers leaned against the doorjamb. "I'm not quite sure yet, but I can tell you that I'm a busy man. I've got things to do. Better things than sitting around watching you lie in a pool of blood." He opened the door. "I'd get up if I were you."

The door shut behind Carruthers, but not before he'd given Col a grin and a wink. His voice came like a fading echo. "Find Kallista. She'll help."

Damn the man, Col thought.

He looked around. There was no blood. Only a widening pool of ink in the moonlight shafting through the open window. It ran over the smooth tiles of the floor, glistening darkly. Why, it was even on his shirt. He touched it. Slightly sticky.

Warm as blood.

He cried out for Carruthers. "Come back! I need your help."

A voice echoed softly around the room, although it might have been nothing but the wind, soughing through the trees. "Find Kallista! Find Persephone!"

Col was tired. He was sick of riddles. He would just close his eyes for a few minutes . . .

What was that? The door opened again. He turned his head, expecting to see Carruthers. It was only a dark, hooded form. "I thought that was only an artist's conceit," he told it, but his voice had changed and nothing came out but a long sigh. He heard the figure moving about the room. Papers scattered and notebooks fell. Death was making a terrible mess of the place, he thought.

Carruthers was talking to him again. This time the voice was in his head. *Damn your eyes, Col, wake up! Find Kallista before it's too late.*

Good advice, Col was sure, but it was already too late. The ink had spread to cover the floor and walls and ceiling. It filmed the open window, thickening like clotting blood, until it blotted up the last of the light.

12

REVELATIONS

Notes from a lady's diary

> *There are few crosses to bear that are worse
> than the knowledge that you have made the
> wrong choice, and that those you love have
> suffered for it.*

    The sun was scarcely over the horizon when
Richard rode over to the *castello* to report the theft
to his patrons. The gray walls of volcanic rock
matched the heavy clouds rolling in from the sea.
The air was pregnant with the coming storm. As he
dismounted and went up the stairs to the imposing
gothic door, a gust of wind whipped through the
tops of the trees.

A most superior servant answered his sum-
mons, looking affronted at the early hour. "I
regret to say that the count is not at home. He and

Sir Horace sailed on with their party to Lipari yesterday afternoon. They will be away at least three days."

There was nothing Richard could do, except gnash his teeth and leave a note for his patrons to call upon him at the earliest possible moment. He thanked the servant and left, cursing beneath his breath. But by the time he returned to the Court of Three Sisters he'd decided that it might work to his advantage.

The air was growing thick, the sky a steely gray. He spurred his horse into a canter. By God, all they needed was an early rainy season to muddle everything!

He returned to the villa and assembled his daughters and Cynthia Morville in his study. It was a subdued group. Thea was tense, Fanny apprehensive, and Summer lost in silent self-recriminations.

"It will be difficult, perhaps impossible," Richard told them, "but it is absolutely essential that we continue as if nothing untoward has happened. Cynthia, you must go alone to the temple complex to begin the day's work. Tell them I will be detained until the afternoon, and ask Symington to take charge in my absence. I have other matters to attend to."

From the grim way he said it, they all guessed that Col McCallum was one of those matters, and that he would be dealt with harshly. "I am counting on you to hold up your heads and pretend that nothing is wrong," he added quietly. "Perhaps it would be a good idea to have a small dinner party this evening—the Symingtons, Forsythe, and Angus Gordon."

Thea gave a little gasp of dismay, but rallied. If it was necessary to her father's plans, she would gladly do her part. She spoke the fear that had preyed upon her through the long night.

"Should you go alone, Father? If you intend to beard Mr. McCallum, it might be wise to have one of your colleagues with you."

"No. This must be kept close to the vest. If I can take care of this dilemma before Sir Horace and the count return from Lipari, none of it need ever be made public. If the slightest word leaks out, I am ruined!"

They sat down to breakfast in the loggia as usual, but only he and Fanny managed to do justice to the meal. Cynthia looked pale and tired. She pushed her food around her plate, and ended up feeding most of it to the cats. Summer ate nothing at all. Richard left them and rode out, without further explanation. Cynthia departed for the temple site shortly afterward, leaving the sisters alone.

Thea withdrew for an hour to write her endless letters. Letters she never sent. Summer had seen them neatly stacked in the inlaid chest in her sister's room, each addressed to Martin Armstrong in Thea's firm hand.

The rain held off but the sun stayed hidden behind the ominous clouds. Summer paced the terrace restlessly, watched by the lazing cats, until the uneven sound of her footsteps wore on everyone's nerves. If Col had been responsible for the theft, then it was all her fault; but try as she might, she could not imagine that he had done it. The evidence, so damning by moonlight, seemed insubstantial by morning's light. Logic said that Col was the most likely culprit. Her heart refused to listen. The more she tried to follow the threads of probability, the more her thoughts tangled into knots.

Thea felt she would scream if Summer made the circuit of the terrace one more time. This brooding was no good. They all needed to keep busy.

"Fanny, you have been wanting some of the wild-flowers for the gardens. I think we should go out and dig some up before the rain comes. Then they won't dry out before we can replant them. And, God knows, it will do us all good to get outside these walls for an hour or two."

"Yes." Fanny brightened a little. "That is the very thing to take our minds off the th—off our problems."

She went to fetch the buckets and handspades they would need for transplanting while Thea rounded up old gloves to protect their hands. Although Summer had no interest in digging up flowers, or in much of anything, at the moment, she went along with her sisters.

Thea was used to organizing. She pointed out which flowers were suitable and which were likely to grow too tall for the raised beds of the courtyard. She was afraid that Fanny would turn mulish when she advised against a certain dark-eyed purple bloom. To her surprise, Fanny took her advice.

Summer seated herself in a flower-strewn patch of meadow. A few weeks earlier she would not have been up to the task, but hours spent uncovering her mosaic had strengthened her. Soon more than a dozen clumps of wildflowers rested in the bottom of her bucket. It was a mindless task, one that left her thoughts too free. She was sure if she could just see Col, she would be able to divine the truth.

Suddenly she became aware of hoofbeats, drumming in the distance. Could it be? . . .

Disappointment was replaced with curiosity.

There were two women crossing the far meadow on horseback. She'd thought from her father's remarks that the entire *castello* party had gone to Lipari. Evidently some had stayed behind. They were apparently trying to reach the *castello* before the rain came.

Both women were dressed in the height of fashion, one in a smart, blue military-style habit, the other in buff faced with white. Their hats were trimmed with long, gauzy scarves that billowed out behind them like angel's wings.

Something about those filmy, trailing scarves was so familiar. . . .

As she tried to figure out why, Summer was suddenly jolted. The door to *Before* swung silently open and the scarves became drifting seaweed beneath reflecting water. She stiffened, fighting against what she felt was coming. The seaweed faded. The wild meadow came back, shifted, and became a sedate green lawn edged by giant oaks. The scene was quintessentially English. Summer recognized it: The long drive at Kingsmeade, on a fresh spring morning.

As she watched, confused and spellbound, a woman in blue cantered up the lane toward her. The ends of her long scarf trailed gracefully, fluttering like gossamer wings. Eager yet afraid, Summer strained to see the woman's face. Her heart pounded because she knew, oh, yes, she knew who it was!

Summer laughed happily and reined in her dappled pony. "Mother! I rode down to meet you. I knew you would be coming back soon!"

"Summer! My dear child, what on earth are you doing sitting out here?"

The voice altered in timbre. Became altogether different. Breathy. Sly. "Why, Summer, whatever are you doing about so early in the morning?"

Summer looked around, bewildered. This wasn't England. This was Greece. There was no mistaking the honeyed light or the whitewashed houses in the distance, climbing up the dusty hills that grew purple with distance. She accepted it as the strange logic of dreams.

"Does anyone know that you are up and out of the house?" the voice asked.

"N—no. The others are all still asleep," she confided. "I always awaken before the others, but today I got up earlier than usual."

She didn't say that it was because she had heard her mother moving quietly through the rooms as she lay awake beside Fanny. Or that when she had tiptoed from her bed she had glimpsed Mama's black-and-white silk dress swirl through the door as it shut.

"I heard the gulls screaming and I thought it was much later. They don't generally make such a racket so early. Since I was already up and dressed I went down to the strand and collected a bucket of shells. I'm making a garden of them. It's a surprise. I thought I had enough, you see, but I find I shall need many, many more."

"What an enterprising child you are! Did you see the fishing boats go out?"

"No, they were already gone by then. But I saw you on the cliffs. Did the gulls awaken you, too?"

The voice became smooth and sweet as toffee. "You shouldn't be walking around so early, especially down by the water. It could be dangerous. The moon is full and the water is much higher than usual. There is only a thin crest of land at the foot of the cliffs."

Summer was disappointed. She sighed. "I suppose I could go up to the meadow and look for buried treasure."

That was her favorite game. Someday she would be an archaeologist like her father, if she didn't decide to be an artist. Fanny said that only men could do such things but Summer knew better. She had told Fanny that she was a silly child, and Fanny had burst into tears.

"I know," the voice said softly. "I will take you down to the shore myself. I have discovered a special place just littered with shells of every description. Hundreds and hundreds of them."

A hand reached out and Summer put hers into it, trustingly. They started through the trees toward the cliffs. "Not that way," Summer said. "It is much too steep. Mother told me never to take that way down."

"Oh, that is when you are by yourself. You'll be perfectly safe with me. Hurry, now."

By the time they reached the cliffs Summer was panting. "You are going too fast for me," she said. She wanted to say that her hand was being held much too tightly, but was too polite to do so. They would be at the steps cut into the rock in a moment and then they would have to go single file.

Summer was eager to see the place with all the shells; but as they reached the cliff path her feet began to lag. The sun was already warm but she felt a chill. "Perhaps I should go back to the house."

"Nonsense. Come with me. I have something interesting to show you."

"I had better go home. Nana will be worried. I don't believe I need any more shells after all."

It was too late. They were at the head of the cliff path, and the hand was pulling her along, down the steep, narrow stairs. Then they were halfway, at the spot where you could see nothing but sea and air. The water was figured silk in emerald hues and the air was as cold, as hard as crystal. It stabbed at Summer. "Please! I want to go back. I want—"

She stopped. Something lay crumpled below in a pool of still water. Black-and-white silk folded in upon itself in a pool of water, shining like a looking glass amid the pale gray rock. Her heart turned over. "Mama! Mama!" Something hit her in the back with terrible force.

And then she was falling, too terrified to scream, falling, flying, like a gull over the edge of the cliff. She spread her wings but they were only arms. Useless, flailing arms.

It took hours, days, years to fall . . . it was over in seconds. The smooth white ground became the hard shingle of the beach, flying up to meet her. If she hit it she would be dead.

Dead like Mama, lying in the shallow pool of water.

Tears filled her eyes, spilled over onto her cheeks. Small, stinging tears. They covered her face like a mother's kisses.

It was starting to rain.

"Summer? It's starting to rain. Summer! What on earth?"

The door to *Before* shut softly. Incompletely.

Summer shook her head to clear it. The implications were clear: She was not losing her mind, she was—she really was—*remembering*.

A different kind of fear filled her. She took a deep breath.

The vision of Greece was gone and the reality of the women in the meadow was gone, but the illusion of her mother, riding up the drive at Kingsmeade to meet her, came back for a few brief moments. Then the scene shimmered and her mother's transparent image faded like the leafy oak branches framing her against the glorious blue sky.

Summer was bereft. She blinked against the sudden flood of light. Her eyes were dazzled and her brain felt numb.

Thea was kneeling beside her, pink with concern. Drops of rain spattered them. "Are you all right?"

"Yes. Only blinded by the sun." She picked up her straw hat, which had fallen off, and replaced it.

Thea was frightened. "There is no sun."

Summer looked up into a hazy pewter sky. A raindrop fell on her cheek and coursed down it like a tear. Glancing back at the two horsewomen, she saw them vanish over a rise.

Fanny came over, her bucket well filled. "Was that Lady Hamlyn? I couldn't be sure of the other. Do you think it could be the contessa?"

Thea replied. "My view of the second rider was blocked. I believe it was Signora Croccetti, the contessa's secretary. They will be soaked through if they don't hurry. And so shall we!"

The wind freshened as she spoke and rain speckled their gowns. Any moment the clouds would open in earnest. Thea shooed her sisters back to the house.

It was dark inside, as if an angry twilight had fallen over the land. A flare of lightning illuminated the courtyard as they set their buckets in a corner of the loggia and hurried to the safety of the sitting room.

Thea lit the lamp. "How gloomy it is! I hope this passes over quickly." Fanny went off in search of the novel she'd been reading.

Summer had gone very quiet since their return, lost in the effort of trying to remember. She spoke abruptly: "Thea? I recalled something. A dappled pony . . . Sugarplum? Did I ride, before my accident?"

"Oh, my dear." Thea took her hand and pressed it gently. "You were a fearless rider! You rode like the wind. I don't believe you ever took a fall from the first time you were up in the saddle."

Summer relaxed a little. That explained the vision that she had just experienced. It was like *Before*, yet somehow different. She wondered if it had been an illusion, or a true memory. Certainly it had seemed very real.

"Sugarplum was your very own pony," Thea told her. "You picked her out yourself when Father took you to see the foals at the Keaton Fair. You were positively besotted with her. Mother said—" She paused, then went on more strongly. "Mother said she was half afraid you'd smuggle the pony into your room at night, or slip out to the stables and sleep in the straw to be near Sugarplum!"

Summer fixed Thea with an earnest gaze. "Tell me about our mother. What was she like?"

Thea stiffened. "What a peculiar question!"

"No. The only thing peculiar about it is that I hadn't asked it sooner." Summer put her hand on her sister's sleeve. She saw the hesitation in Thea's face.

"Please," she urged, "tell me about our mother. As a person. I don't really know anything about her, except that she was very beautiful."

For a moment she thought that Thea would refuse; but after a long pause, her sister spread her skirts and sat beside Summer on the settee. "What would you like to know?"

"Everything! From your very earliest memory.

What was she like? How did she spend her time? Was she musical? Did she love poetry? Was she . . . was she happy?"

Thea's eyes took on a faraway look and her voice was low and soft. "My earliest memory is of sitting outdoors with her on the grass. I was a little more than two years of age, I believe. A kitten gamboled about playing with the ribbons of my bonnet. Mother was singing and plaiting a coronet of daisies for me. Then father came out to join us. He put me up on his shoulders and carried me back to the house. We were all very happy."

Thea picked at the braiding on her skirt that had come loose. "Mother loved music. She sang like an angel, and she played the pianoforte quite well. We gathered round it and sang together for an hour or so almost every evening."

That surprised Summer. There was no piano now at Kingsmeade, although one was considered an important part of every well-to-do household. Fanny's desire to obtain one a few months earlier had been summarily dismissed.

Perhaps it was too painful for their father to have one in his home. Grief did strange things to people.

"Tell me more, please. Did she share Father's interest in his work? Did she travel with him as Mrs. Symington does with her husband?"

"In the early days. By the time Fanny was born, Mother was ready to put roots down in England. We settled into Kingsmeade quite happily. Then the opportunity came to go to Rhodes for a season. Father said it was too good to pass up, so we all packed up and sailed off for the Greek Isles. We spent four years there."

A tantalizing memory sprang into Summer's mind. "And you met Martin there!"

A sigh from Thea. "Yes. You are remembering! How long ago that seems! We were married the following year, and started out on our honeymoon, while the rest of the family went on to Ilykion." Her voice softened with remembering. "But it was on Rhodes that Mother lost the son she'd been carrying. Father thought Ilykion would be a change of scene."

Thea paused. Rain rattled on the roof tiles. "That was the beginning of the bad times." She worked away more of the loose braid. "Nothing was ever the same after that."

"The accident, you mean?"

"What? Oh, yes, of course. The accident."

Summer realized that Thea was struggling to keep her composure. Tears filled her eyes and muffled her voice. Seeing her distress, Summer was sorry she'd stirred up the past with her questions. And yet, it was almost as if Thea had been speaking of something entirely different.

A sadness had come over her, as if Thea's mood were infectious. "I'm glad we spoke of Mother. Perhaps we can talk of her more often. I think Fanny would like to know about her, too."

"Perhaps you're right." Thea rose, tears trembling on her lashes. "Summer, we were very happy. And we were loved."

She gathered her skirts and left the room with a fleetness that left Summer slightly envious, and more confused than ever.

By noon the rain cleared and the sky had a fresh-washed innocence. Summer was curled up on the chaise in her favorite spot, a book of Rosalind Symington's poetry opened beside her. The poetry was an anodyne to her own roiled emotions.

I am the heart of the dark night
still and silent in my grief.
pierced by sunbeams,
bleeding shadows in the light. . . .

The words echoed in Summer's mind, stark and poignant. She sensed that Rosalind was cursed with the ability to feel everything more deeply than others, but blessed with the power to turn her pain into a moving beauty.

Fanny finished planting the wildflowers while Summer read, and they had just gone in to dine when Zita came bouncing in. "A message from the *castello*," she announced enthusiastically.

Thea looked at the expensive crested envelope. She broke the wafer and removed a single sheet.

"It is from Signora Croccetti. She writes that the contessa is much recovered from the rigors of her journey, and invites us to visit her this afternoon, for tea and cakes in the *castello*'s garden."

"The *contessa!*" Fanny was as excited as Zita. "How splendid that sounds. Do say we may go to meet her!"

Thea smiled wryly. "I see no way out of it."

The hours passed slowly until it was time to meet the contessa. Summer's heart was too heavy to look forward to their visit, but it was better than being all alone with her thoughts.

They found the *castello* as intriguing up close as it was from a distance. It was older than it had appeared, and would not have looked out of place plunked down in the British Isles. Thea reminded them that at one time the Normans had ruled Sicily and the nearby islands. Indeed, as they rode under the machiolated gate, they saw the coat of arms of Richard the Lion-Hearted carved beside that of the DiCaesaris'. Fanny, who hadn't cared earlier to learn anything about the area's history, looked around eagerly.

"Mr. Vance must find this place quite intriguing," she said in a suspiciously offhanded manner. "In addition to his own buildings, he studies the architecture of other lands and times. One can tell a good deal of the people by the style of their homes and cities."

"You sound like a trained parrot," Summer said wryly. "Mr. Vance must have reformed your first impression of him."

Fanny had the grace to blush. "I have learned never to judge by appearances," she said flatly. "In fact, I do not know why I ever thought him anything but attractive, in a warm and genuine way."

Thea knew she should be alarmed. It was obvious that her youngest sister was in a fair way to developing a tendresse for Whitney Vance. Instead she smiled and asked a question regarding him, just for the fun of seeing Fanny's face come alive with radiance.

Ah, well. Even if the architect had no interest in such a young chit, Thea knew that Fanny would come to no harm through him. He would be as gentle with her girlish heart as he had been with her person. Martin had the same sort of goodness about him, she realized with a pang. It was no wonder that the two men were friends.

Their carriage had entered a wide, cobbled yard. Grooms leapt to take the horses' bits and liveried servants handed the ladies down from the carriage.

Summer hesitated at the door. It was ancient, banded in steel, and carved of heavy oak. Exactly like the door she imagined, that barred the way to *Before*. Then it swung wide and she entered.

Signora Croccetti met them in the airy hall and welcomed them. Despite its exterior grimness, the inside of the *castello* was luxurious. This chamber had tall windows all along two sides and was hung with glorious paintings and an assortment of weapons dating back to the time of the first Plantagenets. There were vases and bowls of flowers everywhere, on the mantelpiece and the polished refectory table, which meant that the gardens were maintained in style, even though the count rarely visited his island retreat.

"The contessa will be down shortly. Emiliana is in the gardens. I shall escort you there," the woman said, and led them down a hall, through elegant salons. They went through a conservatory and out into the gardens. They were extensive, a miracle of color and bloom, with arbors and topiary, marble statues in niches, cushioned benches, and a central fountain in an artificial pond.

A young girl, as fair of hair as Fanny, was throwing bits of bread to the ornamental fish that darted in the clear waters of the pond. She was dressed in exquisite continental style, which Fanny immediately envied, and came forward eagerly to meet the guests. She had a high forehead, full mouth, and a gentle, grave demeanor that hinted of natural shyness; her brown eyes were warm with pleasure as she extended her hand in greeting.

"I have so looked forward to meeting you all," she said as they were introduced. "I hope that we may stay the season, now that you are here."

Signora Croccetti invited them to be comfortable. "I shall tell the contessa you have arrived, and see that refreshments are brought out to us."

Within minutes the outgoing Fanny and reserved Emiliana were fast friends. They took Summer off to feed the ornamental fish, but Thea stayed behind to await their hostess. Summer found herself drawn to a statue of a Roman mother with a smiling child. It stood beneath a flowering tree. Its branches were still loaded with blossoms, but the rain had knocked loose petals from them. They littered the ground like pink and white confetti. It reminded Summer of something.

The garden faded. There were white and pink pebbles on a beach. White-hot sun and black shadows under the water. No. Not shadows. It was . . . it was . . .

"Not here! Not here," she whispered, and the vision went away at once. Summer was amazed. Could it be that she was learning how to control the episodes? And if she could banish them at will, could she—should she—conjure them up purposely?

A shiver played over her skin. Her earlier vision of the cliffs in Greece, of falling, had faded away like the echoes of a bad dream. It lingered on the very edge of consciousness and she was afraid to draw it out again, into the light of knowledge.

Perhaps it was better never to know exactly what had happened.

While Summer battled for control of her memories and the two younger girls went off, Thea waited and counted the minutes. Unless the contessa was truly an invalid, her behavior bordered on rudeness. She was wondering how much longer they would be kept waiting, when the secretary appeared at the conservatory door.

"If you would be so kind as to come with me, Signora Armstrong, the contessa would speak with you a moment in private."

An odd request. Perhaps she had suffered a relapse of whatever ailed her. Thea rose. "As you please."

She followed the woman inside and through a door she hadn't noticed earlier. It lead to a lovely sitting room, hung with peach silk and furnished with gilded antiques. Signora Croccetti disappeared, leaving Thea to examine the painted walls and rococo ceiling.

She was overwhelmed. A drawing by da Vinci, simple yet capturing the essence of a young girl, was framed in silver over an inlaid escritoire. In this room of treasures it seemed no more remarkable than the grouping of family portraits along the mantelpiece. And surely Tintoretto had created that masterpiece!

There was so much splendor that her eyes could barely take it in. She drifted toward the fireplace and glanced at a charming photograph of Emiliana in a white gown. Beside it stood a larger one, the man in it obviously a younger version of the count. The next was a woman of haunting beauty, with deep-set eyes of peculiar intensity. On the other end was a family grouping. The picture was creased with white lines and had faded with time and strong light.

Thea picked it up for a closer look—and almost dropped it. It couldn't be!

She took it to the window and held it so the light struck its surface at an oblique angle. Her hands trembled. She had not been mistaken. There, looking up at her from a gilded frame, was a formal family portrait. A Fairchild family portrait. She saw her own face staring back at her, younger and filled with assurance. Summer standing beside her chair, straight and strong. Father smiling proudly. Fanny a baby in their mother's arms. But how had this portrait come to be here? Even as she refused to acknowledge the answer, Thea knew.

She turned at a soft rustle of silk and froze. A woman was framed in the opposite doorway. Although she was in shadow Thea's heart turned over.

"That was my favorite picture. It was taken that last autumn at Kingsmeade, do you remember?" a low voice said. "It has been my solace in exile. It was all I could take of you with me."

Thea couldn't find her voice. The woman stepped into the room, graceful despite her advanced pregnancy. "It was inexcusable of me to lure you here in such a way. I cannot blame you if you turn from me. But please don't go, I beg of you! I must talk to you about . . . about so much!"

"But—" Thea was flabbergasted. *"Mother?"*

She stepped forward slowly, like a sleepwalker. Ten years had passed, yet time had been kind to the woman who had given her birth. Thea felt as if she were walking through syrup, every movement slow and filled with effort. Then she was running across the carpet until they were face to face. In a split-second they were in each other's arms.

Orelia wept as she held her eldest daughter. "I thought you would hate me. I never dreamed . . ."

Thea's face was shining with tears and happiness. Of the sisters, she alone had known that their mother was still alive, somewhere. But she had never expected to find her here, on Ellysia. "How did this come to be? What are you doing here? Oh, the joy of seeing you again!"

"When you hear me out you may not be as glad to see me." Orelia's tear-ravaged face grew composed. She led her eldest daughter to a sofa. "I never dared hope that I would be granted this chance, yet I have prayed that somehow we might meet again." She paused a moment to collect her thoughts.

"We were at our home in Palermo and had planned to pay a visit to Ellysia, to see how the excavations were coming along. John Carruthers had remained a friend to me over the years. Then I learned that Richard—that your father was coming to join him."

She took Thea's hand and held it like a lifeline. "I had no intention of setting foot upon Ellysia under the circumstances. I have caused your father enough sorrow. But then I heard—" She stopped, swallowed, then went on. "I heard that Summer is very ill, crippled, someone said." Her face contorted. "Oh, my dear! I had to come. I had to know. . . ."

They sat together, matching one another tear for tear, and poured out their histories of the ten years since their parting.

Summer looked around for Thea. She seemed to have vanished. Fanny was still enchanted with the colorful fish and her new friend. Now the two girls had run out of bread, and amused themselves by scattering petals on the water to watch the curious fish rise up and investigate.

Summer wandered along a path past a topiary unicorn and back toward the conservatory. The contessa certainly had a strange way of entertaining guests, she thought. Something caught her attention. Was that Thea's voice? Moving beneath an arbor, she found herself in a garden of ornamental herbs. The air was rich with early lavender.

Suddenly she felt dizzy and reached out to support herself on the iron gate. For a few frightening moments she relived the earthquake and its aftermath. The *castello* quivered like aspic and dissolved into an empty meadow, where girls were gathering flowers to garland the shrine above the village.

Their short tunics flashed around their bare legs as they turned to look up at the sky. A puff of dark smoke lifted above the tip of Hades's cone, just visible over the trees. It spread rapidly outward. Within seconds the air smelled of sulfur and tiny flecks of pumice rained from the sky. The children squealed and ran toward Cliete and . . .

Summer struggled and won. Whatever the origin of the strange scene, she had managed to send it back to its source!

Her confidence was almost her undoing. Then the facade of the *castello* dissolved into a gray wall of enormous stones. The garden became an area of disturbed ground, mounded into weathered hills and riddled with trenches.

She had fallen and skinned her knee. It was bleeding badly. She knew she shouldn't have been climbing around the excavations. It was dangerous and forbidden. Father would be very angry with her for disobeying. It would be better to go to Mother. She was here somewhere, sorting through baskets of potsherds. She would take care of it.

Yes, there she was, behind the wagon. "I'm sorry I didn't mind. I'm sorry I fell . . . I'm sorry. . . ."

Summer came to her senses with a shock. The

scene faded. She recognized it suddenly. *Greece. Ilykion!* She began to shiver. With every trace of memory she came closer to the fearful things locked away in her heart.

She thought that she was hearing voices. Belatedly she realized that it wasn't from memory. Her feet moved of their own accord. She followed the sounds to their source.

A pair of glass doors were opened to the herb garden, and they came from just inside.

"I am so sorry. So very sorry," a gentle voice murmured. "My dear Thea, perhaps if I had been there to guide you, you would not have gotten yourself into such a fix."

Thea's voice came, low and anguished. "You mustn't blame yourself! It was all my doing. But what shall I do? Oh, what shall I do?"

"My poor child, I am the last person to advise you, when I have muddled my own life so terribly! My best advice is this. Follow your heart. Don't let false pride—yours, or his—stand between you."

Summer cocked her head, puzzled. The voice was oddly familiar. It drew her. Drew her against her will. She was filled with longing and fear, yet the voice was a siren song, leading her on.

The voice had dropped to a murmur. Was that weeping she heard now, or was she falling back into *Before*? Summer stopped and almost turned away. Something compelled her on. She stepped through the doorway and saw Thea sitting on a velvet sofa, her head against a woman's shoulder. The woman was stroking her hair, comforting her.

At first Summer thought the other woman was Cynthia Morville. Then the woman looked up and straight at her. Summer gasped. Thea jerked away.

The woman rose to her feet. She held her arms out imploringly.

If not for Thea's presence, Summer would have thought it was one of her strange visions. Yet the same breeze that stirred the ribbons of Thea's skirt and brushed her own cheek wafted the draperies of the woman's exquisite gown. Summer crossed the rug, her lame foot scuffing the nap. One step. Two steps. Three.

Orelia burst into tears. "Oh, Summer! My darling Summer! What have I done to you?"

Summer looked into her face, the forgotten-familiar face that she had seen every day at Kingsmeade. Older now, more fragile and even more beautiful, but still the face that stared out at her from the portrait over the mantel in the drawing room at Kingsmeade. She trembled violently with reaction.

Was it possible? How could it be? Yet here she was, only a few feet away. At first it was only a woman with the face from her mother's portrait. Then some psychic stricture loosened, and suddenly Summer remembered.

Her breath caught in her throat. She stumbled forward and threw herself into the woman's arms. "Oh, Mother! Mother! I thought you were dead. They told me you were dead!"

There were tears on Summer's cheek, but whether her own or her mother's, she couldn't tell. They were both shaking, clinging, touching as if each wanted to assure herself of the other's reality.

When they finally broke from their embrace Summer's mind was awhirl with questions. "I don't understand . . . how . . . *why?*"

Her mother's face was anguished, her voice choked with tears. "You remember me, but not—not *that?*"

It was true. She knew her mother's voice and scent. There were jumbled fragments of memory like the pieces of the mosaics she'd been trying to piece together. But nothing that she could hold on to. It was like trying to grab handfuls of fog.

"No. There is so much missing . . . most of it, in fact. But, oh! Mother, I do remember you!"

Summer turned to Thea. The answer was in her sister's face but she asked it anyway. "You knew, didn't you?"

"Yes. I—"

"How long?"

Thea was very pale and quiet. "From the time I returned from my honeymoon. Father told me then."

"Father? Father knew?"

It was all too confusing. Summer put her hands to her temples. "I don't understand any of it!"

The silence was appalling. If Thea was pale, their mother had gone white and bloodless. Orelia sat up very straight. "I must tell you the entire truth. I owe it to you. My darlings, try not to think too harshly of me. I was wicked. Wicked and foolish."

She lifted her chin and tried to meet her younger daughter's eyes. "Your father and I were . . . unhappy. We were ill suited from the start. I was only sixteen when we were wed. I tried to understand his life. Tried and could not. I was sick of living in tents and hovels. We quarreled.

"Richard—your father—tried to accommodate to me. He did try. We went back to England but the academic life was not for him. Eventually he went back to excavating and we went along. Your father thought it would be educational."

"To Greece," Summer said softly.

"Yes. To Greece." The pain in Orelia's voice was

blurred with a layer of sorrow, like a coating of thick rust. Her eyes were dark with remembering, and neither daughter dared disturb her.

"Conditions were poor at Ilykion," their mother said. "I didn't want to be there. There was much illness that season. I was with child. I lost him in the sixth month, after a bout of fever—a beautiful, well-formed boy. The rift between us deepened. Your father and I could scarcely be in the same room with one another."

She looked from Thea to Summer. "I am not telling you this to excuse myself. I acted inexcusably. If I live a thousand years I cannot forgive myself for the pain I have brought upon those I love."

She walked to the window and stared out blindly, unable to meet their eyes. "A certain member of our party comforted me in my grief. He was attentive and flattering. I was vulnerable and alone. Eventually we . . . became lovers." She turned back abruptly. If she had not faced her family then, she must find the courage to do so now.

"This is difficult for me to say. So very difficult. My . . . lover . . . and I decided to fly away together. I slipped away from the house to meet him. You must have seen me leave, Summer, and followed me. I cannot imagine why you would have been out so early and alone.

"That was the day that you suffered your terrible accident, Summer. And all for nothing. He never came. I waited and waited. Later I learned that he had died. So you see, it was all for nothing—and I am to blame. For everything. Although I didn't know you'd been hurt. It was only a few weeks ago that I learned of it. My God!"

She went into some inner, private hell. Her beautiful features twisted into tortured lines. The effort she made to pull herself out of it was visible. "You mustn't blame your father for telling you I was dead," Orelia told Summer, "for to you, I was. He only meant to shield you—all of you—from the scandal. And the truth."

Thea twisted her handkerchief between her fingers. "Does Father know that you are a guest at the *castello*?"

Orelia laced her fingers together. "I didn't want to rake up old angers. I meant to plead illness and stay out of sight, but my darlings, I couldn't bear to be so close to you and not see you, even from a distance!"

Her beautiful, ravaged eyes silvered with tears. "I never intended to reveal myself to you." Her gaze fell on Thea. "I thought I could watch you from afar. We rode over the meadow this morning. It was in hopes of catching even a glimpse of you, nothing more. But after I saw you I'm afraid that I let my instincts overcome my sense of what was right."

She took a quick turn around the room. Despite her gravid abdomen she was graceful as a flower in her trailing gown. She stopped by the mantel and rested her arm along the marble shelf.

"Edmundo warned me against coming to Ellysia. He was afraid that once I saw you, I would want to talk with you. Edmundo is a wise and good man. I only pray that I have done no harm to you, or to him, by divulging my presence."

Summer's stunned brain came out of its paralysis and began considering the implications. "But I thought that . . . that your lover had died? Surely that is what you said earlier?"

"Yes. I met Edmundo afterward. In Naples."

Thea's thoughts were whirling. Edmundo was the name of the count. "Then, are *you* the *contessa?*"

Orelia saw that her pride must suffer still more. "The people of Ellysia and at Edmundo's estates in Tuscany know me as the *contessa*," she said in a low, level tone. "I am his wife in all but name."

She winced as her daughters gasped, but did not lower her eyes. "I am Edmundo's hostess in Rome and entertain his friends. There, they address me as Mrs. St. James, although our true relationship is known by his friends. I am received everywhere, except the Vatican. The Italians, like the French, understand such arrangements."

Summer saw how painful it was for her mother to speak so frankly of her private life. She spoke up, more sharply than she'd intended. "Why has the count given you everything but his name?"

"He would if he were able. Edmundo already has a wife, you see."

She let them absorb that before continuing. "I beg of you not to judge him too harshly. The woman who married Edmundo twenty years ago, and bore Emiliana and Vitorio, is as good as dead. They are very kind, and have accepted me as their stepmother. I love them both dearly.

"Their mother is mad. Dangerously mad. She lives in a well-appointed house with several trusted servants. The doors are always locked, the windows barred. All knives and sharp implements are kept under lock and key, as well."

Thea was appalled. "Has she tried to—to harm herself?"

Orelia closed her eyes a moment. Although Edmundo had given her permission to share his history with her daughters, if the necessity arose, she found it extremely difficult. As if it were a betrayal of the man who had loved her and made her an integral part of his life, sharing with her everything he had except his name, which was—and would always be—forbidden by the laws of church and state.

She decided to speak. Not to vindicate herself, but so they would understand Edmundo, and why this most generous, most loving of men had entered into an illicit relationship with her. She took a deep breath and told them about the beautiful, fey young girl who had become a sly, murderous creature that was something less than human, of Edmundo's anguish and his resolve to care for her despite the responsibility.

Thea was too sickened to move. Summer went to her mother and took her hand. "I think I see why you love him."

Orelia raised her eyes. "Do you? Oh, my dear!"

Bootsteps scraped on the threshold, startling them. "Well, well," a deep, familiar voice said scathingly, "isn't this a cozy little scene! A family reunion, Orelia?"

She stiffened and released Summer's hands, setting her away. "Hello, Richard."

He advanced into the room. "By God, you have a bloody nerve!"

He stopped when he saw her pregnant state and the automatic gesture of protection she made to guard her abdomen. His face went so ruddy that Summer feared he'd suffer a stroke of apoplexy.

"When you left, Orelia, you swore that you would never shatter our lives again!"

"I thought it only right—"

"Right! *Right?* You do not know the word! And you gave up all rights to see your daughters ten years

ago. Your gall amazes me, but not your perfidy. You
never were one to honor your vows, were you?"

His voice lashed her like a whip, but Orelia
accepted it as her due. She signaled her daughters to
leave. They protested, but she shook her head. "Your
father will not harm me. There are things we have to
discuss between ourselves. Please go."

Thea looked from one to the other, frightened and
unsure. "We shall only go as far as the garden. If we
are needed . . ." She left it unsaid. Richard could not
meet their eyes.

Orelia waited until they were gone. The room was
filled with the sounds of his harsh breathing and the
dry rustle of memory and unresolved passions. She
stood erect, her skin exceedingly pale.

He faced her in hot fury. "How dare you. How
dare you!"

"I had to see my daughters. I had to! After all this
time I had to know how they were. I never meant for
them to know who I was."

"You are a fool!" he thundered.

"There is nothing you can say to me, Richard, that
I haven't said to myself."

"Isn't there, by God? What of the word *harlot*? Or
do you prefer *whore*?

She didn't even flinch. "I will own up to the name,
if it makes you feel better."

"God *damn* you," he said viciously, "how dare you
come back into our lives as if nothing had happened.
Especially now, when I am just picking up the pieces
of the life you shattered, and making a new one!"

For the first time her facade cracked. "I thought—I
thought you would recover quickly. You didn't love
me, Richard. It was only your pride that I hurt."

He looked stunned. "Didn't love you? I loved you

so deeply that it nearly destroyed me! After you left me, I went back to Kingsmeade and buried myself alive there. Brooding and bleeding inside. I turned to my work and found it scarcely mattered to me."

His hands knotted at his sides and he turned away. "I knew that I had failed you. And by doing so, I had failed our daughters as well. I can never look at Summer without thinking that, if only I had made you love me, you would not have left me, and she would not be crippled as she is!"

A cry from Orelia made him turn back. She looked as if she'd been struck a mortal blow. Tears spilled over her thick lashes and down her cheek. "Oh, Richard! If only I had known, how different our lives might have been!"

"I thought," he said brokenly, "I hoped, that you would come back to me when Lawton died."

Her hand fluttered to her throat. "I wanted to. I wanted to, but I knew your pride. And I knew that what I'd done to you, to our daughters, was unforgivable."

Silence spun a fragile web of grief between them. She turned her back to him, but met his gaze in the mirror. "Tell me the truth, Richard. If I had come to you on my knees, would you have taken me back? Could things have ever been the way they were before I became infatuated with Lawton?"

Richard could not meet her eyes. A deep sigh came from him, as if he'd been holding his breath for ten long years. "No. Not then. Not even now." He turned away.

"Your husband," he said suddenly. "Do you love him?"

"Yes. He is a good man. A wonderful man. I hold him in the highest esteem."

She was trembling with reaction. He brought her a

chair. "Sit down. I don't want to be responsible for your losing this child, too."

He'd wanted that child as much as Orelia had; yet he'd insisted on going to Greece that summer, despite her pregnancy, and he'd left her more and more alone.

He went to the window and looked out over the sunny garden, not really seeing it. "I was fighting for my professional life, for our future. We had been living on my expectations, but our expenses were overcoming them. Getting the concession at Ilykion had been—so I thought—a marvelous stroke of luck. I knew that if I were successful, I would be given a chair at the university and we would be set for life. And so I was, although by that time all the joy had gone out of it."

He faced her once more. They looked at each other across the patterned carpet, across ten years of bitterness and pain and deadly misconceptions. There was nothing left of their rage and their passions but ashes and dust, and a pervading sorrow for what they had lost, and could never regain.

Orelia clutched the cold marble of the mantel. "I never meant to tell you this. I had broken off with Lawton and never intended to see him again. That last evening I had made a vow to put things right between us. To dedicate myself to making you happy.

"Then you came in, bursting with rage and the news that I had betrayed you with your colleague and rival. I knew that it was hopeless. Nothing I did or said would make any difference. And so, you see, I had no choice but to go with him after all."

She turned slowly at the sound of a muffled sob. Richard had covered his eyes with his hand. She had never seen him weep before. He sounded as if he were choking. It was worse than anything she'd endured before. He would never pardon her for seeing him like this. She strove for a diversion.

"I have always wondered how you found out about us," she said. "Was it Cynthia?"

"No. No, she never knew. Cynthia thought Lawton Morville was killed in a tragic accident. To this day she doesn't realize that her husband had intended to run off at all, much less with you."

"I see." Her mouth twisted. "How like Lawton, not to leave even so much as a note."

Richard was relieved that Orelia didn't probe further. No good would come of opening old wounds.

"Are you going to marry Cynthia? That is what Sir Horace tells me."

"We've applied for the forms. But to be legal, we need the services of a Protestant minister. One is coming through soon, bear leading a young cub on his Grand Tour. We hope to persuade the reverend to tie the knot for us."

"I hope she will be a better wife to you than I was."

Richard took a half step toward her. "You tried. You were very young. And I was married to my work. I see that now. Now that it's too late."

"You are making a fresh start with Cynthia. I wish you well, Richard. I have always wished you well." She lifted her head and offered him her hand. He started to take it, then stopped. His hand dropped to his side.

"I wish you well, also. But I think it is best, Orelia, if we don't see each other again for the duration of your stay. I will explain the matter to Cynthia." A shadow crossed his face. He turned it away from her gaze.

"There is only one question . . . I have wondered for years. Is Summer my child?"

She winced as if he'd struck her. "Of course she is! Why would you even think of such a thing?"

"She is so unlike the others."

Color flooded Orelia's cheeks. "Is that why you became so cold and distant all those years ago? Because she is so dark when they are so fair? Oh, you fool! I see it now. You thought I had been unfaithful to you years earlier. No wonder there was such strain between us!

"Summer is the very image of my Welsh great-grandfather. Except for his gray eyes, Owen Griffith was as dark as a gypsy."

There was a soft rustle of skirts behind him. When he looked again, she was gone.

Richard buried his face in his hands. He should have asked that question years ago. No, he should never have even thought it. Orelia was right. He was a bloody fool!

It took him a few moments to recover himself. Perhaps it was better that everything was brought out into the open. Now he would be able to close the door on a long and dreadful chapter in his life. He could go on from here, and truly make a new start.

He crossed to the door and went out into the garden in search of his daughters, leaving behind the room that was still scented with Orelia's perfume.

While doors were closing for Richard, they were opening for Summer, and onto amazing vistas. She wandered blindly through the garden, while Thea went off to fetch Fanny. The shock of seeing her mother—of seeing her alive and well—had wedged open the door to *Before*.

She sensed that it would never close completely again, no matter how much she might wish it to, in the end.

Images—vivid, disturbing—flickered through her mind like will-o'-the-wisps, illuminating her past. A whitewashed room. A leather box, stamped with her father's initials, and the sharp white square of an envelope propped against it. Then, hot sun, dark cliffs, and whitecapped seas. And, always, *the tide pool*.

A line from Rosalind's poem ran through her mind: "I am the heart of the dark night."

She shivered and wrapped her arms around herself for warmth. It was coming back to her. Whatever *it* was. It would be terrible, she knew, but she would survive it. And when she did, she would be whole, entire. Complete at last.

A Leap of Faith

The chief angel poked her head into the celestial weaving room. The light from her wings spangled the floor like stardust. "Almost finished? Good. Expect a Heavenly Presence to stop by soon. There seems to be a good deal of interest in this pattern."

The apprentice Fate almost dropped one of her threads in alarm, and snagged another. "But I'm not nearly done! And it gets more complicated as I go along—I really expected it to get easier."

"Haven't you learned by now? Ah, I see what the problem is. You are trying to force the pattern into ways it was never meant to go. Close your eyes a moment. Listen to your inner voice. The pattern is all there, waiting for you to see it."

A wink, a swirl of cosmic dust, and she was gone.

The apprentice peered doubtfully at her handiwork. How could the pattern be there, when she was making it up as she went along?

But suddenly something shifted in her thinking. Ah! It was true. The pattern *was* there if only you looked. . . .

13

THE LOOM OF FATE

Notes from Summer Fairchild's journal

Until we came to the Court of Three Sisters, I never gave much thought to my own mortality. Today, as I was watching the petals fall from the almond trees, I thought of how each one returned to the earth, to enrich the soil. And it occurred to me that the essence of those petals would someday become a part of the almond trees, or perhaps blades of grass or wildflowers. Nothing in nature is wasted.

Now I think of Cliete and Kallista and myself, of the entire human race. And I wonder. Yes, I wonder.

Richard Fairchild stood at the balustrade on his terrace, watching another storm sweep in. His emotions were as ragged as the windswept clouds. He heard the sounds of the carriage in the outer courtyard. Two hours had passed since he'd left his daughters at the *castello*. He didn't know what to expect from their return.

Thea and Summer found him there. A long silence stretched out. "Are you very angry with us?" Thea asked at last.

"Not with you. With *myself*. I have made some grievous errors in my life. I am sorry that you have had to pay the price for them." Especially Summer, whom he loved dearly, and whom he had wronged by thinking in his heart of hearts that she had been fathered by another man. "I hope you will find it in you to forgive me."

They went into his arms.

The dramatic meeting with her mother had driven everything else from Summer's mind. But later, when she was alone with her father, she asked what had transpired when he confronted Col McCallum.

Richard looked confused for a moment. "Nothing," he said finally. "He wasn't there. It was clear that he'd absconded during the night. The place was in great disorder, with things thrown everywhere so that I could hardly see the floor."

"So you learned nothing at all?"

Richard looked very grim. "I learned that Carruthers was murdered! He didn't have a good sense of smell, you know. Something to do with a brain sickness he'd suffered as a child. That's why he loved spicy dishes and strong cigars, and he often reeked of garlic. I assumed it was from an attempt to add flavor to his food, since it was all bland to him."

Thea and Summer exchanged looks, wondering if meeting with Orelia today had unhinged their father. What did murder and garlic have to do with one another?

Richard frowned, remembering. "I found a box of his cigars lying on their side and, well, damn it, I took one. Carruthers didn't need them anymore. I imagined he would roll over in his grave if he knew. He was very peculiar about his cigars and only smoked them when he was alone. He would share anything else, but never his Havanas!"

He shook his head, smiling sadly. "His valet once said that Carruthers credited his longevity to them. It turned out to be quite the opposite. The moment I lit the cigar I realized that he had been poisoned. The rich taste was overwhelmed with the odor of garlic."

He looked into their astonished faces. "Arsenic, when burned, gives off the strong odor of garlic. I checked the open tins. The cocoa was similarly tainted."

"But who—?"

Reaching into his pocket, Richard extracted a note. "Someone who knew Carruthers's love of a cup of hot cocoa and a good smoke, and knew that he couldn't smell much of anything. Someone who'd spent a few months in Havana, and who had an eye to Carruthers's fortune. I mean no other than that thieving scoundrel, Col McCallum!"

Summer was stunned. "I cannot believe that. He spoke to me of his relationship with Carruthers. Their bond was one of love and mutual respect."

"And the moon is made of green cheese!" Richard relented. "Why else would he go by his family name, rather than his title? Yesterday I was upset over the theft of the statues. Today I am only glad that no harm came to any of you because of FitzRoy, or McCallum, or whatever he may call himself. You are more important to me than all the treasures of the ancients. That's why, the moment I suspected that Orelia was at the *castello*, I went there immediately."

Thea was puzzled. "But how could you possibly guess? I was absolutely floored when . . . Mother . . . appeared."

"I went up to the site to discuss my discovery with Symington, and enlist his help. I learned there that the contessa was at home, that she was an Englishwoman, and not ill at all. And that her name was Orelia. My intuition took a great vault forward and I realized why DiCaesari was so stiff with me, and why the contessa was avoiding a meeting. It went against all logic, yet I knew—I *knew* that it had to be. . . ."

He looked around, suddenly realizing that his youngest daughter was absent. "Where is Fanny? How is she taking this?"

Thea smiled faintly. "Fanny is taking it very well. She is a most adaptable young woman. I hope you will not mind, but she has decided to spend the evening with Emiliana. She needs time to take it all in, and we thought it best to let her have her wish."

"Take what in?"

They turned as one, and saw Cynthia enter almost on their heels. Summer was too exhausted, emotionally and physically, to answer. Thea felt it was not her place. Their father went to Cynthia and took her hands in his. Not knowing how to ease into it, he spoke baldly. "They have spent the afternoon with their mother."

"I—I beg your pardon?"

"Yes, my dear, they know all," Richard said. "Orelia is here. At the *castello*." Her mouth opened but no sound came out. He turned to his daughters. "If you are both all right, I should like to speak with Cynthia, alone. We have much to talk about."

"Of course," Thea said hastily, edging Summer to

the corridor. "It has been an exhausting day. We can discuss this among ourselves later."

The sisters parted at Thea's bedroom door. Summer was glad to reach the sanctuary of her own room. So much had happened. And there was so much more to sort out. Dropping her bonnet on a chair, she removed her pearl earrings. One fell and rolled to the edge of the floor. The sable cat leaped from its resting place on her bed and batted it across the floor. Summer scolded him and put him out of the room.

She got down awkwardly to look for it but it seemed to have disappeared. No, there it was, wedged between the floor and the wall. She hadn't noticed the gap there before. Summer reached up to the dressing table beside her and grabbed her button-hook. If she wedged it just right, she could flip up the pearl without damaging it, she hoped.

It was stuck fast. She tried another angle, and the tiny molding around the edge of the wall loosened. It was a short strip, she saw, only a foot long between the joints. If she removed it she could get at the ear-ring without scratching the smooth nacre. Jamming the buttonhook between the wall and the molding, she pried it away.

Yes, there was the pearl, unharmed. As she pulled it free her eye was attracted by color beneath. She squinted. There appeared to be a mosaic floor beneath the wood. First the one in her secret garden beneath the plaster, and now this! It was very odd.

Now that she knew what to look for, she saw gaps in some places between the wall molding and floor. Her curiosity aroused, she forgot her tiredness and went to work. A quarter hour later she'd removed half the molding. In some places the gap was almost six inches long.

The plank at the very end of the room, beneath her window, was loose. Summer pried it up. It was heavy and very difficult for her to move. She slid it up and got a splinter in her palm for her pains. Sucking her hand, she managed to get it out with her teeth. When she took the time to examine the floor beneath the plank she was astounded. Instead of the usual decorative picture, the mosaic seemed to be a map.

She got up and bathed her bleeding hand in the water from her basin. The task had used up her reserves of energy. She decided that her curiosity would wait, while a nap would not. In any event, she had neither the strength nor the motivation to pull up an entire floor. It was older than the others, with larger stones and brighter colors.

Stretching out, she lay upon the bed, fully clothed, and stared up at the ceiling. Something had been puzzling her. Since her mother was alive and well, why was she still haunted by terrible images of her mother's body, lying still and broken at the foot of the cliffs? Were they nothing more than products of her imagination?

She had to know.

For the first time Summer purposely tried to conjure up the tide pool. Hot sun. The smell of the sea. The honeyed voice. Then flying, falling . . .

She fell into *Before*. It was dark and cold. It stank of decayed fish and seaweed but there was no place else that she could go to hide. She heard footsteps and tried to wriggle in deeper. The pain slammed her into the damp sand. *My legs my legs my back my legs!* Everything went blacker.

When she came to, she heard footsteps crunching

over the rocky shore. She was wedged into a cleft at the base of the cliffs, behind a boulder. All she could see was a narrow crack of light, and blue that might be sea or sky. By moving her head with infinite care, she managed to see past the boulder. Something black and still. White fabric, fluttering in the breeze. A crab, tiny and pale, clambered over it. A gull screamed and dived down, but whether after the crab or something else was unclear. Someone was blocking the slit of light.

"Summer? I know you're here, hiding. Come out. I won't hurt you."

She held her breath. *Don't breathe don't breathe don't move don't cry.* It was easier not to cry now. The pain was ebbing, replaced by a dreadful numbness in her leg.

She tried to hold the scene, but it fragmented and slipped away. Summer wondered how she could see things that weren't there? How could she see a tide pool, how could she have seen . . . something . . . someone . . . nibbled by crabs, when her mother was alive and well?

The day's events, the attempt to remember, had exhausted her. Summer fell into a disturbed sleep, and dreamed of crabs outside the door to her secret terrace, scrabbling at the wood with evil little claws. Scrabbling, scrabbling . . .

Some time later she woke up fully, heart pounding. She thought she'd heard a sound. A cat's plaintive cry? Throwing back the sheet, she swung herself over the edge of the bed. She was wide awake now. Summer took the pins from her hair. Picking up her brush, she drew it through her tangled hair until it was smooth as satin.

Something was nagging at her. It had to do with

Cynthia. With Cynthia's expression when she had heard that Orelia Fairchild was at the *castello*. It came to Summer all at once. It had not been merely shock written on the woman's features: It had been fear. Poor thing, she had lost her husband, and now was afraid that she would lose the man she loved again; but if Cynthia had seen her father and mother together it would have relieved all her fears. Whatever had been between them was only a bitter-sweet shadow.

There was that cry again, so soft and faint she wasn't really sure she'd heard it, and it sounded as if it were coming from behind the hidden terrace door. The tapestry moved slightly, as if the heavy weaving were stirred by a draft. Summer went to it and pulled the chair away.

The door swung open, pushing aside the tapestry and knocking Summer back against the bed. She tried to save herself by grasping the quilt. Although she managed to break her fall, Summer still ended up on the floor beside the bed, and facing the tapestry.

Something clunked to the floor beside it. She gasped and recoiled. A hand, raw and blackened with dried blood. As she drew in a deep breath to scream for help, reason came to the rescue. The person was injured and therefore no threat to her, and there was only one person who knew the way up from the sea stairs to her hidden sanctuary.

She sprang forward, although the movement cost her pain, and pulled the tapestry away. A man lay stretched across the threshold, his face gaunt and gray, his shirt covered with a crust of old blood.

"Col!" Her voice was little more than a whisper.

He heard, and opened his eyes. A beatific smile illuminated his face. *"Kallista!"*

Then he passed out cold.

She touched his throat. His pulse was thin, but steady. Seeing him again, looking into his eyes, had vanquished all her doubts. No matter how bad things looked, she could not believe that he had stolen the statues. She was ashamed that she had entertained the possibility, even for a minute.

And no one would ever make her believe that he had killed Carruthers, regardless of how the circumstances looked.

He was too heavy for her to lift to the bed, but she couldn't leave him wedged across the threshold. Someone would surely find him. Instinct warned her that she must keep his presence hidden for now, at least until he regained consciousness. Using all her strength, she managed to haul him out to the terrace sufficiently to close the secret door; but first she brought out a pillow and blanket and her thickest quilt to fashion a makeshift bed.

After dressing his wound, which was beneath the shoulder and had bled most dreadfully, she moistened his lips with water. The bullet that had struck him from behind had obviously missed anything vital. The important thing now was to keep him warm and free of infection.

She debated furiously with herself about whether to try and enlist Thea's aid, and risk discovery. She was afraid of her father's reaction and of what he might do to Col. Afraid to acknowledge the fear that her father might be the one who had shot him. At the moment discretion seemed the wiser course.

He was shivering with cold. Her gown was stiff and bulky. She stripped it off, and her unwieldy corset with it, until she stood in nothing but her shift. Summer curled up beside him and pulled the blanket to his shoulders and warmed him with the heat of her own body.

Later Summer asked for a supper tray in her room, but Thea felt they should join their father at table in a show of support. Col was in a deep sleep and Summer decided to chance it. She must keep appearances as normal as possible.

As she dressed for supper she thought of how coming to Ellysia had changed her and opened her eyes. Was there anyone at all, past the age of childhood, who did not wear a mask?

The dinner was a stew of lamb with rice and turnips and a thick soup of beef stock and vegetable marrow. Thea had long given up teaching the English ways to their housekeeper. There was no way that Summer could pour any of it into her pocket for Col, so she tucked away some bread and made plans to raid the kitchen later. The soup was exactly what he needed. Warming, easy to wash down, and strengthening for a man who'd lost a good deal of blood before staunching it with a wadded pillow slip.

After the meal ended everyone seemed tired and drained, and she didn't have to make up an excuse to go back to her room early, for they all retired.

Summer found Col propped up against the wall, hollow eyed and burning with fever. He was lucid and recognized her. Thank God for that, she thought. She brought him water to drink and to cool his brow and went back to steal some broth to strengthen him. His bandage was dry and she was relieved to know the bleeding had stopped. She hoped that it was only loss of fluids that made him so hot and dry.

The effort was enough to exhaust him, and she let

him sleep. He was restless the first two hours. Finally he dropped into a slumber so deep that it frightened her. He didn't open his eyes again until sunrise.

Summer was stiff and sore from lying so carefully all night, but they'd been warm and snug enough. She had liked sleeping beside him, listening to his steady breathing. Knowing that he was only a hand's touch away. She felt his forehead. It was blessedly cool. After dosing him with more broth and a draught of laudanum, he slept through until after luncheon.

The house was quiet. Her father and Cynthia Morville had gone off to the site to work. Fanny had stayed at the *castello* and Thea was busy with her endless letters. Summer knew she was writing to Martin again, telling him of all that had occurred; and that this letter, like all the others, would end up in the wooden chest on Thea's dresser. After that one weak moment of unburdening herself to Summer, Thea had refused to speak of it again.

When she returned Col was resting quietly, his breathing soft and even. Since she had nothing better to do with her time while he dozed, Summer went to work at uncovering her mosaic. This time she'd brought along some gardening utensils to make the work go faster. Once he recovered, she would show Col her latest discoveries, and then tell him about the suspected mosaic under her bedroom floor.

She worked quickly, putting the force of her agitated emotions into her efforts, and was surprised at how easily the powdery plaster came up now. It showered everywhere, covering up the design even as it was revealed. Well, she decided, a full view at the end would be more meaningful than trying to decipher each foot-wide swatch as she went. It became a game, like finishing a novel and trying not to glance at the last page.

She realized that her muscles no longer ached as they had, and even her back and legs felt stronger. She would never be cured of her physical problem, but she could certainly live a more active life than she'd been doing in the past. Perhaps she would try the mineral baths at the foot of the sea stairs some time. The so-called healing waters might do Col good, as well. Summer realized that she was already planning for the future. She had never done that before.

Before she knew it the mosaic was free of its concealing layer. When it was finished she felt a rush of elation. She had done it, and she had done it by herself, without help from anyone.

The powdered plaster covered her hands and arms. Mixed with her perspiration, it was beginning to harden. If she didn't remove it immediately, it would be difficult to get off at all.

Summer went into her room and bathed away the dust, then slipped a fresh gown on over her shift. She didn't bother with the cumbersome corset. She was sore enough without it.

Summer went out to check on her patient and found Col awake, clear-eyed and cool. He was sitting against the wall, fiddling with her bandage to make it tighter. "I see that you are the angel to whom I'm indebted. I might have known."

She smiled but didn't answer, returning shortly with a glass of fresh water and a bowl of soup. He held down the water and took a few sips of soup. "I feel dry as a bone," he said. "I could drink a river and still be thirsty."

"You must have lost a deal of blood." Summer fingered the pearl buttons of her dress. She could put off the moment of truth no longer. "What happened?" she asked him quietly. "Who did this to you?"

"I don't know for certain, although I have my suspicions. I was deeply into one of Carruthers's notebooks." There was more in it about the map he'd found and hidden. Enough to make Col go back to an earlier note about the Venus of Ilykion. He sipped the cool water that Summer held to his cracked lips.

"My back was to the open window. I heard a rustle and started to turn. That saved my life. Otherwise the bullet would have gotten me through the heart. Whoever did it was a crack shot. When I stumbled up I lost consciousness and hit my head when I fell. The assassin must have thought that I was dead."

A crack shot. For some reason the words echoed in Summer's head. She saw a flash of black and white, felt a fluttery sensation of falling and heard a shot ring out. *All for you.* Her breath hissed out beneath her teeth. The words and phrases joined together, became sentences, became a voice, low and filled with hatred. *You can't get away. I'm a crack shot. It's over. To think I did it all for you . . . did it all for you . . . and you planned to betray me . . . me . . . me.*

She was standing on the cliff at Ilykion, at daybreak. The speakers were below her, on the stairs carved into the cliff face. By a trick of the wind and rock, their voices were blown back to her, echoing from the overhang. "Don't be a fool, the child will see . . . the child will see."

Col grabbed her hand. "See what? What is it? What has frightened you?"

Summer was back in Persephone's garden, kneeling

beside Col. She was shaking violently. He put his good arm around her and held her tight.

Summer didn't want him to let go. Not ever. Because if he did the memories would all come back, rushing in like a tide. The overwhelming fears of the child she had been warred with the need to know of the adult woman she had become. She had to know, once and for all, what had happened. Had to know who had pushed her—yes, it had been a shove that had sent her over. Had to know exactly what she had seen in the tide pool that fateful morning.

With Col's arm around her, Summer found the courage to face the dark secrets of the past. She gave up fighting them.

Sounds, sights, impressions crashed over her, thrusting her into a deluge of memories. They swept her away in an emotional tidal wave.

Tidal wave. Yes. The cone of Hades had blasted away in the earthquake, but it was the greater cataclysm to the west that had darkened the sky for hundreds of miles in all directions. It was as she had foreseen it, doom and loss and infinite destruction. The air was thick with ash and pumice and her lungs were choked with them. But that was not the worst. Even in the darkness she could hear the water hissing back from the shore, drawn away as the sea rushed into the gaping hole where the island capital of the empire had been. But Kallista was no more.

And soon the gathering waters would swell and grow, once, twice, a hundred times their height. Then they would come crashing back with a force unknown since the creation of the world, drowning everything within its path, washing away ships and cities and whole nations, as if they were bits of straw.

Washing over the high walls of the villa and pouring down into the hole between the roof and floor where she and her sister lay buried in rubble. She called out Cliete's name, but there was no answer. No sound at all except for the constant rain of tiny grains of pumice, and the sucking sounds of the retreating sea.

She prayed to the Great All-Knowing, for help. Fear and faith gave her the strength of ten. She pushed up with all her might and the fallen timbers shifted, just enough so she could wriggle through. There was a great pain in her back and shoulder, and her one leg dragged behind her uselessly. She pushed and pulled herself along, working always in the direction where she had last seen Cliete. Where she sensed her lying beneath the collapsed roof in a terrible stillness.

She reached and reached and finally touched flesh. Her sister's arm, still warm. Still alive!

Forever passed in the wink of an eye as she tugged at Cliete's sash. Beyond were the stairs that led up to the terrace where she sat to receive tribute from the people. Where she watched and waited for her lover to appear. If they could only get up to the terrace they might be safe. And if they were safe then he would surely find them, and take them home.

Home! She longed for it. But no, she remembered now. Kallista was gone. She had seen it in the altar flames as surely as if she had witnessed it. Not three seconds later the volcano on the far end of the island had blown up with a sound like the cracking in two of the world.

"Cliete, can you hear me? Cliete, we must find the stairs. We must climb up them before the tidal wave sweeps back against the land. Come, sister." Or was it the tide pool? No! That was another life, another dream.

The goddess will not abandon her priestesses now. She pulled and clawed her way forward until she touched the bottommost step. "Keep hold of my hand. Don't let go . . . don't. . . ."

"I won't." Col held Summer against him, ignoring the searing pain of his injury. He was afraid to let go of her, even for a moment. Afraid that if he did, the consuming terror would wash her away, leaving nothing but an empty shell.

He didn't know how to help her. Summer's face was turned up to him and her eyes were closed. Fear stabbed through him. He didn't know how or why, but he knew that he was losing her.

Summer fought with all her might. It was like a whirlpool of spinning memory fragments. She was caught in a web between worlds. A psychic space were time met and mingled and didn't exist. It was too much for her human mind to contemplate.

Col called her name. Her body stiffened. Summer was torn between past and present, drawing on his strength to raise herself above the maelstrom of memory.

Her rambling words were mixed with the names of her family, with old nightmares, and with phrases he had heard on Crete. Her skin was cold and he thought that she was dying. He pressed his mouth to hers, as if his kiss could call her back from the edge. As if both their lives depended upon it.

Gradually her flailing ceased. Her lips warmed to his. His blood sang with triumph. She was awake, lying in his arms as if she belonged there. As if she always had.

He cupped his good hand over her breast. Her

heart beat strong and true beneath his palm. Bending his head, he kissed her again. Once before he had touched her like this, only to turn away when he saw her twisted bones. She couldn't bear it to happen again.

Col smiled faintly. He always had the most damnable timing. He wanted her so badly, yet his wound made him awkward and weak. He knew that there was no force of life greater than the act of love. She needed that to keep her locked with him in the here and now.

He knew that he must choose. If he made love to her now, while she was vulnerable, he knew that she would hate him someday, and he would lose her forever. If he didn't, he feared that he would lose her anyway.

In the end, he realized that there was no choice at all. What was meant to be must be, and he was meant to love her. From the time of their first meeting, perhaps even before, their lives were fated to entwine, just as her arms were twining round his neck. Their lips were meant to meet, just like this. Soft, tender, opening to one another.

His hands were at the bodice of her dress, pulling at the buttons and breaking the loops of thread that held them. Sliding away the fabric to reveal her soft skin, her rounded breasts. His mouth skimmed her throat, the hollow at its base, the fragrant cleft between her breasts. She smelled of wildflowers and honey.

Summer floated on billows of sensation. The warmth of Col's mouth, the rasp of his jaw, the slippery heat of his tongue filled her with joyous pleasure. He slid his hand around to her back and let his fingers trail down her spine. There was none of the shrinking she had imagined before. His touch was sure, and filled with reverence.

Her fingers twined in his hair, pressing his mouth harder against her. As long as they were together the shadows could not touch her. Cliete and Kallista, tidal waves and tide pools, had diminished to tiny dots of awareness, off in a distant corner of her mind. There was nothing but herself and Col and the melding of their souls.

Her hands touched his naked shoulders, felt the bandage she had made on one, the sleek, supple shape of the other. It seemed that she had always known exactly how he felt—the texture of his skin, the play of muscle and tendon, the curves and hollows and angles. As familiar as—more familiar than—her own.

Col could not get enough of her. He wanted to give her the most sublime of first experiences.

He eased himself up beside her, no longer aware of the aching in his shoulder. The throb in his loins was far greater. And they had only begun. He trailed his fingers across her breast while he took her mouth in a melting kiss. She shivered and moaned when he touched her.

He meant to be gentle, but found he could not hold back completely.

Summer was lost in total ecstasy. She had never known, never guessed . . . Oh, yes! Yes! She didn't know if she'd spoken aloud. Her breath came fast and hard. She wanted . . . she wanted. Oh!

She was falling through air as she had fallen at Ilykion, then soaring, soaring with his mouth against her breast. Up and up and up until she almost touched the sun.

Then she was falling once more, and afraid. She

would hit the ground and die. But no, Col was there to catch her. To wind his arms and legs around her. To enter and fill her and pin her to the ground with his solid strength. To keep her from falling.

Col hung on to her as he lunged. A slight pressure of resistance and then release as he breached her hymen. He was enfolded by her. For a few moments he lay atop her, savoring the first seconds of their union. They were joined. She was his. His! His!

He pushed deeper with every thrust, lifting her hips so he could plunge even more. He had never known anything like this before, this merging of longing, this complete and full giving of self. In return she had given him her trust, her innocence.

He thrust deeper, harder. Her gasps of pleasure urged him on. They became the rhythm of the waves crashing on the cliffs below, they became the sound of each other's hearts, so intimate and integral that there was no boundary between them. They were one, soaring together on the heat of their passion until, this time, they fell into the fiery heart of the sun.

They lay joined for longer than either of them could guess. When he withdrew she made a low sound of protest. Col leaned over and kissed her mouth, already swollen and rosy with his kisses. "Don't go," she whispered against his mouth.

He laughed low in his throat. "No fear of that, my darling. I love you, Summer. I will always love you. There is nothing that you can say or do that will ever drive me away. I will never leave you."

He cradled her in his good arm until she fell asleep, smiling.

*   *   *

Evening threw its lavender shawl across the sky, muting the colors of the inner courtyard. Summer wandered past the fountain, listening to the last call of the birds as they settled in for the night. Wondering if Cliete and Kallista had stood somewhere near where she was standing now, and listened to the same songs. She thought perhaps they had.

That made her feel better. She didn't think she would be caught up in their memories as often or as deeply as before. Although she didn't understand it, Col's theory was that she, either due to an inherited talent or in trying to remember her own past, had somehow gone too far. That she had merged memories with those of a woman who had once lived in this very same place in ancient times. Perhaps all the way to the first inhabitants of the house that came to be known as the Court of Three Sisters.

Summer turned back toward the loggia. Col had gone away and she was anxious that his strength would hold up. "Don't worry," he had promised. "After this afternoon I feel invincible."

She blushed at the memory, and picked a blossom to tuck at her breast. Her whole body felt as if it were glowing. It was a wonder that she hadn't betrayed herself in some way. She was still amazed. The act of love was such a wondrous thing, she could hardly contain her joy. Why did people hide it and make it such a dark, secret thing, as if such perfect union were a disgrace?

She turned away with a secret smile—and found herself face to face with Cynthia Morville. The other woman looked at her in surprise, then quickly recovered herself. "Why, Summer, even in the failing light I can see that you are positively glowing. You look like a woman in love."

Summer's heart beat faster. Even if it were safe to do, she wouldn't want to discuss her feelings for Col with anyone. They were too private, and too new. "I am happy to know that my mother is alive and well," she said quickly. For so many years I saw . . . I imagined . . . horrible things."

"And none of them were real?"

"I don't know. Some things still seem as if they were." She looked inward, afraid that she would be sucked back into that world; but Col's love wrapped around her, keeping her firmly anchored in time and place. Summer shook her head. "The tide pool, or what I thought was one. For years I saw—*imagined* that I saw my mother lying dead in one, and that crabs were nibbling at her flesh."

"How perfectly horrible. I hope the nightmares will go away now that you know the truth."

Summer frowned without realizing it. "I daresay I won't know what is real and what is not, until I remember everything."

Cynthia patted her hand. "Perhaps it is better not to try. You've gone through a good deal in the past few weeks. I have learned, from my own experience, that it is better to let the past die."

"That is good advice," Summer replied. "I only hope that the past is done with me."

The Symingtons came to visit that evening, along with Angus Gordon and Lewis Forsythe. When Whitney Vance strolled in a quarter hour later, Fanny's face lit up. As she was trying to think of an excuse to move closer to where he was sitting, Vance suddenly got up and changed his seat. He took an empty chair at right angles to hers.

"The view is much better from here," he said mildly. Fanny pinked with pleasure.

The night was warm and the talk desultory. Cynthia excused herself to fetch a book they were discussing from her room.

Summer was impatient. Col had promised to return by nine o'clock and now she would have the devil of a time getting away to let him into her room. She smiled. She was even beginning to think in the way that he talked. But since she'd wedged the door shut from the inside, to keep it from swinging open and revealing itself, he had no safe way in.

For a few minutes she lost herself in happy recollection. When she turned her attention back the conversation had taken a different tack.

"Yes, I remember hearing about Morville's death. Off the cliffs at Ilykion."

"Like that reporter fellow who fell to his death a few weeks ago," Forsythe added. "Adams, wasn't it? Jethroe Adams?"

Richard hesitated. "Yes, that was his name, but as it turned out, the newspaper he claimed to work for had never heard of him! It appears that he was some kind of inquiry agent."

"Like a Pinkerton agent, you mean?" Fanny was all agog.

"I don't know. Perhaps Carruthers suspected that McCallum was poisoning him through the cigars he sent, and hired Adams to investigate. I assume that McCallum thought he would get the concession here, along with any treasures that were dug up, as well as the property I understand Carruthers left to him in his will. Greed is a powerful motive."

"But not Col!" Summer wanted to cry out; but he

had made her swear not to give anything away about their relationship. Cynthia returned.

"He should have been sent to the authorities, to have this McCallum fellow arrested," Symington stated. "And, if he suspected, why did he go on smoking those damned cigars?"

Richard frowned. He hadn't pursued the point in his own mind. "My dear fellow, I don't have the slightest idea. All I could learn, from the letter I received today, was that Adams was hired by John Carruthers, through his man, Evans. He was to meet someone in Lipari, then come on to Ellysia. And he had been in Cairo shortly before, also acting for Carruthers. I cannot make head nor tail of it."

"Ruggieri had been in Lipari only a short time before," Mr. Symington said.

His wife nodded. "Isn't it strange? Like a repeating knitting pattern, all of a piece."

All of a piece. The cliffs at Ilykion. Summer glanced up and saw Cynthia's face. It held the same look it had earlier, of startlement and fear. Pieces fell into place in Summer's mind. A terrible pattern formed. It was like assembling the bits of mosaic that Cynthia had brought back. Once the basic pattern was discerned, the entire picture would be revealed. Her heart literally skipped a beat. Any moment now, she would know, would recall exactly what she'd seen that fateful day.

Cynthia leaned down and murmured something in Richard's ear. He looked up sharply. "Very well. If you'll excuse me," he said to his guests, "there is something that requires my immediate attention."

Summer froze. Could it be Col? Fear for him pushed all other thoughts away. They still thought that he was a thief and a murderer. She held her breath until they went off together and into the inner courtyard.

No one was looking and it was already five minutes after nine. She slipped away into the shadows and down the corridor to her room. Everything was exactly as she had left it. Once inside she bolted the door to keep anyone from entering, and went out to the terrace. A sound startled her.

As she was turning, something struck her from behind, hard. Stars bloomed inside her head before a wave of blackness crashed over her.

A cool draft touched her hair. She was trapped beneath the rubble with Cliete again. She had to free herself. She had to save her sister. This time she was face down. It was wet. Oh, God! Oh, God! she was in the tide pool again. She had tripped and fallen into it. She had been running, running. No, falling, falling. Something . . . someone had hit her in the back, hard. She could still feel the imprint of the hand on her back.

Summer tried to clear her head. She was crouched in a wedge of rock, hiding from the voice. "Come out. I won't hurt you. Be a good girl now."

By moving her head with infinite care, Summer could see better. There was a depression worn in the rock beyond that had filled with seawater splashed in by the waves. There was something just an arm's reach away. Something black and still. White fabric, fluttering in the breeze. A crab, tiny and pale, clambered over it.

She almost screamed in fear. She mustn't, mustn't, mustn't scream. If she did the voice would find her.

A gull screamed and dived down, but whether

after the crab or something else was unclear because she squeezed her eyes shut tightly. It didn't help. She could still see his face. His eyes, wide open and staring. The sea mist sparkling on his dead white face like tears. The gunshot wound at the side of his throat and the crabs . . . Oh, God! The crabs picking away at it, nibbling, nibbling!

She screamed. A voice answered, but not the *Voice*. "Col," she cried. "Col!"

"Don't touch her," he shouted.

A hand nudged her. Summer winced with pain. There was something in her back, a sharp, hot knife of pain. She realized that someone was standing over her and that she was on the edge of the cliffs . . . no, she was on the secret terrace, at the place where the balcony had broken away when the cliff face crumbled centuries before.

"Don't come any closer," someone whispered. "I'm a crack shot!"

"Yes," Col answered sternly. "I've already discovered that, to my sorrow. I was rereading a section of Carruthers's notes when you shot me. I had just realized that I'd misinterpreted something—that when he wrote of discussing the Venus of Ilykion with someone whose initial was C, that it stood for Cynthia, and not for Col.

"And now I have the proof in hand. Evans is in Appolinaria. He came in this afternoon on the supply boat. I figured it all out. It was the motive that I couldn't see at first. I didn't realize, you see, that Carruthers's murder was not your first."

Summer gasped. Cynthia's face was contorted with anger. "You think you know everything, don't you?"

"Oh, but I do. You stole the statue to discredit

Alistair—who would have suspected you?—and sold it quietly in Athens. It would have fetched a fortune in the right hands, but it wasn't the money you were after, was it? It was the fame."

"And why not? We'd worked for it, and seen all the accolades go to the others who were far less deserving."

Summer struggled and the foot on her back pressed down. "I'm so sorry, my dear," Cynthia murmured. "I was fond of you, you know. But there is only one outcome, now. You and your lover must die. And I'm very sorry, but I think that you must be first. It will seem that you fell over the cliff—or that Col pushed you, in a jealous quarrel—and then shot himself in remorse. Good-bye, Summer."

Summer knew she must act. There was a tiny click of a hammer drawn back. The ginger cat shot out of the darkness, startling Cynthia. Lurching up, Summer grabbed at her attacker's leg. She heard Col call out, "No! Cynthia!"

The darkness erupted in flame and noise as the bullet, meant for Summer's head, exploded on the stone floor. Shards of mosaic flew everywhere and the cat yowled in alarm.

Summer was half over the edge of the terrace, unable to save herself. Col dived at Cynthia, knocking the gun from her hand. She broke free and started to run toward the door of Summer's room. Col had only two choices, to go after her or to rescue Summer. He didn't hesitate.

Despite his injured arm he flung himself at Summer, trying to grab her arm or leg. Instead there was a grumble that turned to a terrible roar. The cliff shook and shuddered, and from somewhere inside the villa they heard Fanny scream. Then they went off the edge together.

Summer clutched at Col. Her every nightmare had come true. They were falling, falling toward the dark rocks.

They landed with a thump. Col's body cushioned her fall. He held her safe and tight.

"We're on the outer set of stairs," he said hoarsely. "For God's sake, don't move or make a sound."

The tremor lasted only a few seconds, but felt like an eternity.

Cynthia had made it to the door and was trying to force her way through the heavy tapestry, instead of around it. The earthquake ended just as she freed herself from its cloaking folds. She never saw the outer wall collapse. One minute she was fleeing in blind fury, the next bloody and still beneath the blocks of the broken wall. The others, hearing the uproar, came running. They paused in startlement when they saw the ruined wall, the partially collapsed ceiling, and the secret terrace beyond Summer's room. Richard ran past the rubble without seeing Cynthia pinned there.

Col struggled upright, his strong arm keeping Summer from falling to her death. Inch by inch he worked their combined weight up until they almost reached the top.

Then she saw her father's face, beaded with sweat, as he looked over the edge at them. "Thank God!" he whispered, extending his hand to Col. He slowly levered them up. The ginger cat sat there, purring.

Thea joined them, tense and white with fear. "There's been a terrible accident. . . ."

* * *

It was three hours since the earthquake, when Col gathered with Summer and her family in their sitting room. Signora Perani had taken on the task of laying out Cynthia Morville's broken body in one of the empty rooms.

"Have I not done this task a dozen times in my life?" she had said to them. "I will see to the poor woman."

The house was intact, except for the wall of Summer's chamber, and the archway into the stable-yard. The Court of Three Sisters was built on bedrock. It had survived another disaster, just as it had for centuries.

The map that Col spread out on the sitting-room table was drawn in minute detail, in Carruthers's hand. "Ironically," he said, "it was in the bottom of the humidor. I never realized that he had made a copy of it. I discovered this, rolled up in a sheet of tobacco leaf, when I went to see if the arsenic story was true. Otherwise it might have stayed there for months. I never smoke cigars."

Summer still couldn't believe it. "Then, all the time, the original of the map, from which he made this copy, was under the floorboards of my room! I never thought to wonder why it was the only room in the entire villa that wasn't floored with mosaic. I thought it was plain because it had been a store-room."

Col smiled and leaned down to whisper, "Even if you'd let me into your bedroom, I doubt I would have noticed, since my mind would have been on other things."

She smiled back and examined the map. "So this was his great treasure, not gold at all, but knowl-edge." Past the Straits of Hercules, a great turtle-shaped island spread out, marked with settlements and towns. Inside the straits to the west, between Crete and Greece, was another island, or rather a group of islands. Rays of mosaic tiles marked shipping routes, linking it with the turtle island, and others branched off to mark towns and settlements of the far-flung naval empire that the ancients had named Atlantis.

"Thera." Col put his finger on the island that had once been the empire's capital. "It blew up in a great cataclysm that shook the entire Mediterranean basin and beyond. Layers of ash and soot are found in Egypt and Turkey today. Settlements were abandoned at the same time all over the area. From the evidence, it was a combination of earthquake and rushing waters that destroyed them."

"But it says Kallista here," Thea pointed out.

"That was its ancient name, Kallista, which meant beautiful."

"What does Thera mean?" Fanny wanted to know.

A sadness came into Summer's eyes. "It means fear."

Col poured her out another stiff brandy. "Drink up, and I'll explain it all."

He paced a few steps, lining up his facts. "I've been on the wrong track all along, thinking that Carruthers had been killed over some Ellysian treasure. It was really locating a small artifact that caused his death—the missing Venus of Ilykion."

"What!" The others sat on the edge of their chairs.

"Perhaps from the very beginning," Col said, "Carruthers suspected that the Venus was stolen by someone involved with the dig. He knew that neither Alistair nor I were capable of such an act."

Richard fumed. "He should have said something to me about it at the time, damn the man!"

Col shook his head. "He didn't because he thought that it was either you, Fairchild, or one of your senior team members. His next choice was Symington. The old lion had a narrow view of women, and it proved to be his undoing. He saw them as mere decorative objects, to lighten a man's life. He never suspected Cynthia until the end, and then it was too late. Most likely not until she'd given him the fatal dose of arsenic in a glass of supposed medicine."

Thea shifted in her chair. "I still don't understand. How did she expect to find fame by stealing a statue?"

"She didn't. Let me make an educated guess, Fairchild. Who was the first person actually to see the Venus?"

Richard blinked. "Why, I had always supposed that it was Lawton Morville!"

Summer set down her glass. "No. I see it now, too. Reflected glory. It was Cynthia who found it, I'm sure; but as a mere female trying to learn mosaic restoration, and not officially attached to the project, she wanted her husband to be given the credit for it. Then she could bask in the glow of his success. Her status in the world was linked to his."

"That's right. But the official version and the newspapers credited my brother. It wasn't Alistair's doing. Perhaps Carruthers had seen to it. And Cynthia was outraged. She felt that Alistair had stolen the glory from her husband, so she determined to right that wrong, by stealing the statue from Alistair."

Rising, Summer went to Col's side and slipped her hand through his good arm. "I don't believe she meant to cause Alistair's death. I don't think she even did it to humiliate him. It was purely an act of an eye for an eye, from her skewed viewpoint."

It was Fanny's turn. "Then why did she take the statues that Father had brought here for safekeeping? Was it another act of revenge? Did she feel that she had been robbed of glory again?"

"She did it," Col said, "to be rid of me before I uncovered the truth of how—and why—Carruthers died. And it was the same with poor Dr. Ruggieri."

Richard poured himself another drink. "But why, damn it? I don't see the reason behind her actions, if she didn't know until then that Carruthers had traced the statue . . . assuming she found it when she searched his house for the letter of autopsy findings on Carruthers."

"She knew. He confronted her over the receipt from Cairo, and the fact that he knew she'd sold it there herself. Perhaps she got him to listen to some plausible excuse, not realizing that she'd already given him the fatal dose of poison in his food or drink. She tore his cottage up as he lay dying, in a vain attempt to find the statue. Just as she tore up the cottage after she shot me, looking for the letter from Rome with the autopsy results."

"But where *is* this missing Venus?" Thea asked.

"Here." Richard placed a roll of velvet on the table. "I found it among her things, with the other two statues, when I was looking for her sister's address." He undid it to reveal a small gold object of exquisite workmanship and beauty. "The Venus of Ilykion."

"Such a small thing," Summer said, "to be the cause of so much tragedy."

Col picked it up. "It's not even Venus," he told

them. "This is surely Eris, the goddess of discord, who in mythology causes strife among both gods and men."

Fanny was still trying to puzzle out the answer to one question. "I don't quite understand," she said to Col. "If Cynthia had the statue and Dr. Ruggieri was dead, why was she so frantic to be rid of you? No one suspected her. In fact, none of us suspected that the other deaths were actually murders. What was her reason for all this?"

An uncomfortable silence fell. Col looked at Summer. She nodded. Col took a deep breath.

"Once before Cynthia had lost the man she loved. She didn't want it to happen again."

No one spoke. Richard tossed off his brandy in one gulp. Rising, he went to the door like a sleepwalker. He turned back and they saw the desolation in his face. His wife had loved him too little, his mistress too much. "I must write up today's notes," he said abruptly, and went out.

14

THE WEAVING IS COMPLETED

Excerpt from the preface of *The Minoan Empire,*
by Colin McCallum, Lord FitzRoy, Summer,
and Lady FitzRoy

> *. . . and in the two decades since our first research began on the island of Ellysia, much has come to light regarding this advanced culture of ancient times. The extraordinary work of Sir Richard Fairchild and that of Sir Arthur Evans at the palace of Knossos, on Crete, gives credence to the persistent legends of lost continents and vanished civilizations.*

    Most of the household was assembled in the loggia, drinking lemonade and talking over the events of the past week, when they heard the sounds of an arrival. Richard went to the outer courtyard to see who it was.

Fanny had just taken Whitney to the far side of the court, beyond the fountain, to look at the tiny lilies she had found, so remarkably like the ones in the dining-room fresco, and Summer had gone into the house to fetch her sketchbook, which she'd left in Thea's room earlier.

Col and Thea were alone at the table, talking of Paris.

"I owe you an apology," she said in her soft voice. "You acted chivalrously, thinking that you were helping a damsel in distress. I had sought your help because of your rumored reputation as a rake. My brain was in a muddle. I thought that Martin no longer loved me, and after he saw us together in the shadows he suspected the worst because I had been so cold and distant to him. I felt I had no choice but to flee to you, which made everything worse for everyone concerned.

"And then, when you left to hire a carriage, I panicked and fled yet again because I feared you misunderstood the situation. I merely wanted to go to my friends, but I thought that *you* thought I intended to run off with *you*."

She sighed and traced the moisture that had formed on her glass with the tip of her finger. "Martin found me weeping in the street outside the consulate and took me in, but we were estranged from that point on."

Col's face was in shadow. "And I thought I was merely escorting an abused wife to her friends in Lyons. You were so afraid of Martin's wrath that I pictured him as a fearful ogre, and you a wronged wife. I had no idea you thought I meant to elope with you, and have my way with you afterward as reward for my assistance."

He chuckled wryly. "If you knew my reputation a little better, you would have known that I never forced my attentions upon an unwilling woman."

Thea's face was as red as the enormous trumpet-shaped flowers climbing up the trellis behind her. "If it were not still so painful, I suppose I would find it humorous, but I can't, for my foolishness cost me everything I hold most dear."

"A true comedy of errors," he agreed, "but one unworthy of a play."

"And yet I ruined my life by acting out the very role I most despise, of the foolish, headstrong heroine."

Col was listening to the voices from the outer courtyard. He recognized them both. "Perhaps not ruined yet," he said.

As if on cue, Martin Armstrong filled the archway between the two courts. His gaze fell upon Thea first, and his face was flooded with emotion. Then he spied Col beside her.

"By God, sir, I have come halfway round the world to fetch my wife, only to find *you* here!" He advanced upon Col with fire in his eye. "You shall answer to me for this!"

Col rose with his arm still in its sling. "Don't be an ass. There was never anything between your wife and myself except a minor friendship. Everything else was the product of two stubborn fools, afraid of losing face by admitting how much they cared, and still care, for one another."

Fanny and her companion turned around at the murmur of voices, but the splash of the fountain covered up the words. She was quick enough to guess there was an unresolved problem between her eldest sister and her husband, for Thea had gone white, then very pink, and Martin stood like a ferocious tiger, about to bite her head off, if he did not stop to rip out Col's throat first.

"Martin!" she said, hurrying forward to greet her brother-in-law and dragging Whitney along with her. "How wonderful! Thea has been pining away to nothing over your absence these past months!"

Martin looked at his wife and saw how thin and pale she was. "If she has been pining for me, it is strange indeed that she has never written me a single word since our parting. Not once!"

Tears trembled on Thea's lashes. How her heart had leapt to see him so unexpectedly; but it was no good. The old anger and suspicions were still there like a wall between them.

Then Summer came back into the court. Instead of her sketchbook she had Thea's wooden box stuffed with the letters she had written to Martin and never sent. Summer came forward and placed it in his hands. "Perhaps you should read these before you say anything you will regret. They are addressed to you, you see, so they belong to you."

He stared at the open box filled with dozens of letters on thin onionskin paper, then glanced at Thea. She smiled tremulously through her tears.

Summer turned to the others. "Shall we go inside?" They all filed into the house, leaving Thea and Martin to sort things out between themselves.

Much later, after dinner, the company sat out on the terrace, watching the sun set off to the west. Thea was in her favorite chair with Martin beside her. Richard, Col, and Summer excused themselves to discuss the mosaic that they had found hidden beneath the wooden floor of her chamber after the rubble—and Cynthia Morville's shattered corpse—had been taken away.

The last golden light fell like a blessing across the once-secret terrace, and through the opening where the wall had stood. Every island and continent stood out amid the swirling blue-green of the mosaic waters. Only a portion of the great island of Hesperia—the turtle's head—was visible beyond the Straits of Hercules. Inside, above Crete, the islands that had made up Atlantis, with Kallista as its capital, were nothing but powder. Not even the tiny island of Thera, that still existed, was left.

Summer sighed over it. "If only the wood had protected the mosaic from the falling blocks!"

Col put his arm around her shoulders. "It wasn't fated to be," he said. "But even with the damage, this is still startling proof of the widespread degree of Minoan civilization. And perhaps we will find more proof."

Richard snorted. "Symington thinks we are all mad. But then, he is a man of dogged patience and little imagination. The only way he will ever uncover a great find is if he falls through a hole into a buried city! And then it will still have to be pointed out to him."

"But," Summer protested, "if they look for these port cities around the seas they will surely find Minoan ruins. Or perhaps I should say, Atlantean ruins."

"Pah!" Richard said. "Do not fool yourself, my dear. Schliemann and the rest are sure that the Minoans were mere vassals of Mycenae. It might take a hundred years for the stiff-backed, thick-headed dolts of the academies, who reject every theory that did not come from themselves, to accept it."

Col knelt down to touch the exquisite map. "It doesn't matter. Not in the end. Archaeologists do not deal in mere decades or even centuries. We will write up our find. Time will eventually vindicate our discoveries. And it will, as Carruthers prophesied, forever rewrite the history of the Mediterranean and Aegean peoples, by whatever name they are called."

It was a shame, though, that this mosaic, the only one known from the period, was ruined.

While Summer, Col, and Richard were busy with the past, the rest of the household had their thoughts set on the future. Whitney handed Fanny a platter of the signora's delicacies.

"These apricot crescents are my favorite," he told Fanny as he encouraged her to take some. "Not so very long ago, I ate so many of them at a sitting that the doctor had to be called!"

"You are funning me, sir." Fanny's dimple flashed. "I suspect that it was many years ago, when you were a boy."

He laughed at that. "You may ask the housekeeper when you come to visit us at Audley—" He broke off, blushing, and addressed Thea hastily.

"That is, I have discussed the possibility with Martin, of having you all come to Audely for the Christmas festivities, Mrs. Armstrong. Your entire family, if we can persuade them. Martin said he must, of course, discuss the matter with you before committing himself."

Thea smiled and caught her husband's eye. Martin had vowed he would take her wishes into consideration before making any major plans. He was a man of his word, but then, Thea knew, he had always been, if only she hadn't been so foolish as not to believe it.

Martin grinned a bit self-consciously. "The Audely is very beautiful, especially at the holidays when everything is decked with candles and holly wreaths."

"Now," Whitney said in mock alarm, "do not be imagining that I am planning anything grand. My brother always comes down from London with his family and I hope to get up a small group of congenial souls to make up a house party. Except for the Christmas ball, I'm afraid we have nothing much to offer but sleigh rides and evenings of charades and jackstraws with Norbert's children."

Fanny clapped her hands. "But that is exactly what I enjoy. And I am heartily tired of grand people." Sir Horace came to mind. She turned to her sister eagerly. "Oh, Thea, do say you will consider it? I should enjoy it above all things!"

Thea looked from one to the other. Fanny had never learned to school her features, and it was plain that she meant every word. Without knowing it, she was two-thirds in love with Whitney. Thea suspected that by the New Year there would be an engagement to be announced.

Her eyes met Whitney's. There was such anxiety and hope in them, as only a man deeply in love would reveal. Thea relaxed. He was the kind of person who could see through a facade to the real person within. He valued Fanny's innocence, her quick, if untrained mind, her instincts for beauty and—best of all—her kind and loving heart. He would care for her and cherish her all her days.

Thea's smile was heartfelt and warm. "While I cannot speak for my husband—"

Martin came up behind her and put his hands on her shoulders. "You may speak for me at any time, my love."

It was difficult for Thea to say anything around the sudden tightness in her throat. She reached up to take her husband's hand. "Why, then, we gladly accept your offer to spend the Christmas holiday with you at Audley, Mr. Vance!"

"Excellent! Martin and I have quite a bit of catching up to do."

His eyes crinkled in laughter. "You see, Martin, I did not even have to mention the Audley ghost to get them to agree."

"Ghost!" Fanny breathed in delight. "You have a ghost at Audley? Oh, you must tell me all about it!"

"Very well." He rose and held out his arm to her. "Let us take a stroll through the courtyard. The flowers you planted are lovely." He lowered his voice and leaned down so only Fanny could hear. "And I think these two lovebirds would like to be alone awhile."

Fanny linked her arm through his. How strange to think of Martin and Thea, so old and settled in their ways, as lovebirds; but as they left the terrace she glanced back to see her sister and brother-in-law standing face to face, their hands entwined. The rose-gold light of sunset outlined them in splendor. They *did* look very much like lovers. How peculiar.

And how like Whitney to realize what had been right under her nose without her realizing it. What a remarkable man he was! She dazzled him with a smile and went out with him into the shady courtyard, where they lost themselves among the soft blue shadows of approaching evening.

After Fanny and her swain went off, Martin smiled tenderly down at Thea. "It warms my heart to see them together. Do you remember when we were like that, my dear?"

She raised a gentle hand to his face, noting the

sprinkle of gray at his temples, and knowing that she was responsible for a good deal of them. "Oh, Martin, I still feel that way! Indeed, I think I always will."

"As do I!" He slid his arm around her waist. "I understand there's to be a full moon tonight, and that it's quite spectacular when viewed from here." He kissed her forehead. "Do you care to wait for it, or would you rather retire early for the night?"

She stood on tiptoe and kissed his whiskery cheek. "I have seen quite enough moonrises for a while. What I want to see now is your head on the pillow next to mine." Hooking her arm through his, she led him away to bed.

After Richard left them to go over his notes, Col and Summer strolled out into Persephone's garden. The fountain had been cleared of obscuring plaster dust to reveal its glory. "I still cannot understand why anyone would cover up such a beautiful mosaic."

Col shook his head and slid his arms around Summer. "Evidently the previous owner found half-naked women not to his liking, the more fool he! There is one I would prefer to have totally naked right here and now."

She glanced up at him through her lashes. "That might be arranged, sir."

He kissed her long and deep. There was no impatience in him now. They had a lifetime to love one another. And even that might not be enough.

Summer leaned her head against his shoulder. For so long she had felt unloved, and unlovable. It made her laugh softly to realize how foolish she had been.

There were years of work ahead of them on Ellysia. Once the ruins were fully excavated they would go elsewhere. Together.

Col read her mind. "I think our next task, once this is done, will be to find Kallista. We have already discovered who Kallista was, thanks to you. I am certain the remains of the priestess's original home are somewhere on Thera, perhaps buried beneath yards of volcanic ash."

"I would like that," Summer said quietly. "I would like to see where Cliete and Kallista lived before they came to Ellysia. But I will be more than a little sad to leave this place."

Col kissed her again, this time with mounting passion. There could not be enough lifetimes to love Summer with all the love he had to give. "Perhaps we'll make our home here one day."

They strolled arm and arm toward the mural, lit by the last rays of sunset. "I never guessed who they were until the day of the last earthquake," she said, looking down at the lovely images of the three Fates, with their thread and spindle and golden blade, spinning out the lives of men and women. "I only wish we could know more of what happened to Cliete and Kallista."

Col didn't answer.

"I know what it is," Summer said. "You are afraid that, if this portion of the villa were ever excavated to its foundations, we might find the bones of the priestess and the princess. That is what they were, you know. I saw it all."

She lifted Col's hand to her lips and kissed it. "Don't try to protect me from life. Or death. I have spent too many years locked away." A smile played over her mouth.

"And you need not worry over what happened to them. He came. Kallista's lover. He came and rescued them, just as you rescued me. I am sure of it." Hadn't she seen him once, coming up the outer sea stairs?

Her certainty touched him. Summer was linked to the past—perhaps to the future—in a wondrous way that he believed in, but did not understand. All that mattered was that she was in his arms, here and now.

The sun sank into the ocean, turning it to a glory of gold, then vanishing and plunging them into the sapphire blue of a Mediterranean night. Col lowered Summer to the quilt he'd dragged off her bed earlier, and made love to her while the stars winked overhead. It was more than an act of love, it was a promise of passion and commitment. And perhaps a tribute of thanks to the Fates who had given the Court of Three Sisters its name.

EPILOGUE

The youngest Fate stood proudly by her loom. It was finished, and she knew in her soul that everything had worked out exactly as it should.

The chief angel came in, looking like a tiny spark in the presence of the great, glowing Being from Whom all that existed had come, and to Whom all would return.

"Excellent!" God said, reaching out to enfold the Fates into the Source. "You have all done exceedingly well. I am pleased."

"You see," the eldest whispered as they merged with Glory, "I was right in what I told you—if you only look for the pattern, you cannot go wrong."

"Whatever happens at all happens as it should. You will find this true, if you watch closely."

—Marcus Aurelius, *Meditations, IV, 10*

AUTHOR'S NOTE

Thirty-six hundred years ago, when Thera was still called Kallista, it was a round island, fruitful and green, the setting for a civilization whose great palaces have been excavated on the island of Crete. At the time of the great cataclysm, that society had already existed for fifteen hundred years.

Like the Atlantis of Plato, whose description of an island kingdom that was "red, black, and white," the volcanic island of Thera was destroyed in a monumental disaster. The marks of great tidal waves from the same era have been found throughout the Mediterranean and Aegean, along with layers of ash that must have blanketed entire countries and blotted out the skies, much as happened in Seattle, Washington, after the explosion of Mount Saint Helens.

After the Theran disaster, Minoan civilization was struck down at the peak of its power. Within a generation their cities were in ruins and their culture overrun by the Doric invaders.

The fertile Kallista is now a fairly barren place known as Santorini, but the remains of its glory have been unearthed under the aegis of the late archaeologist, Christos Doumas. Brilliant frescoes, buildings of several stories, terraced gardens, rattan furniture, ceramic pipes, and indoor plumbing with hot and cold running water were everyday affairs for these ancient people, and their love of beauty is well documented.

Those interested in learning the true story of Thera and the effect of its destruction can refer to *National Geographic*, to the articles and books of Christos Doumas, and to Dr. Charles R. Pellegrino's fascinating and excellently researched book, *Uncovering Atlantis*.

Any errors are mine alone, and the great turtle-shaped landmass in the Atlantic is my own invention based on the legends of ancient Greece and Rome, as well as certain stories of the First Nations of North America. Perhaps its remnants are there, waiting to be discovered.

COMING NEXT MONTH

FOREVERMORE by Maura Seger

As the only surviving member of a family that had lived in the English village of Avebury for generations, Sarah Huxley was fated to protect the magical sanctuary of the tumbled stone circles and earthen mounds. But when a series of bizarre deaths at Avebury began to occur, Sarah met her match in William Devereux Faulkner, a level-headed Londoner, who had come to investigate. "Ms. Seger has a special magic touch with her lovers that makes her an enduring favorite with readers everywhere."—*Romantic Times*

PROMISES by Jeane Renick

From the award-winning author of *Trust Me* and *Always* comes a sizzling novel set in a small Ohio town, featuring a beautiful blind heroine, her greedy fiancé, two sisters in love with the same man, a mysterious undercover police officer, and a holographic will.

KISSING COUSINS by Carol Jerina

Texas rancher meets English beauty in this witty follow-up to *The Bridegroom*. When Prescott Trefarrow learned that it was he who was the true Earl of St. Keverne, and not his twin brother, he went to Cornwall to claim his title, his castle, and a multitude of responsibilities. Reluctantly, he became immersed in life at Ravens Lair Castle—and the lovely Lucinda Trefarrow.

HUNTER'S HEART by Christina Hamlett

A romantic suspense novel featuring a mysterious millionaire and a woman determined to figure him out. Many things about wealthy industrialist Hunter O'Hare intrigue Victoria Cameron. First of all, why did O'Hare have his ancestral castle moved to Virginia from Ireland, stone by stone? Secondly, why does everyone else in the castle act as if they have something to hide? And last, but not least, what does Hunter want from Victoria?

THE LAW AND MISS PENNY by Sharon Ihle

When U.S. Marshal Morgan Slater suffered a head injury and woke up with no memory, Mariah Penny conveniently supplied him with a fabricated story so that he wouldn't run her family's medicine show out of town. As he traveled through Colorado Territory with the Pennys, he and Mariah fell in love. Everything seemed idyllic until the day the lawman's memory returned.

PRIMROSE by Clara Wimberly

A passionate historical tale of forbidden romance between a wealthy city girl and a fiercely independent local man in the wilds of the Tennessee mountains. Rosalyn Hunte's heart was torn between loyalty to her family and the love of a man who wanted to claim her for himself.